Queen, King
ACE

Queen, King
ACE

Olivia Hayfield

One day, a King will come, and the Sword will rise again

TreeHouse

Published by Treehouse Books, 2024
Ponsonby, Auckland, New Zealand

ISBN: 978-0-473-70263-2

www.oliviahayfield.com
www.suecopsey.com

Cover design and internal layout: Cheryl Smith, Macarn Design,
www.macarndesign.co.nz

For Chris Jones
A dear and nutty friend

I think that we
Shall never more, at any future time,
Delight our souls with talk of knightly deeds,
Walking about the gardens and the halls
Of Camelot, as in the days that were.
I perish by this people which I made—
Tho' Merlin sware that I should come again
To rule once more …

~ ALFRED, LORD TENNYSON (1809–1892)
Morte d'Arthur

THEN

Cornwall

Isla

The past is another country, someone once said. Another landscape, a foreign place. One we can never return to.

My memory of that summer is vague, the figures dim shapes, glimpsed through a mist. There I am, that past me, created by others, before I knew who I really was. I wanted to sing; I wanted people to love my music. But they wanted more than my voice.

I was headlining at Glastonbury, along with Oasis and The Cure, after two number ones and an album that was the fastest selling in UK history, until Adele's 25 stole that spot, but not for another twenty years.

More than seven hundred thousand in a week. Actual CDs back then, in 1995. I used to picture them stacked up. How tall would that tower be? It would touch the clouds. All those people, the length and breadth of Britain, listening to my songs. Kids lying on their beds, girls dancing with their hairbrushes in front of the mirror. Singing along to me in the car. It was intoxicating, knowing my music would forever be the soundtrack of their summer.

What's a young woman to do with all that love? Truth be told, I don't properly remember. Yes, it was *that* good. (Apart from when Duke was home. But we had a plan, my friend Merle and me.)

The Glastonbury after-party was wild. I remember going in, but not coming out. I got pregnant that hot summer night. Not proud to say, I have no idea who by. There are brief, intense flashes of memory – champagne from the bottle, strobe lights, crowd surfing, popping something. So high, so happy, like this was the pinnacle of *being*.

Later … it's quieter; the music is somewhere outside, and there's a beautiful man. Were we in a trailer? I don't know. Could've been a tent. I remember flickering golden light on pale walls, an earthy smell. He seemed familiar, but like I said, I don't know who he was. It wasn't off-your-face, mindless sex, though. It was … sublime. There was something different about it, like being in another dimension, a bliss I'd never experienced before. *Ecstasy*, I suppose would be the best word for it.

The guy; all I remember is his beautiful eyes, and afterwards I looked at every photo I could find of every band member and singer at the festival, but none had his eyes. Who was he? The father of my child, born nine months later. Conceived on that magical night, beneath that sacred tor, where legend says King Arthur is sleeping until Britain needs him again. It felt right that we'd created a life, as if the universe – the stars, as they wheeled across the heavens high above Worthy Farm – said, see here, this moment deserves an outcome.

People said I should terminate. My career was skyrocketing, there would be no father in the picture. My parents were still working, didn't want to be landed with a baby.

But they – everyone – had turned me into this person, this pop princess who had no time to be her real self, no opportunity to find her own path. That was all being laid out for her, so quickly she could barely keep up.

I decided to take a breath. I said no, I was having this baby. Something deep inside said, *they're not taking this from me*. Someone who'd love me for who I really was, not this version I'd become.

I attempted, month after month, to find the father, thinking I should let him know, and … I wanted to see him again. The memory of him; it would return to me in the early hours when I couldn't sleep. His silhouette in the dark of that long, hot summer night; entwined, connected. The touch of his skin, his gentle fingers, his warm, soft lips; the beauty of it. The magic.

Who were you?

But discreet enquiries among the Glastonbury crews led nowhere. People remembered seeing me at the after-party, but strangely, no one could remember who I was with; nobody saw me leave, and then I was gone until the next morning, when I stumbled into my trailer to the relieved cheers of my team.

I carried on performing until I began to show, and then I disappeared back here to Cornwall, where my beautiful baby boy, Arthur, was born.

NOW

Chapter 1

London, July 2021

Eliza

'Is this guy for real?' said Terri, frowning at the front page of the *Guardian*. She dropped the paper on her desk and peered over her glasses at Eliza, who was staring out of the office window at the Thames.

A year ago.

'Sorry.' Eliza turned her attention to Terri. 'Guy? What guy?'

Terri stabbed at the paper with a long, black fingernail, and Eliza spotted the winning smile and tousled golden hair of a man holding high the Wimbledon men's singles trophy. Perking up she replied, 'Ah, the rather delicious Ace Penhalagon. Dad was beside himself with the win.'

Eliza's father, Harry Rose, chairman of Rose Corp, was a tennis fanatic, and the family had attended the Wimbledon final yesterday.

'Are you suspicious of Ace's charming smile, Terri?'

'I don't buy it,' replied *The Rack*'s editor. 'He's far too good to be true.' She smiled, and it was wicked. 'I can't fuckin' *wait* to interview him tomorrow.'

Arthur Penhalagon, known to the British public as Ace, had come out of nowhere to win Wimbledon – elegantly, with no grunting, no arguing with the umpire, no fistipumps, no petulance over questionable line calls. He was gracious in victory, smiley and warm, and from the frenzied media coverage it would appear that not only was he an exceptionally pretty face, he also cared deeply about racism, inequality, climate change, and holding to account the current government which, in recent times, had pinged like a pinball between disasters, sleaze, scandals and shortages. Covid-19 and Brexit had left the country exhausted, and yesterday's Wimbledon victory had been just the pick-me-up Britain needed.

'Says here he's donating half his winnings to charity,' said Terri. She tucked back the stripe of white hair that edged her cutthroat black bob, and picked up the paper again. 'And he'll be – wait – *using his voice to call for change.* God save us. I bloody *hate* it when celebs do that.' She peered more closely at the photo. 'Even if they look like that.'

Eliza chuckled. 'Be nice. Don't Terri-fy him. Britain badly needs a hero right now. Maybe this time we'd like to discover he is in fact genuine? No hidden agenda? Seriously – just this once, leave your hatchet at home.'

'You calling me jaded?'

'Totally,' said Eliza. 'I desperately want there to be no murky past, no inflated ego. I want him to be for real.' Her face broke into a delighted smile as she had an idea. 'Why don't you get Will to interview him? He'd love that, and he's got some downtime.'

Will Bardington, RoseGold's Head of Drama and Eliza's closest friend, had just finished work on their latest TV series, the logistics of which had been a massive headache thanks to the complications thrown in its path by the Covid pandemic.

'Will deserves a treat,' said Eliza. 'He's had one hell of a year.'

'No way,' said Terri. 'Will would fall in love with him.'

'True. But it would make a cracking piece. C'mon, Terri. Let's give the readers a break. All they've had is depressing stories and carping and moaning and the world is ending. Let's give them their British hero, make it a love piece. *Imagine* – Will's words, describing how Ace moves around the court. And *think* of that front cover.' She fanned herself dramatically with a hand.

Terri shook her head. 'Jesus, Eliza. How you manage to stay upbeat in the face of Britain's current level of shite, I'll never know.'

'You'll talk to Will, then?'

'I'll think about it,' said Terri. 'Now for fuck's sake go and be positive somewhere else.'

❀

In her top-floor office, high above Southwark, where people were trickling back to sit outside Thameside cafés and pubs, to queue up once again at The Globe, Eliza looked at her calendar to see what the day had in store. The usual meetings, mostly on Zoom.

Online be damned. What she needed today was physical, meaningful human contact. Yesterday's day out had been such a treat, a return to old times – almost. There had been no traditional Rose Corp marquee at Wimbledon this year; corporate hospitality had been on hold for so long now. After the ravages of this terrible pandemic, everyone was relearning how to be social, how to do going out.

The priority of Eliza's top management team: herself as CEO, Harry as chairman and 'consultant' (a misnomer – her father *never* waited to be consulted), and their COO, Cecil Walsham, had been to keep Rose Corp forging ahead, to adapt to the new business landscape created by the pandemic. Many staff were still wfh (or wfy – working from yacht – as Harry often called it) and the goalposts were forever moving. It was exhausting trying to keep things on track.

But today, Eliza would cut herself some slack.

A year ago.

As she sat alone in her office, feeling her positivity ebbing away, she needed a hug. And she knew who she needed it from.

A lump formed in her throat. Exactly a year ago, she'd lost her soul mate.

She'd learned how to skirt that void, how to exist with the gaping hole he'd left in her life, in her heart. Today, though, it was all too hard.

She stared out at the Thames. *Same river*, he'd once said. Where they'd scattered his ashes, in Oxford's moonlit watermeadows.

Goodbye, sweet Kit.

Blinking away tears, she picked up her phone: *How u doing? Shall we get v drunk?*

Will: *That would seem entirely appropriate. Sleepover?*

❀

'I brought his favourite.' Eliza handed Will the six pack of beers as she stepped across the threshold, following him into the cosy, book-lined living room, dropping her overnight bag on the sofa.

Before she could stop them, her eyes lit on the spot where they'd found Kit, the knife in his neck, the pool of blood creeping across the floor as the life drained from his body. She flinched as the flash of those colours and textures seared her mind's eye – the shiny, dark red slick oozing over the richly polished wood.

Eliza had been in this room many times since, but today … Her heart beat uncomfortably as the image of Kit's lifeless body pushed its way in. His long, pale hair lying in the pool of blood, the light in those beautiful eyes snuffed out.

Kit had been killed by one of his father Andre Sokolov's hitmen, after Kit had tricked Andre into confessing to Eliza's mother's murder. Sokolov was now serving a life sentence.

Will noticed her discomfort. 'Kitchen? Or outside?' It was a sultry summer's evening, and out of the window, dusk was sucking the colour from the red bricks of the Victorian terraces on this quiet East London street.

'It's okay, I'll be fi–' But her voice caught and then her hand covered her mouth. The tears she'd been fighting all day broke through.

'Oh, poor love. Come here.' Will pulled her into a hug, and she clung tightly to him. He rested his head on hers, rocking her gently.

'Shit, why is today so hard, Eliza? It's just another sad day of another sad week.'

Will had been Kit's partner. Or as close to a partner as anyone had ever been. They'd bought this house together, lived in it as a couple.

Neither spoke for a while, then Eliza sniffed, drew a deep breath and pulled away. 'Oh boy, I needed that hug.' She gave him a watery smile and dabbed at her cheeks.

'Me too. Far better for that. But the kitchen would be wiser, I think.' He moved towards the door, calling, 'Romeo! Wherefore art thou?'

Eliza snorted, and the mood lightened. 'How is your new significant other?' Will had recently adopted a handsome amber-eyed cat, which for some reason had taken an immediate dislike to Eliza.

'He is the master now.' Will pushed open the French doors to the long, narrow back garden, calling again. Shadows were swallowing the herbaceous borders, leaving pale flowers floating in the twilight.

'Beer or wine?' he said, going over to the fridge.

'Let's have the Greene King.'

'I ordered Thai – all right with that?'

'Lovely, thanks. How have you been today?' She hopped onto a bar stool and flicked back her curly red ponytail as Will poured her beer. Romeo sauntered in from the garden, grey and round and fluffy, and looked at her with disdain before butting his head into Will's calf.

'Just something to be got through, is it not? A year – can it really be?' He clinked his bottle against her glass. 'To Kit,' he said. 'How dare he leave us because Fate said it must be so.'

Eliza looked at him. 'You don't believe that.'

'But *he* did, and apparently he knew better than us.'

'True.'

Kit had also told Eliza he knew he'd die young. And that the concept of time is an illusion, that it isn't linear – it bends, twists and loops.

She considered her next question carefully. 'Will, do you ever … I mean, being here on your own. Do you ever … *sense* him?'

The tobacco scent of nicotiana drifted into the kitchen.

'I talk to him all the time,' he replied.

'So do I, but that's not what I meant.'

'No. Number thirty-four is ghost free, of that I can assure you.' He tickled Romeo under the chin. 'Just me and this lovely boy.' He raised his bottle again. 'To Kit, much loved, much missed. Now let's cheer the fuck up. He wouldn't want us to wallow.'

Will, Kit and Eliza had been fellow English undergraduates at Oxford. Eliza had been intrigued by Kit's brilliant mind, his understanding of human nature, especially its darker side, and frustrated at her inability to work him out. He'd been a compelling enigma; a beautiful, wild, outrageously slutty boy who'd lived without boundaries. It was only on the day before he died, when he told her the truth of his life, that she finally understood him.

In their second year, Kit had thought it perfectly natural that he and Eliza should be more than just mates. But her father had demonstrated – and how – the consequences of infidelity which, for his wives and mistresses, had included depression, insanity, murder and suicide. Eliza had been determined to hold out for a man who knew the meaning of the word faithful. Not Kit.

But just once, after a few too many ciders, she'd let her guard down …

'Eliza?'

She looked up. 'Sorry, I was having a moment.'

Will raised his eyebrows. 'I can see it was a happy one.'

'I was thinking about that night at Oxford, do you remember? When we left the pub together, me and Kit. *Together* together.'

There was an awkward pause, even though the night in question had been way before Will embraced his gay side.

'Of course I remember. You almost succumbed, but you were too sensible. That was probably the first time anyone had said no to him.'

'Not *exactly* a no.'

It was time to clear the air – it had taken them a year to work up to this conversation.

'We … um, well, we kissed, but when he tried to take it further …' She grimaced. 'That was when I found out I had issues. You know – *body* issues. Mostly to do with trust. It was a long time before I could … get intimate. With anyone. Kit didn't tell you?'

Will held up a hand. 'That's probably TMI. But no, he would never talk to me about you on any meaningful level.' He looked her in the eye. 'But my god, that boy could kiss.'

Eliza felt herself blush. 'Best ever. Work of the devil.'

'On how many occasions?' Will's smile faltered as he waited for her response.

She shook her head a little. 'Only that once.' But then she found herself saying, 'Sometimes, a kiss, though … you remember it more than even …' The memory of it still hummed in her veins.

Her eyes slid away from his, settling on Romeo, sitting by the doors, blending in with the dusk. 'I told him later, my reluctant virgin moment probably had something to do with Dad's treatment of women, especially Mum. And … you remember his uncanny knack of spotting connections? That was when he put two and two together, about our dead mums and their mutual killer – when I told him Mum died of toxic shock. Same as his.'

Will sighed. 'If only he'd shared that suspicion with us at the time.'

'He knew it was too dangerous, his dad being an actual *psycho*.' She watched her thumb as it drew a line down through the condensation on her glass. 'But yes, only that one kiss,' she said, circling back to his question. 'And then, just quickly … quick-*ish* … the night before he died.'

They'd been waiting for a taxi, and she'd twined her arms round his neck.

Kit …

You love me, I know.

Will's eyes held hers, the question still there.

'You know he loved you, in his own strange way.' She smiled, and touched his arm. 'You were the only one he stuck with. Ever.'

There was a knock at the door. Will held her gaze a moment longer, then slid off his stool.

Over their meal and on into the warm night, they shared more memories. And more beer and wine. As darkness crept across the living room, Will flicked on a lamp, creating a cosy pool of light.

Eliza was lying on the sofa, her head on the armrest and her feet in Will's lap. Romeo was also in Will's lap. 'Stop!' she squeaked, as the cat grabbed her foot in his fat, grey paws and clamped his teeth around her big toe. 'He really doesn't like competition, does he?'

'One learns to live with it, if the oppo is your dearest friend.' Will's brown eyes were glassy with alcohol and sentiment.

'I wasn't your oppo.' She poked him with her free foot. 'Anyway, I was with Rob by the time you two finally hooked up.' Rob Studley had been Eliza's long-time boyfriend, until she'd realised they wanted different things from life. They remained close, as far as was possible with a continent and an ocean between them. He was now head of RoseGold's US operation.

'Current status on your love life?' asked Will. 'Is the delectable François still *un petit ami*?'

'*Non.* He was *charmant*, but I couldn't handle Dad's disappointment. You know his opinion of the French.'

'Ah, *bien sûr*. And I take it Dev's been banished to the annuls of Eliza history, filed under *Enormous, I-told-you-so Mistakes?*'

Eliza winced. The exuberant Dev, a Rose TV presenter, had been her most recent … what would she call him – favourite? But it had soon become clear he was in it for the publicity. When she'd cooled things, he'd sold his kiss 'n' tell to a tabloid.

'Never trust an Essex boy,' said Will. 'I pegged him as a chancer from day one.'

'I hate it when you do that.' Eliza didn't want to dwell on the treacherous Dev. She'd fired him, of course. 'And you? Anyone new in the picture?'

'Nope. I don't even know what I am.' Will sighed dramatically, flicking back his long, chocolate curls.

'You're a lovely man, Will Bardington, and the most talented writer in all of England, maybe the world. And you're my best friend and I love you very much.'

'You're drunk, Eliza Rose.'

She raised her glass to him. '*In vino veritas.*'

'Yes, I am a lovely man and a passable writer. But am I gay, am

I bi, am I straight? Do I Tinder, do I grind, do I bumble? Or just loiter hopefully at the Groucho bar? I was into girls until I met Kit, and then I got confused. Now everyone assumes I'm gay, but I don't know anymore.'

'You're still grieving. You'll know when you meet the right person. Give it time. Actually ...' she smiled mischievously, 'you may be getting a call from Terri. Did you watch the Wimbledon final?'

'I most certainly did. What a banger. How do you like the divine Ace? Lord, what that beautiful man can do with a ball. Ah, wait ... you're going to tell me–'

'Terri's interviewing him tomorrow. I told her you should do it.'

Will sat up straighter. 'Oh, I would be *so* up for that.'

Eliza grinned. 'Thought you might be. She said she'd think about it. But you know what? Who's the boss here? I might just apply some pressure.'

'Grind her beneath your boot, Eliza. And now ...' Will looked at the antique clock on the mantelpiece, 'we should away to bed. If I am indeed to sit down with the epitome of physical perfection, I don't want to be grey faced and hung over. Do you want the sofabed in the office, or Kit's room?' He paused. 'I'm afraid I still haven't been through his stuff. Can't face it.'

'Kit's. I'll sleep with Kit tonight.'

Chapter 2

She let herself into Kit's bedroom and looked around her. It was exactly the same. The walls were painted deep red, the space above the bed dominated by a poster advertising Christopher Marlowe's *Doctor Faustus*, starring Kit Harington.

As she changed into her pyjamas, Eliza thought back to when she, Will and Kit had been to see the play, smiling at the memory of Kit's brilliant-but-baffling critique in the pub afterwards. How he'd insisted it was no coincidence the play was at the Duke of York's Theatre, because Kit (Harington's) character in *Game of Thrones* was of course the bastard son of Ned Stark, who was based on the Duke of York, as in the Wars of the Roses, and *these things are never not connected.*

And Kit Harington's mum had named her son after Kit Marlowe, so *of course he was destined to play Doctor Faustus, it's not that hard, Eliza – work it out.*

She lay down on the bed and pulled up the duvet Will had given her. Flicking off the light, she noticed a faint smell of cigarette smoke, even now.

I wish you'd give up. Do you have a death wish?
Possibly.

Eliza's mind drifted back to their tutorials – trying to follow Kit's ramblings on Elizabethan plays and modern poetry and American literature and all the rest of it. Happy days. And then, as her eyelids grew heavy, her brain of its own accord fast-forwarded to their last night at Oxford, sitting with Kit beneath a moonlit oak, her head on his shoulder as he shared his thoughts on time. And then … making time stop.

Whatever happens, me and you – we're forever.

Did she just whisper that out loud?

His softly spoken reply: *Forever, now. It's all the same.*

She was falling sleep; her head was spinning. She was glad she'd had the presence of mind to drink a large glass of water in an attempt to mitigate tomorrow's hangover. Had she set the alarm on her phone? She tried to remember, but sleep was claiming her, she couldn't muster her thoughts …

What are you doing in my bed, Eliza?

❀

Her alarm woke her and she held her breath, waiting to find out how bad the hangover was … not too serious. She sat up, blinking, pushing back her hair. Daylight was spilling into the room; she hadn't drawn the curtains last night. Cool, damp air drifted in through the open window, along with the background hum of London traffic, the guttural rattle of an old black cab passing on the street below.

Her eyes roamed around the room. Bookshelves, a chest of drawers with a dusty stack of literary journals on it. A desk; an old oak wardrobe, Kit's backpack lying on the top, empty. No photos, no awards, even though he'd won a fair few. He'd always called them 'pointless'. *You do realise, it's all bollocks?*

She smiled. Pretty much everything had been 'pointless' to Kit, apart from his writing, through which he'd attempted to make sense of human existence, all the while somehow knowing his own would be cut short.

Last night, she'd dreamt of him. *What are you doing in my bed, Eliza?*

She threw back the duvet and swung her feet out of bed, feeling somehow renewed, invigorated. Yesterday had been cathartic; now they were past the anniversary, she and Will could move forward again.

But then, as if putting that to the test, her eyes returned to the chest of drawers. Ignoring her panicked inner voice – *Don't! Just don't!* – she slowly pulled one open … and froze. His T-shirts. On top was a black one she remembered well. She could see him in it, sitting on the riverbank at the boat races, sharing a Pimm's. Shuffling closer to him, pushing back his hair, slipping her straw between his lips. The look in his amber eyes, just before he'd surprised her with a minty kiss.

She lifted out the T-shirt and buried her face in the fabric … it smelt of him. She breathed in; a long, shaky breath. 'I miss you so much,' she whispered, pressing it to her cheek. 'I'd give *anything* to have you back.'

A stillness filled the room; the back of her neck prickled. *Kit?*

She glanced over her shoulder, her eyes drawn to the Doctor Faustus poster.

The heavy silence was broken by a soft knock on the door and Will's muffled voice saying, 'Are you conscious? Coffee or tea?'

She kissed the T-shirt and put it back in the drawer, pushing it firmly shut, resolving to talk to Will about sorting out Kit's things.

'Morning! Coffee please. Um, can I have a shower first?'

'You may, but make it quick. We need to leave in half an hour – Terri just phoned. I'm interviewing Ace Penhalagon.'

'Whoop!'

'Do you want to come with?'

Eliza pulled open the door and poked her head out. 'Yes! Give me fifteen, then rendezvous with coffee in the kitchen?'

❀

If there had been any upside at all to the pandemic, Eliza reflected, as their train clattered south, it was the anonymity afforded by masks on public transport. She no longer had to taxi everywhere; she just put on her mask and sunglasses and … no more Eliza Rose, head of Britain's biggest media corporation, daughter of the country's most famous billionaire. Instead, she was just another commuter on her way to the office.

'*If there's a skeleton, dig it up,*' Will read out from his phone. 'My god, Terri's brutal.'

The new Wimbledon champion was coming to The Rose for a photo shoot, then Will would interview him over lunch. Terri had emailed a list of questions she wanted Will to include, and it was clear she was suspicious of Ace's golden-boy image.

'No – don't search for a skeleton,' said Eliza, 'just get to the heart of him.'

Will's eyebrows rose. 'I'm happy to probe deep.'

Eliza giggled. 'I *so* want you to discover he's as nice as he seems. Like, the Tom Daley of tennis.'

'Oh, Tom,' sighed Will. 'Can I interview him too, please?'

'One gorgeous man at a time, Will. Bottom line as I see it, is that Britain needs someone to believe in, right now. If Ace genuinely cares about the things he says he does – racism, inequality–'

'He's clearly woke–'

'So it would seem. I want him to be for real; I want a big, fat, good news story. A new hero for Britain. Find out exactly how he intends to push his agenda, if he's genuine about using his voice for good. If he is, we can help him with that. But if you detect anything off, like a power trip, proceed with caution.'

'Right you are, boss.'

'And enjoy it.' She patted his knee. 'I pushed for this because you deserve a treat. What you've done with *Twisted* – fantastic work, and I know it wasn't easy. I'm so proud of you.'

Will had recently adapted Rowan Bosworth's ground-breaking play from a decade ago. It was a classic piece of theatre but a difficult watch, full of emotional and physical violence. Will had worked closely with Bosworth to bring it to the screen.

'I'm so glad we've wrapped,' said Will. 'Rowan's brilliant, but he's the very devil to work with. It's done me in.'

'Gritty Yorkshireman?'

'He's a cool guy, he just seemed to take a dislike to me, at least at first.' Will frowned. 'I'm not entirely sure why.'

'Then, I dislike *him*, on principle.'

'And he didn't take to Terri when she interviewed him,' said Will, 'although I appreciate that's not unusual. But they're similar – both from Yorkshire, down-to-earth champions of the common man. It's odd they didn't get on.'

'Terri's so hard to please.'

'Anyway, here's our stop. How do I look?' Will whipped off his mask as they left the train.

'Bloody gorgeous. Are you gay today, then?'

'I'd say that very much depends on Ace.'

✹

At the office, Will exited the pink glass lift at the RoseGold floor, and Eliza carried on up to the top. She walked past the crèche, smiling at the sight of children rampaging around it again. The deserted crèche had been a sorry sight, as staff and their families sat out the pandemic at home, waiting … and waiting … for life to return to normal.

But Rose was bouncing back, and Eliza was feeling positive again. She'd got through yesterday's difficult anniversary, and tonight she was off to a special screening of a new RoseGold romcom with her father. It would be the first time she'd glammed up since … she couldn't even remember.

She stopped at her PA's desk. Eliza had sorely missed Pippa's chirpiness, her sing-song Welsh accent and her motherly concern for Eliza's welfare (or, more accurately, her insatiable interest in her private life) during their time working from home.

'Hi, Pippa! Everything under control? What do I have to look forward to today?'

'Good morning! You're seeing Cecil at eleven thirty; I blocked off this afternoon so you can get ready for tonight. Your hairdresser's confirmed for your place at three.'

'Great, thanks.' She lifted a hand to her unruly bun, hastily pinned up at Will's. 'Best of luck to him with that.' Danny was the only person she trusted to tame her wild red curls into anything resembling sophisticated.

In her office, Eliza clicked on her email inbox and opened one of two from Rob. His weekly report on US operations was attached to the first. She saved it for later.

The other was to her personal account:

Hi Lizzie – Facetime this week? Personal not work? Missing you, would love to chat. R xx

Dear Rob. She'd thought he was The One. They'd lived together; Rob had proposed, but their relationship had faltered, floundered, and then imploded in the face of the obstacles thrown up, the pressures they'd faced – the death of Rob's depressive ex-wife, Amy; the fact that Eliza was Rob's boss, his prolonged absences in America, and the final, horrible, nail in the coffin, his affair with the beautiful Letitia Knowles, an actress in the production he'd been overseeing.

And then there was Rob's blind spot when it came to Kit. He'd been unable to grasp that a man and woman could be soul mates, but not bed mates. At least, when that man was as notorious as Kit. He'd hated their closeness, was infuriated at how Kit understood Eliza on some deep level he couldn't.

But even though they'd split, on the occasions they saw each other … well. They were both still single, loved the very bones of each other, and Eliza was only following Kit's orders: *Be with him but don't commit. Live like a Marley.*

As Eliza pressed send on her return email, her desk phone rang. 'Terri just called,' came Pippa's voice. 'Says they're in studio three if you want to pop down.'

Eliza had only read two emails, and her productivity yesterday had been abysmal. 'I probably won't; I'm behind.'

'But Eliza!' said Pippa, several vocal tones higher. 'It's Ace Penhalagon!'

'I know, I know.' Eliza looked through to the outer office and saw Pippa grinning at her, nodding enthusiastically. 'Well, if you insist. I'll do it for Dad.'

Eliza dealt with her urgent correspondence, then took the lift down to the studios. Pushing open the door to number three, she peered in.

Ace was posing in front of a black backdrop, dressed in a beautifully tailored pale-grey suit. His golden hair glinted in the studio lighting, and a spotlight was trained on his classically handsome face, accentuating lofty cheekbones and a jawline chiselled by the gods. In his hand was a tennis racket.

'No – don't smile!' called the photographer, who Eliza recognised as Allessandro Giordano, London's great celebrity portraitist. The stylist had made Ace look like an Armani model. Although … Eliza swallowed. She wouldn't have had to try that hard.

'Hold up your racket,' called Allessandro, 'and look through it into the camera – serious face. I want, *I just won Wimbledon, but you don't know me yet.*'

Ace looked confused, and a little awkward. He held up the racket and …

'No! Don't smile,' repeated Allessandro.

'Sorry,' said Ace. 'I'm not great at this.' He gave the photographer an apologetic, lopsided smile, and something squeezed Eliza's heart.

'Ace!' came Terri's Yorkshire tones from some dark spot beyond the bright lights. 'Give us the face you gave Bianci just before you demolished him in the tie-break.'

'Oh, right.' Ace squinted in the direction of Terri's voice. 'Got it.' He squared his shoulders, narrowed his eyes slightly and fixed the camera with a stare.

'YES! Hold that look!' called Allessandro.

Oof. Holy Mother of God. From goofy-gorgeous to warrior-king in the blink of an eye.

'Yeah, baby,' called Will, also not quite visible behind the bright lights.

Ace glanced over at Will, and the smile was back.

'Shut up, Will,' called Allessandro, 'or you're out of here.'

Trying not to draw attention to herself, Eliza edged round to where Will and Terri were sitting. 'How's it going?' she whispered.

'Beautifully,' said Will, at the same time as Terri said, 'He's not a natural.'

The photographer pulled the camera over his head, set it down and went over to Ace. 'Maybe this is all a bit corporate?' he called to Terri, fingering the lapel of Ace's silk jacket.

'I like it,' said Terri.

'The suit's great,' said Will to Terri. 'But maybe he should wear it more casual?'

Eliza couldn't help it. Still full of that surprising lightness she'd woken up with, she moved out of the shadows and into the spotlight, suddenly glad she'd stopped off in the Ladies to touch up her make-up and liberate her curls from their bun.

Allessandro took a step back as he spotted her moving towards Ace with intent. 'Eliza! Great to see you again!' He'd photographed her, Will and Kit for the cover of *The Rack* during the launch of RoseGold.

'Hi, Allessandro. I couldn't resist popping down to congratulate our new champion.' She stopped in front of Ace. 'Hello there. I was at the final on Sunday. That was the most *incredible* win, and just what Britain needed. Well done.' She gave a quiet little clap, looking up at him.

Oh, he's so tall!

Eyes the blue of the open ocean, fringed with long, dark lashes, gazed down into hers. 'Hello, Eliza. It's a pleasure to meet you.' His voice was as warm as his smile, and there was the tiniest trace of a West Country accent. 'I'm an avid reader of *The Rack*; can't quite believe I'm going to be in it.'

'And on the cover!' said Eliza.

'Thanks for your kind words. I'm still coming to terms with being Champion – rather unexpected, to be honest. Last week hardly anybody knew me, this week everyone seems to.' He gave a small shake of his head, looking slightly bewildered. 'It all feels a bit surreal.'

Eliza laughed, then glanced over at Allessandro, raising her eyebrows. He motioned to her to continue.

She lifted a hand and let it hover in front of Ace's tie. 'May I?'

He shrugged. 'Be my guest.'

She took a step closer; he smelt of something ... woody, with a hint of spice. Intensely masculine. She inhaled a slow, secret breath. Feeling a little giddy, she loosened his tie, and the back of her hand scraped the stubble on his jawline. 'Sorry,' she whispered, briefly meeting his eye.

She pulled off the length of silk with a swift movement, throwing it to one side, then carefully undid the top button of his shirt, sliding her fingers down to the next, and then the next, their tips brushing his warm skin. She took the two sides of the shirt and gently eased them apart, revealing a glimpse of the tanned, muscular chest beneath.

'There. Smart-casual.' She tilted her head up again, and there was no mistaking the expression in those deep blue eyes as they locked on hers. Neither looked away. Then she smiled. 'Okay with this?'

She could hear his breathing, which had quickened.

'If that's what you want,' he said, quietly.

She stepped back again. 'Allessandro?'

'Perfect!' he called. 'Let's do it.'

Eliza made her way back to Terri and Will.

'Fuck's sake, Eliza, what was that?' said Terri. But she was grinning.

'He's not gay,' said Eliza to Will.

'Well, no,' he replied. 'Eliza, you little minx. That was *not* CEO-appropriate behaviour. Although I have to say, you've nailed the look.'

Allessandro looked happy with the looser version of Ace, who was now once again posing with his racket.

'I don't know what came over me,' Eliza said. 'Or maybe I do …' She winked at Will. 'But I should get back; I'm seeing Cecil. Enjoy your interview. Remember – I want a hero.'

As she pulled open the studio door she looked back at Ace; he was watching her. She gave a small wave; and he lifted his racket in response.

Well, that was nice!

Then she wondered what she'd been thinking. Will was right, that was not appropriate behaviour for a woman in her position. She'd given in to her inner flirt. But then, she was her father's daughter.

❀

As Danny fixed her sophisticated up-do with a blast of extra-hold, Eliza received a text from Will. Her face broke into a grin as she read: *Hype does not lie. You have your Mr Perfect. Genuine, humble but VERY sharp, and with a social agenda. I'm in love.*

She was about to reply when her phone rang – *Dad*.

'Hi! Looking forward to tonight?'

'I was indeed, Lizzie,' came Harry's deep voice. 'Very much so. But I've been Corona'd, as your brother would put it.'

Eliza's heart leapt into her mouth. Last year, her father had suffered a serious heart attack. Two operations and a weeks-long coma later he'd seemed as good as new, but when Covid-19 had struck, Eliza's concern had skyrocketed again.

'Dad! You mean … you've tested–'

'No, no. Sorry, should've made that clearer. I've been pinged – close contact. Just when we thought life was getting back to some semblance of normal, heh? Would you credit it.'

Eliza sighed. Would this dreadful virus ever be done? 'I'm just glad you're okay. Don't frighten me again. And no problem with the preview, I'll ask Will. Not *quite* as dashing as you but he'll do.'

They said their goodbyes.

She phoned Will. 'Hi. Look, Dad's cried off the screening tonight. Want to come?'

'But of course. When and where?'

'Come to mine, soon as you can. Wear a suit.'

Half an hour later she was ready, in a beautiful dress organised for her by *Hooray*'s fashion editor. It was silvery grey and off the shoulder, tightly fitted with a full, feathery skirt. No necklace, just long, silver filigree earrings to offset the scraped-back hair; a few silver bracelets and rings. Her trademark red lipstick to finish.

She snapped a selfie in front of the mirror and messaged it to Rob. *Do u like?*

Rob: *I do. What's the occasion?*

Eliza: *The romcom preview*

Rob: *Of course. Sad now. Arm candy?*

Eliza: *Will* ☺

Rob: *Less sad. Enjoy – u look beautiful XXX*

She smiled and sighed. She missed him.

Another text pinged in.

Will: *Forgive. Couldn't resist!*

Eliza: *?*

No reply.

She loaded her silver clutch – phone, lipstick, tissues …

There was a soft tap at the door and she opened it to see Will, still in his work clothes, and next to him … Ace.

'Oh!'

'Your car's here,' said Will, gesturing towards the street. 'Look, I'm bushed after our big night. Sorry, I just don't have the energy. But I asked Ace, here, if he might step into the breach, and if you can face the media explosion that will tiresomely and inevitably follow …'

Chapter 3

Ace

Ace would never forget the moment he first set eyes on Eliza Rose. She'd emerged from the shadows of the studio into the spotlight, the red tones of her dress flaring in the beam, her long auburn hair blazing as it caught the light, contrasting with her porcelain skin. Those full, red lips, the tall, slender body moving gracefully towards him. She was like the firebird in the ballet, and in that moment her image burned itself onto his memory and he knew it would never, ever fade.

Those intelligent, deep-brown eyes, gazing directly into his as she asked, her voice full of mischief, *May I?*

He'd been aware of Eliza before the photo session, of course – the young, glamorous head of Rose Corp, apparently as brilliant as she was beautiful. The younger daughter of billionaire businessman Harry Rose, who got through wives as quickly as Ace went through tennis rackets. Metaphorically speaking.

A whiff of scandal trailed Eliza, too: a relationship with a married colleague, whose wife, Ace seemed to remember, had been found dead soon after their affair became public. And more recently, a racy kiss and tell from that full-of-himself TV presenter Dev Noble, who'd nicknamed her Iceberg Rose.

But there had been nothing cold about the woman who'd stood looking up at him that morning. The warmth of her smile, that playful twinkle in her eye. Then, as he held her gaze, the air between them had charged, and a pulse of electricity had arced from her fingers to his skin as she slowly unbuttoned his shirt.

Ace wrenched his attention back to Will Bardington, sitting opposite him in The Rose's café. Ace had been expecting Terri, *The Rack*'s infamously aggressive editor, to interview him, but she'd said, 'Change of plan, Ace, love. The boss says Britain's had enough of angry and grim, so Will's here for your heroic and nice. Enjoy the easy fuckin' ride.' With a disgusted shake of her head, she'd left the studio.

'You were saying?' prompted Will, biting into a falafel, 'how it feels to be Champion?'

Ace smiled as he met Will's lively brown eyes. The famous writer was camper than a day out at the seaside, and utterly charming with it.

'Honestly? Like I said to … to Eliza, it's kind of surreal. I'd never even made it to a Grand Slam final before this year, and now, winning the French and Aussie Opens and then Wimbledon – it's like someone sprinkled me with tennis fairy dust.'

'I'm using that.' Will glanced at the phone sitting between them, recording the conversation. 'Let's rewind to the backstory – you were fostered, correct? A tricky childhood there, perhaps?'

Will clearly hadn't done his homework. As soon as Ace had reached Wimbledon's final rounds, his background, as far as it was known, had been splashed all over the papers.

There was a flash of irritation. Ace didn't enjoy dwelling on his past. 'You'll already have the bones of it from your research? Can we talk about something the tabloids haven't already hashed to death?'

Will looked embarrassed, and now Ace felt bad. The writer was far too likeable. But Ace had to beware of a possible trap. This whole *Britain needs a hero* angle, as Will had described it, could be an attempt to open him up and tease out the parts of his past he'd rather keep private. Act like a friend, then move in for the kill.

'I have to confess,' said Will, 'I'm woefully ill-prepared. This gig was sprung on me last minute, and sport is not my natural habitat.

I know nothing of the superiority of the two-handed backhand or the speed of Ace's ace. Please forgive.'

Ace wrinkled his nose. 'The two-hander is a blunt and thuggish cudgel; Roger would agree with me on that.'

'If you say so. But in all honesty, Ace, the *Rack* reader does not need to know more about your racket skills. That's the job of the BBC's commentary box. No – they want to know about your childhood, your likes and dislikes; whether there's an Ace love interest. The true version, by the way, not the stuff *The Sun* made up.'

Ace wondered what that had been. His manager had shared only selected highlights of the recent press coverage.

He went quiet, frowning at his water glass. This was how things would be, from now on. The trade-off. If he wanted to be a force for good, he would have to open himself up to scrutiny. And the results would often be mis-reported or made-up bollocks.

'Nothing much to see here. I've always been too busy training to do anything that would titillate your readers.'

'What a shame.'

'And no serious love interest. The tennis circuit … it's difficult.'

'But look at you!' Wills eyes drunk in Ace's hair and face, slowing down as they panned across his shoulders and chest. 'I would imagine a certain amount of crushing from the lovely leggy ladies of the tennis scene? And the men?' he added, hopefully.

'I'm not into men, Will,' said Ace with a smile.

'How very sad. But of course, I'd worked that one out already.' Will nonchalantly picked at his salad. 'How did you like our Eliza?'

'She's … quite something.' Ace also looked down, focusing on slicing a sliver of tuna.

'Well, yes.' Will paused. 'And if you tell me more of your background, I shall tell you more of hers.'

Ah. So that was how this was working. Evidently, Will had noticed the spark that had flown between the two of them. It had probably been hard not to.

'I see.' Ace had the distinct impression he wasn't only being interviewed for *The Rack*. 'You two are friends, right?'

It was no secret. Last year, the pair had been all over the media when the third member of the famous RoseGold trio, Kit Marley, *enfant terrible* of the arts world, had been murdered. Intrigued as he was, Ace thought it was probably best not to bring that up.

'We are. You may think of me as her minder.'

'I see,' Ace repeated. 'Fair enough – every queen needs her knight.'

'You'll have to solve my riddles to even get over the moat.'

'Oh, trolls – I know how deal with them. You should check out my social media campaigns.'

There was another pause, and a sense of squaring up.

'We'll come to your opinions later,' said Will. 'I promise to ask you about racism and climate change if you will *please* stop being mysterious about your background.' He cocked his head to one side. 'Well?'

'Right.' Ace drew a breath. 'As you may be aware, I was fostered as a small child. Permanently, as it turned out. My foster mother, Merle, was a sports coach and recognised I might have potential.'

'Oof,' interrupted Will. 'She must've thought she'd won the foster-child lottery.' He apologised as Ace gave him a look.

'My foster father wasn't around much. I guess you could say it was a matriarchal household – my foster sister, Faye, is a … um, strong woman too.'

The discomforting image of his sibling slid in, and he wondered for a moment if she knew about his Wimbledon win. Probably not. Since leaving Merle's, Faye had lived on the margins of society, disappearing for long periods, travelling with fringe, off-the-grid communities. When the pandemic hit, she'd hooked up with a group of conspiracy theorists and melted into the woods of the West Country.

As a teen, Faye had been diagnosed with 'conduct disorder'. She'd ricocheted between foster homes, one carer after another throwing up their hands in despair, until Merle had taken her on, determined to be the one who'd make a difference.

'I have a foster brother too. He left to travel just before Covid, he's sitting it out in New Zealand.'

'Sensible chap,' said Will. 'Why were you fostered? What happened there?'

'That's classified. Sorry.'

'You're famous, now. It'll come out, eventually.'

'It's not important.' Ace's tone was exasperated.

'It *so* is, to your fans.'

Ace put down his knife and fork. 'Right. Off the record?'

'Ace. If you don't tell, the tabloids will dig. If you're uncomfortable discussing it, give me the barest bones and I'll fudge. I'm good at writing words that keep secrets.'

Ace looked doubtful, but recognised the sense in Will's words. 'I have no idea about my biological parents. For all I know, I could've been found sleeping in a cave. I've never especially wanted to find out; I'm happy with who I've become, and grateful to my foster family.'

He stopped talking; he was saying no more. He held Will's gaze as the silence stretched out, and when Ace didn't fill it, Will finally nodded. 'Thanks for sharing that. I'll probe no further.' He checked his phone then carried on, questioning Ace about his rise to tennis stardom.

Ace explained, patiently, how he'd competed in fencing before switching his focus to tennis. He'd been Britain's number one youth fencer, and had won gold at the 2012 Olympics.

Will's eyes widened in surprise. 'Olympic gold? Oh my lord, you are an actual golden boy!' But then he pulled a face. 'Fencing, though?'

'An ancient and noble sport, Will.'

'What got you into that? I mean, swords are quite sexy, but the head-to-toe onesie things … not so much.'

Ace leaned forward. 'I think you might enjoy this tale.'

'I'm all ears.'

'My foster father, Hector, is a keen coarse fisherman. Those people you see huddled under giant umbrellas on wet Sundays, avoiding their families? That was Hector.'

'*Wear out thy youth with shapeless idleness.*'

'Something like that. When I was little – about five or six – he found an ancient bronze sword in the shallows of a lake up on Bodmin Moor. He was reeling in a fish when a glint in the reeds caught his eye. He waded in and there it was, just lying there on the bottom.'

'Treasure! How thrilling.'

'I was fascinated by it.' Ace pictured the beautiful sword, which Hector had kept in a custom-made cabinet. One of Ace's earliest memories was of pressing his nose up against the glass, gazing at that weapon, longing to swing it above his head, to run his finger down its gleaming blade. But it had been kept under strictest lock and key.

Museum experts had identified the sword as Celtic. The grip was embellished with moulded swirls, and in the pommel was a space where a precious stone would have sat.

'It's Hector's pride and joy,' said Ace. 'Every visitor to our house has to hear the tale. Merle – my mum – was terrified we'd be burgled because of it, but the display case is museum grade. No way could anyone break into that cabinet.' He grinned. 'Apart from me.'

Will chuckled. 'Do go on, *Arthur*.'

'When you live in a Cornish backwater, you welcome a supposedly insurmountable challenge.'

'You mean you worked out where your dad hid the key.'

'Oh no. No key.'

'Then …'

Ace tapped the size of his nose. 'A touch of magic. Opened it up, pulled out that sword.'

'And now you're going to tell me Hector called it Excalibur.'

'He didn't, but I did. Secretly,' said Ace. 'And when I liberated it, I took it outside, and by the time Hector came home I was hooked on the feel of a sword in my hand. He discovered me feinting the elderberry tree. He was furious, and couldn't believe I'd worked out how to take it from its case. But he knew how fascinated with that sword I'd always been, and in return for my promise never to touch it again, he paid for fencing lessons. Of course, I didn't compete with a heavy sword like Excalibur, I fenced with an epee.'

'An epee?'

'It's a light, thrusting weapon. And the entire body is a valid target.'

Will met his eye. 'Indeed? Now that's a sport I could get into.'

Ace laughed and sat back in his seat, his meal and his story finished. 'I think we had a deal, Will.'

'You want more on Eliza.'

'That would be nice.'

Will looked at him for a long moment, and appeared to reach a decision. 'She's everything she seems. Exceptionally bright, genuine, feisty but kind-hearted – a pussy cat in a tiger skin, my late-lamented partner once called her. Also something of a square peg in a round hole, if you'll pardon the cliché, in that she's a creative person living a corporate life. Her only failing is probably that she's a workaholic. But she's been through a lot. Business battles, family dramas, splitting up with her long-term boyfriend ...' He paused. 'And ... Kit's death. Kit Marley.'

He stared out of the window. 'The three of us – we were a close-knit team. Eliza and I are still somewhat adrift without him. Eliza maybe even more so than I.'

'That was a terrible business,' said Ace. 'Andre Sokolov was involved in sports broadcasting, so I came across him. But ... back to Eliza?' Even saying her name made his heart beat faster.

'Right. Yes. Close to her father. They've had their moments – all the wives and mistresses and the scandals. But they've worked through that and – well, Ace, should you ever find yourself on her slender arm, know that Harry Rose's good opinion of you is the deal-clincher. *However*, as he's a tennis fanatic, you have something of a head start there.' Will shook his head. 'Honestly, Harry acts as if he invented the game.'

'Useful to know. What's he like?'

'Utterly charming and very charismatic; *wicked* sense of humour, but – shit, you wouldn't want him as an enemy. He's ruthless as they come. Verging on the tyrant, at times.'

'I see.' Ace looked out of the window at the Thames twinkling in the sunshine, then back at Will. 'And Eliza ... there's no, um–'

'Love interest? Not currently. She's still close to Rob, her ex. It's something she's good at,' he said, as if the thought had just occurred to him, 'keeping on good terms with people who have … let's say, let her down. And there have been plenty of those, especially in her crazy extended family: psycho sister, devious cousin, an out-of-control half-brother – he died; a heinous uncle, as well as all the business enemies she's had to deal with. But somehow she sails through, comes out the other side sparkly as ever.'

Ace wondered if this woman had any flaws at all, but as he went to ask, Will said, 'Your turn. You've said in the press that you want to *use your voice for change*. Tell me about that.'

Fair enough. Will didn't want to say too much about Eliza to an over-interested stranger. Ace took another drink of water, then began sharing his thoughts on how those in the public eye had an obligation to use their time in the spotlight to push for change. People didn't trust politicians, he said, but they idolised sportspeople, calling them heroes. And that particularly applied to the working classes, who were often denied a voice.

Will stifled a yawn; his gaze had drifted out of the window again.

'Am I boring you, Will?'

The writer's eyes snapped back to his. 'Never, Ace. I'm beyond delighted you're good at heart. We all *desperately* want to believe you're the white knight you seem.'

'Probably not a good metaphor – I'm taking a stand against racism.'

'Oh. The black knight, then?' Will adopted a pose. '*I move for no man.*'

Ace grinned. '*Tis but a scratch …*'

'*I've had worse.*'

They both laughed.

'Classic movie,' said Ace. 'Shall I continue? Or are my thoughts on social injustice going to be edited out to leave space for speculation on why I was abandoned at birth?'

'Indeed. I'm just anticipating my editor's deletions on the piece we'd in fact both like me to write.'

Ace thought for a moment. 'But isn't Terri Robbins-More all about fighting for the common man?'

'She is. But she's also deeply suspicious of people's motivations. She's been around for a long, long time, watched the very best of them collapse under the weight of their own ambition and success. The whole *power corrupts* thing.'

'I'm good at hitting a ball,' said Ace. 'That doesn't mean you have to listen to my opinions on equal rights, racism, whatever. But the fact is, when you become famous, people want to know what you believe. And the person on the street will often take more notice of what, say, Harry Styles thinks, than the PM or the leader of the opposition. You're giving me a platform here. I'm not going to waste it.'

Will leaned forward, warming to his theme. 'But how are your opinions likely to change anything? A tennis champ who cares about racism, or climate change. So what? Aren't we all already concerned about these things? Why not do something practical, like, set up a charity to give poor kids the opportunity to play tennis?'

'Others already have. Sportspeople are great at bringing through talent that otherwise wouldn't have the chance. I want to be more about changing attitudes. Look – that photo shoot. You think that's what I want to be doing? It's bollocks. How is it important whether or not I look hot on your cover? But you know the answer to that. It sells more copies. People will read it mostly to find out who I'm dating, and maybe how much money I won on Sunday. I tell you that, and then I get to share–'

'But you haven't told me who you're dating.'

'No one, right now …' It was *almost* true. 'And in return I get to share my thoughts on, say, diversity in sport. You get the picture?'

Will smiled. 'Indeed I do. Right you are – feel free to share more opinions. I just hope you're prepared for what this feature might unleash.'

'Bring it on.'

'Well,' said Will, some time later. 'I have all I need and that was an absolute delight. And when I report back to our dear leader –'

The phone in his hand rang. 'Speak of the devil …'

Chapter 4

Ace

A different Eliza answered the door that evening. Where before she'd been like a bright flame, all wild red curls and flirtatious smiles, now she was cool and shimmery in a pale grey dress, her hair tamed, pulled back. Delicate silver earrings swung beside her slender neck; the only splash of colour was her red lips.

And that expression that skipped across her beautiful face, sandwiched between surprise and pleasure: wary.

His heart dropped.

'Oh … Ace!'

'Will thought this might be fun,' he said, hesitantly. 'But if you'd rather–'

'No, no, it's just –' She glanced at Will. 'I guess … the press.' He saw her thinking quickly. 'Come with us, Will. You can sneak out as soon as we've gone in. Please?'

'Tsk. It's totally the opposite direction to home.'

She raised an eyebrow at him.

He sighed. 'Okay, boss.'

She swept up a set of keys from a table by the door, and he and Will moved aside as she locked up. While her back was turned, Will gave Ace a wink, but Ace wasn't so sure. Will had been carried away with the moment, earlier, and Ace had grabbed the opportunity to get to know this intriguing woman a little better. But now, here at her home, uninvited, it felt as if he were intruding into her private life. She seemed … guarded. Slightly remote. A little voice inside him said, *What were you thinking?*

Ace had been properly famous for a matter of months. His background was every sort of ordinary. Until he'd won Olympic gold, he'd been Mr Nobody from Nowhere, then he was that young lad who'd won the fencing. But it wasn't one of the sexy events, so he'd been quickly forgotten. When he'd started to do well at tennis too, his sponsors – sports gear manufacturers, mainly, plus a fuck-off watch brand – were there for his accident-of-birth good looks, rather than his hard-won sporting achievements.

He's not just a pretty face, Merle had snapped at Camelot's marketing people when they'd wanted to use him, shirt-free, in a campaign to raise awareness of the National Lottery's support for the Olympic team.

And then, *boom*. The two Opens, and storming to the Wimbledon final, winning it for Britain. Catapulted into the spotlight, an unfamiliar place, one he was feeling his way around, a day at a time.

Whereas Eliza … a life lived in the public eye. The Roses were probably Britain's most famous family after the royals, and one of the richest. The two of them were worlds apart; Eliza was way out of his league.

He checked himself. He was overthinking it. This was one date – not even a proper date. Ace was a last-minute fill-in for Eliza's father, that was all. Will had put her on the spot, and she was too polite to send Ace away.

'Sheesh, you're lofty tonight,' said Will to Eliza as they set off walking, past the Dickens Inn, its tiered wooden balconies hung with pots of gaudy flowers. The yellow-brick apartments of St Katharine Docks glowed gold in the evening sun, and the ropes of the boats bobbing in the marina clinked, soft and melodic, against their masts.

'Nearly six foot with these on,' she said, looking down at her silver high-heels as they tip-tapped on the stone pathway. She hooked an arm through Will's.

'I like,' said Will. 'And the dress is spectacular, wouldn't you agree, Ace?'

Ace turned to look at her as she walked between the two of them. Her eyes met his – properly, for the first time since he'd shown up on her doorstep.

'Spectacular, yes,' he said. And when her full, red lips curved into a smile, he lost control of his words. 'In fact, you look incredibly beautiful.'

'Oh.' She was taken aback. 'That's sweet of you. Thanks!'

He grimaced. 'Sorry if that was a bit much. It just came out.'

She bit her lip, then laughed. She was unwinding, softening, in front of his eyes. 'I'm here for your bit much,' she said, and hooked her other arm through his.

'Gorgeous,' said Will, beaming.

At the car Will held open the door and Eliza slid in, Will letting himself into the passenger seat. Ace sat down next to Eliza. The driver recognised him, and as they drove west along the embankment, shared his opinion of the Wimbledon final.

'Just what we needed. Really picked us up it 'as, your win. Well done, sire.'

'Thanks,' said Ace. 'It feels great to have given everyone something to be cheerful about at the moment.'

Unfortunately, this prompted a monologue on Brexit and the mishandling of the Covid pandemic.

Ace glanced at Eliza and rolled his eyes a little. She gave him a conspiratorial smile. He was acutely aware of their closeness; she smelt as beautiful as she looked, and her dark eyes – who did they remind him of? It clicked. Princess Jasmine, in Disney's *Aladdin*. She'd been his first crush; he must have been four or five years old.

He just wanted to stare at this woman, to drink her in, but he tore his eyes away, letting them settle on her hands where they rested in her lap. Long, delicate fingers, tipped with pale nail polish. He noticed a beautiful silver ring with a red stone. *I wonder who gave her that?*

'How did your interview go?' she asked in a low voice, leaving Will to enjoy the driver's opinions.

'It went well, I think. Happy I got the good cop, not the bad one. I want to start a few conversations, but I don't want them to be all about me. I just hope Will doesn't get too carried away with this whole *new hero for Britain* angle.'

'The British press – they build you up to knock you down. Do you have decent media training? Because you'll need to know how to play this game, as well as the one with the racket.'

'Both need a good set of balls,' commented Will, earwigging from the front.

'My mum, Merle – she's also my manager – she handles most of the PR.'

'Your *mum*?' said Eliza.

'Foster mum. She's a sports coach, a bloody good one,' said Ace, defensively. 'I've got a top tennis pro now, too, but Merle still handles the management side of things. I'm looking forward to Will's write-up, I think he gets what I want to try and do.'

'Indeed I do,' said Will. 'It'll be a rave, and if Terri cuts out the white knight parts – white knight, black knight, knight in shining armour –'

Ace grinned. 'Knight who says "ni" …'

Will spluttered.

'What?' said Eliza.

'Monty Python – Holy Grail,' replied Ace.

'– whichever shade of knight Ace, in fact, is,' Will continued, 'should my words be sliced and diced, then my wrath shall know no bounds.'

They'd arrived at Leicester Square. 'Wait,' said Eliza, as Ace went to open his door. 'The story. Will was interviewing Ace for an *unmissable* piece in the *Rack*, and invited him along tonight. I'm delighted to be meeting Ace *for the first time*. Are we clear?'

A posse of photographers and a growing crowd of passers-by surged forward as Eliza and Will exited the car.

'*Eliza!*'

'*Over here!*'

Eliza and Will approached the pack, wearing wide smiles.

The car door was open, but Ace remained inside. No one had spotted him yet. He watched Eliza, completely at home in front of the media.

As if sensing his stare, she half turned, looking at him over her shoulder. Her eyes met his, and that flirtatious twinkle was back. She raised her eyebrows, smiled slowly, then lifted a hand and beckoned. The gesture was undoubtedly for the benefit of the press, but it was still a spectacularly sexy move.

He slid out of the car and grinned across at her.

As one, the crowd let out a gasp.

'*Ace!*'

'Oh my *god* – it's Ace Penhalagon!'

Eliza laughed in delight.

It was a beautiful moment, and he revelled in it. He raised a hand, waving at the onlookers, acknowledging their cheers.

'*Congratulations, Ace – we love you!*' called a loud voice.

He made his way over to Eliza. Will was explaining to a reporter, his voice raised above the cheering, how Ace had come to be here this evening.

'And here's the hero of the moment!' Eliza trilled, waving Ace to her side. 'Aren't we just *so* lucky with our special guest tonight!'

This was the picture they all wanted. The photographers jostled for position, and Ace noticed Will take Eliza's elbow. It was touching, the way he looked out for her. Will smiled over at Ace, and he sensed he'd passed a test today, that he would be allowed across the moat.

'Yes,' Eliza was saying to the reporter, 'you did see me at Wimbledon on Sunday, but today is the first time I've had the pleasure of meeting Ace. *Such* a privilege, and hasn't he just cheered us all up with his sensational win?'

Then she adeptly switched the conversation to the movie, as the two lead actors appeared behind them. He recognised the glamorous film star who hurried over, giggling, opening her eyes wide. 'Wow – Ace! I'm totally your biggest fan! Can we get a selfie?'

The crowd snapped their own photos as the pair leaned in and smiled into her phone. The click and whirr of camera shutters filled the air.

Catching Ace's eye, Will cocked his head towards the entrance. Eliza wrapped up her chat, and they made their way to the Odeon doors.

Inside, guests were milling in the lobby, attempting awkward, socially distanced air-kissing, and more often than not, *oh-fuck-it* hugs.

'Right, my darlings, I'm going to love you and leave you,' said Will. 'I was kidding-ye-not when I said I was all done in.'

Ace noticed dark circles beneath his eyes, and realised the exuberant Will was indeed about to run out of steam.

'Yes, you get off home,' said Eliza, putting a hand on his shoulder. 'Snuggle up with Romeo and watch something trashy. Get food delivered. Promise me you'll eat?'

'Yes, yes. Don't fuss.'

'And give Romeo a stroke from me, but don't say it's from me, otherwise he'll bite you.' She turned to Ace. 'Will's cat hates me. He's terribly possessive, doesn't like to share.'

'As opposed to his predecessor, the other Kitty, who, shall we say, enjoyed sharing.' Will gave Eliza a small, sad smile. 'Ace,' he said, perking up a little. 'Meeting you has been beyond a pleasure. This will be the first Olympics about which I have given even the slightest of fucks. I will be glued to the screen and cheering you on.'

Ace was leaving for Tokyo in a few days' time – probably. The way this year was panning out, a last-minute change of plan wouldn't take anyone by surprise.

'Thanks, Will. I've had a great day too. Anything more you need – you have my direct number.'

Eliza's face was concerned as she watched Will leave. 'He's shattered, poor thing. And I *know* he won't bother to eat.' She tutted. 'He's worked so hard this year, under really difficult circumstances, and last night we had rather too much to drink, hence his sudden crash. We were ... it was the one-year anniversary of losing his partner.'

'Kit Marley,' said Ace, thinking back again to the shock death of the controversial writer.

'Yes.' Pain flickered across her face before she looked away, scanning the room. 'Drinking too much seemed appropriate. I hope I don't fall asleep in the movie. Please nudge me if I start to droop – or snore.'

'I will.' Though Ace couldn't imagine this dazzling woman emitting such a sound.

Later, as the film began, he breathed out, relishing the moment of peace after the relentless training, the matches, the Wimbledon PR circus. The romcom wasn't his cup of tea. *Not Loving This*, it was called. Apt. But he doubted he'd have registered any of it, even if it had been his favourite blend. How could he focus on the screen when he was sitting here, next to the enchanting Eliza Rose, who had entered his life only this morning, like a wrecking ball. Ace was hyperaware of their elbows resting together on the armrest between them; he shifted in his seat, and his leg touched hers.

She glanced at him. Her eyes were illuminated by the screen, and he saw the question in them. Opening the little handbag in her lap, she took out her phone, typed something in, then angled the phone towards him.

Boring! Want a drink?

He smiled in the dark, and nodded.

Side door in 5 mins. Ask security for directions.

Luckily, Eliza was on the end of the row, and when the movie grew noisier she slipped away. A few minutes later, he followed.

The security guard asked for a photo, then led him to a fire exit opening onto a quiet side street, where Eliza was waiting. Finally, he was alone with her. But now, like a schoolboy with a hopeless crush, rational thought flew, taking with it the simple task of asking if she'd like to go for a bite to eat. Instead, he blurted, 'Um … did you really want to get a drink? Or were you just bored and tired and wanting to go home?' He gave himself a mental slap.

'Oh – these so-so, middle-of-the-road movies,' she said, shaking her head. 'We have to make them, they earn well. But give me a dark, emotional drama any day.' She smiled. 'How about we go somewhere I can ask about *your* favourite movies. Apart from Monty Python.'

Her dark eyes were like whirlpools, drawing him into their depths, tying his tongue in knots.

'Where are you staying?' she asked, when he didn't reply immediately.

'Westminster – the Plaza. I'm staying on a couple more days, to do the publicity stuff.'

'Well, it'd obviously be hopeless, going to a bar,' she said. 'We'd be all over Twitter in seconds. We could just walk your way? Along the embankment – I love walking by the river.'

'In those shoes?' He eyed them doubtfully.

'I'll give it a go.' She fiddled with her little bag, taking out a silvery chain, looping it across her body. 'May I?' she said, moving her hand towards his arm.

He grinned. 'Last time you asked me that, you started undressing me. But yes, my arm is your arm.'

Eliza giggled and took it, and Ace gained another foot on top of his six two.

'I'd duck in there and get you a thick shake,' he said as they passed McDonald's, 'but I have an inkling I won't be able to do that again for a while. How weird is that?' He wondered whether Eliza had ever been in a McDonald's.

Ace was pleased to find he'd regained the ability to speak coherently, and they chatted easily as they walked down to Trafalgar Square, ignoring the double-takes of passers-by, Ace smiling in a leave-us-alone way at people calling their congratulations.

The air was warm as they crossed the square, the day's heat still radiating off the stone buildings with their colonnades and domes and porticos and general British Empire pomposity.

'My feet –' said Eliza. 'Can we stop for a minute?'

They perched on the wall of a fountain, sitting close. Slanting sunbeams brushed Eliza's bare shoulders with gold as the sun dipped towards Canada House, and her earrings flashed as they caught the light.

'Shall we have a stab at tomorrow's headline?' she said, trailing her fingers in the water. 'I'm going to say, *Eliza Serves an Ace*.' She looked up at him and raised her eyebrows. 'Your turn.'

He laughed. 'Good one. I'll go for … *Game, Set, and Love Match for Ace*.'

'Excellent.'

'And how about, for the first paragraph –' He held up a hand, palm outwards, and swept it across the air in front of them: '*Tennis champ Ace Penhalagon got a taste of his own medicine when he met Eliza Rose. The beautiful media queen's fearsome ace hit him straight in the heart*.'

She snorted, and flicked water at him. 'Wow, Ace. That's top tabloiding. When you tire of tennis, can I hire you for *Hooray*?'

'Admirable alliteration. Advantage Eliza.'

'Ha-ha.' She leaned on him for a moment. 'This is fun. Thanks for stepping up tonight.'

'You're more than welcome. Probably *The Lord of the Rings* and *The Hobbit*, by the way.'

'What? Oh – interesting choice. Are you a fan of fantasy?'

'Not as such. But I love a good quest, a full-on battle between good and evil; death and immortality, Fate and free will …'

'Also dragons.'

'Always love a dragon,' he said, smiling down at her. He flicked a little water back, and a few drops landed on her shoulders. They sat there, sparkling at him in the evening sun, like tiny dome-shaped prisms. Unable to resist, he gently brushed them off. Her skin was warm and smooth beneath his fingers.

Her flirtatious smile faltered as she met his gaze. She bit her bottom lip, and Ace's words ran away with him again. 'What I said before – it was kind of true.'

'Which part?'

'The heart part.'

There was a pause, and neither looked away.

'Eliza … can I see you again?'

She hesitated. 'Well … that would be nice. Just … casual. I don't really have time for much else, I should probably let you know that.'

It wasn't a no, and she was being honest.

'I've got the Olympics, and then the US Open, but somewhere in between I'd love to …'

What those eyes did to him. He leaned forward and kissed her.

Eliza went rigid.

Oh, shit. Mortified, Ace went to pull away … but she lifted her hand to the back of his head, keeping him close, and he felt her soften … and melt.

Briefly.

'Stop …' she whispered, dropping her hand. 'Someone will see.'

Stopping was so hard. 'Sorry, I keep forgetting. I can't get used to this.' He moved away a little. 'Shall we carry on down to the river? I promise to keep a respectable distance.'

There was a note of exasperation in that last sentence. When he'd kissed her, the world had faded away, and he couldn't have cared less if they'd been livestreamed on Facebook.

Eliza stood up, smoothing down her dress. 'That sounds like a sensible plan.' She winced as the weight returned to her feet. 'Ow, bugger.' Then, noticing a group of people looking over at them, hearing someone call Ace's name, she cursed again. Bending down, she slipped off her shoes then looked up at him with a grin, holding out a hand. 'Run, Ace!'

He grabbed it and they hurried across the square, past the lions, past Nelson's Column, the one-armed admiral gazing sternly down at them from his lofty pedestal.

They stopped at a pedestrian crossing. Looking behind them, Ace was glad to see they weren't being pursued. As they waited, Eliza slipped her shoes back on.

They continued down to the river at a slow walk. Eliza was beginning to hobble.

'How about we stop off in here,' he said, as they reached the gardens along the embankment. He took a quick look round as they reached the entrance – there was no one here.

'I might take my shoes off again.'

'No need.' He bent down and scooped her up.

She let out a delighted squeak, putting her arms around his neck. 'Wow, what a way to travel – swept up in the arms of Britain's hero. This romcom is panning out *so* much better than that lame thing we just watched.'

'It really is. Hold on tight.' He carried her along a gravel path bordered by neat lawns and pretty flowerbeds, their colours fading as twilight crept across the city. Across the Thames, the giant O of the London Eye was lit up in scarlet.

'Not too heavy?'

'Eliza, I spend a tedious amount of time working on my upper body strength. Here?' he said, as they drew level with a bench.

'I don't want you to put me down. This is too lovely. Can you carry me all the way home, please?'

'Easy.' He hitched her up a little. 'I'm at peak fitness right now.'

Her fingers crept up the back of his neck, playing with the curls above his collar. 'Fit indeed. How are you single? All those beautiful tennis girls.'

She was fishing. He was enormously happy that she was fishing.

'Lovely girls, yes. But do I want to spend time with women who talk mostly about tennis when my life is already all about tennis? Probably not.'

She stroked a finger down his cheek, then turned his face towards her. 'So …' she said, looking into his eyes.

He was aware of his heart thumping, and wondered if she could feel it.

'So yes, I am–' He'd been about to say 'single' when she interrupted.

'– adorable.'

He gave a small laugh. 'Puppies are adorable.'

'A lovely man, then.'

'That's sweet, but you don't know me.'

'Intuition. And Will told me.'

'He's met me once.'

'Will's an excellent judge of character. So …'

The Earth seemed to hold its breath. Then she pressed her soft lips to his, and Ace's senses reeled as he inhaled her musky perfume, felt her fingertips tracing his skin. The kiss quickly became intense. Ace slid his arm out from under her knees, holding her tight against him with the other, and lowered her slowly to the ground. He brushed aside an earring and trailed kisses down her neck, before his lips moved to the irresistible hollow above her collarbone. She tipped back her head with a sigh, and pushed her hips into his.

His body's response was fierce. 'Eliza,' he said, into her warm skin, 'we should probably stop, before …'

'Before we can't stop,' she whispered.

They made their way to the bench, and Ace sat quietly beside her, waiting for his heartbeat to slow. His head was spinning; he had the strangest impression, of something out there in the ether, whirring, clicking, ushering him on to another level, another phase in his life – one that revolved around this woman beside him, that had her at its core.

'When can I see you?' he said. 'I'm back here between the Olympics and the US Open?'

Eliza took her phone out of her bag. 'What's your number?'

She typed it in, then suddenly sat up straighter. 'Oh – I've just had the *greatest* idea!'

'What?'

'My dad. He's a tennis nut. He was so thrilled with your win. How about …' she stroked her chin, a little theatrically, 'you come to Richmond – the family house – but we don't tell him. I'll just say I'm bringing a friend for Sunday lunch.'

Her father's good opinion of you is the deal-clincher … he's as ruthless as they come.

'And I'll let Clare in on the secret.'

'Clare?'

'My step mum. You'll love her.'

He smiled. 'You sure? I mean … meeting the family?' He was charmed to see a faint tinge of pink on her pale cheeks.

'We don't have to let on about … well, I can just say we're friends?'

'I don't mind the truth if you don't.' He gently pulled her towards him. 'Eliza – what even is the truth?'

She put her arms round his neck. 'I guess the truth will make itself known, somewhere in the madness of our lives.'

He moved to kiss her again, but her eyes went over his shoulder and she pulled away, saying, 'Quick … masks.' Someone had appeared by the park gates, starting to pull them shut, waving across at them.

They made their way over and, unrecognised, slipped past him onto the embankment.

'I suppose we should get you a cab,' he said.

'Probably should.'

'For … just you?'

She raised her eyebrows. 'Never on a first date. What kind of girl do you take me for, Mr Penhalagon?' Her cheeky smile softened the disappointment.

'A cruel one. But tonight has been amazing. So – I'll see you after Tokyo?'

'You will. Tell me, what does one say to a departing Olympian?' she asked, flagging down a taxi. 'Break a leg?'

'One says, good luck, and the Olympian replies, if I lose it's all your fault, because I might just be trying to get home sooner.'

'Win for me, then, Ace.' She kissed him quickly on the lips. 'Make it your quest. Go forth for Eliza, for Britain. Bring us back some gold.'

Chapter 5

Eliza

Rob's face appeared on Eliza's laptop as she sat on the sofa the following evening. The balcony doors were open, and the soft murmurs of people strolling around the marina floated upwards.

'How goes it, Snow White?' He was in a suit, all LA film exec, his dark curls neatly styled, his sharp jawline shadowed by designer stubble.

As ever, seeing his face brought a big smile to hers. 'Good thanks, Roberto.'

'Oh – I spot a skimpy top,' he said. 'Is it one of your three days of summer over there?'

'I'll take less of the smug Californian, thank you.'

'You do look hot, though,' he said, his brown eyes twinkling. 'But then you look hot in the middle of winter too.'

She tutted. 'Cut it out, Rob.'

'Sorry, boss. So – all's well?'

'It is. Apart from the you-know-what.'

'The Virus That Shall Not Be Named?'

'Yes, that. We've gone from pandemic to pingdemic. Dad got pinged–'

'So I heard.'

'You did? How is that news?'

'The no-show at the preview? But you served an Ace instead. Nice one, Lizzie – it sure gave our romcom the push it needed.'

Photos of Eliza and Ace had been everywhere today. Headlines had covered all the expected variations on the theme, the most cringeworthy probably being *Ace of Hearts,* courtesy of the *Mirror.*

Harry's text had read: *Scored yourself an Ace, Lizzie? Your father approves.*

'Please tell me Penhalagon's a complete douche,' said Rob. 'Like, stupid and vain and he hates animals?'

She smiled. 'Sorry, he's adorable.'

'Fuck – really?'

'Yep, a solid ten. We got bored with the movie and ran away, just the two of us. It was a blast. And it was indeed a lovely warm evening, even by your city-carved-out-of-a-desert standards.'

Rob's smile faded. 'You like him? Properly like him? Are you seeing him again?'

Eliza considered her answer. She'd finished things with Rob because she couldn't bring herself to commit. He understood that. But the last time he'd been over, he'd asked if they could get back together – again. He meant the world to her, and she hated saying no to him, but he simply wouldn't accept that, deep down, where it mattered, their life goals were different.

'I've only met him once, Rob. He's off to the Olympics soon, and he's always travelling so … probably a non-starter.' She quickly changed the subject, telling him about her evening at Will's, and why she'd been there.

'I can't believe it's only a year,' said Rob. 'It seems much longer – like another lifetime. Everything pre-Covid seems like another lifetime.'

They went quiet.

'Lizzie …' he said, hesitantly. 'I've got something to tell you.'

'Ah. I did wonder.'

'You did? Why?'

'Your email, it just gave me that vibe. What's up? Don't tell me you've been headhunted by Disney, or that Mac's turned traitor again?' Eliza's Scottish cousin, Mackenzie James, was now VP of the US operation and was doing great things, but only last year she'd attempted to wrest control of the Rose throne from Eliza.

'Not work. Personal.' He raked his fingers through his hair, looking uncomfortable.

'Personal?'

'Yep. I'm … I wanted to tell you myself, before you saw it online, which will happen sooner rather than later, seeing as she's quite famous now.'

'She?'

'Letitia.'

Eliza's heart plummeted. Rob's fling with the beautiful actress had been what finally killed their relationship. He'd claimed it had never amounted to anything, that he'd been trying to make Eliza jealous, to force her into committing once and for all. It had hurt – badly – and she still didn't know if he'd told her the truth about how far things had gone.

'Letitia,' she said, her voice flat.

'We're dating.'

'Again.'

'No, not again. We didn't date before, we just –' he shrugged, '– kind of hung out and a bit more.'

Eliza said nothing. Her head told her she had no right to even know who Rob was dating, never mind pass judgement on his choices. But her heart disagreed.

'I see. So you actually like her, then? For more than her pretty face?'

'She's a lot more than a pretty face. You'd like her too, but look, it's early days. I just wanted to let you know.'

'I appreciate that.'

They went quiet again.

'Work's all good?' Rob said, awkwardly.

'Fine.' Why was she so upset? What had she expected? 'Sorry, Rob. I guess … not going to lie, it hurts a bit. A lot. Because it's her.'

'I understand. And for you, it's probably all tangled up with that terrible time. Everything happened at once and you don't need reminding of it all. Look – I'll call again when you've had a bit of space. Shall I?'

'Okay.'

'Cool. Well, I'd better get back to work. Speak soon – yes?'

'Yep.' She blew him a kiss and snapped the laptop shut, with far more force than was necessary.

Letting her head drop back against the sofa, Eliza couldn't stop the memories flooding in. She and Rob had been so happy together, briefly, after all the waiting – for his divorce, for her therapy to work, for Rob to come to terms with Amy's death – until Eliza had been forced to think about what she really wanted from life. Which didn't include being a wife, or having children. Her career – Rose Corp – was her priority. But how many men would be prepared – no, it needed to be *happy* – to come second in her life? Not Rob.

Kit was the only person who'd ever understood. *He wants a degree of power over you. Don't give it to him.*

She smiled as she remembered the next part of that conversation.

And you know what, Eliza? It's no fun sticking to one. Chrissakes, girl – how many boyfriends have you actually had?

One.

Fucking hell.

They'd spluttered with laughter.

Oh my god, Kit. It's pathetic.

Tragic. There's a world out there full of beautiful men, and you're its queen.

So after the break-up she'd dated one beautiful man after another, but had let none of them emotionally close. She was still too raw after the split, and Kit's death. She needed to keep her heart safe.

There was a moment of clarity as she acknowledged she'd deliberately dated glamorous men who had little else going on to hold her attention.

The evening had cooled. As she closed the balcony doors, her thoughts turned to Ace. He was on a different level. He had depth. What had Will said? *Genuine, humble, but very sharp.* And he wanted to use his fame to do good, to make a difference. Like her, he wanted to change the world.

That little squeeze of her heart again.

She was thankful his schedule was so busy; it would give her time to decide whether to take this forward. After the preview, she'd sent him a text: *Thanks for tonight, it was absolutely lovely. Wishing you huge success at the Olympics, I'll be watching! With love and hugs XXX* She thought it struck the right tone between friendly and 'a bit more', as Rob had put it.

His reply had taken her by surprise: *You took my breath away. Hope I'm thinking straight by the time I get to Tokyo. Will do my very best to win you your gold. Won't contact you again before I return because I need to stay focused. Please take that in a good way ☺ xx*

That seemed quite intense, after only one sort-of date.

But that was part of his appeal. There was no pretence. That was why Britain loved him.

❀

'My god,' said Chess, as they watched Ace demolishing his opponent in the men's singles final. Eliza's cousin, who was also a close friend, had stayed over so they could watch the game, and they were sitting in their pyjamas sipping cups of tea. Eliza's hair frizzed wildly around her shoulders, while Chess's well-behaved version of the Rose family red was neatly tied back.

Much of the Olympics had taken place in the middle of the night, UK time, but thankfully this match was post-sunrise and on a Sunday. A little on the early side, but so far, well worth getting up for.

'*What* a shot,' gasped Eliza. Ace, in stunning form, had just blasted a forehand down the line, not only reaching the unreachable but turning it into a winning shot the Romanian hadn't a hope in hell of returning. 'Ace is on fire.'

'He's so cool with it, though,' said Chess, as he played yet another blinder. While his opponent accompanied every shot with a loud grunt, Ace played silently, like a cat, the only sound the squeak of his trainers on the court. And his expression gave away nothing; there was just a narrowing of the eyes as he prepared to serve.

'Look at that focus,' said Chess. 'There's absolutely no hint of nerves. It's like he's completely fine with the whole of Britain being desperate for him to win gold.'

'He will,' said Eliza. 'I told him to.'

Chess spluttered into her tea.

Eliza's cousin was right – there was no indication whatsoever that Ace was feeling the weight of Britain's expectations. This was a different man from that tongue-tied version in Leicester Square. He was in full warrior-king mode, owning the court, his serves so powerful they were only properly visible in slo-mo. As Eliza watched him kill a lob with a brutal smash, she could hardly believe those were the same arms that had held her close in the park; that the fingers tightly gripping that racket had gently brushed spray from her shoulders in Trafalgar Square.

Chess nudged her. 'Well, cuz, I have to hand it to you. You really scored this time. He's incredible. And not very ugly.'

Eliza laughed, not taking her eyes from the screen. 'True. But … well. There's a lot more to him than …' She paused, holding her breath as Ace spun a backhand that dropped the ball just over the net, where it refused to bounce. '– that.' The Romanian stared at the dead ball in surprise.

'How did he do that?' said Chess, eyes wide behind her glasses. 'I'm actually starting to feel sorry for Nicolescu.'

There was a smattering of claps from the tiny number of people in the arena. It felt so wrong; Ace should have been getting roars of applause for a performance like this.

'The way he uses his racket,' said Chess, 'it's like a wand, controlling the ball. I strongly suspect sorcery.'

Eliza chuckled. 'Did you read the article?' She glanced at the latest issue of *The Rack*, lying on the coffee table. Ace was on the cover, looking deadly but relatable. Clever Allessandro – he'd got him just right.

'Not yet, I only looked at the photos.' As the players swapped ends, Chess picked up the magazine and read the front-page headline out loud: '*Is Ace Penhalagon Perfect?*' She raised an eyebrow at Eliza. 'Seriously? Who wrote that?'

'Terri. She meant it ironically. She instructed Will to dig up dirt

– Terri thinks Ace is too good to be true – but he fell in love instead. You should read it. Ace isn't just a brilliant tennis player …' she glanced at the cover again, 'with outstanding upper-body strength.'

Chess flicked through, going quiet as her eyes scanned the piece.

Eliza returned to the TV. Ace was sitting on his chair, swigging water, towelling his neck. His gaze was fixed on the ground; he was in the zone, preparing for the final battle – one set up and winning the second 5-1, serving for the match. It looked like being one of the speediest finals on record.

The players made their way back onto the court.

'Watch,' said Eliza.

'Reading. Heck, is he for real? All this stuff about giving away his winnings.' She read out: '*Britain's powerful, entitled elite, making merry, lining their silk pockets while the country flounders in chaos … skipping over the cracks in society they have driven ever deeper, wider …*' She looked up again. 'He said that?'

Eliza smiled sheepishly. 'Will might have edited …'

Chess carried on. '*Where's the diversity? Tennis is probably the ultimate country-club sport. By which I mean white …*'

'Shh – watch!' said Eliza, as Ace paused in bouncing the ball, fixed Nicolescu with that stare, then threw it high and served. *Served?* It seemed an impossibly polite verb for what Ace had just delivered. *Dinner* was served; Ace's opening shots were fired, like bullets.

Nicolescu returned a weak forehand, which Ace immediately killed, swivelling on his heel, thinking about his next serve before his opponent had even attempted to reach the shot.

'He's absolutely crushing it,' said Chess, as the camera zoomed in on the Romanian's stunned expression.

'Fifteen love,' said Eliza. Her heart was in her mouth. Superstition dictated nothing should be taken for granted, while rational thought acknowledged this match was all but over.

Another ace whipped past Nicolescu, who shook his head as he swapped sides.

'Thirty love. Oh my god.' Eliza shuffled to the edge of her seat.

Ace's next serve hit the net and dropped out. His second serve was good, but the Romanian reached it and managed a decent forehand; Ace's return was long.

'Thirty fifteen,' said Chess.

'Forty fifteen,' said Eliza, seconds later. She put her hands over her eyes, peeping out between her fingers. 'Match point.'

'Olympic Championship point.'

You could have heard a pin drop in that arena. Although, given the number of people watching, you might have been able to hear that anyway.

Ace did the stare again, then served. Nicolescu returned with a powerful backhand; Ace ran into the net and deflected the shot deep into the corner. Nicolescu managed to reach it, flipping it high over Ace's head; Ace ran backwards, leapt up and swept his racket down, smashing the ball at the Romanian's feet. Nicolescu brought his arm up quickly; the racket connected with the ball, sending it into the net.

'Yes!' shrieked Eliza, jumping up. 'Oh my god, he's done it!'

Chess leapt up and they hugged each other, bouncing up and down.

Ace fell to his knees and covered his face with his hands, dropping his head to the ground. When he raised it again, Eliza saw his tears.

'Oh god, look at him,' said Chess, putting a hand on her heart.

Eliza was choked; she sank back onto the sofa, wiping a tear from her eye. 'I wish I could hug him,' she said. 'I wish I was there.'

☙

The three medal winners took their spots on the podium for the victory ceremony. As per Tokyo 2020 regulations, when the medals were brought out on their cushions, the winners picked them up and put them round their own necks.

'Contactless medal delivery,' said Chess. 'Such times.'

Ace held his gold medal up as cameras flashed to a quiet ripple of clapping.

'It's so sad,' said Chess. 'No roaring crowd, no having the medal put around your neck. But he looks very happy.'

Smiling widely, Ace lifted his disk of gold and kissed it, then waved to the crowd that wasn't a crowd, before turning to the camera and blowing it a kiss.

'Oh, my poor heart,' said Chess. 'He's bloody gorgeous.'

'That kiss was totally for me,' said Eliza.

The players left the arena and Eliza stood up and stretched, then went over to the kitchen to make them breakfast.

'Come on then – spill,' called Chess. 'For my ears only; I promise not to repeat to Gil.' Chess was married to Gil Studley – Rob's brother – and the two men were close.

'Well, I guess you could say he swept me off my feet,' Eliza replied, breaking eggs into a bowl. 'We went for a walk, but I was wearing silly shoes, so after a bit he carried me. Honestly, it was like I weighed nothing. The strength in those arms.'

'How delicious. And then?'

'He asked if he could see me again, after the Olympics.'

'And … before he asked that?' Chess raised her eyebrows.

'Well, yes, there was a kiss. Or two.'

Chess gave a little squeak. 'And?'

Eliza went quiet.

'C'mon. I've been married forever, I need the occasional vicarious thrill in my life.' Chess had married young; as far as Eliza knew, Gil had been her only serious relationship. Eliza had always felt that her cousin, who had excelled academically and was now a production manager at RoseGold, disapproved of Eliza's 'creative' friends – one in particular – and the men she'd dated since Rob.

Eliza put down the whisk. 'It was … quite intense.'

'Really?' Chess's expression grew serious. 'What will you say to Rob?'

'He already knows. But … well. He's dating Letitia.' Eliza met her cousin's eye. 'Did you know?'

'No,' said Chess, looking surprised. 'News to me. It must be recent – he and Gil have been FaceTiming a lot.' Gil and Chess had few secrets. If there were any developments in Rob's love life, Eliza usually got to hear about them.

'It hurts, Chess, I'm not going to lie.'

Chess gave an exasperated huff. 'You can't have it both ways. You knock him back, then jump into bed with him again, then hold him at arm's length. The poor guy still has no idea where he stands with you.'

Chess had always been fond of her brother-in-law, and had thought he and Eliza were perfect for each other. 'He's not going to hang on forever. And Letitia's nice – I know, I know,' she said, holding up a hand as Eliza opened her mouth to interrupt. 'She's a blonde sex kitten so we should hate her, but she's actually very nice. A bit like Amy, but much sassier.'

Rob's wife, a nurse, had been quiet and fragile, prone to depression.

'What? Amy was a mouse!' flashed Eliza. 'Letitia doesn't strike me as a small, timid rodent.'

Chess sighed. 'Amy was sensitive …' She stopped, and there was an awkward silence.

'Sorry,' said Eliza, calming a little. 'I know my jealous streak isn't pretty.'

And Eliza knew, without ever having heard it from her lips, that Chess didn't believe Amy's death had been an accident. That she thought it too much of a coincidence Amy died the week her divorce came through, the day after Eliza and Rob had first been photographed in public as a couple.

'Maybe we're both moving on,' said Eliza quietly, and as she pictured Rob, tears threatened. 'Sorry again. I shouldn't have said that about Amy.' She sighed. 'I can't seem to let go of Rob. Maybe it would actually be best if he found someone else, and just said no to me.'

Chess smiled. 'I don't think he'd ever say no to you. So maybe it's up to you to do the moving on?'

'I don't know.' Eliza's eyes settled on the magazine cover. 'I'm not an easy person to be with. So much baggage, and I'm already married – to the job.' She started slicing bread for the toast. 'Can you make us some coffee?

'Sure.' Chess came over.

'You know what? I wish I still had Kit to talk to. I miss him more than ever. It's been a year.'

Chess frowned. 'God, Eliza. That man … '

'Sometimes I feel like I've lost my … I don't know. My flame. Something at the very heart of me.'

Chess tutted. 'He was so wild, though. Pretty disgraceful.'

'True,' said Eliza with a small laugh.

'He was a bad influence. If you ask me, the only good thing Kit ever did was getting Andre Sokolov convicted.'

Eliza's smile vanished. 'What about his work? He was brilliant!'

'I'm talking personal.'

'No. You're wrong. Kit was a beautiful person–'

Chess opened her mouth, but Eliza spoke over her, '– just quite messed up. I didn't realise, until he wasn't there anymore, how much I depended on him. Now, when I don't know what to do, I still talk to him. Like, with Ace. Do I take this forward, knowing how complicated that could get?'

'You can talk to *me* about it. Not a bloody ghost! About anything. You know that.'

Eliza sighed. 'I know I can. And thanks.'

'So … what *is* the plan, with Ace?'

'Oh, I had the greatest idea,' Eliza replied, perking up. 'I've invited him to Richmond, but I'm not going to tell Dad. Can you *imagine* his face!'

Chess laughed. 'That's brilliant. Uncle Harry will be thrilled. Watch out, though. Harry told Dad he despaired of ever having grandchildren.'

'Oh god.'

'I'd imagine Harry would be rather pleased at the introduction of some top-notch tennis genes into his dynasty.'

'Hey,' said Eliza. 'Not everything I do is an attempt to win my father's approval.'

Chess gave her a look.

Eliza's smile faded. 'Is it?'

Chapter 6

Eliza

The two Opens, Wimbledon, and now Olympic gold. The British public, most of whom ignored tennis outside of Wimbledon fortnight, couldn't get enough of their champion. The Ace Penhalagon edition of *The Rack* sold out almost immediately, and was quickly dismembered by schoolgirls (and boys), the photos pinned up on their bedroom walls. Mums (and dads) hovered, gazing, when they ventured into their teenagers' rooms.

On the iconic cover, the rim of Ace's racket was on fire – a nice, devilish juxtaposition to the halo above his head – and his deep blue eyes, staring through the strings, were a striking contrast to the orange flames.

Will's writing was poetic, telling the story of a little Cornish boy who knew nothing of his roots, fostered by a gifted coach who worked her magic to turn him into a sporting king for Britain.

'And he seems so *nice*!' said those teens and their parents.

Will had followed up the life story with quotes from Ace about his hopes for Britain, and how he wanted to be part of the change. The tennis champ came across as passionate, genuine, and not at all preachy. No doubt Will's input had helped present Ace's point of view so eloquently and persuasively, but still …

In her office, Eliza closed the magazine, her eyes falling on Ace's open shirt. A little thrill ran through her as she remembered undoing it. She chided herself, and pulled her focus back to Ace's 'Wish list for Britain', as Will had called it, typing a quick email to Terri:

Shall we find out if Ace can write? And if he can, shall we give him a column? Seems to have interesting opinions and a way with words?

Terri: *Good morning Eliza. Are you sure it's his opinions you're interested in? Asking for a friend.*

Eliza laughed out loud. She typed: *What friend?*

Terri: *Let's say your mother.*

Terri and Ana had been close friends.

Eliza: *OK, I might *possibly* be interested in more than his opinions. But I think his views esp social/politics are in line with yours and you might like to provide a platform. Plus think of the sales. Strike while the iron's hot. (And this iron is VERY hot. Sorry.)*

Terri: *If you believe he's for real we can discuss. But let's see if he can write first.*

Eliza: *If not, Will can 'edit'* ☺

Eliza knew Ace was back in the country. There had been scenes on the news of him emerging to a rapturous reception at Heathrow this morning, hoisted on the shoulders of his team mates, draped in a Union Jack.

She picked up her phone and typed: *Welcome home! Hope radio silence now lifted. No words for how proud we all are. How does it feel to be Britain's super-hero? (Sorry for cheesy words but it's true!) xx*

She hadn't mentioned Richmond, but hoped he was still open to a visit. This Sunday, maybe. (But what were the chances? Everyone would be wanting a piece of him.) She had no idea where Ace lived, though. Cornwall? Or did he have a place in town? She knew nothing of his life.

Ace

Ace reread Eliza's message as he sat with Merle in the garden of the Hounslow house they were renting. This morning, Merle had bought a sun umbrella from the local B & Q for them to sit under, fed up of the neighbours trying to photograph Ace from their upstairs windows.

How does it feel to be Britain's super-hero? he read. *Conflicted* was probably the best word. This whole fame thing was beginning to wear him down. His daily runs around the local streets were no longer possible. Even if he wore a mask and sunglasses, people somehow recognized him. And anyway, no one was wearing masks for a run round the block anymore.

He couldn't nip to the corner shop for a paper; he couldn't kiss a girl in public. His private life was being picked over by the media like seagulls on a rubbish tip. The hum of unease never left him now.

But … he reminded himself of what he'd achieved; how he'd felt when it had sunk in that he'd won Wimbledon, and then Olympic gold. The rush, the elation, the sense of being on top of the world.

Not to mention the sudden wealth. His winnings, plus the hike in sponsorship monies and a flood of new offers would mean that, even earmarking a sizeable chunk of his income for the common good, he'd be able to buy a place near London – somewhere not too far from the airport and the National Tennis Centre. It would be wonderful to have a base, a proper home, instead of renting places like this, short term.

His eyes scanned the overgrown little garden, and he pictured a lovely rambling house with a tennis court, enough room for Merle, and Hector when he came up from Cornwall. His foster brother, Lockie … maybe. Or maybe not. Perhaps Lockie would never come back. Ace glanced across at Merle.

Also, if he bought near London, he wouldn't be far from … *You've met her once. Once!*

He reread Eliza's message. Again.

'Sorry, what?' he said, realising Merle, lying on her stomach on a sun lounger, had asked a question.

'I said, are you still jetlagged? You don't seem to be all here.'

'No, I'm good.' He lowered the back of the deckchair a couple of notches, stretching his legs out in front of him. 'But maybe I could take a few days off now?'

'We'll see. We can't let things slide.' Ace, Merle, and his coach, Tristan, would be departing soon for the US Open.

She picked up her iPad, flicking through the media enquiries, her long purple nails making little tapping noises on the screen. She read them out – everything from TV chat shows to women's magazines (lots of those) to serious dailies and sports publications. 'We need to work out which are the most useful, and how to fit them around your training.'

'Whatever you think. Bearing in mind I want to talk about more than just tennis. *The Rack* piece was the perfect launch pad and I don't want to lose the momentum, so pick the people likely to be open to that. I want to–'

She made a tutting noise. 'I *know* what you want, Arthur.' Merle and Hector were probably the only people not using his nickname now. 'But you're new to the fame game. We have to give the media what *they* want. It's important to keep the sponsors happy. For the time being, it's all about your sudden rise to stardom, your personal life; how it feels to be champ, and … well. You're a pin-up now.'

She laughed – a strange, high-pitched giggle, falling off into a sigh that dropped an octave on its long journey down. 'Oh my word,' she said, and cackled again. 'That funny little boy, Arthur Penhalagon, now champion of the world and every schoolgirl's crush. That's the power of my magic, right there.'

He shook his head. 'Stop it. I'm also hoping to see Eliza again, maybe this week, if she's free. While I've got some downtime.'

Merle's expression changed in a flash. 'You're too busy–'

'Mum …' Ace stopped. He hardly ever called her Mum, now. Technically, her role as foster parent had ended four years ago, when he reached twenty-one, but sometimes he reverted. 'I need some time off. I want to see Eliza again.'

She pursed her lips. 'What about Catriona?'

He'd been seeing a cute Scottish player for a few months, until Wimbledon, when he'd cooled it, not wanting the distraction. But as far as Merle was concerned, his relationship with Catriona was the correct level of serious. As in, not at all serious.

'Me and Catriona aren't together. Not properly.' He stared at his phone, scrolling through a sports news app. He should contact

Catriona. He'd sent polite replies to her congratulatory messages, and now he needed to end it properly.

Feeling the weight of Merle's stare, he looked up.

'So …' she said, 'you think you've earned yourself a girlfriend upgrade? For heaven's *sake*. Eliza Rose? Do you honestly think she'd be interested if you hadn't won Wimbledon?' She flicked her long silver plait over her shoulder. It settled along her back like a thick coil of rope.

'Don't judge until you meet. And now, if you don't mind, I'd like a bit of peace to message my crush.'

Merle tried not to smile, and failed. 'Okay. But don't say I didn't warn you. That girl's got heartbreaker written all over her. She's her dad all over again.'

Ace shivered, and looked up. The sky had clouded over, as is the way with British skies when the patio furniture makes an appearance.

From nowhere, a chilly gust of wind breezed into the garden, threatening to topple the sun umbrella. Without turning her head, Merle stuck out a hand, pushing it back to vertical. 'Stay,' she commanded.

The wind died.

'How do you do that?' said Ace. He returned to his phone.

Greetings, Eliza. I bring you gold. When can I show it to you? XX

To his joy and surprise, a reply arrived immediately. *Ace!! Well hello there, golden boy. I expect everyone wants a piece of you. Don't suppose you're free on Sunday? Where are you staying? What are your plans? I know nothing of your life! XX*

Then Merle's iPad beeped. 'Tristan's organised training at Roehampton for the rest of the week.'

'Okay, as long as I can have Sunday off. *All* of Sunday.'

'Why?'

Ace grinned and wiggled his phone at her. 'I have plans.'

He typed: *Staying in Hounslow until I leave for US next week. My Sunday is your Sunday XX*

The garden was ringing with the sound of message alerts.

Wonderful! Would noon suit? Richmond Lodge, Queens Rd, just by gates to Richmond Park. Do you have a car?

Ace: *Yep. Should I bring tennis gear?*

Eliza: *We have plenty but prob not up to your standard. When you get here don't press intercom – text me* ☺ ☺

Ace: *Got it. Roll on Sunday! X*

Chapter 7

Ace

Richmond Lodge, read the sign beside the enormous wrought-iron gates. Security cameras winked at him from the tops of stone pillars either side.

Beyond the entrance was a driveway running uphill, bordered by sweeping lawns and tall trees.

He texted Eliza; the gates swung slowly inwards and he drove through. Rounding a corner, a panoramic view over the green expanse of Richmond Park opened up, its meadows scattered with people and dogs enjoying Sunday walks. And on the rise overlooking that view was an enormous, centuries-old house.

Ace swallowed. *Holy shit.* The last time he'd visited such a place there had been an entrance fee and a gift shop.

He swung the Lotus onto a large area of gravel, switched off the engine, then turned his gaze on perhaps the most beautiful residence he'd ever seen. The mellow red brick frontage was criss-crossed with ancient timber beams, and along the undulating clay-tiled roof, sagging under the weight of its years, sat tall, ornate Elizabethan chimneys, their burnt-orange bricks fiery against the blue sky.

Climbing roses of palest pink rambled up the walls and across the tops of leadlight windows that had buckled and bowed over the centuries. Several of the upper rooms were topped by carved wooden gables.

Who had this house been built for, and when? A Tudor hunting lodge, maybe?

As he climbed out of the car, the ancient front door opened and Eliza came skipping down the steps, wearing a floaty green dress and an enormous smile. As she flew across the gravel, tall, slender and light-footed, her mass of fiery curls catching the sunlight, she reminded him of a wood nymph, or a Celtic princess, maybe.

All the greetings he'd carefully rehearsed evaporated at the sight of her.

'Hi!' she said, breathlessly. They stood smiling at each other. It seemed neither had a coherent word to say.

'Well!' she said, finally. 'Here you are!'

'Here I am.' He smiled down at her. 'Yes.'

She laughed, and came closer. 'Sorry, attack of the fangirl – I'm a bit lost for words.' Then she punched him on the arm. 'Ace, you did it. You bloody did it!'

'I did. I got you your gold.' He punched her arm back, gently. 'And I blew you a kiss.'

'I *knew* that was for me!'

'It really was.'

As they gazed at each other, the urge to pull her into his arms, touch her hair, breathe her in, press his lips to hers, was overwhelming. Every single cell in his body was begging him to. But – his eyes flicked over her shoulder – there were an awful lot of windows in this house.

'Did you bring your medal?'

'I did. It's …'

'Oh –' Her eyes went to his chest. 'I see it!'

He'd wanted to wear the medal for her, but thought turning up with it hanging round his neck would be showing off, so he'd tucked it beneath his shirt.

'May I?' she said, her fingers moving towards his buttons.

He grinned. 'Chrissakes, Eliza – not again.'

She giggled as she undid the top half of his shirt.

Her fingers grazed his skin, and he inhaled the subtle, remembered scent of her perfume. His pulse quickened.

Never mind those windows; never mind the medal.

'Come here,' he said, pulling her into his arms.

She slid hers round his neck, standing on tiptoes, and he hugged her tight.

'It's so good to see you again,' she said, her warm breath tickling his cheek. 'And I'm so, so proud of you.'

She dropped back onto her heels. 'Oh – and here it is!' She pulled out the medal, holding it up by the ribbon. It twirled and twinkled in the midday sun. 'Wow, an actual Olympic medal. It's so … *gold*. And weighty!'

He reached behind his neck and lifted the ribbon over his head, handing it over. 'About half a kilo.'

She weighed the medal in the palm of her hand.

'I worked hard to get you that. The least you can do is kiss me.' He put a finger under her chin and gently tilted her face up to him.

'Ace!'

Eliza shot backwards at the sound of the deep voice behind her. Over her shoulder, Ace saw the tall, unmistakable figure of Harry Rose striding towards them. Where had he appeared from?

His trademark sandy hair was streaked with silver; Eliza's famous father must have been knocking on sixty, but looked ten years younger. Above his ruddy cheeks, piercing blue eyes swept over Ace.

Harry didn't look at all surprised to see him.

'Dad!' said Eliza, a wide smile on her face. 'Surprise! Look who's come for lunch!'

Harry's smile was amused. 'Well, Lizzie. This is something of an honour. How do you do, Ace. Are we hand-shaking or elbow-bumping?' Harry looked at Eliza. 'I'd say an elbow bump would be rather pointless. I don't see a lot of social distancing going on here.'

Eliza blushed and took a step further away from Ace.

Harry held out a hand, and Ace shook it. 'It's a pleasure to meet you, Sir.'

'The pleasure is most certainly all mine – and it's Harry.'

Ace glanced at Eliza. Her wide smile had vanished.

'Dad? I wanted to give you a big surprise, but you don't seem … surprised.' Her words dripped with disappointment.

Harry raised an eyebrow. 'Sweet pea, when I saw those pictures of you two at the preview, I knew an invitation to Richmond would be forthcoming.'

'Oh.'

'Also … Terri.' He winked, and made a small clicking noise, like he was encouraging a horse.

'Oh my god,' Eliza muttered.

Harry turned back to Ace. 'Which doesn't diminish in the slightest the very great privilege of meeting you. My heartiest congratulations on your wins. You've given Britain just the shot in the arm it needed. The booster, maybe.' He grimaced. 'Please, someone stop me using the Covid words.'

Ace laughed, and clocked himself responding to this man's overwhelming charm. 'Yes, the timing was pretty good, cheering everyone up.'

I hope you're game for a set or two after lunch?'

'Absolutely, S– Harry.'

'Hard or grass?'

'You have both?'

'We do.'

'Maybe you should choose?'

'Hard it is, then. I wouldn't have a hope in hell on grass. Or on hard, no doubt, but I look forward to giving it my very best. Good. I'll see you on the terrace for pre-lunch drinks. A beer, Ace? Or do you never drink before a match? Bearing in mind there's wine with lunch.'

'I brought some.' Ace ducked into the car to retrieve the bottle.

'Interesting car.' Harry ran an eye over its sleek lines.

'Lotus is a new sponsor,' said Ace, emerging again. 'But I'd only agree to drive their EV.' He handed over the wine.

'Splendid,' said Harry, glancing at the label.

Ace winced. He'd popped into Tesco Express and grabbed a reasonably expensive bottle of white, having only the sketchiest knowledge of what would be acceptable. Back in Cornwall, Sunday lunch was accompanied by whatever was on special at Sainsbury's.

'Cloudy Bay,' said Harry. 'Good man – one of my favourites.' He clapped a hand on Ace's shoulder. 'Shame you're driving, we should really be cracking open a bubbly too. What a magnificent pair of wins. You did Britain proud. Right, Eliza, you give Ace the garden tour, then he's all mine. See you on the terrace.' He raised a hand and started back towards the house.

'Bloody hell.' Eliza scowled at his back. 'He's impossible. *I knew an invitation to Richmond would be forthcoming,*' she said, in a passable imitation of Harry's clipped tones. 'And Terri. Traitor. I can't do *anything* without him knowing about it.' She huffed a breath.

Ace laughed, and at last felt himself relaxing. He ducked into the car again. 'I got you these.' He held out a bouquet of orange roses and white … other flowers. He wasn't familiar with the names. He'd thought the roses were very Eliza – bright and exuberant and beautiful.

'Oh.' She gave a little laugh. 'Roses for Eliza Rose.'

His face fell. 'I thought … the colour, they reminded me of …'

'My hair?' She raised her eyebrows.

'No – they're pretty, and a bit fiery, and …'

'Orange.'

He shut his mouth.

Her face broke into a grin. 'I'm teasing you! They're perfect – thanks so much.' She kissed his cheek.

'That was mean,' he said, smiling.

'Sorry. You really are adorable.' She put the bouquet down and tucked a hand under his arm. 'I'll pick them up on the way back. Come on, let's go see some more flowers.'

They set off along a path that snaked downhill towards the park. Ace looked about him at the enormous grounds. 'I thought Richmond Palace had been demolished, but here it is, still standing.'

Eliza laughed. 'You know about that? A small part of the palace is still there – the gatehouse, down by the river. We bought this place twelve, thirteen years ago. After Dad's third wife died, before he married his fourth.'

Ace wasn't sure how many wives there had been. Five? Six?

'The older parts date back to Tudor times. It was a hunting lodge. Local legend says Elizabeth the First slept here. In my bedroom, obviously. Look – here's the tennis courts.'

They'd reached a high fence, beyond which were two courts. And beyond those, the turquoise waters of a swimming pool.

'Harry seriously wants to play me?'

'Of course he does! And he's bloody good, although not by your standards, obviously, so please be gentle with him. He wasn't at all well last year – he had a heart attack. And he's so competitive, he'll do his darndest to win a point or two.'

'I see.'

'We should probably go back now,' she said.

Ace turned to face her. 'Before we do …' He rested a hand on her arm.

She glanced over his shoulder to the house.

'Would it really be so terrible, if he saw?' He bent down and kissed her, and after a moment's hesitation her arms came round his waist.

He brought her closer, exploring her soft lips; her mouth opened beneath his and she let out a soft moan. The sound sparked a fire inside him, and he slid his hands down to the small of her back, pulling her hard against him.

She gasped, putting her hands on his chest. 'Ace, it's Sunday lunchtime!'

He gave a low laugh. 'Your fault – you're completely irresistible.'

She gazed into his eyes. 'Oh god, so are you.' She took a step back. 'Shall we pick this up later?'

'I really think we should.' Then his eyes moved up to the house on the hill. 'There's just the small matter of winning your father's approval. Honestly, if it's not your best friend making me solve his riddles, it's your father challenging me to a duel. Do you also live in a tall tower?'

'Practically next door to one. And maybe when you come over, I'll be lying on my bed, waiting for a kiss.'

Chapter 8

Eliza

'Cornwall?' said Harry, sitting at the head of the table set out under the pergola. He sipped his Cloudy Bay, watching Ace over the rim of the glass.

And so begins the inquisition.

Sunlight trickled through the roses above them, dappling the white linen tablecloth. Eliza was on Harry's left, Ace on his right, and at the other end sat Clare, looking summery in a yellow linen blouse and white jeans. Eddie, now fifteen, and Marcus, a schoolfriend staying for the holidays, made six for lunch.

Like Eliza, Clare seemed to be having trouble concentrating on her food. A few peas had just toppled off her fork onto the table without her noticing.

'Cornwall, how lovely,' she sighed, gazing at Ace.

Eliza couldn't blame her. Suddenly, there was a man at the table with charisma to equal Harry's. And a gold medal. She was still buzzing (and, if she was honest, wriggling a little) after that moment in the garden. That kiss. It had been like one of his serves – so powerful there was no opportunity for considered reaction. This was a different Ace to the man who'd kissed her gently in Trafalgar Square, who'd been unsure of himself. This was warrior-hero Ace, returning home triumphant, claiming his reward.

Truth be told, in spite of halting the kiss, she wouldn't have objected if he'd hauled her into the nearest shrubbery.

His eyes darkened as they met hers, and a high-voltage spark shot across the table. He blinked, and turned back to Harry, clearing his throat. 'Yes, Cornwall. Camelford. Do you know it?'

'I'm not familiar. I rarely venture west.'

'Stop it, Harry,' said Clare. 'Sorry, Ace. He's equally annoying about my neck of the woods – I'm from Cumbria. Harry thinks civilisation stops at the M25. Whereas I'd say Cumbria and Cornwall are England's *loveliest* counties.'

'Pasties and Poldark,' said Harry.

He's jealous!

Eddie frowned at his father, then smiled at Ace. 'I've heard Cornwall's really cool.'

'Fair to say there's not a lot going on in my town,' said Ace, returning his smile, 'but the pasties are actually great, and it's not too far from the coast. There's some good surfing beaches. Ever tried surfing?'

Eddie went a little pink. 'Yes. I had lessons in Bermuda, at our house there.'

Ace paused in lifting his fork to his mouth. 'You have a house in Bermuda?' He glanced at Eliza.

'We do, yes.'

'Also France,' said Harry.

Stop it!

'But I'm not a fan of the French.'

'Harry!' said Clare. 'Would you listen to yourself.'

'Traditional enemy. Like the Scots.'

Eliza huffed. Dad wasn't funny today.

Harry's face broke into a wicked smile. 'Seriously, Ace, my family are so easy to wind up. Please know that I am not in fact a bigot – except for the French part – and I wholly support your stance on diversity.'

'That's good to hear,' said Ace, and the fork carried on to his mouth.

'Bardington's piece was excellent,' said Harry, 'and I'm in fact wondering how I might help with your – what did you call it?'

'His wish list for Britain?' said Eliza.

'It seemed rather … far-reaching. A lot to tackle at once. Have you considered tightening your focus?'

Ace's face lit up as he explained his vision to Harry. Yes, it was a broad list, but it was all connected, he said. For example, poverty and climate change were intertwined.

'My focus has mostly been on diversity in sport,' he said, 'but now people are listening, I want to talk about wider issues too. Britain's lost its way, become more divided. And people don't have faith in our leaders anymore.'

'But did they ever?' said Clare. 'People are always suspicious of politicians.'

'Britain's ruled by an elite,' said Ace. 'Social mobility has gone backwards.'

'*Plus ça change*,' said Harry. 'If you'll pardon my French. Eliza – would you pass the potatoes please?'

Eliza looked at Clare, who gave a little shake of her head.

'Oh for Pete's sake.' Harry had been on a controlled diet since his heart attack last year.

Ace grinned. 'You have my sympathy, Harry. My manager is also a potato Grinch. She controls every morsel of food that passes my lips.'

'Matriarchal households are hard places to be. But my apologies for interrupting. Do continue.'

'Yes – we need to redress the balance,' said Ace, 'in society, I mean, not just in matriarchal households. We need to level the playing field. Well-known sportspeople – they can make a real difference. Look at Marcus Rashford. There are a lot more of us out there thinking the same way. Supposing we all joined forces; a group of sporting names, putting our voices – our star power – to good use.'

'A think tank?' Harry looked sceptical.

'Sort of. An organisation the media can canvas for opinions and comments, who can visit schools, talk to sporting bodies, lobby politicians–'

'I think that's a *fantastic* idea!' said Eddie. 'I bet my school – Eton – would love to have you visit and talk to us.'

Eliza swallowed a laugh at the irony of Eddie's words.

'Future leaders, yes,' said Ace with a kind smile. 'It would be great to chat with them, tell some stories from the real world, be like a bridge. And members would walk the talk, like reducing their carbon footprints, endorsing ethically produced sports goods, collectively saying no to, let's say, trainers produced in sweatshops … if we *all* said no, with one voice, and publicised the reasons for that, those companies might actually make the change.'

'You know about Eliza's charity?' asked Harry.

Ace turned to her. 'No, I didn't?'

'The Ana Rose Foundation,' said Eliza, 'named after my late mother. We seed fund women around the world setting up small businesses, and we support my sister's work with victims of sex trafficking. Other stuff too – all for women.'

Ace's eyebrows had shot up. 'That's amazing.'

'Surprised to learn not all wealthy people are selfish bastards?' said Eliza, with a smile. 'Even Dad has his philanthropical moments. He does a lot for medical research, and he funded a new neonatal unit at our local hospital.'

'David Attenborough's probably rich,' said Marcus. 'And he's trying to save the planet.'

'He's my hero,' said Ace.

'Mine too,' said Eliza, Clare and Eddie, together.

'All the best people live in Richmond,' said Harry.

'How are you at writing?' said Eliza to Ace.

'Writing? I'm no Will Bardington, but I can string a sentence together. Why?'

'Terri and I were wondering about giving you a column in *The Rack*.'

'Eliza – that would be perfect!'

His gorgeous smile was infectious. Eliza noticed Ace's positivity infusing everyone at the table.

'*Ace on the Case*?' said Harry. '*Face to Face with Ace*?'

Eliza shook her head. 'Thanks for that, Dad. Maybe I'll talk to Ace about it later.'

❀

That afternoon, everyone took a turn playing tennis against Ace. Harry lost 6–1, and although it was clear Ace was holding back, Harry emerged with his pride intact, having held Ace to some spectacular rallies. He was already boasting about winning a game off the Wimbledon and Olympic champion.

The boys' heads were bent over their phones as they furiously updated their Instagram stories with action photos of each other playing Ace Penhalagon.

Eliza hadn't had a moment alone with Ace since before lunch. Now, finally, as they made their way back up to the house, they slowed their walk until they were well behind the others.

'That was fun – your family's awesome.' Ace's hair flopped boyishly over his forehead, and Eliza found herself gazing at the damp tendrils curling into the nape of his neck, suddenly overcome by a desperate urge to kiss the skin on which they rested. To taste its saltiness.

Her gazed travelled upwards, to that chiselled jawline, to his lips … his cheeks, flushed with colour after two hours of tennis; his eyes – so very blue against his tanned skin, their long, dark lashes … so long. So thick. An absolute forest of them. And they even curled up at the ends.

Ace Penhalagon was *ridiculously* handsome.

Their pace slowed further, and he lifted a hand, brushing her fingers with his. Even that lightest of touches … a pulse of electricity zipped up her hand, fired along her synapses, and came to rest, fizzing, at the very heart of her.

His eyes burned into hers. 'Can I drive you back to town?'

'Wouldn't that be completely out of your way?'

'That's kind of beside the point.' He laced his fingers through hers.

'Yes please. I'd love a lift home.'

The air between them hummed with tension, like the string on a longbow pulled taut. In an attempt to ease it, they chatted lightly as the Lotus made its way through Fulham, Chelsea, and Westminster, then along the embankment to Tower Hill. Ace shared tales of the Olympics; Eliza described how Harry had met Clare, spoke of Eddie's plans to study medicine … but each time they paused, the tension resurfaced, wound ever tighter, ready to snap. This arrow was desperate to fly.

Eliza's heart was thumping in her chest. She'd never been this strongly attracted to someone. *Never.* With Rob, it had been a gradual thing, a progression from childhood friendship to grown-up love. Familiar, cosy, like going home. And Kit – well, that didn't count. She'd been a naïve student, while he was a louche sexual adventurer. In spite of her deep love for him, she was never going to let that happen.

The men she'd dated since Rob had been little more than arm candy, when it came down to it. Good company, easy on the eye, occasionally staying the night, but more often just a kiss goodbye on the doorstep.

And those who'd stayed – it had been mostly about honouring Kit's memory. 'Live like a Marley,' he'd said. She'd made him a promise, given it a try, but casual sex wasn't for her, and she was still getting over Rob. And Kit. Plus she was forever wary of her reputation, especially considering her father's notoriety when it came to women.

Her eyes settled on Ace's strong hands on the steering wheel. The way he handled this car; the way he handled that racket. Eliza suppressed a shiver. What might those powerful hands be able to do to her?

Anticipation, nerves … *desire*. An ache. A very insistent one. She was practically a puddle in her passenger seat.

At last, as the sun began to set, they drove into an undercover car park close to Eliza's flat. At the Pay and Display machine, Ace's hand hovered as he was asked to select the number of hours.

He turned to look at her. 'Two? Three?'

She met his gaze, her heart in her mouth. Every nerve in her body tingled at the intensity in those eyes. 'How about overnight?'

'Overnight?'

'It's a very secure car park.'

Ace smiled, then leaned down and brushed his lips against her cheek, then her lips, for just a few seconds.

He turned back to the machine. 'Twenty-three quid. If you're going to change your mind, best be quick about it.'

'I won't be changing my mind.'

He pressed OK, and then he was kissing her like he'd die if she changed her mind. Desire raced through her; her lips parted and she moaned as his tongue flicked into her mouth.

'Let's go,' she murmured, nuzzling his jawline, kissing the skin beneath it, tasting him … not salty.

A door slammed with a metallic clang as someone entered the car park, and they pulled apart.

'Take me to your next-door-to-a-high-tower,' Ace whispered in her ear.

He draped an arm round her shoulder as they walked the short distance to the marina. People were noticing them; a couple gaped. 'Ace!' called the woman. Her partner told her to shush.

Ace looked at Eliza and she nodded, slipping her arm round his waist. 'That's it. We're official,' she said, as another passer-by snapped them, blatantly, on his phone.

'Are you okay with it?'

'I think I probably am.'

His face broke into a gorgeous smile, and he planted a kiss on her head.

Eliza unlocked the door to her apartment and let them in. 'Would you like something to drink?' she said, for propriety's sake.

As anticipated, he ignored the question, taking her in his arms. 'What was that about lying on your bed, waiting for a kiss?'

'Can't wait that long,' she said, pulling his head down to hers.

They made their way to the bedroom, leaving a trail of shoes and clothes in their wake. By the time they reached the bed there was nothing left to take off, except for the medal. Ace lifted it over his head and put it around Eliza's neck.

She lay down and closed her eyes. 'Wake me up, lovely Ace.'

He stretched out beside her, propped up on one elbow, and her heart raced as he picked up the gold disc by its ribbon, dangling it above her, then drew it across her skin, following the contours of her chest, circling round and round, brushing it across her nipples before letting it lie between her breasts. Then he trailed kisses over her body, pausing to stroke, to explore with his fingers, with his lips, before moving down …

'Is this okay?' he said, stopping for a moment.

In reply she gripped his golden hair and lifted herself against him, moaning as he resumed, until she thought she might explode with the intensity of it.

'Come back up here,' she breathed. 'Kiss me.' He moved on top and then he pushed into her, and Eliza gasped, stretching her hands over her head like a cat as he moved slowly, slowly, then faster, harder … playing her like he played that ball, completely in control, intent on her pleasure, until she died a little death. Then with a groan he let go that control, dropping his face into her cloud of hair.

They lay quietly for a while, her head on his chest, Ace idly playing with her curls, which were taking up far more of the bed than was polite. She stroked her fingers across his chest and down his bicep, experiencing a moment of wonderment as she remembered this same muscular arm sending spectacular shots across the net in Tokyo.

'I can't believe you're here, in my bed.'

He was too drained to respond; he just let out a contented sigh.

Later, summoning her last dribble of energy, she said, 'I should draw the curtains,' meaning, she needed the bathroom. Telling him she had to pee felt like it would break the magic. She took off the medal and hung it over the bedhead.

Outside the window it was almost dark, and when she returned she flicked on the bedside light. Ace had rolled onto his front, and …

Holy Mother of God.

Eliza's skin prickled. Across Ace's broad, muscular shoulders, and all the way down the valley of his spine, glinting with sweat, was the spectacular tattoo of a Celtic sword. It began just below his neckline, the grip decorated with intricate swirls, then its wide guard spread partway across his shoulders. The blade ran down the length of his back, tapering where his waist narrowed, its tip level with the twin dimples above his buttocks.

Eliza wasn't normally one for tattoos, but this? It was undoubtedly the most beautiful thing on a man she'd ever seen.

Moving closer, she noticed curlicue lettering running down the two sides of the sword. She sat down on the edge of the bed and quietly spoke the words: '*Take me up … Cast me away.*'

She remembered the tale in Will's article. 'Is this your Excalibur?'

When he didn't respond, she realised he was asleep.

Eliza couldn't tear her eyes away; those golden curls at the nape of his neck, this sword, embedded in his shoulders, inked into his spine.

He stirred, and his eyes flickered open.

'This is incredible,' she whispered, trailing her fingertips lightly along the tattooed valley. 'I love the strength of it. It speaks to me about you.'

He smiled lazily and rolled onto his back, and the sword was gone.

'Come here,' he said, and she lay down beside him, wondering if anything could ever make her want to leave this bed again.

Chapter 9

Ace

On Monday morning, as he slowly came to, Ace reached out an arm for Eliza but his hand met only empty air, and then the rumpled bed sheet. He opened his eyes a fraction and discovered yes, he was alone; shut them again, hoping she was in the bathroom, or making coffee to bring back to bed, maybe. He wasn't yet ready to let go of last night.

Morning sounds from the marina below slipped through the open window: the tapping of heels, the murmur of voices, the occasional distant blast of a horn from a boat on the Thames, the ever-present thrum of London traffic.

From inside, the hiss of the kitchen tap, the clink of mugs.

He opened his eyes, wider awake now. His medal hung over the bedhead; his clothes, abandoned last night with frantic haste, were neatly folded on a chair. Eliza was clearly up and doing.

Disappointment, that this night, with its magic, its intimacy – its heat – was over, that they had places they needed to be, back in their busy, separate lives. There would be unread messages and missed calls. He anticipated Merle's onslaught, and probably Tristan's, and mentally blocked them, instead replaying yesterday in his mind:

That's it – we're official.
You okay with it?
I think I probably am.

They were together. The glorious, incredible Eliza Rose was his. Wimbledon, Olympic gold, and now her. The power of three.

Ace smiled, and stretched luxuriously.

Eliza was something else; he'd never met anyone like her. Beautiful, brilliant, passionate; a powerful businesswoman, yet surprisingly down to earth, given the family billions – her tot-up of residences had gone on to two hands. 'Six, if you include the yacht,' she'd said as they talked, limbs entwined, in the early hours.

'Yacht?'

'Of the super variety. I'm sure Dad will invite you.'

'I don't even have my own place,' he'd said. 'I still live with Merle and Hector when I'm in Cornwall. But I have plans. Thought I'd buy somewhere, maybe in Surrey.'

'Oh, I could help you look!'

Her assumption that she'd be part of his future had made him feel all kinds of wonderful.

Ace's body stirred as he thought back to the night they'd just spent together. Eliza had been on fire, reaching for him time and time again. From the moment they'd met, those dark eyes had hinted at the flame inside, but her powerful, uninhibited response had still taken him by surprise.

She'd told him, as they lay in the dark, how she'd had to overcome a psychological problem to be able to 'enjoy physical intimacy'. He'd smiled at the coy expression, given her creative and enthusiastic approach to what they'd just done.

She hadn't told him the cause of the problem, alluding only to something in her family past.

'Families can be seriously fucked-up places,' he'd said. 'Even adoptive ones, where the parents have to jump through hoops to be allowed to care for unwanted children–' He'd stopped himself.

'Do you know why you were adopted?' she'd asked carefully. 'If that's not a really intrusive question?'

'No, it's natural to wonder why. Everyone assumes I want to find out, but I honestly don't, right now. I wasn't adopted, though, I was fostered.'

'But doesn't that imply you should have been returned to your original family at some point? Or have I got that wrong.'

'All I've been told is that my mother died and my father's identity was unknown. My grandparents – I don't remember them – were friends with Merle and she was a foster-carer. The grandparents wanted to spend time abroad, so Merle offered to foster me for a while and Social Services approved it. When my sporting talent made itself known she was keen to keep me on, and the grandparents wanted to settle overseas, so … everyone was happy.'

He was grateful for the dark when he said those words. He'd quickly switched the focus to Eliza – in particular, her love life.

Rob had been her only serious relationship. That was it, nothing more to tell.

Eliza's head appeared around the door. 'Ah, you're awake!'

Ace shut his eyes. 'Not fully. In the name of equality, I demand to be woken up in the traditional manner.'

When he felt her soft lips on his, he pulled her down onto the bed and rolled on top of her.

'Stop!'

Opening his eyes, he realised she was dressed. More disappointment.

'You're the very definition of temptation,' she said, tracing his lips with a finger, 'but I have to be at work in less than an hour. Come and eat some breakfast – I'm making eggs. Normally it's cereal, but I think we deserve better this morning.' She sat up and smoothed her hair, which hung around her shoulders in glossy waves.

He ran a hand down it. 'How did you do that? It's only taking up a quarter of the space it was last night.'

She laughed. 'I have a magic wand. See you in the kitchen.'

He quickly showered and dressed, and went through to the airy living area of this beautiful warehouse loft apartment, which he'd barely glanced at last night. The morning sun flooded in through huge arched windows looking out over the marina. The walls were of exposed yellow brick, and a row of giant pendant lights hung down from the high ceiling above the kitchen island, where Eliza was busy with a saucepan. There was a glass table and six chairs next to the windows, two leather sofas and an enormous TV.

The furniture was mostly white, the floors were polished wood, and bookshelves, rugs, modern art and posters for RoseGold productions were splashes of colour. Fresh flowers sat on the surfaces; everything was immaculate. Ace assumed Eliza didn't do her own cleaning.

He went over and swept her hair aside, nuzzling her neck. She smelled fresh, of something fruity; her skin was cool and silky smooth against his lips.

He let out a theatrical little moan. 'You should've woken me earlier.'

'Oh, you have *no* idea how much I wanted to,' she said, turning to face him. 'But you looked so peaceful. And a bit worn out.' She smirked.

'What have you done to me?'

'But worth the twenty-three quid?'

He smiled. 'Last night was incredible. *You're* incredible. I don't want to play tennis today. I don't even want to go out. I just want to be with you.' He kissed her, wanting her all over again. 'Can't you work from home?' he muttered against her mouth. 'Everyone works from home now.'

Eliza tutted. 'Ace, you slacker. That's not the spirit that won Olympic gold.' She kissed him on the cheek, then turned back to the stove. 'I really can't today. Coffee?' She nodded at an espresso machine that brought to mind an aeroplane cockpit. 'I ground some ready, just press that button. I'll grab you a mug.'

Ace frowned slightly at her back, clocking her distraction. She was thinking forward to the day ahead, not back to the night they'd just shared.

She passed him a mug. On the side was the word *BOSS*.

He slipped it under the filter. '*BOSS*. You sending me a message there, Eliza?'

'That was a present from your predecessor. His little joke.'

'Dev Noble?' said Ace, as the machine purred and the delicious aroma filled the air.

'Oh my god, no.' Eliza looked horrified. 'Never speak that heinous man's name again. That wasn't a relationship, it was a lapse of judgement. No, I meant Rob.'

'Ah yes, of course.' Ace looked around him. 'Did he live here with you?' He registered how much that thought bothered him.

'Yes, but he was in the States a lot. And this place is really Dad's, not mine.'

She paused; he saw her wondering whether to say more. 'We did look for a place of our own, but … well. Nowhere ever seemed right, and then the penny dropped, for me, that it wasn't the properties that weren't quite right …' She turned away from him, busying herself at the hob.

'Will said you're still mates?'

'Good mates, yes. Since we were kids. Rob's lovely – you'll like him. That's him in that photo, the one on the right.' She gestured to a collection of framed photos on the wall.

'He works for Rose too?'

'Yes, he started as a sub-editor on *The Rack*, now he's head of RoseGold's US operation.'

Ace wanted to ask why they'd split, but Eliza glanced at the kitchen clock. That was clearly a conversation for another day.

He took his coffee over to the photos and saw Eliza picnicking on a rug, a dark-haired man stretched out next to her. She was laughing down at him; they looked happy and carefree.

'That's St James's Park,' she said, 'with Chess – my cousin – and Gil. He's Rob's brother. We were celebrating their engagement. Rob was still married then, so nothing much happened for a while.'

His eyes scanned the other photos grouped with it and … his heart skipped a beat.

Holy shit.

'Is that …?'

Eliza looked up; her eyes went to the photo, then returned to her pan. 'Yes, that's Kit,' she said quickly.

'Kit,' Ace repeated. For a moment …

But no. This boy's eyes were an unusual hazel colour, almost gold. Not blue. And there was no vulnerability, no shyness in them. Quite the opposite.

'He loathed having his photo taken,' said Eliza, concentrating on her pan of eggs. 'It's sad – I don't think I have any of him smiling. He had a lovely smile too. If mostly a wicked one.'

Ace peered closer. Kit was sprawled on the grass in front of an old honey-coloured building, leaning back on his elbows. A cigarette dangled from his lips. Messy blond hair fell to his shoulders, and those strange, amber eyes were slightly narrowed as they stared into the lens.

His features, especially the full, pouting mouth, were feminine. But Kit was most definitely male. His legs were splayed wide. Whoever had taken the photo must have been sitting between them.

That look he was giving the camera.

'Did you take this?'

'Yes. When I snapped it, he told me to fuck off.' Eliza smiled at the memory.

'Well – he obviously didn't mean it.'

'What?'

Ace looked again at that beautiful, sensuous face. 'That expression doesn't say "fuck off" to me. It says, "Come to bed."'

Eliza didn't miss a beat. 'Of course it does,' she said, spooning scrambled eggs onto toast. 'That was his default setting. Breakfast's ready – let's eat.' She carried the two plates over to the table by the window.

Ace joined her, mulling over the fact that Eliza was a … *passionate* person, and this man, to whom she'd apparently been close, had looked at her like that. Interrogating her about past relationships at this early stage probably wasn't cool, but he couldn't help asking, 'Kit was Will's partner, right? He was gay?'

Eliza shot him a glance as he sat down. 'Bi, pan; whatever you want to call it. He didn't give a toss about gender. Will fell in love with him at Oxford. They lived together, wrote together. Though, frankly, Kit often didn't deserve his love.' She sighed. 'Or maybe he did. Kit was hard not to love. The reasons for his behaviour – it was complicated.'

Ace was quiet, waiting for her to continue.

She met his eye, and her smile was sad. 'It's a long story, one I don't have time for right now.' Then she perked up. 'Or the energy. I'll be doing well if I make it to lunchtime without crashing.'

Ace registered the change of subject. Talking about Kit was making her unhappy.

He followed her cue. 'Yup, I suspect my tennis will be less than stellar today. And I haven't even switched my phone back on yet.' He made a scared face. 'Merle and Tristan are going to crucify me.'

'Tristan?'

'Tristan Knight – my coach.'

'I remember him! Wasn't there some scandal?'

'Yes, he ran off with his doubles partner's wife. Planet Tennis can be pretty incestuous.' Which reminded him – he needed to speak to Catriona, before he and Eliza became common knowledge.

There was a niggle of worry. Catriona could be quite intense. It was why he'd been putting this off; he hadn't wanted the drama during Wimbledon and the Olympics, especially with the burgeoning media interest.

'While I think of it,' said Eliza, 'that column we spoke about yesterday. Do you want to send me, say, fifteen hundred words on your wish list for Britain?'

The burst of pleasure that she'd remembered was quickly swamped by crushing doubt. Eliza was surrounded by great writers and media people. Even Rob had been an editor. Would she take one look at his work and think he was a badly educated ignoramus? Just a good-looking bloke with some unoriginal ideas who was good at whacking a ball? Dare he even show her his writing?

During his teens, Ace had been completely focused on sport. He'd barely scraped through his GCSEs. He'd read few books – mostly biographies of sportspeople – had struggled to write essays, and had almost no clue what to do with apostrophes (that hadn't changed).

Eliza had told him she'd achieved a first in English at Oxford, along with her two clever-boy pals. Much of her working life was devoted to bringing great drama to the screen, to the world.

The gulf that had opened when he'd set eyes on the family mansion had just widened.

She reached over and squeezed his hand. 'Hey – don't sweat the small stuff. We have a fabulous team of editors, and Will can help you set the tone, the style. He's bonkers about you, he'd love to do that. Just give us your vision in your own words, don't try and make it fancy. Your voice, your passion – that's what's important. Leave the rest to us.'

He blew out a breath. 'Right,' he said, still feeling way out of his depth. 'Thanks.'

'I have to go,' she said, collecting their plates. 'If you want, you can stay for a bit and let yourself out.'

'No, I should be on my way. I just need to check my phone and no doubt make a grovelling call or two.'

'Ten minutes,' she said, heading back to the bedroom.

He switched on his phone, setting it to silent in anticipation of the barrage of alerts, then opened Merle's most recent email – today's schedule, beginning with training at Roehampton at ten a.m. Normally he was in the gym by seven. *Thanks, Merle.* It was uncanny how she always knew what he was up to.

It was eight fifteen. Plenty of time. He relaxed, and read an earlier email from her. There was an attachment. Opening it, he sighed.

Two photos: a screenshot from Instagram, and one from the *Daily Mail*'s website. The first showed Harry squaring up to an Ace serve, watched by Eliza up on the umpire's seat. The profile was @MarcusCrawford, and the caption read: *Better than Wimbers! Harry Rose vs @AcePenhalagon at Richmond!!* There were thousands of likes.

The second was of Ace and Eliza arm in arm, heading through St Katharine Docks last night, with the headline: *Ace and Eliza – It's Game On!* Merle had cropped off the rest of the words, and he didn't need to know what those were.

Well, that was quick.

He read Merle's email, which was along the lines of, you might have told me, I've been fielding a trillion media calls since yesterday afternoon.

A word of warning, it continued. *Trolls are on the attack and it's vicious – mostly against Eliza. You're the golden boy, she's the rich bitch etc. I've been deleting and blocking but I can't keep up. Warn her not to read. I'm sure she's an old hand at this but some of it's disturbing nonetheless.*

Ace shook his head. What was *wrong* with people? He felt a moment's rage at Marcus for posting the picture and tagging him, but he was just a kid. And the story would have been out there anyway, by now.

He followed Eliza into the bedroom. She was in the ensuite, and through the open door he saw her leaning in to the mirror, applying lipstick.

He knocked softly and pushed the door open the rest of the way.

Her eyes met his in the mirror.

'Maybe don't do that just yet.'

After considering his words, she smiled slowly, plucking a tissue from a box on the shelf. Holding his gaze she dabbed at the lipstick and ran her tongue over her lips. Then she bit the bottom one.

The gesture hit him right in the groin. He moved behind her and pulled her against him. God, it had been *hours*.

She swivelled in his arms and he kissed her.

'Ace, I'll be late,' she whispered, but there was no conviction in her words.

'You want quick?' he muttered. 'I can do quick.' He pushed up her skirt.

She inhaled sharply. '*Yes* … quick. *Now.*'

At the speed of light, they dealt with underwear and zips; he hoisted her against the sink and seconds later was deep inside her, all the way, every last little millimetre of him.

'*Oh god,*' she breathed. '*Yes.*'

It was quick, but it was mind-blowing. And afterwards, when

she flopped against him like a ragdoll, he was so overwhelmed with feeling that he blurted out, 'Eliza … I think I'm in love with you.'

She went still. 'Oh, that's … lovely.' She wriggled, and he moved back as she slid her feet to the floor, pulling her skirt down.

She looked up at him, her expression serious. 'There's so much I need to tell you, about why this – me and you – might be difficult. I really like you; I like you a *lot* …'

'But?' He braced himself. He'd said too much, too soon.

'I'm complicated. I have a ton of baggage, and a very large empire to run.'

She'd had only one serious relationship, and it seemed to have ended amicably. Why would she have a ton of baggage?

He stroked a finger down her cheek. 'Which make you all the more interesting. How about I help unpack your bags? Next time I see you?'

She gave him a grateful smile. 'Well, if you put it like that … Yes, lovely Ace. You can. And we should … look, the press. It's bound to happen–'

'It already did.'

Her eyebrows shot up. 'Seriously?'

'Merle sent me a couple of things. Social media, *Daily Mail* website. And she said to tell you, don't read the comments.'

'Oh, I never do. I hardly bother with social media, apart from the occasional Instagram. But the story – tell your people they can confirm we're seeing each other, but they must say no more than that, okay?'

'Fine by me.'

She headed back to the bedroom. 'I'll walk with you to your car.'

'Can I drive you to work?'

'No. I always walk. It's when I do my thinking – it centres me. By the time I get to work, I'm good to go.'

Chapter 10

Eliza

'Dammit,' Eliza muttered as she spotted the photographers. Half a dozen of them, in a huddle on the footpath. She should have realised they'd be door-stepping her today. It was annoying, but she could hardly complain; several of her own magazines were enthusiastic supporters of the paparazzi.

She turned to Ace. 'Maybe you could drive me till we've shaken them off?'

'Right. Obviously I've spent the night, so there's no point in being coy about it.'

'No.' She opened the entrance door. 'Smile, but don't engage – okay?'

The photographers surged forward as Eliza exited first, slipping her hand into Ace's.

'Good morning, everyone,' she said with a smile, not slowing down. 'Please take your tiresome photos quickly and then kindly piss off.'

Ace put a protective arm around her as the pack followed them all the way to the car park, before melting away.

'How's your schedule this week?' he asked as he unlocked the Lotus. 'Dinner one night?'

'Lovely,' she said, getting in. 'I haven't got used to going out again. Now, with you, would be a good time to relearn the art of being social.'

'I think I'm doing *The One Show* one night. Maybe after that?' He clicked his seatbelt and switched on the engine.

'*The One Show*? Fun! I've lost count of the number of times we've tried to poach Alex Jones. Are you on our morning show? *Rose Breakfast?* If not, someone's going to hear about it from me.'

'Not sure,' said Ace as they drove up the ramp. He glanced over. 'Eliza – can I ask? You're a media person. Merle says no one will want to know about my campaigns, they'll just want to hear about the Olympics and … I don't know. My love life and my favourite things to eat. What do you reckon?'

Oh god, this man. This gorgeous man, with his sincerity; his genuine belief that he could use his fame for good. What were the chances?

But then, Eliza became aware of something deep inside, stirring, pushing back against the version of herself Harry had nurtured, as he instilled in her the survival tactics needed to maintain her position at the top. Always suspicious, always second-guessing. Forever on the lookout for hidden agendas, questioning people's motives.

Like, with her Scottish cousin.

And Rob, maybe. *What?* Where had that thought come from?

She dismissed it, and homed back in on that feeling, encouraging it, blowing gently on the flame. Yes, there it was, still flickering … that sense she'd had at Oxford, and when she'd started out at Rose, that she could change the world, make a difference. Before the realities of life as CEO of a megacorporation had stripped her of that naiveté.

And those dreams had been big – visions of influencing society through drama; challenging attitudes through storytelling, as great writers had done all through the ages. And the Green Rose brand she'd created, which was going to be a trailblazer for ethical, sustainable consumer goods. Until her sister Maria had shut it down during her draconian reign, labelling it 'off brand'.

But at least Eliza had made a stellar start on the drama, thanks mainly to Kit's incredible, seminal work, *My Dark Soul*. Since

Kit's death, however, RoseGold had produced nothing with even a fraction of the impact. Rob was focused on the bottom line, on ratings and deals, and she'd been happy to leave him to it as she concentrated on steering the company through the pandemic.

'Ace,' she said, as the flame flickered higher, 'stick to your guns. Yes, of course people want to know how it feels to win Olympic gold, and what you eat for breakfast, but they are also really fed up right now. Covid, Brexit, the cost of living, climate change …'

Ace nodded.

'What you said in your interview with Will, about feeling let down by our leaders, how the cracks in society are getting wider – you struck a chord. Your ideas, your vision … the timing's perfect. *Carpe diem*, Ace.'

'Car– what?'

'Seize the day. You have the platform – the stage – right now. People are listening, and they love you. Engage with them while they still do, tell them how you're going to address racism in sport, workplaces – everywhere. Lobby for more action on climate change. Why are we still using coal, for chrissakes. What else? Come on, Ace, what else?'

'Inequality. And family violence,' he said, picking up on her energy.

'Right, yes. But like Dad said, that's going wide.'

'It's all connected, though.'

'Okay, well if we go with the weekly column, which will be a great start for you, there'll be time and space for all of it.'

Ace gazed at her. 'I can't believe I've found you. You're from another world, but you care, and … you get me.'

Her throat tightened as she looked into his earnest blue eyes.

They were almost at London Bridge, and Ace pulled over into a bus layby. The people waiting glared at the supercar and the arrogant, entitled City-boy no doubt driving it. Then their expressions changed as they recognised the guy at the wheel.

But they weren't about to embarrass themselves by gawping, so they pretended Britain's sporting crush pulling up in a Lotus was no big deal, and carried on staring at their phones, surreptitiously angling their cameras.

He pulled her in for a kiss, and as she melted against him, she wondered why on earth she wasn't 'working from home' today, as he'd suggested. Was she insane?

A red double-decker blasted its horn behind them.

'Oops,' she said, reaching for the door handle. 'Remember – send me your words. And copy in Will. We can tweak before letting Terri see. We'll make them sparkle. The three of us are going to be one *hell* of a team. Right – best be gone.' She slipped on her mask and sunglasses. 'Call me soon, lovely Ace!'

She slammed the door and he raised a hand, and then, with an almost-silent whoosh-whine that seemed completely at odds with an Olympic warrior departing in his Lotus, quietly merged the EV into the traffic.

As Eliza crossed London Bridge, she let her mind off its leash, hoping that by the time it returned it would bring with it some useful perspective on the situation she found herself in.

There was a chasm between her and Ace, in spite of his recent success. And she knew he felt it too. Eliza was, as he'd joked, a princess in her tower, high above his world, of which, if she was honest, she knew little. Who was she to presume she knew what the person on the street was feeling?

She read about the real world, she observed it, but she didn't live in it. Not really. She had no first-hand experience of the sorts of struggles most people faced in their daily lives. Her rose-petal-strewn path had been laid out for her from the day she was born, and she'd tripped lightly along it, stumbling from time to time, but there had always been a soft landing ready for her, a cushion of wealth, a loving family; job security.

Ace's background, what little she knew of it, couldn't be more different. He'd grown up motherless, with no idea who his father was, in a tiny town in a far corner of England. His grandparents had dumped him with foster carers, disappeared abroad and never come back.

How would that feel? To have no real family at all. No one. It was hardly surprising Ace avoided thinking about that, focusing instead on the stroke of luck that had seen him fostered by a sports coach.

But … should the differences between them matter? No – they didn't have to. Eliza couldn't help her background any more than Ace could help his. They cared about the same things; they just came at them differently.

She remembered that breathtaking tattoo on his back. Its beauty and symbolism had spoken straight to her heart, of the strength of purpose at the core of this man.

That inscription – what had it said? Her lips formed the words: '*Take me up … Cast me away.*'

Out of nowhere, a cool blast of wind leapt up from the Thames and whirled around her head, grabbing her hair, spiralling it upwards, whipping it across her face. The sky ahead darkened, throwing the silvery spike of the Shard into relief, like a towering, menacing inversion of that sword.

Eliza shivered. Her sleep-deprived mind was playing tricks on her.

The wind sped away, the sun reappeared, and she picked up her daydream, focusing on that tattoo again.

Oh. It came to her. The front cover of *The Rack*, to introduce Ace's new column. Just his beautiful tattooed back, artfully lit against a dark background. The headline: *Ace – A Force for Good*.

Her fingertips tingled as she recalled tracing the smooth valley of his spine … all the way down to those irresistible dimples above his buttocks. She pictured his sleepy eyes opening, focusing on her; remembered how he'd rolled over and pulled her to him.

And then her mind tossed in the question she'd been hitting away, like Ace deflecting a volley at the net. Would she feel this overwhelming attraction if Ace had been some regular guy she'd met in the pub, at a party?

He was Britain's hot hero, and she – Eliza Rose – was the object of his desire. It was all deliciously sexy, something any girl would find impossible to resist. Was she just swept up in the excitement and glamour of it all?

While Ace was, apparently, in love with her, was she mostly … in lust?

Oh for heaven's sake, Eliza. She was overthinking things again. They'd had two dates – *two.* He'd be off to the States soon, and then somewhere else, jetting around in his life she knew little about.

She should take her own advice. *Carpe diem.* Enjoy this for what it was, now, and worry about the future if and when she had to.

And yet – there went her mind again – a weight was settling around her shoulders. In her heart, she knew she was already in deep. His impulsive *I love you* may have been prompted by that spectacular moment in the bathroom, but it had also been a response to the beautiful, unforgettable night they'd spent together. And not just the … she grew warm at the memory. No, not just *that.* The quiet moments, too.

Talking in the dark, getting to know each other. In spite of his success, there was no self-importance, no conceit. Only that appealing bewilderment, at finding himself in this place, and with her. She couldn't face the thought of hurting this genuine, exceptional man the way she'd hurt Rob – never committing, always putting her career first.

She needed to work out her feelings. Was she still in full heart-protection mode, after Rob's infidelity and Kit's death? Or was it time to let her guard down, to allow herself to love again? But if she did, would she end up in the exact same place she'd reached with Rob?

❀

It came as no surprise that Eliza's focus was hard to pin down this morning. It wandered around the office, hovered for long stretches by the window, took her down internet rabbit holes as she googled *Ace Penhalagon.* But it was important to be well informed. If there were things for the press to find out, she needed to find them out first.

Her phone buzzed, and Cecil asked if she was free for a word.

Anticipating his arrival from the office next door, she quickly shut the window of images that had popped up under *Ace Penhalagon girlfriend*, the most recent showing him with a strikingly attractive brunette. Eliza just had time to read her name: Catriona Macleod.

A soft knock on her open door, and there was Cecil, waiting to be invited in, in that way he had. Always respectful, professional, but with a strong dose of fatherly concern.

She waved him over, and he settled himself down opposite her.

Here we go.

The hitching up of his neatly pressed trousers, crossing one leg over the other, a little chin stroke, a glance out of the window as he considered his words.

She smiled. Cecil was her rock; he took care of matters corporate, enabling her to focus on the bigger picture. Although, there had been scant strategic thinking this past year. How could you forward plan when there was a virus hell-bent on sabotage?

'Everything okay, Cecil?'

His wise brown eyes met hers, and she saw him searching for words. 'Fine, yes, fine. All good. And you?'

'Excellent, thank you!'

'Right. I thought it would be worth a quick word, about …' He paused.

'Ace Penhalagon?' That little squeeze of the heart again.

'Yes. What an *incredible* player he is.' Cecil's face was unusually animated. 'Harry must have been delighted to meet him. And play against him!'

'Yes indeed. Yesterday's little surprise which, in fact, *wasn't* a surprise, because Dad is all-knowing.'

He chuckled. 'Not me this time.'

'I suspect Terri.'

'You and Ace …?'

'Two dates, Cecil. *Two*. But yes.' She smiled. 'And there's a lot more to him than incredible tennis skills.'

'You should probably talk to the PR department. I understand they're swamped with calls.'

'Fine, I'll give them some words, get them to square it with his people.' She frowned. 'Who even are his people? We should probably find out. His foster mum, I think.' She pulled a face.

'Merle Innes. A force to be reckoned with, apparently.'

'*Cecil?*'

He grinned. 'Come on, Eliza. You knew Harry and I would be watching your back.' His expression returned to its customary serious. 'What do you know of Ace? His background?'

She pursed her lips. Sometimes Harry and Cecil were too much. 'Not a lot.' Her tone was clipped. 'Like I said, it's been two dates.'

'Right. The thing is, he clearly has a political agenda. If you're going to be associated with him, you need to be well informed about that.'

She bristled. 'It's not so much political. He just wants to do some good. He cares about things – about people, and the planet–'

'Which is all well and good. It's just … by *aligning* yourself with him, you're endorsing. Be careful. And have you considered … if he's positioning himself as standing up for the little man–'

'and woman–'

'Quite. What will people make of him hitting the big time and immediately dumping his unknown-tennis-player girlfriend for the high-flying daughter of a famous billionaire? A woman with a media empire he can use to his advantage.'

Girlfriend?

'And as far as your *own* reputation's concerned, people might assume Ace is, well –' he looked awkward, '– the latest in a string of glamorous men you've dated? A trophy?'

Ouch.

'I'm sorry – you realise I'm playing devil's advocate, of course.'

She sighed. 'I know you are. It's always about the spin. But this … thing – it's more than that. Ace is a genuinely good person, and I like him very much. *Very* much.' She paused. 'I really do,' she added, with a note of surprise.

So – it seemed she wasn't just in lust, after all.

He was still looking worried.

'Is there more, Cecil?'

He uncrossed his legs and leaned forward in his seat. 'I know we can dismiss it all as unworthy of our attention, but I prefer you to be informed. There's been something of an online attack. On you. I'm not especially familiar with social media, but our people who handle it all, they've had to freeze our official accounts. It's been vicious. Um … there was also a death threat.'

'*What?*'

'I know. It's crazy. According to the PR department, it's not that unusual if you're the love interest of a celebrity. Ace's superfans – their hearts are breaking, it would seem. And some of them are very angry.'

'Jesus wept.'

'We usually ignore this nonsense, but the PR folk – they just felt, this time, we needed to keep an eye. These trolls, they're spewing all sorts of hate, trawling through your past – Amy Studley's death. And Kit Marley's–'

Eliza breathed in sharply. '*Kit?*'

'He had a huge fan base – still does – and …' He stopped.

'What, Cecil. What do they say?'

His expression was troubled. 'Well … it's along the lines that … he died because of you.'

It was as if she'd been winded. For a while, she couldn't speak. Cecil was quiet.

It's true. He died because of me.

'My god.' Her voice was shaky. 'I had no idea people were saying that.'

'I'm so sorry.'

'Right.' She blew out a long breath. 'So – was that what you wanted to talk about? The fact that there's a new level of Eliza hate?' Her tone was lighter, but her stomach was churning, and there was a foul taste in her mouth.

'Let it bounce off you, Eliza. You've done it before.'

In an attempt to neutralise the bile, she conjured up thoughts of Ace. 'And I'll do it again. Ace Penhalagon is worth it.'

'He seems like a very genuine person,' said Cecil. 'And such a talent.'

'Oh yes. Very genuine, and *very* talented.' She gave him a

mischievous smile, in an attempt to end the meeting on a less-serious note.

Cecil gave a small cough and got up to leave.

'Sorry. I do appreciate the heads up, and please – don't tell Dad about the death threat?'

'Already did, I'm afraid.'

'Oh. Okay, well – any idea where it came from?'

'No. But female, is the PR department's informed guess. They're investigating the most persistent trolls, the names that crop up time and again on Ace's various fan sites. And Kit's. I don't expect it's anything to worry about. Avoid it – don't even dip your toe – for the sake of your mental health.'

She nodded. 'Good advice, as always. Thank you.'

He left, and her eyes went to her computer screen. No way was she checking out any of those sites. You could never unsee the comments.

Hate. Why?

He died because of you.

Her heart twisted as she pictured Kit, the day before he'd been killed – the first and only time she'd seen his vulnerable side. He'd shown her a photo of himself as a little boy, with his mother.

She was an angel. My father killed her. And he killed your mum too, Eliza.

And later, when she knew it all, she'd said: *I wish you'd told me before. I could have …*

Maybe.

She squeezed her eyes tight shut to stop the hot tears leaking out.

What had she been about to say?

Kit had always scoffed at the notion of romantic love, dismissing it as 'absurd'. Growing up in that dysfunctional household, he'd come to associate love with control, power – with abuse – and had lost all belief in it.

'Love is a lie, an evolutionary trick,' he'd said. 'And sex is the bait.' He'd never connected with his lovers on an emotional level.

I could have … made him believe.

Chapter 11

Ace

'Christ on a bike, Ace,' called Tristan from the base line. 'What feckin' planet are we on today?'

Ace had just sent another volley wide. His prediction that he wouldn't be on form this morning had turned out to be an understatement. The players on the adjacent courts at the National Tennis Centre were now so over throwing back his tennis balls, the stars in their eyes had well and truly fizzled out. Ace could almost hear them: *He's not so flash when he's not competing.*

'Sorry, Trist,' he said, shaking his head. 'Shall we take a break?'

Ace sat down next to his coach, who gave him a long, hard stare. And he felt Merle's eyes burning into the back of his head, from where she loomed on the spectator balcony.

'Sorry,' Ace said again, massaging his temples. 'Problem with focus.'

'Because?' said Tristan, adjusting the sweatband holding back his floppy red hair.

'Lack of sleep, mostly.' He looked Tristan in the eye, then laughed. 'Fuck it, Trist, I think I'm in love.'

A smile pulled at the corners of Tristan's mouth. 'Ah, right you are. I thought as much.' It came out as *I tort as much.*

'Please, say nothing to Merle. She's pissed off with me as it is.' Ace glanced over his shoulder. Although she was way out of earshot, he had the uncanny notion she could hear every word he was saying.

'Mum's the word.' Tristan picked up a ball and bounced it idly in front of him. 'So, Ace. In love, you say?'

'Yup, I reckon.' Ace leaned forward, his elbows on his knees, and gazed ahead. 'I know it's only a couple of dates, but honestly? I never felt like this before.' Tristan was his friend and confidant, as well as his coach.

Tristan let out a small, wistful sigh. 'Well, *obviously* I should be telling you not to let it mess with your focus. But for sure I'm not one to talk. Just–'

'It's fine,' said Ace. 'I know how to keep my head in the game. I met her before the Olympics, remember? I guess … yesterday, she just kind of drained me of all energy.' He gave Tristan a wink. 'Like a spectacularly beautiful vampire. A good night's sleep'll see me right.'

'Hm. So – this is Harry Rose's girl, am I right?'

'Eliza, yes.' He said her name slowly, rolling his tongue around it, and the *yes*, came out like a sigh.

Tristan's soulful green eyes misted over. 'Sheesh, would you look at you. I remember that.'

For many years, Tristan had been a regular on the tennis circuit, a solid player from Ireland who'd maintained a reasonable ranking in spite of never winning a major singles title. But he'd won several tournaments, including Wimbledon, with his doubles partner Mark Cornish. Then, five years ago, Mark's new wife, Izzy, had joined her husband on the circuit.

Ace remembered Tristan saying that when he met Izzy for the first time, the attraction had been so strong, so impossible to resist, it was as if someone had slipped him a love potion. (Tristan had the Irish gift of storytelling.) He'd been powerless, stripped of free will.

'Honestly, I felt all the levels of terrible – *all* of them,' he'd said. 'My heart did the two things, when I set eyes on Izzy. It leapt with joy, and it also sank, because I knew – I just *knew* – I was lost, and there was no way back. I could tell, before either of us had said a word, she felt the same, and that we were about to hurt a good person, someone who was a true friend to me. But I just couldn't stop this thing.'

Tristan and Izzy had indeed been powerless to resist whatever force was at play, and ran off together during the Monte Carlo Masters. Incredibly, after the dust settled, the three of them managed to make peace. Mark and Tristan eventually resumed their doubles partnership, until Tristan retired from competitive tennis and became Ace's coach.

'So … you're all loved up. That's grand, *if* you don't let it mess with your game. No reason why it should – if you can channel it into your tennis, maybe it'll even work to your advantage.'

'Worked for me at the Olympics,' said Ace. 'She commanded me to bring her gold.'

Tristan chortled. 'We are forever questing at the behest of our true loves. So, let's take some of that with us to the US. Okay, we'll call it a day. Go lift weights instead, or run, whatever. Just make sure you're back on form tomorrow. We can't afford a slip up, not now, while you're at the top of your game. Or *were*, until today.'

'Still am,' said Ace, firmly. 'Minor blip. Also …'

'Also what,' said Tristan. And when Ace didn't reply immediately, '*What?*'

'I've got to write something.' Ace's face creased into a frown. 'Something important. It's worrying me. Do you know much about writing?'

'Jesus, Joseph and Mary,' Tristan muttered. 'Writing, is it now? Writing what, exactly?'

'Fifteen hundred words for *The Rack*, on what's gone wrong with Britain, and how those of us in sport with loud enough voices might help put it right.'

Tristan let out a bark of laughter. 'You think you can explain what's wrong with this benighted country in that many words? What does fifteen hundred words even look like?'

'Good point,' said Ace. 'One page? Two? Christ, I have no idea what I'm doing. Help me. Eliza's got a degree in English from Oxford.'

'She's going to think you're an eejit.'

'She will. I can't bloody write.'

'What about your voice app thing? You're good with words, just not at writing them down. Say them into your phone.'

Ace's face lit up. 'Trist, that's bloody genius.'

Merle appeared beside them. Neither had seen her approach, and they jumped.

'Merle, could you not do that, please,' said Tristan. 'We're having a man-to-man, here.'

'Tristan,' she said, fixing him with a stare. 'I don't pay you to give out fatherly advice, I pay you to teach Ace how to hit the ball in a way that will conquer the world.' She turned to Ace. 'That was the worst session I've seen since you were sixteen. Terrible. The sooner we're out of London –' she gave Ace a pointed look, '–the better.'

Ace and Tristan went quiet.

But nothing – not his appalling morning's tennis, not Merle's thunderous expression, not even the thought of having to produce fifteen hundred well-reasoned words for *The Rack*, could dampen Ace's spirits as he pictured Eliza's beautiful face, her wild curls spread across the pillow, her–

'Ace!'

'Sorry, coming.'

❀

'Where are you staying?' came Will's voice down the phone.

'Hounslow,' answered Ace, with a note of embarrassment. He wondered where Will lived. If he had to take a guess, he'd say East London.

It was a warm afternoon and the windows were thrown open. Sunlight fell across the kitchen table, where Ace was sipping a cup of tea. As he answered Will's question, he glanced around at the small 1990s kitchen, comparing it to Eliza's acres of polished oak worktops and snow-white cupboards and shiny gadgets that probably cost the equivalent of a working-class family's quarterly food budget. Each.

'Right. See, Ace, it's … all here,' said Will, hesitantly, 'but we need to make it more about *you*. You sound like a reporter.'

In spite of Will's words, Ace was delighted to discover he could 'write' like a reporter. He'd emailed the voice recording with an apologetic note explaining he didn't have time, right now, to type it up. And he'd sent it only to Will, hoping he'd help refine his words before it made its way to Eliza.

'Too many facts and figures, not enough emotion and passion,' said Will. 'I can only do so much with this. Look, can we meet? I can't abide Zoom. I'll fit in with you.'

Ace's heart sank. While he enjoyed spending time with Will, he didn't want a writing lesson that would expose his less-than-adequate education. Plus, he couldn't take more time out from training. The media attention was already causing problems.

'Your first line, for example,' Will went on. '*I'd like to talk about how we can widen the appeal of tennis to a more diverse audience, and how we can get more kids from different backgrounds interested in the sport.*'

'Is that okay?'

'It's boring. Maybe, *Too posh and too white. Let's talk about why tennis needs to change.* You see?'

'Oh.'

'And then, we need to know what it is to *you*, why you care. I mean, there you are, white and posh – a cynic might say you were virtue signalling.'

'Not posh. I have plenty of money now, but I am *definitely* not posh.'

'But you're dating a very rich, very posh, exceptionally white girl.'

Will had a point.

'C'mon, Ace, you have to anticipate the reader's response. Will they believe you're genuine in your concerns? And why would you focus on racism? It's up to the black players to own that space, and for you to *support* them, surely. Not the other way round?'

'So you think white players shouldn't take the knee?'

'Of course they should.'

'Then it's a matter for all of us.'

'Fine, yes, and honestly, your words aren't bad. But look, *The Rack* doesn't do "not bad". *The Rack* only does the best. Terri will bin your piece if it's not up there. Opportunity blown. You're an outstanding sportsman, a stellar person, now we need to get that star quality into your writing. It's easy enough once you know how. Shall I come to you?'

'That might be—'

'Our dear leader has spoken; Eliza wants this to work. She's ordered me to make your words as powerful as your … lord. Stop me before I stray into double entendre territory. The well of tennis puns runs deep. In fact, don't be afraid to add in a few – lighten the tone. It's all a bit *earnest*. I'm not getting genuine, caring, Ace; the relatable champ with a good sense of humour. I'm getting solemn, *slightly* preachy. Voice is the hardest thing to get right. It has to give us the *heart* of the writer. So – when's good for you?'

They organised for Will to come to Roehampton tomorrow lunchtime.

And now … Ace was fast approaching exhaustion. Will's onslaught had left him reeling. But he couldn't put off the next call any longer.

Catriona was due to fly to Chicago for the WTA125 tournament, and they'd made a tentative arrangement for her to join him afterwards at the Cincinnati Open, then on to the US Open. Meantime she was at home in Glasgow. It was only a day or two since photos of Ace and Eliza had begun appearing in the media, but he needed to sort this out. It would be unkind to let her find out the hard way.

He finished his tea and called her number.

Five minutes later he ended the conversation and slumped forward onto the table, resting his head on his forearms. God, he needed sleep. The call had finished him off.

Catriona's Scottish accent had intensified when she got angry, to such an extent he'd missed half the abuse she'd spat down the phone at him. But he felt like a complete shit.

She'd seen the reports on the internet, of course. And she clearly believed that as soon as he'd hit the big time, he'd dumped her for a top-of-the-range model.

The insults he could handle. Catriona was ever a feisty woman, and he'd liked that about her. But when she'd run out of rant and burst into tears, quietly sobbing down the phone – that had been horrible. Ace hated upsetting people. And while he understood her anger, he was hurt she'd believe he'd dump her for someone just because they were more famous, more beautiful. A '*rrrrich bitch*'.

A shadow fell across the table. 'Told you it'd be too hard,' came Merle's voice behind him. 'Writing was never your strong point.'

'The writing's going fine,' he said, his voice muffled against his arms. 'Will Bardington's giving me some tips tomorrow – it's okay, he's coming to Roehampton,' he continued quickly, as Merle opened her mouth to protest at yet another distraction from his training. 'I was … I just broke up with Catriona.' He sighed. 'I didn't realise she cared that much.'

Merle went over to the sink and filled the kettle. 'Course she does; she's mad about you. Hells bells. And now we wait for the media to find out. Let's hope she does a queen.'

'What?'

'Responds with dignity, says nothing. Just gets on with her life. Though, I'm not at all sure Catriona will go quietly. You've really been a bit of a shit there, Arthur, haven't you?'

Ace turned to look at her, his head still resting on his arms. 'Merle, I wasn't expecting to … to fall in love.'

'In *love?* Really? With Harry's Rose's little princess?' Merle rolled her eyes.

'I'd feel this way if Eliza was just a girl I'd met on the bus.' Although, he wondered if Eliza had ever been on a bus. 'She's amazing, a really good person … genuine and–'

'Spare me the love bomb. Eliza Rose is a product of her exclusive upbringing. You don't meet girls like that on the bus. You're from different worlds.' She paused. 'On the other hand, maaaybe –' she drew the word out, '– she could be just the incentive you need to stay at the top. 'Cos if you're knocked off your throne, she'll disappear in a puff of smoke – you mark my words.'

Enough!

All at once, physical exhaustion, guilt for Catriona's tears, and frustration at Merle's blinkered assumptions formed the perfect storm, which bowled in and blew away the rosy fug Ace had been drifting around in since yesterday.

He lifted his head from his arms. 'Shut the *fuck* up, Merle. Are you worried someone else might get a say in my life? That there's a threat to your *control*? From someone who sees beyond my ability to smash a ball hard and make shitloads of money? Someone who won't *exploit* me?'

Merle's eyes narrowed into that laser glare as she poured boiling water into the teapot. The water would find its way without her actually watching it.

'Well, there's gratitude for you. After all I've done–'

The words exploded out of him before he could stop them. 'You're not my mum! You don't really care about me. Nobody ever has, not properly – *nobody* – except Faye and Lockie. And look what happened to them. They're gone. Lost to me. Because of your … *incompetence.*'

She flinched, but he carried on – he couldn't help himself.

'Fucked up. Both of them. Two fucked-up kids who were even more fucked up by the time they left you. You're a great coach but you're the worst foster mum in the history of crappy foster parents. And you know *nothing* about Eliza. She's kind, caring; she gets me. I won't let you wreck this. I *won't*. Now butt out.'

He held her gaze; he wasn't going to drop it. Not this time. Though … Ace was already regretting the ferocity of his words.

Her eyes saw his soul. After a pause she looked away, and her chest rose and fell in a sigh. 'I see. Well, if that's how you feel.'

He said nothing, breathing quickly.

She met his eye again, and … something had shifted. 'I regret what happened. Of course I do. I misjudged the situation. I apologise. Maybe we can make it right.'

He shook his head. 'It's too late. I don't think Lockie will ever come back now.'

'He will. In the meantime … fine. Be with your new girl, I hope it works out. But something tells me it won't.'

'Merle … Mum.' He swallowed. 'I'm sorry–'

'You know what, Arthur? It's not easy, being a foster parent. And having this … intuition. We have our ups and downs, you and me, but believe me when I say, I've always got your best interests at heart.'

He sighed. 'I know.'

'Truce?' Her dark eyes were full of concern, now. And maybe a bit of love.

'Sorry,' he repeated. If he'd felt like a shit before, there were no words to describe how he was feeling now. 'I shouldn't have said all that.' He raked his fingers through his hair. 'Truce, yes. And I want you to meet Eliza. Then you'll know, the things people say about her, they're way off the mark. She's an awesome person. It's early days, but … I already know. She's the one.'

Chapter 12

Eliza

Eliza was walking home past the familiar, imposing walls of the Tower of London, when Will rang. Moving out of the flow of people, she stopped at the parapet above the Traitors' Gate.

Will filled her in on Ace's first draft. 'He wanted my feedback before showing it to you. His personality's nowhere to be seen. I'm going to give him some coaching.'

Eliza smiled. 'One on one? There's a surprise.'

Will chuckled. 'Guilty as charged – total fanboy. Look, I could just rewrite, but that would be doing him no favours, correct?'

'Yes, Will. But be sure not to contaminate his voice–'

'He appears not to have one, when it comes to writing. He's avoiding anything personal, and my intuition tells me that's deliberate. I think … Eliza. What has he told you of his background?'

She thought back to their night together, that conversation in the dark. 'Not a lot, really. We haven't talked much about his childhood.'

'Hm. While it's deliciously mysterious, it's also a problem. I think he's deliberately fudging. We can't get to the heart of him if we don't know who he is, where his motivation's coming from. Why don't you come with me tomorrow? I'm going to his tennis place. If we make it a pincer attack, he might open up.'

Eliza was conflicted. While the thought of seeing Ace tomorrow was most appealing, she wasn't comfortable with Will's use of the word 'attack'.

'We'd need to tread carefully,' she said. 'If we put him on the defensive, we won't get the words we're after.'

'Why's he got such a bee in his bonnet about racism and inequality, anyway?' said Will. 'Is it just because it's cool to care about those things? It won't wash. It's got to be relevant to him.'

'Okay, okay. I'll come. Text me the details.'

She ended the call and looked around her, thinking. It was high tide on the Thames, and the muddy waters were eddying below her, slapping against the ancient embankment walls.

The memory came at her out of nowhere – voices echoing in her head. Hers and Kit's.

I walk past this every day, but it still gives me the creeps.

This whole place screams.

Time slipped. The air temperature dropped, the crowds faded away and they were alone here, on this very spot, in the dead of night. The floodlights were reflecting off the Tower walls, silvering Kit's pale hair.

That wasn't a cold shiver, but let me warm you up anyway.

She froze as she felt the pressure of his arm across her back, his hand squeezing her shoulder.

'*Kit?*' she whispered, breaking out in goose bumps.

That night, he'd just returned from spending the summer in France, with Will.

When you're not around, I feel lost.

The dark silhouettes of nighttime barges lumbering along the river, thrumming quietly … she'd asked his advice about Rob.

Babe, nobody's good enough for you. Apart from yours truly, but I'm a fuck-up.

You are, Kit. Maybe you should have therapy too?

No one could sort out my shit, believe me.

The voices faded, the pressure on her shoulders lifted, warmth displaced the chill and she was back in the present, on a late-summer's evening, among the milling crowds.

Eliza carried on home, shaken, her shoulders tingling from that ghostly touch.

It had happened once before, when they'd scattered his ashes – she'd sensed his presence. The soul; the spirit. Could it live on? Exist outside the body?

Harry had had an out-of-body experience, and Eliza was the only person he'd ever told. He'd been on the operating table after a near-fatal shooting, watching himself from above, while shadowy forms discussed whether he should live or die, whether he'd atoned for his wrongdoings – in a past life, in this life? He wasn't sure.

Harry had ever been the sceptic when it came to matters spiritual. He'd put it all down to the mysterious workings of the brain. But when it happened again, last year, when he'd been in a coma, he and Eliza had reached an unspoken understanding. Something was at play. Something they would never comprehend. Weren't meant to.

But Eliza knew, deep in her heart, that Kit's death and Harry's recovery were connected.

He died because of you.

❀

Later, as she hung up her jacket in the wardrobe, her eyes fell on the bed and she smiled, remembering Ace demanding to be woken properly with a kiss. That look in his eyes.

Ace. Anticipation at seeing him tomorrow pushed aside the final echoes of that unsettling moment by the Tower. She would talk to Will on the way to Roehampton. No way did she want Ace to feel cornered, or worse still, embarrassed about his upbringing.

She went through to the kitchen and switched on the oven. Her daily, Molly, had left her a salmon meal that just needed heating through.

As she waited, she turned on the TV and picked up her mail. There was a padded A4 envelope, the address written in sprawling black felt tip:

Eliza Rose,
Ivory House,

St Katharine Docks,
London EC3

Someone – the Royal Mail, presumably – had added her apartment number in blue biro.

An internal warning light flashed on as she stared at the bold lettering. Something about this felt off.

She turned the package over. The sender window was empty. It weighed very little; she squeezed it. Inside was something long and thin, tapering at one end.

She put it down on the coffee table in front of her, stared at it some more. Anxiety was creeping along her veins; a sense of dread, spreading its chill, immobilising her limbs. Her heart started to thump as Cecil's words about hate slithered in: *it's been vicious … a death threat …*

Eliza stood up quickly, wrenched open the balcony doors and gulped in a lungful of air.

What's wrong with me tonight?

First she'd imagined Kit had popped in from the other side to relive their chat by the Thames. Now, a simple package apparently contained something sinister, something … cursed.

Calm down.

But the panic wouldn't leave; bile was rising up her gullet.

… don't read the comments.

She needed to talk to someone. She grabbed her phone and called Harry.

'Lizzie! How are we this evening? I very much enjoyed yesterday, with Ace. Top chap. Well done.'

Eliza sank onto the sofa and took more deep breaths.

'Is everything all right?' he said, when she didn't reply.

She picked up a cushion and hugged it. 'Actually, no. I … I'm feeling scared.'

'Scared? Why, sweetheart?' His deep voice was already steadying her. 'Because of all the press interest? You've–'

'Not that. Did Cecil tell you about the online hate? The death threat?'

There was a short silence. 'Psh, come on.' His voice was teasing.

'Since when have you let any of that nonsense get to you? You've never let it ruffle your sensible feathers before.'

'But Cecil said–'

'Just because you've captured the heart of tennis's latest pin-up, and in the process incited the jealous wrath of female Britain, that's no reason to start worrying about the crazies.'

'No …'

'And male Britain, I suppose, because it's fine for us to find him attractive too, now. Correct?'

Eliza laughed. Good grief – Dad joking about a man crush? She felt better already.

'Okay, I'll try and be cool. But can you stay on the phone while I open this thing I got in the post?' She described the package. 'I don't know why it's making me nervous – it's just giving off this vibe.'

'Right. Switch your video on and we'll open it together.'

She set down the phone so it was showing the table. Harry's face popped up. She ripped open the envelope and peered inside.

A Barbie doll, its long hair coloured Eliza-red.

'Shit.' Her hand began to shake. A cold gust of wind slipped through the balcony doors to touch her arms, her face. 'It's a doll,' she whispered.

'Take it out, Lizzie. Touch it as little as possible. And stay calm.'

She pulled the doll out by its hair – and dropped it immediately, as if it had burned her.

A tiny knife was embedded in its neck. Crimson streaks of paint dribbled their way down its chest and onto its clothes – a copy of the dress she'd worn to the preview at Leicester Square. The doll's lips had also been coloured crimson, the smeared outline giving it a grotesque smile.

'Oh my god.' Eliza's skin was crawling, as if a million tiny wriggling things were grappling to get out.

She picked it up again, holding its hair between a thumb and forefinger, and showed it to Harry.

'Jesus Christ.' She saw the flash of fear on his face. 'That's sick.

Right … put it in a bag, envelope and all, and give it to Cecil. We'll get it looked at. Is there anything else in the envelope?'

She shook it, and a folded piece of paper dropped onto the table. Picking it up by a corner she read out: '*THE DEAD ARE NOT DUMB.*'

What? The words sent another chill through her veins.

'Keep that with the doll.' Harry's voice was soothing. 'You always hated Barbie. Perhaps she's out for revenge.' He was doing his best to calm her.

It was true, she *had* hated Barbie. The vacuous blondeness of her; the tiny waist, pointy breasts and unfeasibly long legs.

'I did,' she said, with a weak smile. 'Remember the Year 9 debating cup?' She'd won, arguing the motion – she recalled it out loud for Harry – '*This house believes that Barbie's proportions are a manifestation of the patriarchal agenda that aims to subjugate women by subliminally encouraging the low self-esteem that will ultimately impede their attempts to achieve positions of power.*'

She'd ended her argument by snapping the head off a Barbie. Her speech had brought the house down, and her teacher had told Harry his daughter would one day be a feminist icon. (But then, Eliza's teachers had always said lovely things to Dad. He had that effect on them.)

'What an insufferable little madam I was.'

'I was always rather fond of Barbie myself,' said Harry. 'She's a bit like Caitlyn.'

Eliza couldn't help laughing. 'Tsk, Dad.' Caitlyn had been the wife before Clare; the stunning, much younger, mid-life-crisis wife. The tragic one. *One* of the tragic ones. *God.* Harry had kicked her out for cheating on him, in the worst display of hypocrisy since Henry VIII had beheaded Catherine Howard.

'And now forget about it,' he said. 'Eat something, watch TV.'

'I don't know if I can …' The thought of that salmon's pink flesh almost made her gag.

'Do you want me to come over?'

She could have used the company. 'Thanks, Dad, but you're

right. I can't let a crazy person, a troll – whoever sent this – get to me. I need to put it out of my mind. I'll be fine.'

'You will. Our family has attracted more than its fair share of nutters in its time. This is just another in a long line.'

Her eyes fell on the doll again. 'Dad – the knife in the neck. The words. Maybe it's nothing to do with Ace. Maybe someone hates me because of Kit.'

Harry was quiet for a moment. Eliza knew he still carried a burden of guilt for Kit's death.

'Someone with a dead guy obsession, perhaps,' he said, 'like the Jim Morrison groupies. These strange people will always be around. Look, we'll get you some additional security. I'll send someone over tomorrow.'

'Yes, please. I don't feel safe, Dad.'

❀

After two or three bites of the salmon her stomach rebelled. *Sorry, too busy churning here*. She threw the rest away and decided on an early night. She was done in.

The lack of sleep (a small smile, as she remembered the reason), a long day at work, including the disturbing conversation with Cecil; the unsettling moment at the Tower, and that package – that *thing* … all at once she was whomped by exhaustion. The tasks of taking off a dress with a rear zip, hanging things up, the faff of the skincare regime; it all felt Herculean.

Eliza turned her mind to Ace, deliberately daydreaming her way through the bedtime rituals, and when she was finally in her PJs she went round the apartment making sure all the windows and doors were secure, putting on the chain, sliding bolts, drawing curtains and blinds, even in the spare rooms.

Her phone rang in the bedroom, piercing the quiet, and she jumped, letting out a small squeak.

Chrissake! She was jittery as a … very jittery thing. Exhaustion had robbed her of similes.

Switching off the living area lights, she went through and picked up the phone. *Ace!* What a joy; what a relief.

'Hello! I missed you today.' She climbed into bed, pulling the duvet up to her chin, arranging the pillows behind her head. She let her body go limp, and settled down with the phone to her ear.

'Missed you more,' came his voice with its cute hint of a West Country burr. 'How was your day, princess?'

A comforting warmth was spreading through her, pushing away the panic.

As they caught up, she said nothing of her meeting with Cecil, or the surprise in the post. She didn't want to give those worries oxygen. Neither did she let on that she was planning to see him tomorrow. She wanted it to be a surprise.

Ace described his morning of terrible tennis. 'I collected the full set of Irish curses from Tristan, and some top-of-the-range death stares from Merle. I'm surprised I'm still alive. I'm in serious need of my zeds, but I wanted to say goodnight first.'

'I'm so pleased you rang. I really needed to hear your voice.'

'Same.' There was a pause. 'Also … there's something I wanted to let you know about.' His voice had turned serious.

Eliza frowned. *What now?*

'I'm hoping it's no big deal but just in case … with the media interest and everything.'

She sighed. 'What is it, Ace? Just tell me.'

'Right. Until quite recently … well, until today, I guess … I was kind of with someone. Catriona. Catriona Macleod.'

'Ah.' She wouldn't share how she'd googled the Scottish tennis player, even though – surely everyone googled the exes?

'It wasn't serious. I was going to end it even before I met you, but I put that off because I didn't want any hassle during Wimbledon or the Olympics.'

'Right.'

'The thing is, she didn't take it at all well. And she jumped to the wrong conclusions – about why I'm dating you.' He paused again. 'We *are* dating, right?'

Her heart squeezed at the note of panic in his voice. 'Of course we are, you numpty.'

He released a breath. 'Thank god. I thought I might have put you off, coming on all intense, like.'

The way he said it, almost *loike*. It was adorable.

'Not too intense, Ace. And Dad thinks you're a *top chap*, by the way.'

'Good to know.'

'What wrong conclusions, though?'

'She'd seen it – us – on the internet. She called you some nasty names, just because you're rich and famous. She may talk to the press. I'm obviously hoping she doesn't, but …'

'You thought you should warn me. I appreciate that. But honestly, if she does, it'll only be a small addition to the ever-increasing mountain of hate. Turns out being your girlfriend brings with it all sorts of … let's say, unwanted attention.'

'Seriously?'

'My team at Rose are keeping an eye. Our COO has warned against any social media or fansite toe-dipping, and indeed I don't intend to sully my pedicure.'

'Your what?'

'Tarnish my pretty feet. I had to wait long enough to get them done, what with lockdown.'

Another pause.

'Can I see? Your feet?'

She giggled, kicked off the duvet and switched to video.

'Oh, look at those toes. Eliza … I *really* want to kiss them. And suck them.'

Oh my god. Eliza squirmed.

And then, he asked to see some more.

A little while later, Eliza switched off her bedside light, pulled the duvet back up, and slipped contentedly into a dreamless sleep.

Chapter 13

Eliza

'New shirt?' said Eliza, as the cab quietly hummed its way to Roehampton. (She had decreed Rose would from now on use only electric vehicles.)

'This old thing?' Will pinched the pale-blue flowery fabric between a finger and thumb.

She lifted a hand and ruffled his lovely chocolaty curls. 'Is that product, William?'

'Hey, mock ye not,' he said, swiping her hand away. 'Yes, I have made an effort, given we're meeting our crush. But it also remains a delightful novelty to put on clothes that aren't joggers and a T-shirt.'

'So true. And you look very nice.'

'Why thank you.' He ran an eye over her. 'Likewise.'

She'd chosen a white sleeveless blouse and wide-leg beige trousers, with a new pair of shoes made from organic cotton and natural latex rubber. She'd been looking into sustainable fashion, after Ace's comment about sweatshop trainers.

'Change of subject,' she said. 'Without giving you the context, can I ask what you make of a sentence? Don't think too hard about it, just tell me what it immediately says to you.'

'I love it when we play games.'

She kept her tone neutral. 'The dead are not dumb.'

He put his head on one side, then said, 'Pft, I hate ambiguity.'

'But what if it was deliberate?'

'Then … quite clever. Someone has died, and not only can they speak from beyond the grave, they can be clever about what they might do with those words.'

'Or get someone else to speak through the living?'

He turned to look at her. 'What are we talking about here? A new RoseGold thriller?'

She opened the photo she'd taken on her phone, and was dismayed to feel panic welling up again. She tried to swallow it down. 'According to Cecil, I'm currently the target of a barrage of online abuse.'

His interested smile vanished. 'What? Why?'

'From hard-core Ace fans. I haven't looked myself, of course. But this handwritten note was in my mailbox.' She turned her phone to show him. 'Honestly, Will, it's really frightened me. And …' She hesitated, then reminded herself to be strong. 'It was with this.' She swiped to the photo of the doll.

His mouth dropped open. 'Holy *fuck*.'

'I know.'

'The knife … sweet Jesus.' His face had turned pale. He said nothing for a while, frowning at the photo, then staring out of the window. 'Obviously a reference to Kit. That's … horribly disturbing. Are you okay?'

'Not really. But Dad and Cecil have already got someone on the case. And they're beefing up security on my flat.'

'Good. That's good.' He took her hand, gave it a squeeze. 'What a nasty shock – you poor thing.'

Eliza swallowed. 'I think you're right. Surely she means Kit.'

'She?'

'Oh. Could be a he, I guess. It's just – the hate seems to be coming from Ace's female fans, and they're also dredging up my past, which of course means reminding everyone that Kit … that Kit died because of me.' Her voice caught on the last few words.

'No, don't ever say that. Don't even *think* it. Kit died because of his father. As did Kit's mother. And *your* mother. Kit avenged them both – he did it for them, as well as for you.' He exhaled, then said quietly, 'And of course, he wasn't expecting to die.'

She looked at him. 'But he was.'

Will shook his head emphatically. 'No. He knew his father was dangerous, but he wasn't a man who'd order a hit on his own son. It was a theft gone wrong.'

That was true – probably – so Eliza said no more.

Will had never bought into Kit's dark obsession with Fate, his uncanny ability to see patterns of events. And she was fairly sure she'd been the only person who'd witnessed his prescience – his sense of things to come.

'Putney,' said Will. 'We're nearly there, and we've hardly talked about Ace.'

'We know what we need to say.' Eliza redirected her thoughts to the matter at hand. 'I'll let you do the talking; I'm probably too involved now. If I started poking into his background under the guise of work, it'd feel off. But look, if he clams up about his past, don't push it, okay? Softly softly.'

'Right. Let's open with a nice gentle serve, see what comes back.' He turned to her again, his expression serious. 'But … about the unfortunate doll.'

Eliza snorted. She felt lighter for having shared it with Will. 'Barbie got what she deserved.'

'If you don't want to be by yourself, come stay at mine. Until the hate dies down. Christ – what's *wrong* with people? I take it … we haven't properly talked … you and Ace *are* together?'

She smiled. 'God, yes. I'm not letting him get away.'

'That's great. I think.'

'You *think*?'

He gave her a sad little smile. 'It's been you and me, this past year. I'm worried I'll lose my best pal.'

Darling Will. Sometimes, wrapped up in her own concerns, she forgot what he'd been through, and how he was always there for her.

She leaned her head on his shoulder. 'Never, silly. You'll always be my best pal. No outrageously handsome, genuinely lovely, Olympic-medal-winning Wimbledon god could possibly come between us. And thanks for the offer. Ace is off to the States this week, so–'

'Oh no. It's you and Rob all over again.'

'Good point. But let's have a few sleepovers. Tonight, though … well, I'm kind of hoping I won't be alone tonight.'

❊

The tennis centre receptionist looked Eliza up and down. 'I only have Will Bardington on my list.' There was a strong note of disapproval in her tone, as if to say, this is a sports facility, not a social club. Or was Eliza just imagining every woman she encountered was burning with jealous hate?

'Last-minute change of plan,' said Will. 'I can assure you Eliza's intentions are entirely dishonourable.'

'Will! I'm so sorry,' she said to the receptionist. 'Would it be all right if I sneaked in too? We're interviewing Ace for *The Rack*.'

The receptionist pursed her lips and tapped something into her computer – probably *Will Bardington, The Rack*, and *Eliza Rose, Rich Bitch* – and passed them visitor lanyards. 'They're on the indoor courts. Follow the signs to the spectator area.'

Eliza tingled with anticipation as they set off along a corridor.

Stairs led to a balcony overlooking a brightly lit, aircraft-hangar-sized space. Eliza spotted Ace on the closest court, his focus intense as he played low, deep, blisteringly powerful shots from the baseline. She recognized the red-haired player who was somehow returning them – former Irish number one, Tristan Knight.

Will leaned on the barrier; Eliza hung back, not wanting Ace to spot her and lose concentration.

She loved to watch him; he was such a graceful player. She remembered Chess's words: *I strongly suspect sorcery*. His skill *was* almost supernatural – the way he anticipated his opponents' moves, as if he could read their minds; the physics-defying angles he found; the way he span the ball so it gave up the will to live.

Will cocked his head and mouthed at Eliza, *Who the fuck is that?*

She thought he meant Tristan, then realized he was looking at someone hidden from view below her. She moved forward, peering over. *Oh!* Was that …?

'I thought it was Venus Williams!' hissed Will.

It was an easy mistake to make. Standing back from the court, watching the play intently, was an imposing woman in a purple track suit. She must have been almost six foot tall, and had a long, thick, silver braid hanging down her back.

Then suddenly, she disappeared.

'What?' said Will. 'Where'd she go?'

She appeared through a door behind them.

'Will, Eliza. I'm Merle. Arthur's manager.'

Eliza just managed to stop her jaw dropping open as she took in the Amazonian figure in front of her. Merle Innes was ageless, beautiful, and black. Eyes of jet glittered in her smooth face – her skin had an almost iridescent sheen. Her thick, silvery hair was tinged with mauve, echoing the tones of her track suit.

Will briefly met Eliza's eye, and she saw him swallow a smile.

'Merle,' he said. 'It is the very greatest of pleasures to meet you. I have heard much about you from Ace.'

'And it's my pleasure too,' said Eliza, finding her voice, holding out a hand.

Merle gripped it with fingers tapering to long, purple nails.

Ouch.

'Eliza.' Merle's dark eyes saw way beyond Eliza's smile. It was like being X-rayed. 'We weren't expecting you.' There was a slight emphasis on the 'you'.

She had an aura about her, like a magnetic field. One that would repel anything – any*one* – who came close to her charge.

'Oh, I'm just tagging along. Will's the wordsmith, I'm more the fan.' Eliza winced inwardly. That hadn't sounded professional. She glanced down to the court. Ace had spotted her, and his face had broken into an enormous smile. He quickly disappeared, too.

'You got an hour, max.' Merle's accent was difficult to place. Somewhere between the West Country and Jamaica.

Her unsmiling gaze was still fixed on Eliza; she narrowed her eyes. 'I know you're keen to …' she paused, and her lips made a strange, quick, sideways pout as she considered her words, '… *champion* his causes. But that is *not* what Arthur should be focusing on right now. If he can maintain this form, he could win the Golden Slam–'

'The what?' interrupted Will.

'Olympic gold and all four Grand Slam events in one year. It's the Holy Grail of tennis. No one's ever done it in the men's singles.'

'That would be amazing,' Eliza said. 'He's certainly capable.'

'I'm going to be blunt here, Eliza. He doesn't need the distraction of a relationship. Especially one that's attracting so much media attention. You'd be doing Arthur an enormous favour if you told him to cool it.'

Will sucked in a breath. 'Merle?' The name seemed so ordinary, so *suburban*, for this imposing woman, this force of nature. 'I interviewed Ace.' He was leaning casually on the rail, but his voice was as determined as Merle's. 'And in my humble opinion, no way should anyone be attempting to dampen his warrior spirit. It's part of him, part of his tennis, and it extends way beyond hitting a ball in spectacular fashion which, while admirable and no doubt lucrative at this level, won't change the world. And the world is something about which Ace obviously cares – deeply. If we can provide a platform for him to use his voice for good, then we fully intend to do that.'

Will – you beauty!

Merle said nothing; her gaze was inscrutable, but that aura had darkened.

Will continued, uncowed. 'And Eliza is *just* the woman to make that happen. Together they'll be an unstoppable force – positive, good-hearted, full of ideas – let's face it, the leaders we've got are making a complete dog's dinner of it. One thing Ace and Eliza can do is publicly hold them to account.'

He turned to Eliza and smiled. 'Eliza won't be a distraction, she'll be a motivator, a great support.'

The door behind them opened again, and Ace blew in. '*What* a surprise!' He swept Eliza off her feet into a bear hug, then kissed her on the lips.

Oh god. Professional Eliza gave a final wave and left. She just wanted to breathe him in, savour the sensation of his arms around her. Kiss him back.

'I hope it was okay to bring a friend,' said Will.

'Way better than okay.' Ace let Eliza go, and beamed at Will. 'You've both obviously met Merle,' he said, remembering his manners.

Before they had chance to respond, the door opened a third time, and Tristan materialised.

'And here's my tennis pro, Tristan Knight.'

Ace's coach had dreamy green eyes fringed with pale lashes, a friendly, freckled face, and fiery hair held back with the trademark bandanna Eliza remembered from his heyday as a Wimbledon doubles champion.

'Well hello there – if it isn't Eliza Rose,' he said, in a strong Irish accent. 'What an absolute treat to meet you. And Will Bardington, too. I love your work, Will. *Most Human of Saints* is one of my all-time favourite series, so it is.'

Will went a little pink. 'That's extremely kind, Tristan.'

What a shame Tristan was already very much committed, romantically.

Ace had taken hold of Eliza's hand, and was stroking her palm with his thumb, liquidising her insides.

Merle looked pointedly at her Rolex. 'I want you back on court at one thirty,' she said to Ace and Tristan. Then she looked Eliza in the eye. 'Think on what I said.' She gave them a nod loaded with meaning, then disappeared.

'Psh, don't you be taking notice of mardy Merle, now,' said Tristan. 'After yesterday's little hiccup, Ace is back on deadly form today. As long as you don't cut off Samson's hair, so to speak –' he winked at Eliza, 'we'll be all good for the US. I'll see you back on court, Ace. Grand to meet you two lovely people.'

Given Tristan's words, not to mention Merle's, Eliza wondered if she should abandon thoughts of Ace staying the night again. But when she looked at him it was, in fact, almost *all* she could think about.

'Café's this way.' Ace dropped Eliza's hand and set off along the balcony. 'Apologies if I'm sweaty and a bit whiffy, no time to shower.'

'We'll take you hot and steamy,' said Will.

Eliza giggled. 'Sorry about my friend.'

Ace grinned. 'Also, apologies if my writing efforts weren't up to scratch, Will. Well – obviously they weren't, otherwise you wouldn't be turning up here with reinforcements.'

'We look forward to whipping you into shape,' said Will.

A little later they were seated in a quiet spot in the café. Happily, it seemed famous-people-watching wasn't a thing here in Tennisland. Everyone was studiously ignoring the trio in the corner.

'So, Ace,' said Will, switching on his voice recorder. 'What I was saying, about making it personal. Your column won't have real impact unless it relates to you in some way. Think 'own stories'. *This needs to change because this is how it was for me*, sort of thing. The racism part makes more sense now.' He took a bite of his panini, and waited for Ace to respond.

'I see. Merle – yes. Well, growing up as a white kid with black parents – Hector's black too – me and my foster siblings were given a hard time at school. We were the unwanted kids with a black mum and dad. Got bullied about that. Sport was my way of fighting back.'

'I bet,' said Will.

'Having black parents – we were totally cool with that. It was only a problem outside the home. Merle and Hector were kind, caring – they'd have done anything for us … in the early years …' He stopped.

'And in the later ones?' said Will, carefully.

'Things changed once I became successful. How could they not? Everything got complicated. Merle was so busy with my training that the other foster kids … well, she had less time for them, and it all started to slide.' He sat back in his seat; he was shutting down a little.

'Ace?' said Eliza.

When he turned those blue eyes on her, she almost forgot her words. 'Um, can you maybe give us a little more on what it was like having black parents when you were white? How the other kids reacted to that?'

Ace prodded his salad, thinking. 'It wasn't just the kids; Merle and Hector were getting it from other parents. Like, why would Social Services place white kids with black parents? Merle used to say, "Families don't have to match," but some didn't agree. I remember the surprise – shock, maybe – on the faces of people who didn't know my parents were black.'

'And did that carry on into your tennis? The prejudice?' asked Will.

'The Williams sisters moved things on a *lot*, but it's still largely white and middle-class. Most people are surprised when I introduce Merle as my foster mum.'

'Guilty,' said Will.

Eliza nodded. 'Me too.'

'Honestly, Ace,' said Will, 'she's *magnificent*. But quite terrifying.'

'That's about right. She's copped unbelievable amounts of racist shit over the years. It's made me hyperaware of it all. But believe me, Merle's more than capable of dealing with racists.'

Will leaned forward. 'I would *love* to see that. What's her modus operandi?'

Ace smiled. 'She hexes them.' He looked Eliza in the eye. 'Tell me, how many non-white British tennis players can you name?'

'Um … Heather Watson? Dad would know more.'

Neither she nor Will could name another.

'Yep, there's maybe a couple more with decent rankings,' said Ace. 'There's around half a dozen black players in the world's top one hundred, men's and women's. None of them are British. We've got to make tennis a more welcoming space. Sport changes things – it's where kids find their role models. When they see black people conquer the sporting world – look at football, athletics – they believe they can win too, whatever they choose to do in life.'

'How can you move this forward?' said Eliza.

'By changing tennis's image, campaigning for more facilities for kids from deprived backgrounds. Profiles of black players in the media will increase their sponsorship chances – that's where people like you come in.'

The conversation continued, Ace touching on social inequality, too, but Will wanted them to stick to one topic at a time.

'I suggest an introductory column to tie in with the US Open,' he said. Eliza nodded. 'We'll have to decide how regular, given everything you've got going on. I have enough from your first interview, plus today. We'll email it to you first, make sure you're happy with it.'

'Sounds good.'

Will switched off his voice recorder. 'And now I'll go see about a cab back. Ace, an absolute delight, again.' He stood up. 'I'll leave you two to chat.'

'Was that okay?' Ace said, as Will departed. 'Honestly, I have all the ideas, but words seem to escape me when I try to write them down.'

She smiled. 'Will's brilliant. The best. Don't for a minute compare yourself to him. Just grab this opportunity for him to take your wonderful thoughts and put them into a piece that will smash it. And don't worry that it won't sound like you. He'll make sure it does.'

Ace nodded.

'Then you're going to have to think about what to do with all that support. How to turn those words into actions. Maybe we end your first column with an invitation for others to join you – who do you want? How do you get them on board? Sportspeople? Captains of industry? Even politicians? Think about the who, as well as the what.'

'Right. I guess you know about this stuff, how to make it work.'

'I was brought up to know.' She stopped as Barbie gave her a nudge, and she remembered the hate. And then there was Merle's attitude. 'Mostly I think of the power and the influence I have, and everything that brings, as a privilege, but … you know what? There are times when I just want to run away and hide, live in a shack on a beach.'

He smiled, and reached for her hand. 'Me too. The pressure, eh? It gets to you. But guess what? Our family does in fact have a shack on a beach, in Cornwall. I could take you there.'

What an enticing thought. Just the two of them, tucked away on a hidden beach. 'Yes! Although I was thinking more a tropical island.'

'Well, there's the Australian Open in Feb.' He raised his eyebrows.

Was he asking her to come see him in Australia? While it would no doubt be impossible, given her work commitments, her spirits rose again, knowing he was thinking this way.

'Oh, I love Australia. I sailed up the coast on Dad's yacht one year, all the way from Sydney to Cairns. The islands, the rainforest – it was a slice of heaven.'

'Hm. I wonder what the carbon footprint of *that* trip would have been?'

Eliza grimaced. 'Good point. Bit of a gas guzzler, is *Janette*.' Heck, a green audit of the Rose family wouldn't be pretty. 'Named after wife number three, in case you were wondering.'

'Probably not wise for me to advise your super-capitalist father to downgrade his yacht to a sailing boat – not just yet.'

'I am not my father. But I do love his yacht.'

He smiled. 'I need to go. What are your plans?'

'I might just head home and work from there … Evening in front of the telly …' She waited, hopefully. 'And you?'

'I have to drop Merle back to Hounslow later, but …'

'You could keep me company. Or would Merle hex me?'

Chapter 14

Eliza

Eliza stayed for the afternoon, watching Ace from the balcony while answering emails and making calls. Harry phoned about the new security, explaining passcodes and alarms and a panic button. In the bright lights of the tennis centre, the memory of the defaced Barbie was less menacing.

She could feel searing beams of disapproval pulsing like lasers from Merle's eyes, from where she stood down below. When she found out Ace was intending to take Eliza out for dinner, she seemed to take the news as a personal affront, as if Eliza was making a deliberate effort to sabotage his tilt at the Golden Slam.

The gauntlet had been slapped down, and Eliza was dismayed with this turn of events. Because in spite of Merle's overt hostility, Eliza couldn't help admiring her. She'd always been drawn to strong women, like Terri, and Clare, who was softer but with a deep well of strength and wisdom. Could Eliza win her round?

She needed to figure out this foster relationship. Was Merle's interest in Ace mostly about her own personal ambition?

'Merle really doesn't like me,' she said, as they drove back into town. 'She thinks I'm a distraction, that I'm going to scupper your chances in the US.'

'She's overprotective,' said Ace, 'but that's understandable. We've worked so hard for this, for so long. I'm sure she'll come round.'

In the marina car park he turned to her, eyebrows raised, when they revisited the *how long?* part of the payment process.

'All night – every last little minute of it,' Eliza said, ignoring the memory of Merle and her aura, and at last he pulled her into his arms for a kiss. She gave herself up to the warmth of his lips, the sensation of those powerful arms around her. This time she felt a rush of emotion, as well as the familiar heat, rising like magma.

They walked arm in arm through the dock, and Eliza was aware of smiles as people recognized them. The world seemed a more welcoming place tonight.

On reaching her front door, Eliza took out her phone and studied the instructions Harry had forwarded.

'Do you have an app, or something?' Ace asked, watching her.

'A new code. I had some extra security installed today.'

'Oh? I hope that's not–'

'Wait,' said Eliza, trying to work out the instructions. There was a loud, insistent beep as she unlocked the door; she pressed keys on the new box and the noise stopped.

'What an absolute pain. I never bothered with an alarm before, what with the security on the main entrance.' She shut the door behind her, locked it twice, and put on the chain.

'Expecting trouble?' Ace said, in a jokey tone.

'No, I … I just get spooked sometimes, living by myself.' She hung the keys up on a hook.

Ace put his arms round her waist. 'I'm here to protect you, princess.'

He kissed her again, and it was beautiful, and hot, and it melted her until she thought her knees might completely fail her.

'Do we really want to eat out?' she whispered. 'Or shall we get something delivered? Later?'

❀

Darkness was creeping in by the time their thoughts turned to food. Eliza was drowsy, her limbs entangled in his.

'Shall I order something in?' she mumbled into his chest. 'If I don't feed you, Merle will *know*. What are you allowed? I suppose pizza's out of the question?'

'Pizza would do it for me. After that workout, I think the restorative properties of cheese would be of great benefit.'

She roused herself enough to sit up, pick up her phone and order: '… and extra cheese, please.'

Ace grinned, then rolled over onto his front, resting his head on his arms. She trailed a finger down his spine, her eyes drinking in his tattoo. 'It's so beautiful – so powerful.'

Outside, the sky to the west burned in shades of orange, the colours diffusing through the sheer curtains into the darkening room, touching Ace's skin with fire.

'Never mind your hair,' she said, remembering the Samson analogy. 'This is where your power lies. It's like …' She closed her eyes; her fingers were tingling. '*Magic*. Can I make a wish?'

'You may. But you're allowed only one. So think carefully, princess.'

'One wish.' She concentrated, and her head began to spin, flinging away her thoughts, emptying her mind.

'One,' came Ace's voice, from somewhere far away.

She drew her fingers slowly down his warm spine, feeling her way from the top to the bottom, and the strange tingling intensified.

The wish arrived of its own accord, like a whisper on the wind, the words manifesting in her head: *I wish Kit could come back.*

'Eliza – hello?'

Her fingers slid sideways as Ace rolled onto his back.

She opened her eyes. It was like waking from a fleeting dream. The sun had set; the room was monochrome, the glow had faded.

'Look at you – so serious.' He ran a finger down her arm. 'What did you wish for?'

She blinked. 'Surely that would spoil the magic, if I told you?'

'The power is mine, though.'

'All the stories say you shouldn't tell.'

Ace flicked on the bedside light. He looked at her again. 'Are you okay?'

Eliza was shaken – she wasn't sure what just happened. 'Fine.'

'Good. Well – are we going to give up any semblance of civilized behaviour and eat pizza in bed, or shall we put some clothes on?'

✸

It was just before ten o'clock, and Eliza was drifting off when she was pulled awake by the sound of a bugle and distant shouts.

'What the fuck's going on?' muttered Ace.

Eliza laughed. 'It's just the neighbours. The Ceremony of the Keys at the Tower. It happens every night – some serious locking up's required when it's the Crown Jewels. Nothing stops it – not wars, not Covid.'

'Ah, I see.' Ace twisted a lock of her hair around his finger. 'Is it any wonder you get spooked? I mean, you live next door to the most haunted spot in England. Imagine them all coming out after dark. Headless Tudors, phantom boy princes, the duke who was drowned in a vat of wine …'

'Ace – you knows your history!'

'One subject I didn't flunk. I love history.'

'Imagine,' said Eliza, picking up on his theme, 'Anne Boleyn and Catherine Howard catching up for a bitch about Henry. Elizabeth floating up from Richmond on a ghostly barge to see her mum …'

'The two little princes pranking Cromwell and More,' said Ace. '*Tales from the Tower*. Someone should make that animated movie.'

'I'll get Will on it.'

They lay quietly, Eliza snuggled into his chest.

'Eliza?' His tone had changed. 'What I said before, last time. I do love you. From the moment I saw you. It feels like it was meant to be, like it's fate.'

Oh god.

The F word. Kit's conviction that we have little or no control over our destiny.

Haven't you noticed, Eliza? Fate loves to fuck with us.

'Gosh. That's such a beautiful thing to say, and it means so much. I'm …' She mulled over her words. 'I'm more cautious than you, for various reasons. I do have feelings for you – strong ones. Getting stronger by the minute.'

'That's giving me hope.'

'I can't stop thinking about you when we're apart.' It was true.

'Honestly?'

'Truly. Ace, that baggage …' He was curious about what had happened with Rob. She owed it to him to explain.

'My split with Rob. It left me confused, I guess. Shaken. I loved him very much, but I couldn't give him what he wanted, which was all of me. I thought, at the time, if I couldn't make it work with him, I couldn't make it work with anyone. Now, I'm not sure. I don't want to get hurt again, and I don't want to hurt anyone. It's why there's something of a wall around my heart.'

'And a moat.'

She looked up at him. 'A moat?'

He smiled, and tweaked the tip of her nose. 'Sorry – carry on.'

'Well … maybe this could work? You wouldn't be pressuring me to put you before my career, like Rob did. I think you understand – you're driven, like me. Your goals are similar to mine. Rob and me, our goals were different.'

As she spoke the words, they were making perfect sense. Maybe this really *could* work?

She laced the fingers of one hand with his.

'You never take this off,' he said, touching the silver ring on her middle finger. 'Did Rob give it to you?'

'No.' She went quiet. 'Kit. It's a replica of one that belonged to Anne Boleyn. He gave it to me one Christmas, when we were working on *Most Human of Saints.*'

He stared at it. 'It's beautiful.'

'Yes.' She sighed, thinking back. 'We could never agree if Anne was a victim or a villain. I'm an Anne fan; he was intrigued by Henry and his conscience.'

She pictured Kit, sitting cross-legged on her living room floor as they ran through the script, Will striding about. Suddenly, it seemed so long ago.

'But you and Rob – you split because he couldn't handle you being his boss?'

'What? Oh, yes – well, partly. But it was more about those life goals. I want to make a difference, to build on Dad's legacy. That wasn't important to him. He's ambitious, but for different reasons. And then he messed around with someone in LA, mostly to make me jealous, to force me to commit. It backfired badly, because fidelity's important to me.'

'And is that why you never hooked up with Kit? Because he was promiscuous? You wanted all or nothing?'

What?

'Is Kit part of your baggage too?'

Eliza curled into herself. She didn't want this conversation.

'No. Well – not in the way you're implying. Though having someone die because of you, I guess you could call that baggage.'

'What happened, with Kit?'

Back off! She didn't want to open up about his death. Not yet.

She saw the uncertainty in his eyes. He deserved some version of the truth, something to be going on with.

'It's difficult to explain. No one's ever got my relationship with Kit. Not even Will. Definitely not Rob. His behaviour was pretty out there, whereas I've always been that good girl. But we had this … connection. Rob misunderstood it. Most people did.'

She hoped that covered it. 'Are we done with the baggage? Of course, we haven't unpacked yours, but maybe it's best we wait, until you've won the US Open and claimed the Holy Grail.'

'No pressure,' he muttered.

'None at all, lovely Ace. And about what you said, before. Give me time. I have a feeling it'll come.'

Ace kissed her hair. 'I appreciate your honesty. And now we should get some sleep. I need to prove to Merle and Tristan you're not sapping my strength.'

She snapped off the light and let out a long sigh of contentment as he tightened his arms.

Chapter 15

Ace

Ace was in the gym at just gone seven, giving it his all on the bench press. This was how he honed the muscles responsible for the serve that had earned him his moniker.

As he lay on his back lifting Tristan's prescribed weights, he was pleased to discover his strength remained intact – unsapped – contrary to Merle's dark predictions. He was in fact killing it this morning. His time with Eliza had invigorated him.

He rested the weights and relaxed, thinking back to her visit here yesterday. It had been disappointing, in that he'd believed Merle would be won over when she met Eliza. How could anyone not be? But the exact opposite had happened. Ace didn't fully understand why. He appreciated her concerns – she didn't want him to lose focus – but he'd proved at the Olympics this wasn't an issue.

No, something else was at play here. He suspected it was Merle's rarely glimpsed softer side. She wanted to protect him. After all, she'd cared for him since he was a small boy, and in spite of the enormous wobble a few years ago, their bond remained strong.

Merle thought Eliza was going to break his heart. She'd said so, more than once. And all because she was a rich girl, and he was basically an ordinary boy. She believed Eliza was interested only in superstar Ace, not in the real Arthur beneath.

This morning he'd left Eliza in bed, insisting she didn't need to get up, taking her a cup of tea. While the kettle boiled, he'd looked again at that collection of photos. He knew he shouldn't have – he didn't need reminding of her life of luxury: too many residencies to count, Daddy's yacht, Oxford uni with her famous friends, and a long-term boyfriend from that same world who was, apparently, very much still part of her life.

He also wished, now, that he hadn't blurted those words about love at first sight. Stupid. Too much, too soon. Again. He remembered her awkward, embarrassed response, progressing to an almost total shut down when he'd clumsily turned the subject to her dead friend. Why did he always do this with her? Why couldn't he just be cool?

Like Kit, he thought glumly, picturing that louche-looking student smouldering at the camera – at Eliza.

Why did he get the strongest impression the dead boy was key to understanding her recent past? He'd been Will's partner, not hers. Rob had been Eliza's long-term love. Kit had been her friend.

But as he resumed lifting weights, he remembered Will's slip-up, when Eliza had gone off to the restrooms during lunch. The slip-up that had prompted last night's questions about Kit.

'You and Eliza,' Will had said, leaning forward. 'It's all on, then? I heartily approve. No more riddles, you're over the moat.'

He'd laughed. 'Thank you for waving me across, Sir Will.' Then he'd grabbed the opportunity to find out if Eliza had discussed him with Will. 'Forever in your debt. But … I'm worried I won't pass muster. We're from very different backgrounds. I barely scraped my GCSEs for a start, whereas she–'

'Pft, don't worry about that,' he'd said. 'It'll be her cautious nature. Just give her time. I mean – you've known her less than a month, right? She's not an impulsive person; she thinks everything through, weighs up the pros and cons. Never lets her heart rule her head. And she's extra cautious now, after last year–'

He'd stopped, and fiddled with his phone. Ace saw him wondering whether to say more. Eliza was his boss, after all.

'Last year …' prompted Ace. 'She told me about it – the bones of it, at least. Why the relationship could never work. Said she still talks to him all the time, though.'

Will had looked troubled. 'She can't let go … I'm in fact worried about her state of mind. I hope you can help her move on.'

'I'm doing my darndest.'

'I guess it's not easy, competing with a dead guy.'

'*Dead?* There was silence. 'I thought we were talking about Rob.'

Will had gone pink. 'Sorry, sorry. Yes, of course you were. Honestly …' he'd given Ace a weak smile, 'I think I'm losing it myself. *I* still talk to Kit, too. We're both a bit lost. It's hard to accept someone you love's gone – just *poof* … gone. Yes, she and Rob do still talk a lot, but much of that's for work, for RoseGold. I provide the drama, he provides the dosh. Seriously, you shouldn't worry about Rob.'

At last, Will had stopped gabbling.

'Right.'

'I do think, honestly, she's ready to move on. To you.' He'd smiled. But his words about Kit couldn't be unsaid.

'Also, this … what would you call it … hate campaign? She's largely protected from it, never reads it, but just knowing it's going on, that's not helping.'

'The social media?'

'Mostly online, yes,' said Will. 'If there's anything you can say to dampen it, on Twitter or whatever; if these fans of yours hang on your every word, maybe remind them to be kind.'

Mostly online. What else had Will meant?

Focus! Ace intensified his lifting in an attempt to empty his mind, to stop the dark thoughts that were trying to nudge their way in again.

'Well isn't that a lovely sight to see.' Tristan had arrived, and perched on an adjacent piece of gym equipment, his legs swinging.

'You look like a leprechaun,' said Ace.

'And there was me thinking you were all against the stereotyping. How was your evening with the lovely Eliza? My, but she's a dinger.'

'She is. And it was great. And my strength and focus are intact.

Just got to get Merle on side, now. Your help with that would be much appreciated.' He rested the weight. 'Seriously, Trist. What's she got against Eliza?'

Tristan moved over to the pec deck, gripped the handles, and began pushing the arms in and out. 'Power struggle, I'd say. It's never pretty, when that's between two beans.'

'Two what?'

'Ladies. Are you seeing her again before we leave?'

'Once more, I hope. Need her to say some magic words, tie a ribbon round my lance.'

'So to speak,' said Tristan. 'Let's go practise then, my man. Two admin-y things, though, before we get into it.'

Ace noticed Tristan's customary brightness dim a little. 'What's up?'

'First off, your ex. Catriona.'

Ace's heart sank. 'Oh no. What?'

'Been mouthing off to the press, sorry to say. My first thought was, what in the name of the Blessed Mother is she thinking? How is that cool? But of course, positioning herself as your wronged ex, dumped with a quick phonecall for none other than the rich 'n' ridey Eliza Rose – well, she'll get some serious exposure from that, and given she's never going to make the big time, she'll milk it for the zillion pounds it's worth.'

'Right.' Ace's good mood was ebbing, disappointment that she'd do this filling its space. Also, 'love rat' wasn't the image he was aiming for, especially when he was about to launch his new column.

'What do I need to know?'

'Just that you're a bit of a cad. Mostly according to *The Sun* and all the Scottish papers and TV. The rest – they're not really bothered. Women's mags will no doubt side with Catriona, though. I'd say ignore. It's the likes of *The Rack* we care about, and you're onto that.'

'Yup.'

'Having said that, the other thing.' He looked awkward. 'A request from them in fact – *The Rack*. They want another photoshoot. Apparently this has come from the top.'

'Terri?'

'Eliza. The art director rang Merle, passed on a very specific request. They want your back. The tattoo.'

Ace smiled. 'Eliza loves my tattoo. But no. It's private. *We must not let daylight in upon magic.*'

Tristan nodded. 'Thought you'd say that. And we don't have the time, anyway. Merle won't want to waste what's left having you poncing around in a photo studio. They'll just have to use something they already have.'

'Good luck telling Eliza that. But I agree. Tell them no.'

❀

Mid-morning, Ace checked his messages.

> Eliza: *Thx for last night. Was extra cheese helpful? Hope you can fit in photo shoot? Will come undo your shirt again ☺ XXX*
>
> Ace: *No time – sorry! Also we Cornish v protective of our magic. Only princesses allowed to see. Can u use pics we did before?*

Message seen. Ten minutes later, no response.

> Ace: *Can I see u before US? Need to collect my favour or will risk tournament death. U don't want to be responsible for that!*
>
> Eliza: *You DO realise how amazing your back wld look on cover?*
>
> Ace: *V sorry. Photo would unman me ☹*
>
> Eliza: *I see. Yes to favour collecting. Don't need more people hating me. Tonight or tomorrow? Either ok. x*
>
> Ace: *Tomorrow good. Downgraded from three big kisses to one small? Forgive? Believe – magic is real XXX*
>
> Eliza: *I know – 'Those who don't believe in magic will never find it.' Could have actual 'going out' dinner? XXX*
>
> Ace: *Pick u up 7? Where would u like to go?*
>
> Eliza: *Will book somewhere. Come to apt first*
>
> Ace: *See u then. PS Will have to go home after sadly –*

flying out Fri a.m. PPS Love you
Eliza: <3<3

❀

That evening, after appearing on *The One Show*, Ace did most of his packing so as to allow maximum time with Eliza on his last night in London.

At least he didn't have to worry about gear. Tennis kit would be delivered in the US, and the technician would be on hand with his rackets before each round.

Ace got through up to nine per match, three at each of his preferred tension levels – tighter for control, looser for power. The tiniest variance in tension made him uncomfortable, and he was equally obsessive with his grip. Always leather – it let him talk to the racket.

His technician teased him about his obsessions, but Ace had his rituals, his superstitions. Another was that he never, ever, took off his shirt during a match. No crowd got to see his tattoo.

Ace's technician cost a small fortune, but … well, he now had a large fortune. Millions. After the US he was going to set up the Ace Penhalagon Foundation and put much of it to good use.

When he was done, he went downstairs, glancing into the kitchen where Merle was preparing a late supper, flinging ingredients into a large, bubbling saucepan.

Sitting on the living room sofa, he opened his laptop and checked the latest tennis news. He was seeded number one for the US Open. As he scanned the page, he was aware of his heart rate increasing. It was becoming ever more difficult to trick his mind into thinking this was just another tournament. The pressure was intense.

He'd avoided the press coverage, but was aware Britain was fixated on his challenge. Everyone he encountered, from the towel guy at the gym to the neighbours putting out their bins, wished him luck. Even next door's black cat, forever on the wall, seemed to command: *Win, Ace, win.*

Only Steffi Graff had ever accomplished the Golden Slam. Could he be the first man to do it? It was a quest the like of which he'd never again face in his career. This was his enormous chance to make sporting history.

As a distraction, he opened Twitter and uploaded a photo of himself lifting weights. He typed: *Feeling the weight of expectation! Full-on training day. Thanks for your amazing support, GB!*

Then, remembering Will's suggestion, he added: *And please remember to be kind today.* He finished it with some hearts and tennis emojis.

Immediately, a vomit emoji popped up in the replies.

Then another reply: *#DitchTheRichBitch*

He closed Twitter with a sigh, and opened Instagram. His sponsors liked him to post regularly, and until recently he'd enjoyed engaging with his fans. Also, he liked to post photos of the beautiful places he saw on his travels, and of his beloved Cornwall, often captioning them with a few words on protecting the environment.

All he had today was the sun rising over the tennis courts, but he uploaded it with the caption: *Never get tired of this.*

The comments started immediately. Lots of hearts and little flames and heart-eyes and Union Jack flags.

Never get tired of YOU!!! Love you so much Ace XXXXXXXX
Good luck in the US Ace! We love you.
#DitchTheRichBitch
King of the court. King of my heart <3

He stopped reading at that point. The internet didn't feel like a welcoming place today.

'Can I help?' he called, attempting to swallow down the acidity leaching up from his gut. It was insidious, the effect the comments had on him.

'All under control,' Merle replied. 'Ready in five.'

He turned his thoughts to Eliza, and immediately felt brighter. Until, with a life of their own, his fingers googled her name, followed by *Rob Studley.*

WTF are you doing? It would seem he'd crossed the event horizon of the internet black hole.

The images popped up, of the pair of them at various events – Wimbledon, film premieres. He clicked on one of her at the BAFTAs. She was wearing a beautiful scarlet dress, Harry on one arm, Rob on the other. He zoomed in on Rob. Classic good looks; wide, self-confident smile; friendly brown eyes. Rob looked like a nice bloke, if a bit full of himself.

You'll like him.

Behind the trio he spotted Harry's wife, Clare, her arm linked through Will's.

There was no sign of the other boy.

He typed: *Eliza Rose Kit Marley* and scrolled through the images.

Why am I doing this? A few minutes ago he'd been trying to distract himself, bring down his heart rate. All he'd done was to increase it.

An Oxford University drama production – cast and crew. He recognised a younger Will, Kit and Eliza; Kit's arm was slung across Eliza's shoulders.

There was the iconic *Rack* cover, which had gone viral. Eliza was seated on a golden 'throne', Will and Kit standing either side. The headline: *New Era for Rose.* He smiled at the image of Will, with his tumbling curls and engaging expression.

God, the other boy. He just looked bored. And effortlessly, wildly beautiful. If you liked boys who looked like girls.

Ace was struck once more by that resemblance – the messy blond hair, the loose-limbed physique, the fine-boned features …

And as he looked again at those unusual gold eyes, he wondered – was Eliza's face the last thing on Earth they'd seen? He seemed to remember she and Will had been present at his death.

He clicked out of the photo and scrolled through the articles. Ace's knowledge of what had happened was sketchy. Eliza seemed reluctant to discuss it, but that was understandable. It wasn't that long ago; it was probably still raw.

There was a piece from *The Rack*, written by Terri Robbins-More. He clicked on it and began to read.

154 # Olivia Hayfield

'Ready!' hollered Merle from the kitchen.

Ace closed the laptop and sat back. *Holy shit.* In the early 2000s, the article said, Russian billionaire Andre Sokolov's investment in Rose Corp had been at risk, because the divorce settlement Harry's wife – Eliza's mother – was seeking threatened to bankrupt Harry. So Sokolov had organised a hit on Ana, without Harry's knowledge, setting things up so the blame would fall on Harry, should the 'death from natural causes' ever be revealed as murder.

Terri, Harry and Eliza had known for years that Sokolov had killed Ana. But it'd been too dangerous to do anything with that knowledge – until Harry had faced a serious heart operation. His 'just in case' last wish was that Terri and Eliza should expose Andre, if Harry didn't make it. He'd told the pair his soul wouldn't rest in peace unless he atoned for Ana's death.

But there had been a problem – there was no proof of Andre's guilt. Only Harry's word.

Kit, Andre's estranged son (a fact Kit hadn't shared with Eliza), had discovered what they were trying to achieve and, under the guise of a reconciliation, had tricked his father into confessing to Ana's murder. But at the last minute, Andre had guessed Kit was wired, and sent one of his lackeys to steal the recording. Kit had put up a fight, and had been stabbed in the ensuing brawl. Eliza and Will had discovered him bleeding to death on the floor of Kit and Will's East London house.

Poor Eliza. No wonder she couldn't forget.

Having someone die because of you, I guess you could call that baggage.

The only consolation was that Will had a copy of the audio file, and Andre had been convicted.

Kit's father killed Eliza's mother.

The concluding paragraph explained how Harry Rose had awoken from a coma to discover his last wish had come true, but that Kit Marley had paid with his life.

So Kit had died for Eliza – and Harry.

I guess it's not easy, competing with a dead guy.

The voice from the kitchen: 'Arthur!'

'Coming!'

'What's eating you?' asked Merle, as they started on her savagely flavoured fish dish.

He looked up, realising he'd been brooding. 'Something caustic. Social media, mainly.' Then down at his plate. 'But also … what on earth have you put in this?'

'A few extra-special ingredients to help with your strength. And some for those nerves – yes, I've noticed. And … other things.'

'What other things?' Ace always worried a test might pick up one of Merle's potions. There was surely a fine line between some of the plant extracts she sourced from goodness-knew-where, and illegal substances.

'Turmeric. Chilli. Cardamom …' She didn't meet his eye as she listed them.

'Hm.' He put his fork down; he had little appetite. 'You know what? I wish I hadn't read those comments.'

'Oh for heaven's sake, you *didn't*. How many times? Just don't. We need to do the posts because of your sponsors, but just leave them to me, right? I'll run them past you first, but for the sake of your mental health and your focus, you *must* avoid right now.'

She muttered under her breath; he caught only part of it. 'I *knew* this would happen … that … girl …'

'Merle. About Eliza. She's–'

'I *know*. I know what she is.' She paused, and met his eye. 'You've passed the stage of listening to me, when it comes to your love life, so I'll say no more. This will play out, the die is cast …'

Ace shook his head. 'I'm dating a lovely girl. She's intelligent, fun; she believes in the same things I do. It's early days, but I think we have a future–'

'Past, present, future …' Merle shovelled a chunk of fish into her mouth and aggressively chewed it. 'Words words words. *Meaningless.*'

God help him, she was in one of her weird moods.

'You either get that, or you don't,' she said. 'Tell me, when you first met Eliza, did you feel like you already knew her? Like you'd met her before?'

He closed his eyes for a moment, so she wouldn't see them roll. 'No, I didn't. I'd seen her in the papers so I was aware of her.' He paused. 'Although – you know what? It was possibly love at first sight …' Then he remembered the feeling he'd had, that time by the river, that there was something at play, out there in the universe.

But he wasn't going to admit that to Merle. She didn't need encouraging.

'Nope. Eliza isn't a past love, reincarnated so we can have another crack at our ill-fated love affair that ended so tragically back in medieval times.'

'How do you know?'

He spluttered with laughter, glad to feel his mood lightening. He changed the subject. 'Do you remember what happened to Kit Marley, that writer, last year?'

'Of course.'

'I was just reading about it – he was Eliza's friend. She was there when he died. It must have been terrible for her.'

'He was one,' she said. She stood up, and went to slice more bread from the loaf on the worktop.

'One what?'

'Oh – by the way,' she said, 'the magazine people confirmed Will Bardington will be emailing your column tomorrow so you can approve it before we leave. They're disappointed about the tattoo, but of course that was never going to happen. They'll use a photo from the session you did before.'

'That's good.'

'But they love the whole sword idea, so they're going to give the cover an Arthurian theme. Britain's warrior hero, uniting the country, leading us out of the millennial Dark Ages, so to speak. I'm not sure Brexit, Covid and climate change equate to a new Dark Ages, but it's quite a clever concept.'

'Seriously?' Ace shook his head in disbelief.

Chapter 16

Eliza

Oh yes. This! Perfect. The cover concept, despite the lack of tattoo, was inspired, and Will had made Ace's words sing and glitter, as she'd known he would.

His covering email to Terri, Eliza and Ace, read:

Greetings, lovely people

Draft of Ace's column attached. All his own words, just massaged, tweaked and buffed, un petit peu.

What shall we call it? 'Touching Base with Ace'? (joking, obvs). Suggest we just give it his byline, and focus on the topic heading. This one could be something like:

[main] "I WAS A WHITE KID WITH BLACK PARENTS"

[sub] WHAT DIVERSITY MEANS TO ACE

Plus an intro from Terri – why you've invited him to write a regular column, etc. A lovely head and shoulders of Ace the Face, of course.

Ace – do you want to add anything more re setting up your foundation?

Warmest wishes

WB

Pippa placed a coffee on Eliza's desk. 'Good to see you looking so full of beans. Hardly surprising, you lucky girl you.' She winked, and whistled under her breath.

'Such a comely one. Do you think he'll do it? The Golden Slam?

Goodness me, he must be under enormous pressure right now, poor man. We Brits are so used to losing at the last minute, but wouldn't it be amazing, if he did it?'

'Timely, too.' Eliza glanced at today's *Guardian*:

ENGLAND'S CRISIS OF CHILD ABUSE, NEGLECT AND POVERTY

'We need a bloody big cheer-up. And Ace? Honestly, Pippa, he's our man. He's as good-hearted as he is gorgeous, and he's on a mission to mend Britain. Wait until you read his first column.'

She clicked on her next email. Oh! A reply from Ace.

Oh my god.

There was a photo embedded in it – a head and shoulders of Amy Studley, Rob's late wife, her eyes doctored to look like a zombie's. Across her neck in red lettering were the words: *THE DEAD ARE NOT DUMB.*

Eliza started to tremble, her eyes fixed on that photo.

'Eliza? What is it?'

When she didn't reply, Pippa swivelled the computer screen towards her. 'Oh no. There's been a lot of this stuff, I don't know how this one made it through. Wait …' She clicked the mouse and read out, '*AceP256@gmail.com.* Obviously a fake account. Don't open anything else from unusual email addresses. We'll have it looked into.'

Eliza still hadn't said a word. Her palms were sweating, nausea was rising. The Amy photo had stamped itself on her retinas.

'Forget you ever saw that.' Pippa's voice seemed to be coming from a long way away. 'It'll just be a stupid stan.'

'A … a what?' said Eliza, coming out of her trance.

'Stan. A superfan. Most of them are harmless, of course, but there will always be a few obsessive nasties. I expect Ace is well used to them.'

She clicked Eliza's mouse a couple more times. 'I've forwarded it to Cecil, and now it's deleted. Honestly, what's wrong with people?' She frowned in concern when Eliza didn't respond. 'Try not to fret, luvvie. Will you tell Ace about this?'

Eliza inhaled a deep breath. 'No.' Ace was under quite enough pressure. 'I'm seeing him tonight. I should just focus on enjoying that, right? Ignore the loonies.'

'You do that. Get him to give you a nice big hug.'

❋

A little later, Eliza rang through to Cecil. 'Can you spare me ten minutes?'

'Of course. Come on through.'

Why did his kind, calm voice suddenly make her want to cry?

She went next door to his office and sat down with her hands in her lap. Her eyes fell on the family photos on his desk. His lovely wife Millie, who was a translator, and their two children, Robbie and Annie. They looked so ... normal.

What would it be like to belong to a family where nobody knew your business, or judged you? Didn't know your family history, had no opinion on your clothes, your hair, your love life? Didn't view you as some sort of public property?

A memory flashed in. Right now, she seemed to have little control over where her mind was taking her. She was with Kit, sitting on the grass at Greenwich Park, beside Queen Elizabeth's Oak. He'd made her play truant from work, knowing she needed time out, and as they'd sat beside the ancient, hollowed-out tree, she'd had that strange, fleeting sensation of being outside of time.

Don't want to go home, she'd said, *or back to work. Not ever. Wish I could just stay here with you. Shall we run away?*

'Eliza?' said Cecil.

She blinked. 'Yes – sorry. Lost in thought. I wondered if you'd had any news on the ... doll. The note. You may have seen, there was an email with a sort of matching theme.' She tried to keep her tone level, professional. As she said the words she dug her nails into the palm of her hand. The pain distracted her.

Cecil nodded. 'I've forwarded it to the private investigator. She'll have technical people who can take a look. On the package ... there's no trail. It looks like it was delivered by hand, to a random mailbox in your building, in the hope it would be redirected to yours. That is, the sender knew your apartment block, but not which apartment.'

'How?'

'Social media, probably. Looking back through your Instagram posts there have been a few off your balcony. Sunsets, drinking wine and so on.'

'Oh no.'

'It wouldn't be that hard to work out where you live.'

They were silent.

They know where I live.

'Just be careful, while this madness is going on.' Cecil sat forward in his chair, rested his elbows on his desk and steepled his fingers, tapping them together. 'Why are people so angry? It seems to have got worse.'

Eliza sighed. 'I don't know. Aftermath of Covid? Maybe it's … a manifestation of fear? A loss of control?'

'Could be.'

'Me getting together with Ace has obviously triggered some people. Probably because I'm this rich, privileged white girl. I seem to have become a focus for the haters. Like, how dare I have the money, the cool job –' she finally managed a cheeky smile, '– the hottest man in Britain.'

Cecil gave one of his little coughs.

'So … the package was delivered by hand, you say?'

'No fingerprints, no clues,' said Cecil. 'The Barbie doll's hair was coloured using a highlighter pen, the blood was interior emulsion paint. The dress – a rough copy. Nothing much to go on, in other words. And probably not serious enough to involve the police.'

'I'd rather not. What about the social media? Did anyone identify any of those trolls – might any be connected to the email that just came in?'

'Still investigating. There's a nasty hashtag that's caught on among Ace's fans. They're trying to identify who started it, the main users, but the privacy laws don't work in our favour.' He paused. 'Honestly, Eliza, I'm so sorry this is happening.'

'What's the hashtag?'

'You don't want to know.'

'A death threat?'

'No, just …'

'Please – tell me.'

Cecil let out a sigh. 'It's on Ace's accounts, mostly. Ditch the rich bitch.'

She gave him a faint smile. 'I can cope with that. But the doll's on a different level. It's from someone who knows how to mess with my head. Because of Kit, and now Amy.'

'It would be easy enough to work out you'd be deeply upset by those two events. Maybe … I don't know. Some people, locked down for months, isolated – they go a bit crazy. Now that's behind us, let's hope whoever it is gets on with their life. And I think the best thing *you* can do is to put it right out of your mind.'

❀

Eliza left work early, too distracted to do anything useful, to risk making decisions. That image of Amy just wouldn't leave her alone.

She headed across London Bridge, wearing a mask and a pair of large sunglasses, plus a new wide-brimmed hat. All in all, a pretty effective disguise.

The dead are not dumb.

The voice inside her head: *Kit died because of you. And so did Amy.*

She glanced at the people she passed, wondering if that person had tweeted about her, or left a comment, used that hashtag. Or just had an opinion, on that rich bitch at the top of her Rose-shaped tower, looking down on the masses below, who were struggling to stay sane and solvent in these difficult times.

Feeling herself begin to unravel, Eliza turned her thoughts to Ace. This morning she'd booked them a table at a favourite restaurant; this afternoon she'd cancelled it, unable to face going out in public. She imagined he wouldn't be *too* disappointed – another nice evening in with delivered food. Or maybe … maybe she should actually cook something. He might like that.

She picked up her pace, more positive now, picturing Ace sprawled on her sofa with a cold beer as she whipped up a tasty dish; soft music playing, asking about his day. Like a normal couple.

Like me and Rob used to be. The memories just kept on coming today. Rob cooking for them, mocking her supermarket-brand ingredients. He'd been quite the gourmet chef, sourcing things from artisan shops and markets, while she'd never been a committed cook, happy with the local Tesco.

The supermarket was just past Tower Bridge, and she bought ingredients for a fettuccine with brown butter sage sauce, plus a bottle of pinot grigio. She remembered Ace's words about Merle's strict dietary controls. Well, the pasta would be a good top-up of carbs after a hard day's training, and sage was high in vitamins and anti-oxidants, and was probably good for … wisdom?

Such were her thoughts as she descended the steps from the shopping strip, when out of nowhere someone barged her hard in the shoulder, sending her tumbling down the steps. Her hat flew off; she dropped her shopping bag and her hands and knees hit the ground hard. There was a sickening smash as the bottle of wine shattered.

A passer-by hurried over. 'Hey, are you all right?'

Eliza sat where she'd fallen, shocked and breathing hard. She looked up just in time to glimpse someone in a hoodie disappearing round the corner.

The woman helped Eliza to her feet. 'Are you hurt?'

'I don't think so,' said Eliza, her voice shaky. 'Everything's intact, apart from the wine and my dignity.'

'Did he steal anything?'

Eliza's handbag was still over her shoulder, unopened. She checked. 'Nothing stolen.'

'Well, that was a deliberate knock, I saw it – mugging in broad daylight! You know what? It's the masks. People have a better chance of getting away with crime.'

Eliza brushed herself down, then peered inside her shopping bag. Broken glass; wine slopping about in the bottom. The packets of pasta, sage leaves and hazelnuts, and the block of parmesan had all survived.

'Wait here,' said the woman. 'I'll get you another bottle.'

As Eliza stood on the steps, she made the connection. She was willing to bet she now had a proper, bona fide stalker. If it had been a mugger, they would have snatched her bag.

Great. Just great.

And then it hit her properly. It could have been the person who'd stabbed Barbie in the neck, who'd deadened Amy's eyes. Someone who enjoyed messing with Eliza's mind, who perhaps held her responsible for Kit's death. Or Amy's. Or both.

'Here.' The woman had reappeared, and was holding out a shopping bag containing another bottle of wine. 'The guy in the shop let me have it for free. You see – not everyone's horrible!' She took the dripping bag and carefully transferred Eliza's shopping into the new one. 'I'll dump this for you.'

Tears were pricking the backs of Eliza's eyes. She wasn't sure whether it was self-pity at being attacked, or the kindness of this stranger.

'Try not to let that get to you,' the woman said, looking in the direction in which the attacker had fled. 'These are strange times, people aren't themselves. Pour yourself a large one from that bottle when you get home.'

'I might just do that,' said Eliza.

Chapter 17

Eliza

She slammed the door shut, put on the bolt and chain, then leaned heavily on the wall, trying to slow her breathing. Every step of the way home, she'd felt as if she were being watched. The skin on the back of her neck was still prickling.

She closed her eyes and took a long breath in … and out.

The quiet of the apartment settled round her and she rallied herself, going over to the kitchen worktop to unload the shopping. As advised by the Good Samaritan, she poured herself a glass of wine. *The kindness of strangers*. There were good people out there too.

She arranged things ready for preparing the meal, then showered, visualising herself exfoliating the negative thoughts, sloughing them off, wincing as the soap made contact with the grazes on her knees and the heel of her right hand.

Trying to put the incident out of her mind, she thought about Ace. She couldn't *wait* to feel his strong arms around her. She put on a simple white sundress and kept her hair loose, the way he liked it.

Her phone beeped: *Here! Machine asking questions again. How many hours? Am I driving us somewhere?*

Eliza*: Change of plan! I'm cooking. Hope this news isn't too disappointing. Number of hours entirely up to you XX*

Five minutes later there was a quiet knock, and she peered through the peephole to see Ace's distorted but hugely welcome image. She dealt with the bolt and chain, opened the door and flung herself into his arms.

'Oof! ' He staggered across the threshold. 'Well hello. Nice welcome.'

She couldn't let him go. The sensation of being held tight against his broad chest – it was like sinking into a hot bath after walking through cold, driving rain. Her anxiety was draining away; she felt safe.

'I can't tell you how good this feels.'

'Same, princess.' His softly spoken reply, his warm voice, dispelled the last of the angst. 'I needed this.'

'I bet. You must be feeling the pressure. I've had … a bit of a time of it, too.'

'Have you?' His concerned gaze made her want to tell him everything. *Everything.*

'I got sort of … assaulted, on my way home. Mugged, I suppose, but nothing was stolen.'

'Shit! What happened?'

'Seems to have been a random nutter. Pushed me down the steps outside Tesco. Just a few steps; I'm fine really – only a little scrape.' She held out her palm, then showed him her knees.

He took her hand and gently kissed the graze. 'Poor thing. Must've shaken you up.'

'It did. C'mon, let's get you a drink. Beer?'

'Sounds good.' Ace shook his head. 'Bloody hell,' he said, as she went over to the fridge. 'The world's gone mad. I made the mistake of checking out my social media. There's a bunch of full-on psychos on there. While I think of it – promise you'll go nowhere near my accounts?'

'As in, hashtag ditch the bitch? I'm aware.'

He looked stricken. 'Eliza … the locks; all your new security. Is it because of me you don't feel safe? Because of my fans?'

She handed him his beer, considering her answer. 'Partly. But it's mostly just Dad and Cecil fussing.' She hoped that made him feel better.

Ace went over to the balcony windows. 'Shall we sit out here? It's a beautiful evening.' It was one of those rare, balmy August nights when the marina could be a Mediterranean waterfront. When you could actually sit out without a cardi.

'Can we stay in?' she said. 'We can open the doors, let the breeze through.'

'But it's–'

'No. I think …' She stopped herself. She desperately wanted to tell him, *I think I have a stalker; there have been death threats; I got something really disturbing in the mail …* but she couldn't land that on him the day before he was leaving for the US.

She pared it back. 'That mugger, and the social media hate. I wouldn't feel safe sitting out there tonight, for all the world to see. Especially not with you.'

Understanding dawned. 'Ah. I see. And that's why you cancelled the restaurant. Shit, Eliza. I'm so sorry.'

She pulled a face. 'It's not *your* fault you inspire demented devotion. And I'm not letting you go, no matter how hard your crazy fans try to see me off. But can we just stay inside tonight?'

'Of course. And at least now I don't have to worry my peasant table manners will let me down.'

She put her arms round his waist. 'It's our last evening together in who knows how long. Let's not waste any more of it thinking about loser fans and weirdos. Let's–'

He silenced her with a kiss, briefly gentle, then passionate, insistent, and her body burst into life, hitting away all the bad thoughts which finally fled far, far away.

'What time's dinner?' he whispered against her lips.

'Afterwards.'

'After …'

'After you take me to bed and do all the nice things to me. Enough things to last me weeks and weeks.'

They lay tangled in the sheets, and in each other, and Eliza experienced a sublime calm. A feeling that nothing and no one could harm her while this man's arms were around her.

'I know we're not supposed to need knight-protectors anymore,' she said, running her palm over his firm, rounded bicep – she realised she had a very specific crush on his arm muscles – 'but I feel so safe with you. Like nothing bad can happen. All my random worries go away when you're here.'

'I'll check in with you every day.'

'Yes please. I'll make sure my toenails are maintained at peak prettiness.'

He chuckled. 'And you can gaze on my tattoo. No sneaky screenshots, mind. Not even for personal use. You *must* promise.'

She looked up at him. 'Seriously? You think if I photograph your back, your forehand will lose all power, or something?'

'You said you believe in magic.'

'I did. Because I do.'

He shifted so he was half sitting, rearranged the pillows, then pulled her head back onto his chest. 'So, Eliza. As a Cornishman, I'm no stranger to superstition. Give me your definition of magic.'

'Definition? Or experience?'

He smiled a wicked smile. 'Other than what I did to you just now, how would you describe magic?'

'Pft. Okay, Ace the Face. I'd say, it's a force that defies the laws of nature. Qualifying statement: the laws of nature as defined by western science.'

He considered her words. 'Very good. But quite boring.'

'It's … something on the edge of our understanding. An energy we're dimly aware of – especially if we're in tune with nature. Like, an animal – a bird or a butterfly, maybe – that for a moment you sense isn't just a bird or a butterfly. I'd say some other cultures are more in tune with it all than ours is.'

'But I'm not talking spirits,' said Ace. 'That's something different.'

'Well … okay. The magic I've experienced.' She smiled. 'Watching

Will and Kit create *Most Human of Saints*. Magic happened when they wrote together.'

'Words have power, but that's not magic.'

'Tsh – it totally is. But okay, proper, completely beyond-science magic – yes. When I was alone with Kit.'

Ace briefly closed his eyes. 'Oh. Do tell me.'

'He made time stop. At least once.'

One eyebrow rose. 'Really?'

'Okay, there may have been alcohol involved, on our last night at Oxford. I was horribly maudlin, sad it was all over. I told him I didn't want it to end, that I wanted time to stop.'

'And Kit waved his lovely big wand? Sorry, maybe I should rephrase that. You *were* just good friends – right?'

What?

'Don't joke about it, Ace.' She pictured that ancient, magical, moonlit oak. 'The college clocks had already struck midnight. We went for a walk, sat under a tree talking drunken nonsense, taking selfies. At least half an hour passed, then he messaged me, right beside him, so I'd see the time come up on my phone. It said midnight.'

'Hm.'

'Fine.' She untangled a leg, shifted away from him a little. 'You can scoff or you can believe. Why should I believe yours, if you won't believe mine?'

'Sorry. Maybe it was the mention of alcohol. Or Kit.'

'Believe it. And … I've sensed Kit, since he died. Two or three times. I don't think he's gone. Not properly gone.'

'That's ghosts, not magic. Or maybe just the power of wishful thinking.'

'Do you believe in ghosts?' she said.

'I've never seen one. Do you?'

Eliza was quiet. 'I think perhaps I do. Not so much floaty white phantoms, more just … a presence, maybe a soul? Perhaps one you were deeply … connected to.'

Ace looked thoughtful. 'Kit had a violent death,' he said

eventually. 'Sometimes you hear that those spirits take longer to leave us. If you believe in spirits. I don't, not really. But my sister–'

'Sister? Oh! You didn't say–'

'Foster sister. Faye – she's a couple of years older than me. She believes in all that. Calls herself a neo-pagan, and a wiccan. There's a lot of it about where I come from. It's mostly nonsense.'

'But you said you believe in magic.'

'Like I say, it depends on your definition. My tattoo – for me, that's magic. Something way beyond the sum of its parts.'

She slid her fingers round to his back; they tingled as they met the sword. 'Tell me its story. I promise I'll never repeat it.'

'I want *two* promises.'

'Oh?'

'The second is that you feed me after I tell.'

She laughed. 'Oh, sorry – you must be starving! Yes, I promise.'

'The bones of it is …' He turned his head away, looking out of the window. 'Eliza …'

'Please tell me?'

'Okay, yes.' He met her eye again. 'I should. Some … bad things happened. Really bad. To my family – my foster family. It was a while ago now; I was in my teens. I'll tell you about them one day. Things weren't properly resolved, it split the family apart. It was a horrible time.'

Eliza gently ran a finger down his arm. 'I'm so sorry.' She'd sensed something like this, in his reluctance to talk about his past.

'My tattoo – I had the sword inked after I won the Olympic fencing, as a reminder of how I'd got through that time and come out a winner. But it symbolised a lot more than that: strength, resilience, and also protection. I resolved that I'd never again let down the people I loved and cared about. I had it done for them, as much as for myself.'

His expression was troubled. Sharing this was hard for him. Eliza realised how closed in he'd been with her, until now.

'Who, Ace? Who's "them"?'

'My foster family; most of all my foster brother, Locryn. We call him Lockie. He's a bit younger than me. His childhood was … chaotic. Not pretty. His mother was an addict; she and Lockie lived in this squalid van up by a lake – the locals call her The Flake by the Lake. Lockie was in and out of care, before Merle fostered him. He's like … a lost soul. Often away with the fairies. But I love him to bits, as much as a real brother.'

Eliza nodded but stayed silent. She didn't want to interrupt the flow, now he was finally opening up.

'And Faye, similar story. Another lost soul. No stability, until Merle took her in. She did well for a while – we were mates. But then …' He shook his head, as if trying to flick away a painful memory. 'It was probably too late for Merle to make a difference. Too damaged. I suppose she tried her best.'

Eliza pictured Merle's strong, self-assured form. 'Why did she take on such challenging kids?'

'Because she's an amazing person. With Lockie – Merle just fell for him.' He smiled. 'He has that effect on people; gets under your skin. He's beautiful, kind of unworldly, a dreamer. Merle wanted to give him a sense of belonging – of *mattering*. He'd never had that. The social workers warned he'd be an enormous challenge, but that didn't put her off.'

'How old was he, when she took him on?'

'Thirteen. God, the state of him. He was malnourished – basically he'd been living off school meals, when he could get himself there. Long, blond dreadlocks – we had to chop them. He kicked off like you wouldn't believe. He was like a skittish kitten. But Merle spotted that he was artistic – he loved to draw.' He paused. 'Lockie was so fragile. We nearly lost him once, when he was fourteen. It was bloody horrible.'

She went to ask what had happened, but stopped when she saw his expression.

'He must miss you. Does he have a partner now?'

'God, no.' He laughed. 'Lockie could hardly bear to be touched.'

Eliza's heart sank. 'Oh no.'

Like me, before …

She was getting a clearer picture.

'Him and Faye, they had so much potential, but … what they had to cope with, to overcome. Makes you wonder how some kids survive.'

She looked up at him. 'Does that include you?'

'No, it wasn't so bad for me; I was fostered early on. But honestly? For a few years there, it was like living in a never-ending storm. What's that word? A maelstrom. It was almost literally a mad house. And in the middle of all this, I was trying to get an education and forge ahead with my fencing and then my tennis.'

'What about your foster dad?'

Ace's expression darkened. 'Hector was hopeless. Spent most of his spare time fishing in an attempt to escape. Merle tried, but ended up turning almost all her focus on me. Lockie completely flunked school; he stopped going, spent most of his time at the beach, surfing, while Faye … holy shit. She was a lost cause who got even more lost. Discovered drugs; shagged every guy in the neighbourhood and then the next neighbourhood.'

'My god.'

'She took off with a bunch of travellers, in the end. Came back, every now and again. She kicked the hard stuff, but then she got into paganism and whatever else …' He paused. 'Tell you what, though. She was good at healing. When I pulled muscles and wiped myself out training, she'd make these poultices, potions. Anyway, they're both gone now, probably for ever. I mean –' he swallowed, '– we're all … grown up.'

'Where are they now?'

'Lockie ran away to the ends of the Earth – to New Zealand. Nobody's heard from him since. Faye's in some West Country woodland with a bunch of conspiracy theorists. As for me – well, I'm lucky Merle kept me on. Look where she's got me.'

'That's quite a story,' Eliza said. 'No wonder you weren't keen to share it with Will.'

'It's my sword's story, really, which is why I'd rather you kept it to yourself. The tattoo was my coming-of-age thing. I had it done – and it fucking hurt – to prove to myself I was now a man, that I'd survived my abandonment, the bullying at school, my dysfunctional family, and now I was going to take on the world.'

He pulled her close and kissed her hair, then looked down at her again. 'Hey … tears?'

'And now here you are,' she said, wiping one away. 'On top of that world. You're absolutely amazing. I think I probably don't deserve you, when I compare my mostly easy ride to what you've been through.'

'Well, I do think I deserve food.'

❀

'I don't want to go,' said Ace, drowsily. He was lying on the sofa after their meal, his head in Eliza's lap, eyes closed. She was languidly stroking his soft, golden hair.

The night was still warm and the balcony doors were open, the sheer curtains drawn across, rising and falling gently on the breeze. The nighttime hum of the city drifted in, a backing track for the music playing quietly from a speaker. The lights were dimmed, the room shadowy.

'To America? Or home?'

'Neither, right now.' He lifted a hand and ran his fingers down her arm.

'There's this old song my step-mum loves,' said Eliza. '*If I could save time in a bottle.* I'd save tonight. And that night after the film preview.'

He opened his eyes and looked up at her. 'I know that song. But it's too sad. And … Eliza, what the fuck's this playlist? Music to die to?'

She gasped in mock horror. 'What? Have you no *soul*? I'd *die* without Radiohead.'

He laughed softly. 'Lockie's favourite band.'

And Kit's.

'You're not the tough cookie people think, are you?' he said. 'There's a sensitive soul in there.'

'Well spotted. Don't out me, though, will you? I'll change this – what would you like?'

'I'm a nineties fan. Love a bit of Blur, or The Cure. Or Isla. Although … what time is it?'

'Eleven thirty.' She sighed. 'Yes, you should probably go. I don't want Merle hexing me for crimes related to crashing out in round one.'

He smiled. 'Nah. Round two. As a top seed I get a bye.'

'Well, aren't you fancy?'

'I'll continue to lobby Merle on your behalf, but yes, I should be off, before she starts sticking pins in an Eliza-shaped doll.'

Oh my god.

'Seriously, I know she'll come round,' he said, when she didn't reply. 'She's just worried you're going to break my heart. *The die is cast*, she said last night, in this *voice*, like some prophet of doom.'

The curtains billowed out on a whoosh of wind, and a door down the hallway slammed. The scent of rain on warm bricks blew in.

'Oh! It's raining. I'd better shut the doors.' Eliza gently moved Ace's head off her lap and stood up, stretching.

'Hey,' he said, sitting up, ruffling his hair, blinking those blue eyes properly awake. 'You promised me a favour, to carry with me to the US. What you got for me, princess?'

'So I did.' She pulled the doors shut, then picked up a little box that had been sitting on the worktop. 'Here,' she said, sitting down beside him. 'It may not be your cup of tea, and you don't have to wear it, but I can say a spell over it if you like.'

He raised his eyebrows as he saw the lettering on the lid. 'Gucci?'

'Because you're worth it.' She kissed his cheek.

He lifted out the long, gold chain, on the end of which hung a little dragon curled around a sword.

'You said you loved dragons … and swords, obviously.'

Was it too cheesy-fantasy? Did he in fact loathe male jewellery? He never seemed to wear any.

He gazed at it, where it lay glinting in the palm of his hand. 'It's perfect.' He kissed her, then kissed her again, until she couldn't have cared less what Merle thought, or even if Ace missed his plane tomorrow.

'Stop … stop,' he said, eventually. 'Put it on for me. Then say your spell, and there it stays until I'm back with you.'

She lifted the long chain around his neck, tucking the dragon beneath the white cotton shirt he'd worn for their restaurant dinner that never was.

'I need some magic words. Abracadabra doesn't seem to cover it.'

'Close your eyes and let them come,' he said. 'Then send your words out into the universe and the tennis gods will listen.'

Eliza unbuttoned his shirt and cupped the dragon gently in her hand. 'Does it need to rhyme?'

'Nope.'

'Okay. *Little golden dragon. Guardian of Ace. Keep my beloved safe as he travels to the lands of the west. Fuel his quest with your dragon fire; may he be brave and strong and victorious, and stay kind and good. Bring my lovely Ace home to me. Thank you, little dragon.*'

He kissed her cheek. 'Enchanting. Top spell. And believe me I've heard a few, growing up in that house.'

She let the dragon settle back on his skin, did up the shirt buttons, then rested her hand on his chest. 'Tattoo on the back, dragon on the front. So many secrets beneath your shirts.'

'I look forward to you undoing more of them on my return.'

'No more buttoned-up Ace. Thanks for sharing so much tonight.'

'You undo me, in so many ways. But now I really must go. Just one more promise, first.'

'What promise?'

'When I get back, let me take you to that shack on the beach. Just you and me, in Cornwall. No work, no training – for a week. Say you'll come?'

'Which week?'

'Does it matter?'

'Probably.' She stopped. 'No. It doesn't. I'll come, no matter what the week.' The thought was absolutely, incredibly delicious. 'Shack, though?'

'Cottage, if you want to be posh about it.'

⊛

She secured the front door with all its paraphernalia, then double-checked the windows. As she went to flick off the living area lights, she glanced at Kit's photo on the wall.

'Well?' she said. 'You gotta approve of this one, right?'

She remembered Ace's reaction to the photo, and peered closer. *God*. Had Kit really looked at her like that?

'Stop it,' she said, with a grin.

His voice popped into her head. *Fuel his quest with your dragon fire? Really, Eliza?*

⊛

The soft, warm night air caressed her skin; his mouth fluttered on hers, barely there. She started to wake – *no, Eliza, stay* – sank back into the dream, moaned quietly in the dark as her body caught fire beneath his gentle fingers, tracing circles, making their way slowly down her body, stopping, stroking; the warm pressure of his lips on her neck, on her mouth. She opened her legs as his fingers found their way between them; soft, feathery strokes; felt the weight of his body as he moved on top of her, slid inside her. He took her hands, one in each of his, stretching them above her head, holding them tight; he kissed her deeply, filling her with love, beauty and truth; whispered in her ear that he loved her, then, and now, that he would always love her, that he would never leave; that he would always be here, in her heart, in her soul. For ever.

Chapter 18

Eliza

Friday the thirteenth, and Ace was flying out this morning. Eliza hoped it wasn't a portent. All this talk of superstition.

She was pleased Ace was competing in Cincinnati first. This would surely ease him into the big one; the one Britain was so hyped for – the Grand Slam tournament in New York. Two of the other big names had pulled out, but Merle, Ace and Tristan had decided Ace should compete while he was on top form. The prize money was more than $650,000, and with the two no-shows, he had a good chance of picking that up.

Last night, over their meal, Ace had explained in more detail his philanthropic intentions for his newfound wealth. As Will had suggested, he'd also shared his plans in his first column for *The Rack*, concluding with a call to like-minded influencers, especially sportsmen and women, to join him.

Eliza wondered what sort of response Ace would get, and whether other media would pick up on what he was trying to do. Or whether they were too preoccupied with his love life to care about his good intentions.

Unfortunately, Catriona Macleod, his most recent ex, had been sharing with the press her 'deep hurt' about their 'out-of-the-blue' break-up. While Eliza was careful to avoid reading things she knew would knock her off balance, Rose's PR department had advised her to take a look at an article in *Heat*, which was apparently typical of what was being published in the gossip magazines. Past experience had proved it was worth knowing the gist of what was being said, otherwise how could they develop a response?

As she sat at her desk with a mid-morning coffee, she slid the magazine towards her, pulling a face at the headline.

ACE BROKE MY HEART it wailed, alongside a picture of Catriona in oversized sunglasses, looking sad (and something about Meghan's White House ambitions).

She flicked through to the piece. Ah. Apparently their split was all *Eliza's* fault. Not Ace's. This was different from what she'd originally been told, that the likes of *The Sun* had been calling Ace a love rat. In this version, Eliza was, in fact, the villain – the seductress.

She sighed. Britain really would *not* hear a word against its perfect hero.

According to Catriona, Eliza, a 'man-eater', had organised for Will Bardington to interview Ace for *The Rack* after taking a fancy to him during Wimbledon. She'd also instructed Will to arrange for Ace to be her date for a film preview. There was a photo of Eliza outside the Leicester Square Odeon, looking over her shoulder and beckoning to him.

'*What Princess Eliza wants, Princess Eliza apparently gets,*' said Catriona.

The article then helpfully reminded the reader that five-times-married billionaire Harry Rose had made his daughter CEO of Rose Corp at the tender age of twenty-four.

Following Ace's success at the Olympics, Eliza had invited him to Daddy's Richmond Park mansion for lunch, asked him to drive her home afterwards, and immediately taken him to bed.

What? How did she …?

But all of this information could have been pieced together from the internet – social media, news websites – in the space of five minutes. Then it was just a case of adding spin.

'*We were going to have a super-romantic few days together in the States before the Open. My heart is broken. I'm devastated that Eliza*

Rose has stolen my wonderful Ace. She treats men like disposable playthings – just ask one of her many exes!'

Many exes? One proper one. One!

'But I wish Ace only luck and happiness,' Catriona nobly concluded. *'Let's hope he comes to his senses. If and when he does, I'll be waiting.'*

Eliza closed the magazine. Ah well, hell hath no fury. Not to mention the fact that until this week, no one had heard of Catriona. *Enjoy your fifteen minutes, sister.*

She hoped Ace would be spared Catriona's bleatings. But would he? Merle might show him the article, to back up her argument that Eliza was going to break his heart, or at the very least, be bad for his image. Perhaps, in fact, Merle and Catriona were in cahoots. Allies in the #DitchtheRichBitch campaign.

Now you're just being paranoid.

Ace would be on the plane now. Which reminded her – she'd had a call from Harry this morning, about Rose Air, which was struggling.

'It's critical, Lizzie,' he'd said. 'We'll need to look at further cost-cutting. Can you come to Richmond this weekend to discuss? Cecil will be here too.'

The two men had been lobbying for a lessening of travel restrictions, and things *were* improving. European travel was picking up, as people became more confident about holidaying abroad again. Meantime, Rose would have to seek further financial support if the airline was to avoid insolvency.

And instigate more redundancies, probably. Great. Inflicting more misery on staff, inspiring more hate. She'd already noticed the change in the way some Rose employees looked at her. More sideways, less face-on. A result of the Catriona business, maybe, and the social media attacks. It was reminiscent of how people had acted after Amy died.

She'd go to Richmond tomorrow. Meanwhile, a quiet night in with the TV – and quite possibly a box of Belgian chocolates – beckoned. A 'be kind to yourself' night, with comforting things to buoy her up for a weekend of damage control with Harry, plus trying to ignore the fact that, when it came to the rollercoaster graph of Eliza public approval, it seemed she was once again hurtling into a deep trough.

'Look what just turned up.' Pippa was holding a bouquet of red roses. 'Some girls have all the luck.'

Eliza perked up. From Ace, presumably. She pulled off the card, opened it … and froze as she took in the words: *WHY ARE YOU STILL ALIVE, ELIZA? PROBABLY TIME YOU WEREN'T.*

'Eliza? What is it?'

She experienced that strange disconnect again.

'Bin the roses.' She showed Pippa the card. 'And pass this on to Cecil. Ask reception which florist they came from … anything at all you can find out.'

'Oh, how horrible,' said Pippa, looking stricken. 'I'm so sorry this got through. I'll make sure anything like this gets checked out first, from now on.'

'Please do.' The dizziness was passing, but she couldn't calm her breathing. She tried a shaky laugh. 'I never liked red roses, anyway. More a York girl myself.'

'Sorry?'

Eliza shook her head. 'Just rambling in an attempt to forget all the … the hate out there.' She was dismayed to feel her bottom lip wobbling.

Pippa put a hand on her shoulder. 'Put that right out of your mind. Don't give whatever lunatic sent it the satisfaction of knowing it might have got to you.'

Eliza decided to go straight to Richmond after work. She didn't want to be alone tonight.

✦

Eliza, Harry and Cecil were strolling in the grounds of Richmond Lodge, taking a breather from their discussions on Rose Air. They were almost done, just a few final tweaks to make to their proposals. They'd need the board's approval, but on matters corporate it was practically unheard of, these days, for anyone to oppose Messrs Rose and Walsham, and Eliza. The board was generally a harmonious entity now, compared to the ructions during Maria's reign, and Mac's tilt at the throne.

Harry looked up into a clear blue sky. 'Remember when that was criss-crossed with contrails? And I never thought I'd miss the sound of planes roaring over the house every minute.'

'I like the less-cluttered sky, though,' said Eliza. 'And the atmosphere must have benefited. We need to consider that too. We've got to be seen to be prioritising the environment.' She frowned. 'No, not just be *seen* to be. We *have* to be. Like I said earlier, when you dismissed me with your *Not now Eliza*s, we should invest more in green aviation technology.'

'Yes,' said Cecil. 'We need to take more of the initiative here. For both business and environmental reasons.'

Harry raised an eyebrow at Cecil. Amazing what this man could convey with one small movement of a facial muscle.

Dinosaur. And look what happened to them.

'A lot of people think it's not okay to flit about the world anymore,' said Eliza, 'while planes are still guzzling fossil fuels. Also superyachts,' she added, before she could stop herself.

'Bless your darling generation,' said Harry. 'People will always want and need to travel. Civilisation would go backwards if we stayed in our own backyards.'

'Would that be so bad?' said Eliza.

'It would,' said Harry. '*Faster* is the thing; efficiency, reducing travel times.' He looked up at the sky again. 'Tell you what, I'm damn jealous of Branson's space plane. Extravagant, but visionary, and will ultimately benefit us all.'

Eliza let out a loud, prolonged *pfft*. 'No, Dad. It's *pathetic*, the man-billionaires and their flying phalluses. I mean – seriously? The world's going through all kinds of shit, and they're having a who's-got-the-biggest-penis contest.'

Cecil chortled quietly.

'Don't knock it,' said Harry, smiling. 'These technological breakthroughs benefit all of mankind.'

'*What*-kind?'

'Chrissakes. Humans.'

'And as for Musk,' Eliza continued, 'instead of these nonsensical ideas about space colonies … imagine, if all those billions were ploughed into reducing poverty, saving the planet–'

'That's not how it works,' Harry said. 'It's not your bleeding hearts who facilitate the great leaps forward, the improved quality of life; it's the drug companies, the tech wizards. Science progresses fastest in times of war … and pandemics. Sad but true.'

'Spare me,' said Eliza. 'Well, can we at least look into investing in hydrogen planes? That research looks promising?'

'We already are,' said Cecil. 'Significantly.'

'Oh,' said Eliza. 'Why did I not know that?'

'Because it's not your bag,' said Harry. 'You get the reports, but you skim-read them. We both know your heart isn't in that side of things, and that's fine. But it's important to remember Rose is first and foremost a business.'

'It's so much more than that.'

Harry threw an arm round her shoulder and gave her a squeeze. 'Lizzie – I do admire your sense of social responsibility, but …' he paused. 'You know I'm a supporter of the Tories. I donate.'

She gave a small laugh. 'How could I forget? The old boy network.' Harry and Boris had been at Eton and Oxford together. '*Boy* being the operative word.' She smiled mischievously. 'You could say, neither of you has properly grown up.'

'Oh dear,' muttered Cecil.

'I support the party, not necessarily various individuals,' Harry replied. 'And in return I'm listened to, given access to people …'

'Is that all?' said Eliza.

'A knighthood doesn't come cheap,' he quipped.

In spite of his tone, Eliza knew it was sore point – Branson had one, so why didn't Harry? Far too much scandal, probably. Too many dead and divorced wives. Not to mention the mistresses.

'Joking,' said Harry. 'Maybe. The point I was feeling my way towards …' His expression grew serious. 'I'm afraid it concerns your delightful Ace.'

'*Ace?*' Eliza hadn't expected that.

'At the moment he's harmless enough; his musings are par for the course – when people become rich and famous, they often feel the need to do their bit.'

Eliza was confused. 'You mean the interview with Will?'

'His column. So to speak.'

'But …' Ace's first piece hadn't been published yet. 'How did–'

'Terri,' said Harry. 'She thought I should be aware. Avoid problems further down the road.'

Terri? Who always challenged Harry on matters of principle? Who always backed her up? The sudden sense of betrayal reminded her of when Harry had told her Santa wasn't real.

'What Ace is saying about the state of Britain isn't much different to the general mood,' he said, 'but Lizzie – if he starts to get properly political, well, that's something else. He's exceptionally popular, people will sit up and take notice.'

'I don't think–'

'If you're his partner, and visibly supporting his political stance, and that conflicts with mine … you see what I'm saying? My position is entirely business focused – I have to do what's best for Rose. And so do you. Sometimes what you personally believe and what you need to do in your professional life – well, the two don't always mesh. Take Terri, for example. Hard left, giving Ace a platform, but she's always got Rose's best interests at heart, which is why she ran this past me.'

Something was shifting beneath Eliza's feet. 'But Dad, the two things, personal and professional, *should* mesh. Otherwise, what's the point? How can you separate your work self and your inner self?'

'That's the real world. That's how most of us do it.'

'Shouldn't work self and inner self be two sides of the same coin?' said Eliza. 'Otherwise you're living a lie.'

They'd reached the high brick wall at the bottom of the garden, where a wrought iron gate led out into Richmond Park. Harry stopped, and turned to her. 'We have a mission statement, and agreed-on company strategies.'

Cecil, listening carefully, stooped to admire the dahlias growing against the wall.

'It's your job as CEO to make sure those strategies are adhered to,' continued Harry. 'All I'm saying is, the column in *The Rack* – fine. Everyone knows the magazine's left-leaning. That's the price I pay for having Britain's best journalist as my editor. Ace's personal beliefs and his wish list thing are a good fit for that. But when he calls for other influencers to join him, and takes aim at certain politicians …' He shook his head. 'You're going to have to make a decision. Having you by his side, supporting him, could be seen as a direct conflict with … well, with Rose. With me, Lizzie.'

'But Dad – we've always had different political views, you and me. You've never said it mattered before.'

'You're still very young, idealistic. One changes as one grows older. Anyway, I've said my piece. Bottom line is, if Ace intends to form a high-profile organisation that aims to influence government, we can't be part of that. *You* can't be part of that.'

'But Dad – I don't want to be a brake on him. I believe in what he's doing. He's so genuine. And people *are* fed up with this government.'

'And they will get the chance to vote on that. That's democracy.'

Eliza scowled. Cecil was looking awkward.

'Don't patronise me, Dad.'

Eliza was conflicted. Her father's words made sense, and Rose was ever her priority. But what this discussion had thrown up was the unsettling thought that her raison d'être – the entity for which she'd chosen career over love – might at some stage need her to act against her own principles and beliefs. If Terri was prepared to do it …

'My guess would be,' said Harry, gentler now, 'that Ace won't have time to get political. Top-level tennis is hugely demanding; he'll be able to do media things and maybe set up this foundation, but beyond that … He might just have to leave it all until later.'

Chapter 19

Eliza

There were only four at the table for Sunday lunch. Harry and Clare hadn't got back into the habit of having friends over, after the long lockdown.

Eddie would soon be returning to Eton, and as the family polished off the last of the apple crumble, he was holding forth on vaccine misinformation.

'You know,' he said, his grey eyes earnest, 'maybe programmes like *Rose Breakfast* should be pushing back against all the nonsense, instead of obsessing over *Strictly*?'

Eliza dropped the hand holding her spoon onto the table with a thump. 'Eddie – give us a break, eh? We're doing our best. It's tough out there. We're up against the Facebook groups, the Twitter haters–'

'I know,' he said. 'It's … god, Eliza.' He looked uncomfortable. 'What they're saying about you on social media? It's–'

'No – not now,' interrupted Harry, giving his son a look. 'And you shouldn't be wasting your time on that rubbish.'

The penny dropped. Her brother had been different with her this weekend. Awkward; not quite meeting her eye. Eliza's stewed apple and custard was all at once disgusting, gelatinous mush. She felt slightly sick.

She scraped her chair back. 'I can't finish this, sorry. I think I'll go for a walk.'

'I'll come,' said Clare. She glanced at Harry who, Eliza guessed, had been about to say the same, but he shut his mouth again.

Eliza wondered for a moment if she'd ever reach such deep, intuitive understanding in a relationship; the ability to read each other's minds.

Well yes, but he's dead.

To her dismay, her nose burned as tears threatened again.

Harry gave Clare a quick nod. 'Eddie, how about a set or two later? Last chance to win a game off me this summer. Girls, place your bets. I'd say fifty to one against.'

Eddie smiled. 'Who's going to lower my self-esteem once I get back to school, Dad?'

❀

Clare and Eliza headed for King Henry's Mound (or Henry's Codpiece, as Harry called it) on the edge of Richmond Park. There was a fabulous view from the top; on a clear day you could see the dome of St Paul's. The mound had apparently been used by Henry VII as a hunting lookout.

By unspoken agreement, they took the lesser-used paths through the deer meadows, to spare Eliza the double-takes. The long grass was turning late-summer gold, and the leaves on the ancient trees already looked exhausted. Eliza sympathised. It had been quite a year.

She gave a secret smile to the old oak beneath which she'd made her 'sexual debut' with Rob, on a warm, moonlit night that now felt like the distant past.

'Did you read that article in *The Rack*?' she asked Clare. 'Apparently we now make our sexual debut, rather than lose our virginity, because virginity frames female sexuality as a treasure to be taken or lost, which is all kinds of wrong.'

'Yes I did. I think it's a bit silly, to be honest. I see what they're saying, but I like the word virgin. It's ancient, and rather noble.'

'*Noble?* Eliza laughed. 'Mine was quite ancient by the time I lost it. I made my debut right there,' she said, pointing.

Clare's mouth formed an O. Then she grinned. 'I remember.'

'You *remember*?'

'Well, strongly suspected. You and Rob came in with pink faces and bits of grass in your hair.'

Eliza snorted, then felt a pang.

'I remember Harry saying it was exactly like when you were kids,' Clare went on, her hazel eyes twinkling, 'when you'd disappear for the day then come back looking like a couple of "unwashed peasant children".'

'*Peasants*?' Eliza rolled her eyes. 'Honestly, to hear Dad, it's no wonder people call me a rich bitch.' She blocked that thought. 'So what do we call Elizabeth the First now? The Queen formally known as Virgin? The Yet-to-debut Queen?'

Clare laughed, then her expression turned serious. 'Eliza ... what Eddie alluded to. This rich bitch business, the–'

'The haters?'

'Yes. I wanted a private word, to make sure you're okay. It's so unfair, that they should target you, the most dedicated, principled young woman I think I've ever known; always wanting to do right by everyone, working so hard all through that horrible pandemic ...'

Clare's sympathy was too much. Eliza burst into tears, flapping a hand in front of her face. 'Sorry.'

Clare pulled her into a hug. 'No, go on – have a good cry.'

Eliza did. She cried a river. Clare was quiet, rubbing her back.

When it slowed to a trickle, Clare led her over to the remains of a toppled oak, and they sat down on its trunk.

Eliza took some shaky breaths. She felt overwhelmed, but she didn't know why. 'I can't believe I'm letting it get to me, Mum. The trolls, they're not worth it, right? And I mean ... look at me. I have *everything*. I have Ace, I have you and Dad, I have–' Another hiccup stole the end of her sentence.

'Yes,' said Clare, putting an arm around her. 'Try and forget the spite, and those silly things that Scottish tennis player said. You've grown up with it, you know how it works. You also know how quickly people forget. And ... Eliza. That's why I think there's more going on with you here.'

'Oh?' Eliza fished a tissue out of her jacket pocket and blew her nose. 'What do you mean?

'If we want to get medical about it –' Clare ran the RoseHealth website, which focused on mental health and wellbeing. 'I think it might be a touch of PTSD.'

Eliza wiped her eyes. 'What? Seriously?'

'Yes. Only last year, you watched your closest friend die. Horribly.'

Eliza's bottom lip betrayed her again.

'And to anyone who doesn't properly know you, it looked like you bounced right back. And other things happened – Harry's heart attack, and your split with Rob. Then you had to deal with the problems created by Covid. And Harry told me what you got in the post. That must have been absolutely horrible for you.'

Eliza nodded.

'When did you last have a holiday?'

She thought. 'Those few days with you in the Lakes.'

'That's it?'

'Otherwise not since Australia, on *Janette*.' That had been two or three years ago. She'd lost track of time.

'Well, there you go. You've been through a lot. You need a break.'

They watched a squirrel hopping across the ground in front of them. It sat back on its haunches, nibbling an acorn.

'How can anyone hate them?' said Eliza, smiling at last.

'I know. Your father still does. I hid that air rifle, though.'

Eliza gave a shaky laugh. 'Good. So … what are the symptoms of PTSD?'

'Flashbacks, I guess. Panic attacks; feeling anxious a lot of the time. Nightmares?'

'I had bad dreams after Kit died, but not now.'

Holy fuck. Her erotic dream of a few nights ago had just ambushed her. Well, *that* hadn't been a nightmare.

'No flashbacks, just vivid dreams.' She felt herself blushing at the memory. 'Anxious, yes. And … I talk to Kit. Out loud, and in my head. Quite a lot. Is that normal?'

'It probably is; you two were very close. And it's not that long since you lost him.'

'But maybe I haven't lost him entirely. Sometimes I feel like he's still here.'

Clare frowned. 'I remember after my mother died, I always asked her opinion before I bought any new clothes. I used to whisper to her in store changing rooms.'

Eliza laughed. 'I shall do the same, many years from now.'

Clare took her hand. 'No need. You have impeccable taste in clothes, just like your real mother.' She winked. 'And in men, just like your real mother.'

'Haha, funny.' Eliza looked down at their clasped hands. 'I think of you as my mum, now. You're the best.'

'Oh, what a lovely thing to say – thank you.' Clare gave her another hug. 'So … maybe it's not PTSD. But obviously it's still haunting you, rather.'

'Yes, it is. *He* is.'

'In a manner of speaking. It does take a long, long time to work through grief. I lost two husbands before I married Harry. I have some idea of what you're going through.'

'No, not in a manner of speaking.' Eliza looked her in the eye. 'Actual haunting. I've sensed his presence, more than once. I think he's – his soul's – still here.'

Clare paused in surprise, then shook her head. '*No*, Eliza. You mustn't think like that. He's gone.' She laid a hand on her arm. 'If you sense his presence, that's the power of the mind, the strength of those memories. You imagine he's still here because you don't want him to have gone.' She stood up. 'Shall we carry on?'

Eliza hopped down off the log and stuffed the sodden tissue back in her pocket. 'Okay. But Clare – do you remember, the things Kit used to say? About Fate, and the soul, and time? The things he seemed to know?'

Clare set off, speaking over her shoulder. 'Just because he explored those ideas in his work – that doesn't mean they were truths.' Her tone brooked no argument.

Eliza's step-mother was a pragmatic woman, her feet firmly on the ground. She probably wasn't the person to talk to about this. Nor was Will – he'd shut Eliza down when she asked if he ever sensed Kit's presence.

Ace? Maybe, with his superstitions, but he was already acting strange, kind of suspicious, whenever the subject of Kit came up. She wondered why that was.

'I think a holiday would help a lot,' Clare said, as Eliza caught her up. 'Maybe next time we sail on *Janette* you could join us?' Her face broke into a smile. 'You could bring Ace!'

Eliza chuckled. 'You'd like that, wouldn't you?'

Clare went slightly pink. 'He is the most *delightful* company. How's that going, between the two of you?'

'Perfectly. He's wonderful. He … he told me he loves me – already!' Warmth blossomed inside as she said the words.

'I'm not surprised – I saw the way he looked at you that Sunday.'

'He wants to take me to Cornwall – they have a cottage on a beach. When he gets back from the US.'

'That sounds perfect!' said Clare. 'And he'll need a break too, after all this pressure.'

It seemed like the very definition of bliss. There was just those three weeks of intense tennis, beneath the crushing weight of Britain's expectations, to get through first.

'And do you think you might feel the same as he does?'

They'd reached the top of the mound, and stood looking across to St Paul's on the horizon. The trees had been lopped to keep the sightline clear; people were snapping the view on their phones, some of them noticing Eliza and not-very-subtly getting her in the periphery of their shots.

'I do have feelings for him. He's everything I could want in a man. I just … I guess I'm super-careful about committing, given past experience. Not many men can handle being with someone in my position.'

'I think Ace could. I remember, with Rob – and you know how much I like Rob–'

'I do.' Eliza raised her eyebrows.

Clare gave a girlish giggle. 'Honestly, you really know how to pick them! But with Rob, I used to think, although you two got on so well, he never seemed quite comfortable with you being the boss.'

'He wasn't. He kicked against it, eventually.'

'But Ace – he seems to admire you very much. And your lives are so different, there's no conflict or competition …'

'Dad seems nervous, though,' said Eliza. 'Like, if I support Ace in any campaigns that have a political edge, that might conflict with my work at Rose.'

'Tsh. Giving Ace a column in *The Rack* is hardly going to bring down the government.'

'But you know Dad, in bed with his Tory chums.'

Clare put an arm round her shoulders. 'Sweetheart, you have to do what feels right for *you*. You don't always have to be seeking your father's approval.'

Eliza remembered Chess saying the same thing.

She thought back to the times she'd fought off challenges to the Rose throne, firstly from her sister Maria and her TV evangelist husband, Phil Seville, and then from Cousin Mac, as manipulated by her fiancé, Hamish Earle. Both strong, intelligent women who'd allowed themselves to be influenced by powerful men.

As she'd approached that second boardroom battle, she'd resolved to fight without help from any man, and after her triumph she'd made a promise to herself – to lead Rose as an independent woman. She needed to remind herself of that now. It was indeed up to her to decide on her goals for herself, and for Rose. No one else. Not even Harry.

Chapter 20

Eliza arrived home to find a padded envelope in her mailbox. Same size as before, same writing as before. *Chrissake!* She took it inside, making an effort to keep her breathing even; turned off the alarm, locked up behind her. Strode into the kitchen, stamped hard on the pedal of her bin, dropped the envelope in, let the lid clang shut, pretend-wiped her hands together: *smack smack smack*.

Unloading the bag of food Clare had insisted on giving her, she discovered a chocolate orange (dark – her favourite) with a scrap of paper sellotaped to it.

Sorry for being a dick. Love from Eddie x

It undid her; the rage flew, its space filled by a familiar exhaustion. She stared at the little pile of goodies. Putting them away suddenly felt too hard. And she really didn't want to be alone tonight, not now.

She rang Will and told him about the package, hoping he'd volunteer to come over.

'Oh no,' he said. 'What was in it?'

'Don't know. Didn't open it – it's in the bin.' She glanced over. She could sense its menacing presence, like a living, breathing thing. 'I know I'll have to pass it on to the investigator, but I'm going to leave it there for now.'

'I'd come over,' said Will, 'but I've got company. Can you come here? You can stay the night.'

'What company?'

'Someone you should meet. If you get yourself here in the next half hour, you'll be in time to share our Urban Turban mixed platter.'

'Are you sure? Honestly, I'm beginning to feel like a burden.'

'Never, my darling albatross. Bring the thing. We'll open it here, drop it with Cecil in the morning so he can sleuth it.'

Eliza fished the envelope out of the bin and threw it into her holdall, along with her night bag and clothes for tomorrow.

Soon she was back on Will's doorstep, intrigued as to who he was sharing a cosy curry with. A new special friend? Male? Female? One of his literary cronies from the Groucho?

She hoped it wasn't that last one; she didn't have the energy to be intellectual and interesting tonight. She wished she could just curl up on the sofa with Will and Romeo and watch something basic on Netflix.

He showed her in, kissing her on the cheek. His own face was slightly flushed. He was wearing his new shirt again.

'I'm beyond pleased you phoned,' he said, his voice low and dramatic. 'He's difficult, but he's *so* worth the bother.'

'Who!' she hissed.

'Come see come see.'

Will ushered her into the living room, which was warm and welcoming as ever with its gentle lighting and familiar walls of books. She loved this place.

On the sofa was a man with curly dark hair, dressed all in black. Romeo was asleep on his lap.

'Oh!' Her eyes widened. 'Hello!'

Narrowed, dark brown – almost black – eyes met hers. He was in his late thirties; charismatic, instantly recognizable.

Gosh.

'How absolutely wonderful to meet you at last!' she said, putting her bag on the floor.

The man smiled – a small, slightly suspicious smile. Those dark, not-especially-friendly eyes assessed her.

'I'm an *enormous* fan, Rowan.'

Stop gushing!

Still he didn't respond.

'And I think Will has done your brilliant play proud. I hope you agree?'

Finally, he spoke. 'Good to meet you, Eliza.' His voice was soft and low, his accent northern – Yorkshire. In contrast to Eliza's (over)enthusiasm, his tone was calm, a little aloof. 'And yes, I do agree. Will's the only person I'd have let mess with my words.' He looked over at Will. 'Even so, I'm afraid I gave your man something of a hard time.' He smiled again; it was a little warmer now.

'Did you?' said Eliza, knowing full well Will had been close to breaking point. 'I know Will enjoys a challenge, being pushed, if it's for art's sake.'

'He had some interesting ideas on where to take the story, but I wanted to stay true to the original. I'd say we reached a reasonable compromise.'

'I concur,' said Will. 'Especially about the hard time part.'

Rowan laughed quietly, then turned back to Eliza. 'I think you'll be happy with the final cut.'

There was something strangely compelling about this man, whose past, she remembered, included an unfounded criminal allegation, as well as a degree of notoriety and scandal. If you believed the gossip. Which – Eliza pulled herself up sharply – one should never do. Ever.

'Can I sit here?' she said.

'I'll get you a wine,' said Will as Rowan shifted along, disturbing Romeo, who flicked Eliza a look of disgust.

'I've wanted to meet you for so long.' Eliza smiled at him. 'I *love* your writing.'

He raised thick, dark eyebrows. 'I'm impressed with the work you do at RoseGold. It's a shame my wife's not here. She'd be interested to meet you.'

My wife. Oh dear. Did he think she was hitting on him? Her words had come out a little breathy. But she wasn't; not at all. He was *very* attractive, but she was mostly … intrigued. What was it about him?

She moved away a little, clasped her hands in her lap.

'Emma's an environmental journalist,' he continued. 'Freelance, since we had our two boys.'

'How old are they?'

'Eight and six. Edward and George.' He looked at his phone. 'I should call them before bedtime.'

'Oh please, go ahead, don't mind me.' She smiled – it was hesitant.

He didn't look up, didn't answer, typed something.

More self-doubt was creeping in. Rowan didn't like her. She was too in his face. Maybe she didn't deserve his respect; she was a spoiled princess-brat of the south, in a position of power thanks purely to her rich daddy. She hadn't worked her way to the top; she'd been gently dropped there by the sparkly unicorn of privilege.

He looked up, and smiled. 'Later. I've no doubt Emma will let them stay up while I'm not there.'

The curry arrived and they tucked in, chatting about recent movies, plays, books. Rowan was well-read, eloquent and *very* opinionated, and Eliza mostly took a back seat, enjoying their conversation. It was clear there was a great deal of mutual admiration, but Eliza guessed that this plain-spoken Yorkshireman found Will's theatrical demeanour just a little too much.

'Feels like old times,' said Will, popping a piece of naan between his lips. 'Eliza, Kit and I were partial to a curry and bookish chat.'

'Kit Marley,' said Rowan with a small shake of his head. 'Fuck me, what an outrageous talent he was. I would've given my right arm to have worked with him.'

'He probably would have,' said Will. 'Fucked you, I mean. As well as worked with you.'

Rowan spluttered with laughter, as Eliza tried not to.

'I'm straight – sexually speaking, anyway,' he said with a wry smile, shrugging his shoulders, which were slightly uneven. She remembered Will saying Rowan had scoliosis.

Now Eliza spluttered, and choked on a piece of chicken.

Rowan patted her on the back. 'All right there, Eliza? But if I was going to give the gay life a go,' he continued, 'he'd have been the one.'

Will caught Eliza's eye. 'Imagine, Rowan and Kit.'

'How delicious. As in, writing together,' she added hurriedly. 'How long are you down here for?'

'A couple of days. Finishing up.' He looked at her, and his expression turned serious. 'Will mentioned you're under attack from trolls and tabloid bollocks and such like.'

'Sadly, that is true.' She glanced over at her holdall.

'Maybe I can help. I've been on the receiving end of all that m'self.'

'Oh, of course.'

It was coming back to her now. How the local newspaper up in Yorkshire had implicated Rowan in the disappearance of two brothers who'd gone missing from the school he was teaching at, and, as a result, he'd been widely suspected of their murder.

'See, I made the mistake of not pushing back right from the start. Instead, I became a recluse. That was because ...' he paused. 'Fuck, it's still that hard to talk about. Those little lads ...' He sat back and raked his fingers through his hair.

'Please, don't–'

'No, it's important.' He looked her in the eye again. 'I felt guilty, for not taking proper care of Freddie and Riv. So I more or less disappeared, when all the stuff came out in the press. But eventually I had to do something – you can't let them hijack your life, Eliza. You need to stay strong. And I know you're a remarkable woman – what you do for British film and TV ...'

He looked over at Will, then back at Eliza. 'I can be an awkward bugger to work with, and I'm aware Will came close to bailing on me, but I know it was you who kept him going, picked him up. And all the logistical problems of filming during Covid. You got them sorted. You did a bloody great job.'

'Oh – thank you.' Tears. *Not again*. She blinked them back. 'That means an awful lot.'

'Those haters,' he said. 'People are angry right now. They need somewhere to vent their frustration. You're an obvious target, and those people don't actually want to believe you might be a nice person; they prefer to think you're a bitch and that they can hurt you. But you have to stand up to bullies.'

'I've been told not to engage, though …'

'No, don't. I mean, learn to ignore it. Have the self-belief to get on with your life; don't ever let them stop you doing what you love. And remember – they don't know the real you, only a distortion. Picture that imagined version, deflect everything her way. Don't allow it to mess with the real you.'

She nodded. 'I was doing okay, at first. But then some other things happened. Like … I think I have a stalker. Someone's sending me things, in the post … flowers to the office. Disturbing messages; death threats. Whoever sent them knows how to mess with my mind.'

'Jesus, that's tough.' He gave a small laugh. 'Sounds like one of my plots.'

Under his pseudonym, R.P. King, Rowan wrote dark, psychological thrillers – a fact that hadn't helped his case when the boys had gone missing.

Eliza's eyes returned to her bag.

'Is it in there?' asked Will. 'Fetch it out.'

She took a deep breath, pulled the holdall across the floor and undid the zip.

'That it?' said Rowan, spotting the Jiffy bag shoved down the side. And before she could grab it, he reached down, pulled it out, ripped it open and upended it. Like pulling off a plaster quickly.

Out fell another Barbie. Again the hair had been coloured red; again a tiny knife was embedded in her. More drops of blood-paint. This time, the knife was in her heart.

They were silent, staring at the doll where it lay in Rowan's lap. But it wasn't the blood or the knife that was making Eliza break out in goose bumps. It was the fact that the doll was wearing a mini version of an outfit Eliza had worn to work this week. Which meant, presumably, whoever sent it had recently seen her in the flesh.

'My work clothes …'

Rowan put a calming hand on her arm. 'From which day?'

For a moment she couldn't think, as she fought off the panic. She blinked, staring straight ahead. *Focus.*

'Wednesday,' said Will. 'When we went to Roehampton.'

Rowan picked up his phone and started typing.

'Is there a message with this one?' asked Will. There was no drama in his voice now.

Rowan threw him the envelope. There was. Will read it out loud: '*He broke my heart. You will break his. I will break you.*'

'Oh my god – Catriona?' said Eliza. 'Could she have been at the tennis place?'

'Who?' said Rowan, not taking his eyes off his phone.

'Ace – my boyfriend. His ex. She's been telling anyone who'll listen – or who'll pay her, probably – that Ace broke her heart.'

'Look.' Rowan showed her his phone. On Instagram, under the hashtag #ElizaRose, was a photo of her walking out to the tennis centre car park with Ace. It looked to have been taken from the road; it was pixelated, but her beige trousers and white blouse were clearly visible.

'Fuck's sake,' she muttered. 'Who took it?'

'Not your stalker, unless they're extremely stupid,' said Rowan. He checked. 'Some random bloke. Hardly any followers. Probably a passer-by who got lucky, or a tennis nerd, lying in wait. So – thanks to that picture, anyone could have found out what you were wearing. What's this Catriona's surname?'

'Macleod.'

He tapped on his phone again. 'She's in Chicago, so unlikely to have been her.'

'Unless she's got an accomplice,' said Will, stroking his chin. 'She could have got someone to deliver it once she'd gone.'

Eliza smiled weakly. 'Okay, Sherlock. We'll give it to Cecil tomorrow. Surely his PI will come up with some answers?'

Rowan put down his phone. 'You said before it was someone who knew how to mess with your mind?'

'I think so, yes.'

'Who are your enemies?'

'Lord,' said Will. 'Do we want to go there?'

Rowan looked at Eliza. 'You okay with this? See – I had to solve the mystery I was at the centre of, mostly by myself. Gave up waiting for someone else to do it. By then, the only person who believed I was innocent was Emma. Even she had a wobble. Sometimes you have to take control.'

'Right. Let's do it,' said Eliza, now over the initial shock. 'Put bloody Barbie away though, Will?'

He slid the doll back into the envelope and took it out of the room.

'Hall table,' he said, when he came back. 'So … enemies. Mostly people suffering the agonies of jealousy, I'd surmise.'

'Pen and paper?' said Rowan. 'Let's do this properly.'

Will fetched a notebook and pen and handed them to Rowan.

'Off you go, Eliza,' said Rowan, gently.

'Okay. Professionally … um. How out there can these be?'

'Totally out there,' said Rowan. 'Anyone with a gripe – revenge, jealousy, let's do all the motives. No particular order, just chuck 'em out, and give me a word or two as to why.'

'Okay. Mac. Mackenzie James – my cousin.'

Will snorted. 'Oh yes. The super-sneaky Scot. Good call. She's *so* got the hots for Rob, too. So many reasons–'

'Will …'

'Sorry.'

'RoseGold Vice President in the US,' explained Eliza. 'Obviously not on hand to slip envelopes into London mailboxes. We're friends now, but let's say, uneasy ones. I banished her to LA, but she's well rewarded, and as far as I know, content.'

'Good,' said Rowan, scribbling. 'Next?'

'Letitia Knowles,' said Will, 'while we're in Hollywood.'

This time, Eliza laughed. This felt ridiculous. 'My ex's new girlfriend,' she explained. 'The catalyst who sped up the end of our relationship. Should imagine she'd also have trouble organizing a quick mail drop from California.'

'And the ex?' said Rowan. 'Who's that?'

'Rob? No-no-no,' said Eliza. 'Not an enemy. Not ever.'

'Ah, Rob Studley,' said Rowan. 'Our producer boy.'

'Lovely chap,' said Will. 'If a bit flash.'

'Also across the pond, therefore unlikely,' said Rowan. But he wrote down his name. 'Next?'

Eliza looked at Will. 'Who else hates me?' Romeo lifted his head. 'Apart from the devil-cat.'

'If we're going with the revenge motive,' said Will, 'then Seymour?'

'Shit.' Eliza sat up straighter. 'But … dolls? Death threats?'

Eliza's creepy uncle had been persona non grata in their circles since her exposure of his harassment. She had no idea what he was doing now. She quickly explained his history to Rowan.

'On the list. Next?'

'How many enemies do you expect me to have?'

Rowan smiled and looked her in the eye. 'Now that I've met you, very few. Maybe just those jealous women.'

Oh. A small frisson, there. 'Okay.' She smiled back. 'Well, Phil Seville, the American TV misogynist – sorry, evangelist. I had a boardroom spat with him. And he called me a temptation sent from God.'

'Did he?' His dark eyes gleamed as they met hers again. 'But the ones sent by the Devil are much more fun.'

She snorted. There were two sides to this man.

'Kit would have agreed with you there. Dad and I saw Phil off. And now – well, there's the small matter of an ocean between us, again.'

'Why do all your enemies end up in America?' asked Rowan. 'Next?'

'Dev Noble,' said Will.

Rowan met Eliza's eye. 'The TV presenter? Seriously?'

'I *told* her–' began Will.

'Look, we're all allowed one enormous mistake, right?' she said, feeling herself blush. 'He kissed and told, he's had his revenge already. It's not going to be him.'

Rowan suppressed a smile. 'Shall I mark him as a mistake rather than a threat?'

'Please do. Next would be … Hamish Earle – but he's in prison. And I hope he rots there.' Hamish had been one of Andre Sokolov's associates, and had organized Kit's attacker.

'Could he sort something like this from prison?' asked Will.

'Probably not his style,' said Eliza.

'Sokolov himself!' Will burst out. 'You were responsible for his conviction, and we know he's a psycho-killer. And … god. He'd still have plenty of contacts on the outside.'

Eliza shivered. 'He killed my mother,' she said to Rowan.

'And Kit's mother – his wife,' said Will.

'But if he wanted me dead, he could just organize that. Why would he do death threats and messages and all the rest of it?'

'For amusement? Must be boring in jail,' said Will.

'I'll give him an asterisk,' said Rowan. 'Make sure your PI knows to check him out, and the other one …' he checked his notes, 'Hamish Earle. Okay, next?'

'Merle,' said Will. 'If we're really blue-skying it.' He turned to Rowan. 'Ace Penhalagon's coach and foster mother. She's terrifying. Thinks Eliza's too distracting. Also, she was with Eliza on Wednesday, when she was wearing that outfit.'

'Merle thinks I'm going to break Ace's heart,' said Eliza. 'But seriously – of course it's not her.'

'What did the note say?' said Will. '*He broke my heart; you will break his* … Well, it's a variation on the theme. But what if those words are meant to throw us off the scent?'

Rowan made a note. 'More ex girlfriends? That's where I'd be looking, if I were a detective.'

'None that he's mentioned,' said Eliza. 'But I don't know much about his life; we haven't been together long. I guess *He broke my heart* would imply an ex, but …' she paused, thinking. 'The first doll was a reference to Kit, and then there was the email with the picture of Amy. The notes with those two said *The Dead are not Dumb*. Like, it was revenge for Kit's death which … well. Some people blame me for that. Perhaps rightly.'

'No,' said Will.

'*The Dead are not Dumb*,' repeated Rowan. 'Hm. Who might have been in love with Kit, or maybe obsessed with him.'

'Just the several hundred,' replied Will. 'Including yours truly, of course.'

Rowan looked up, and Eliza saw him considering it.

'I think we've completed the list,' she said. 'What do we do – pass it on to the PI?'

'Depends how good they are. Like I said, I took matters into my own hands, but you have Rose's resources at your fingertips. I'd get the PI to check out those people – where they are, what they've been up to. But my instinct would be it's an obsessive fan of Ace's. What do you think, Will?'

'Agree. So it looks like it might be down to the computer experts, who can look into the online side of things – trolls, haters, what have you.'

'Rowan,' said Eliza. 'Thank you. I can't tell you how much you've eased my – well, my anxiety, this evening.'

'You'll be fine.' He put a hand over hers. 'Stay strong, believe in yourself. Now I'd best phone my boys, then I'll be off.' He left the room.

'Well?' said Will, in a low voice.

'Oh Will – I *love* him,' she whispered.

He grinned. 'Knew you would. You always were partial to an enigma.'

'True. He's honest; kind, once he lets you in. But at the same time, I don't know … mysterious?'

As they waited for him to return, she glanced at the clock on the mantelpiece. 'Hey – it's getting late. I need to FaceTime Ace.'

'AceTime? Ten thirty – what's that in American?'

'Um, five thirty p.m. That's okay then, no rush. I'll message him, sort out a time.'

'Get him before dinner, fresh out of the shower. Oof.' He fanned himself with the take-away menu.

Eliza giggled. 'Stop it. But yes.'

When Rowan came back, they made him promise to come for

another curry night on his next visit to London. A little later, as they stood on the doorstep, he gave Eliza a hug. 'Let me know how you go.'

'I will. You and Will have cheered me up no end. Thanks for letting me gate crash.'

'And if you're ever in Yorkshire … we live in the Dales, on a farm. Spare room's yours if you need a bolthole. If you don't mind noisy boys and dogs.'

'Oh, thank you! That's so kind. I'd love to, actually.'

'Ahem,' said Will.

'Don't be ridiculous, Will. You'd bloody hate it,' said Rowan. 'Goodbye, my lovelies.' And off he went.

Chapter 21

'I'll clear up, you go make your call,' said Will. 'Are you sure you wouldn't like the sofabed in the study? I still haven't touched Kit's room.'

'We should do that together,' said Eliza. 'Then we can repaint it a more Will-ish colour. Sunshine yellow, maybe.'

'Or prose purple?'

'Never. But is it okay if I do sleep in Kit's room? It was kind of nice, last time. In a good way, not a creepy way. Like … his energy's still there. I dreamed of him.'

Will glanced up the stairs. 'It's up to you. Just … maybe don't let on to Ace it's Kit's bed you're calling from.'

'Oh, right.' She hadn't told Will how Ace had acted odd when the subject of Kit came up. Sometimes Will's intuition was on spot on.

'Hi,' she whispered, as she closed the bedroom door behind her. The silence of the room settled around her. That faint smell of cigarettes again, his favourite French brand.

The night was warm, and she opened the old sash window; it rattled upwards, letting in fresh air and London's hum. She pictured him doing the same, his hands, right here.

She changed into her pyjamas, sat cross-legged on the bed and opened her laptop; clicked on Facebook, waited for it to load.

Nothing happened. Just blank white space. She clicked on the wi-fi symbol: *Looking for networks*. She checked her settings. Her laptop should be remembering Will's password, *BAFTABEMINE*.

All looked in order. She switched the wi-fi off and on again. Still it wouldn't connect. She'd have to use her phone.

No internet connection.

She went onto the landing. 'Will? Has the wi-fi dropped out, do you know?' But her mobile connection wasn't working, either. Odd.

'It's patchy upstairs,' came his voice from the kitchen. 'There's a dead zone. You might just have to come back down.'

She made her way to the living room. Ace finally appeared on her laptop. A little wave. 'Hello, princess.'

'Hello! Did you just get out of the shower?' His hair was damp, and the top of a towelling robe was visible, the gold chain of the dragon necklace peeping out.

'I did, yes. And why is that funny?'

'Just something Will said, about timing this call right.'

'You're ready for bed. I like your PJs.' They were her old favourites, a present from Rob. Pink, with little crowns all over them. 'I have yet to see your PJs in the flesh.'

'Just the flesh without the PJs.'

He laughed. 'I wish I could cuddle you in your PJs right now. Just … snuggle up. I miss you.'

'Me too,' she said, feeling the absence of those strong arms. 'Sorry I'm a bit late. Technical problems. I'm at Will's, and the wi-fi's misbehaving.'

Ace's image wobbled as he settled himself more comfortably against his pillows. 'Why are you at Will's?'

There was no need to burden him with the truth. 'Rowan Bosworth was here – the writer? Will invited me over to meet him. Easier to stay the night.'

His eyebrows shot up. 'Seriously? You and your notorious friends. What's he like?'

'He was … wary of me at first. A bit prickly.'

'Maybe he was shy. I lost the power of speech when I met you.'

She smiled. 'Aw. But no, not at all shy. He has these dark, penetrating eyes, a bit like Merle's. He thawed, once I stopped acting all starry-eyed. He's awesome, actually. Gave me a pep talk about dealing with trolls, and tabloid bollocks, as he called it.'

'Should I be jealous?

'Not at all; he's very much married. He invited me to his Yorkshire farm, which was lovely of him. But I'd rather come to Cornwall with you.'

Ace looked away from the screen, staring into space. 'It's difficult to imagine that, right now. When all this will be over. I wish I could mess with time, like your Kit did. Just fast-forward until it's done.'

'Oh, don't say that. I know the pressure's hard, but this is your moment. You're at the top of your game; Britain's hero. In years to come you'll look back and wish you could live it all again. Try and enjoy it?'

'I'll do my best. With the help of my friend.' He fished out the little dragon. 'He says hi.'

The rest of the conversation was light chit-chat. She finished up wishing him good luck for his first game, assuring him she'd be watching; he kissed the dragon and told her he'd be doing that before every match. They said an affectionate goodnight.

It left Eliza feeling strangely empty.

Back in Kit's room, she hopped into bed, flicked off the light, then lay staring at the ceiling, dimly illuminated by London's glow seeping through a chink in the curtains. Caterwauling erupted from the street below. Romeo, perhaps, in a nocturnal battle with the rival neighbourhood cat gang.

A siren wailed in the distance, then faded away.

She couldn't sleep. The night was now quiet, and the image of the doll hovered. *I will break you.* In an attempt to keep her out, Eliza replayed her conversation with Ace.

The doll was still there. Eliza needed something to read, but hadn't thought to bring a book.

Light on again, out of bed, and she looked around – her eyes fell on the literary journals on the drawers. She picked one up, then, with a will of its own, her other hand pulled open the same drawer as before. Putting down the magazine, she took out Kit's black T-shirt and held it to her face, breathing him in. Then she whipped off her pyjama top, slipped the T-shirt on, and hopped back into bed. Snapped off the light.

'I'm safe now,' she whispered. 'No more stupid doll.'

She snuggled down, and in the warmth of his embrace started to drift off.

You're safe in the dead zone, babe. No one can reach you here.

'Romeo!' called Will, shaking cat biscuits into a bowl. And then, louder: '*Romeo!*'

Eliza was sipping an espresso at the kitchen worktop. They were discussing the timing of Ace's column, and how they were going to handle his call to action.

Will opened the French doors. 'Where's that cat? I hope he hasn't been birding again. He's lethal – dropped a bloody pigeon at my feet the other day.'

'Can you get him a bell?'

'London pigeons love bells. Obviously.'

Will was working from home today, but Eliza needed to go in to the office. She had to hand over the doll to Cecil, among other things on her 'to do' list, none of which were filling her with enthusiasm.

'Ace'll need to get his foundation sorted soonest,' she said. 'People can't get in touch if there's nothing to get in touch with. I was thinking, it could be headquartered at Rose. We have the spare office space, they'll only need a small admin staff.' She ignored Harry's voice in her mind, warning about conflicts of interest.

'It would be a good fit.' Will raised his eyebrows. 'Sounds like you're talking long term, you and Ace.'

She smiled. 'Yes, I think I am. I can't see a good reason not to, other than all this unwanted attention. But that'll die down, right?'

'Once we've milked it for his do-goodery. Did he tell you what he was thinking of calling it?'

'No?'

'Good Sports. Or maybe Sporting Goods.'

They both smiled, then wrinkled their noses.

'More cheese than a three-cheese pizza with extra cheese,' said Will. 'Want some toast?'

'Yes please. He should probably just call it The Ace Penhalagon Foundation. Then they can think of a cool slogan to go with it.'

'Oh, I could do that,' said Will. 'Do you think he'd admit a non-sporty writerly person onto his round table? Would I make the grade as a knight?'

'You want to be part of it?'

'I'd love to, actually. He's very inspiring.'

'Me too,' said Eliza. 'Maybe I could be involved in a behind-the-scenes way.'

'Camelot. Already taken – what a shame.'

'What about Excalibur?' Eliza pictured his tattoo. 'That would tie in beautifully with the Arthurian cover they're doing for *The Rack*.'

'Oh, I *like* it. The fencing connection, fighting for good, uniting Britain.'

'And think of the logo.'

'God, I love *Le Morte d'Arthur*,' sighed Will. 'Crazy-genius medieval dramatics. Remember when we studied it?'

'I remember you and Kit arguing over it.' Eliza pictured them in their tutor's cosy study, which was almost as old as the fifteenth-century text, locking horns in one of their literary spats, this time over whether Arthur had been a made a fool of by Lancelot and Guinevere, and this was at the heart of his downfall (Will), or whether Arthur had known about their affair all along and just didn't think it was a big deal (Kit).

'I think Kit's words were, "Why would you not share your favourite person with your other favourite person?"' said Eliza.

'No,' replied Will, pinching toast from the toaster, dropping it onto a plate. 'What he said was, "Why would you mind if the person you loved most, loved the other person you loved most."' He gave her a small smile. 'For some reason that stuck in my mind.'

For a moment, the quiet of the kitchen hung heavy.

'You have the look of Guinevere about you,' he said, passing her the plate, sliding the butter and marmalade across. 'The Celtic hair, the fair skin … quite the jealous streak, too. Now you're with Ace, perhaps it's just as well Kit's not around to do a Lancelot. Again.'

'Do a *what*?'

'Never mind,' said Will, spreading his toast, not meeting her eye.

'Will!' She stared at him. 'How can you *say* that? And you're *way* off the mark.'

'I am?'

Why was he being like this? 'And anyway, Lancelot was obsessed with God, and doing the right thing. Kit was an atheist who spent most of his adult life behaving badly.'

'Look deeper,' Will muttered, still avoiding her eye. 'Or maybe don't.'

Eliza felt a fierce stab of hurt. Did even Will resent her, deep down? Did he subconsciously blame her for Kit's death?

'Sorry,' said Will, after a pause. 'That was uncalled for.' He finally looked her in the eye; tears were brimming in her own.

'I take up so much of your life, don't I?' she said. 'Never imagine I don't know that, or that I'd take you for granted. Do you even realise what you mean to me?'

He sighed. 'God, I hate Mondays. Come here.' He moved round the worktop and gave her a hug. 'We're still a bit fraught, aren't we? But we'll get there. We lost our favourite person, but you have Ace now, and he's wholesome and wonderful, so life is brighter, it truly is.'

'Yes, you're right.' She sniffed, and wiped beneath her eyes.

'Eliza.' His voice had lost its chirp. 'You have to let him go. He's gone. There are many still here who love you. Focus on them.'

He hasn't gone.

'I will.' She moved away from him. 'And now I guess I should get off to work, find out what shit awaits me today. Death threats, a collapsing airline …'

'Fun times,' said Will. 'Do you want to stay with me for a bit longer? If you're feeling spooked?'

'I might just do that. Thanks. Call you later?'

'Okay. And I'll let Terri know about Ace's piece. Maybe next time you're speaking to him, suggest Excalibur.'

'I will. Tonight.'

'But nicely; we don't want him getting all insecure about his words again – then tell him I would love to be Excalibur's wordsmith, should he consider the pen as mighty as the sword.'

'Well of course it is – mightier.' Eliza smiled at him. 'I guess it's not *all* shit, out there. Maybe even pretty exciting, after these past two years; being able to move on, do something positive?'

'It really is,' said Will.

Chapter 22

Ace

Ace was in the locker room, preparing for the Cincinnati Masters final. His palms were sweating. He twisted his towel between his hands and tried to slow his breathing.

His winning streak had continued unabated, but as the stakes grew higher, his nerves were becoming harder to control. More and more he was relying on Eliza to buoy him up when he felt himself buckling under the pressure, which, in quiet moments like this, would crush him like a cartoon weight dropping with a whistle from a great height.

Merle and Tristan had just left. With ten minutes until he was due on court, he wanted some time alone. During the match, he'd be constantly aware of the pair of them in his peripheral vision. It was forbidden for players to talk to their coaches, but Merle would motivate and instruct via the energy of her stare, or by muttering under her breath – words that somehow reached him via intuition.

She'd spotted Ace's dragon, of course, which he touched for luck each time he changed ends. 'Tacky,' had been her only comment, delivered with a curl of the lip.

Tristan had loved it, though. 'A spell, now? Grand! There's nothing like a love-based enchantment to give you that edge.'

'But she hasn't actually said she loves me, Trist,' he'd replied, finally acknowledging the insidious voice that had been whispering in his ear in quiet moments. 'Believe me, I've been listening out for it.'

Tristan had shrugged. 'Some people just aren't into gushing about it every five minutes.' And when Ace didn't reply, 'Look, when was the last time Merle told you she loved you?'

Ace thought. 'How about never?'

'I rest my case.'

This week, Eliza had been at Will's, her reason being it was fun to watch the games with him. Ace suspected it had more to do with her not wanting to be alone – that anxiety she'd tried to downplay when she'd told him about the extra security.

During one video call, the three of them had had a useful chat about the next steps for his foundation. Excalibur. Eliza had suggested the name, and Ace agreed it was perfect. Good Sports had suddenly seemed embarrassing – uncool – and Ace wondered if the pair of them had had a laugh about it.

Will had said they should wait for the US Open before launching Ace's column. And Eliza had suggested she could help recruit a team of administrators, to be based in The Rose. He loved that thought. The building was a London icon.

Ace looked over at the clock on the wall. It was nearly time. In the quiet of the locker room, he closed his eyes, gripped his little dragon, and manifested himself owning the court, killing his Russian opponent's shots.

There was a knock, and an official appeared.

As he exited the tunnel to thunderous applause, the crowd chanted, '*Ace! Ace! Ace!*' and the pressure magically lifted.

Eliza

'See? There,' said Eliza, as Ace ran a finger along the gold chain tucked beneath his tennis shirt. He was 5–0 up in the first set, and had just played a drop shot that had seen the ball bounce, then hover in the air smirking at the Russian, before flying backwards into the net.

'Good god,' said Harry, sitting forward in his armchair. 'How on *earth* did he do that?'

'Magic,' said Eliza, sitting with Clare on the TV room sofa. 'The dragon around his neck. He asked me for a good luck token, and I put a spell on it. Seems to have worked. I'm a witch! Who knew? Witch bitch.'

'Just like your mother,' said Harry.

'Oh, how lovely!' said Clare, as Eliza frowned at her father. 'He's wearing your favour.'

Harry chuckled. 'Your knight in shining tennis whites. Why a dragon? That's a bit Welsh.'

Eliza rolled her eyes. 'Just a fun conversation we had. And the Welsh don't have a monopoly on dragons.'

She was at Richmond for the weekend – being alone at her apartment still made her anxious.

On Wednesday, she'd finally met with the private investigator, Fran Singh. It hadn't been enlightening. The second Barbie had held no further clues.

As far as the online abuse was concerned, it seemed it was nigh-on impossible to identify trolls and senders of threatening emails without involving the police, thanks to privacy laws. Eliza still didn't want that, and Fran advised it was unlikely to be investigated anyway as, technically, no crime had been committed. The social media hate didn't have a single perpetrator, even if the emails and dolls were connected.

Eliza's head had spun with it all, as Fran attempted to explain IP addresses and fake email and social media accounts. The only worthwhile piece of information was that thanks to CCTV from a local business, there was an image of Eliza's mugger. It turned out to be a young teen, or possibly a tall child. Their face and hair weren't visible because of the hoodie and a mask, so they were judging by height. Jeans, trainers, plain black sweatshirt. Not helpful. But not an adult, they agreed.

Fran's conclusion was that it was a random mugger who, for some reason – perhaps to do with how Eliza had been holding it – hadn't grabbed her bag. Eliza's instinct still said otherwise, but she knew there was a degree of paranoia in that.

'Doesn't Ace look cute in that ninja headband, Eliza,' said Clare.

Harry gave her a look, and the two women sniggered quietly.

'No, shush, it's serious,' said Eliza.

With astonishing speed, Ace smashed, lobbed, volleyed and – as was only to be expected – aced his way to victory, and the crowd erupted as the new champion ran in to the net.

Shaking hands was now acceptable again, after months of unsatisfying racket tapping. There was no emotion in racket tapping, thought Eliza, as the Russian hugged Ace. That was nice. Even scary Russians loved Ace. And Ace's face, gripped by such intense concentration these past minutes, broke into the gorgeous smile that was demolishing hearts all over Britain.

He waved to the crowd; the camera swung to Merle, who was jumping up and down, her long plait flapping behind her, then back to Ace, whose fingers returned to the chain around his neck and pulled out the dragon. He looked into the camera, blew it a kiss, then kissed the dragon.

'Oh my gosh,' said Clare, going pink. 'Was that for you?'

'I do believe it was,' said Eliza, melting.

Harry raised his eyebrows at his wife. 'Well, Lizzie,' he said, getting up from his chair and stretching. 'I'm beginning to wonder whether your special friend is in possession of superpowers. That was extraordinary. Let's just hope he hasn't used up all of that dragon magic before the big one.'

❀

Over the following week, Ace, now one tournament win away from the Golden Slam, was in enormous demand from the media. On US TV, that somewhat bewildered Wimbledon champion was now self-assured, but still humble, unable to believe his streak of success.

Jimmy Fallon wanted to know if his 'super-famous girlfriend' would be flying to New York to watch him play, helpfully reminding viewers that Eliza was a member of the 'Rose Die-nasty'. (Indeed, thought Eliza, several Roses, including her own mother, had met unfortunate ends.)

'She's a very busy lady,' Ace had replied. 'We'll see how things go.'

'You totally should,' said Will, as they watched the recording.

When Ace had told Eliza he was appearing on *Tonight*, she'd arranged for his still-unpublished *Rack* column to be forwarded, in strict confidence, to the production team. As a consequence, Jimmy had questioned him about his views on how tennis could be brought to a more diverse range of young people.

Ace had described his new foundation. 'Excalibur, it's going to be called. Strong, British, a force for good.'

'Excalibur – Arthur's mighty, magical sword! Tell us more.'

'Love to, Jimmy. Sport's given the British people something to get behind this year – the Olympics, the Euro football, the tennis – it's been a uniting force for our increasingly divided country. And sport doesn't discriminate – or at least, it shouldn't – on the basis of wealth, class, colour. It's a great leveller.'

'Sport is often a way out of poverty, here in the US,' said Jimmy.

'Yep. Worked for me. And now I want to give back, give others the opportunities I had. But I'm thinking wider than that. I want sportspeople to use their voices for the greater good. Britain's lost its way. We need to get our Great back, reunite the country …'

The US media couldn't get enough of him. If he won at Flushing Meadows, he'd be a dead cert for the cover of *Time*.

Chapter 23

Eliza

The following week, Eliza stayed mostly at her flat, more confident about being alone now that there had been no further incidents. No emails made it through, nothing sinister crouched in her mailbox, and the Rose social media accounts were defrosted, though Eliza stayed away from them.

In New York, Ace spent the days before his first match training, video calling Eliza in the evenings. During one call he described his practice session with one of the 'big three' – the Serbian one.

'What's he like?' asked Eliza.

'Awesome. And he says we're the big four, now.'

Sadly, neither the Swiss one nor the Spanish one were playing in the US Open due to injury, but at least this upped Ace's chances.

His first column appeared in *The Rack*, and Rose Corp issued a media release to introduce it. The launch received widespread coverage, and the article went viral on social media.

ACE'S QUEST TO PUT THE GREAT BACK IN BRITAIN, said *The Guardian*.

#Ace4PM trended on Twitter.

He dropped only two games in the first rounds. On the Saturday of his third-round match, which she would watch at Will's, Eliza suggested they spend the morning clearing out Kit's room.

'Got to be done,' she said, as they sat in the garden drinking

216 ⊛ Olivia Hayfield

tea. The weather was still warm, and Will's exuberant herbaceous borders were enjoying their final late-summer hoorah.

Her implication was, she'd be helping Will face up to going back into that room. But, she acknowledged to herself, it was mostly for her own benefit. Her compulsion to go through Kit's things grew stronger each time she slept in his bed. He'd been an enigma to her, right up until that last day, and she wondered if she'd find anything that would help her further unlock him. She hoped that if she understood him better, she'd find it easier to let him go.

Eventually. But not yet.

As she faced up to the fact that Kit was still on her mind – or more accurately *in* it – all the time, she wondered about Clare's suggestion of PTSD. She couldn't forget that look in his eyes as he'd died. The faint smile he'd given her, which had seemed to say, *See? I was right. But it sucks that I was.*

⊛

'Shall I take the wardrobe?' said Eliza, ripping a bin bag from the roll.

'Right you are. I'll do the drawers.'

Eliza switched on the speaker she'd brought upstairs, and as it made its warm-up sound, positioned it on the bedside table. She selected an upbeat playlist that should help them through, then, telling herself to be strong, moved over to the wardrobe.

The speaker remained mute.

She checked the settings on her phone. 'Will – if you tell me Bluetooth doesn't work in here either, I'm going to be seriously spooked about your dead zone.'

He stopped dumping clothes onto the bed and came over. 'Odd; it's well within range.'

Eliza picked up the speaker and left the room. As soon as she stepped onto the landing there was a crackle, and the music started playing.

A shiver ran down her spine. 'Okay,' she said, going back into the bedroom. 'Let's just accept the energy in here's different.' She wrinkled her nose. 'And we need to get rid of the cigarette smell. It's unpleasant, even if it is the sexy French ones.

'What?' she said, when Will didn't reply.

'There's no cigarette smell. It's just fusty.'

'Oh,' she said in surprise. 'Maybe you're more used to it than me. It hits me every time I walk through the door.'

Will went round the room, sniffing. 'No. Definitely no smell.'

'Maybe you're getting Covid.' But even as Eliza made the joke, she allowed in the truth of what might be happening here.

Will didn't smile. He sat down heavily on the bed. 'Shit, Eliza. What's going on?' He raked a hand through his hair. 'All that stuff he used to say about the soul. He's still fucking with my mind, even from beyond the grave.'

'He told us enough times,' she said. 'Maybe we should have listened better. I think his soul might still be here. Somehow, in some form.'

And maybe that's because I wished it.

'No, that can't be,' he said. 'Perhaps it's like … an echo of his life. One you're somehow tuned into, because you two were so connected. Maybe … you walk in here, you see his stuff, and it triggers your brain – it sends you the smell of him. Can that happen?'

'It's plausible, I suppose.' Will's words made sense, but he was wrong.

She started removing clothes from hangers, folding them carefully and putting them in bin bags.

Oh god. His leather jacket. She held it to her, and its familiar smell was like a knife to the heart. Her nose stung as tears gathered. 'Do you want this?' It came out as a croak – and then she fell apart.

'I'm not a leather jacket kind of guy,' he said levelly, turning away from her. 'More of a big coat man.'

She was grateful he didn't offer sympathy. 'I'll hang it back up. We can't let this go.'

'Oh shit.' Will was staring into a tin he'd just opened.

Eliza saw glass pipes, other paraphernalia. She looked away quickly. 'Whatever it took,' she said quietly, wiping her eyes. 'To write like that. To feel …'

'Or not to not feel,' said Will. He dropped the tin in the rubbish. 'That can fuck right off.'

Eliza carried on, and soon only the leather jacket remained on the hanging rail.

Next, shoes. And at the back, a shoe box. She opened it, sitting down on the bed. On top was the photograph he'd shown her the day before he died, of himself as a young boy, holding his mother's hand. *She was an angel.*

More photos – a selfie of him and Eliza sitting under the oak on their last night at Oxford, their hair silvery in the moonlight. The three of them slurping noodles at Eliza's flat.

Eliza reclining in a punt. Eliza on Magdalen Bridge on May Morning. Eliza laughing her head off in the college bar. Some from their trip to LA, on board *Janette*, Eliza in Kit's arms as they danced until dawn. She remembered how that felt, her head resting on his shoulder as Thom Yorke's haunting voice sang of death and the soul. 'Street Spirit' had been their song.

The tears returned in a rush. 'Sorry, I can't …'

Will stopped stuffing jumpers into a bag and came over, pulling tissues from a box. He held them out. 'Had an inkling we might need these. Look, we're almost done,' he said, as she pressed a tissue hard against her eyes. 'I'll finish off. Go make us a cuppa.'

She blew her nose, trying to regain her composure.

Will picked up a handful of the photos and leafed through them. Eliza was in almost all of them.

She passed over one of the three of them celebrating quiz night victory at The Dickens, Eliza grinning as she held up their meal voucher prize. 'I love this,' she said, wanting to scream at the universe for all they'd lost. 'You could frame it.'

He didn't respond, as he read a gift tag with glittery green holly and a red ribbon. On it, her writing:

To Kit

ILY

Eliza XXXX

He met her eye. 'It's okay. Never think I minded. Please, go make us a tea. I'm parched. I'll see you downstairs.'

She ducked into the bathroom to splash cold water on her

face. That had been so hard, and they hadn't even touched his desk, or his bedside drawers. There must be notebooks. A journal, maybe.

In the kitchen she leaned on the worktop, dropping her face into her hands. The tears came back, and they just wouldn't stop.

I want you to be here. But I want you to rest in peace.

Needing air, she went over to the French doors, turned the brass knob and pushed, but it wouldn't open. She looked down and saw Romeo's grey fluffy form curled up on the doormat.

'Excuse me, puss,' she called, swiping at her cheeks.

Romeo stayed where he was. Either he was ignoring her (as per) or he was asleep.

She pushed gently, and when he didn't move, she looked again.

Her blood ran cold.

'No,' she whispered, refusing to acknowledge what her eyes were telling her. 'Oh dear god, no.'

She nudged the door open against Romeo's weight, inch by inch. His lifeless body slid ahead of it. Eliza squeezed through and crouched down. His mouth was set in a grimace; a drool of blood matted the fur on his chin. His blank eyes were half-open.

She stroked his beautiful grey fur.

How do I tell Will?

She wanted to give up. Just curl up in a ball and cry. Go to bed for a week.

But then she pictured him upstairs, bravely clearing out Kit's things. He was being so strong; she needed to be the same for him.

'What happened, little boy?' she said softly. Had someone run him over, recognised him and delivered him home? Or a hit and run, leaving him in the gutter to be picked up by a neighbour?

She carefully scooped him up; he was already stiff in her arms. Underneath him was a folded note. An apology, maybe. An explanation.

Unless … *No.*

She unfolded it.

YOUR TURN NEXT, ELIZA.

Will was beside himself. All the emotion from this morning, and now this. It broke Eliza's heart, seeing him cry.

She poured them each a brandy and they sat in silence on the sofa, her arm around him, his head on her shoulder. She hadn't yet shown him the note.

They'd laid Romeo on his favourite cushion and gently covered him with a blanket. There was a deep gash on his neck, almost certainly a knife wound. They'd have to contact the police – this death threat was way more serious than a defaced Barbie or a comment on Instagram. But Eliza hated that thought; reporting it would make it real. *I have a stalker who's threatening to kill me.* She tried to swallow down the panic.

'Could this year be any more shit?' said Will, rousing himself. 'What sort of sick psycho stabs a cat?'

'I'd take a guess the sort of psycho who fixates on a famous person and then stalks his girlfriend. Or maybe the sort who fixates on a dead guy and stalks the person they blame for his death?'

'You think? Seriously?'

She took the note from her pocket and showed it to him.

He stared at it. 'Same writing.'

'Yep.'

'I'm scared, Will.'

'I'm not leaving your side. I'll allow you to pee, that is all.'

❀

They decided Eliza would spend the week at his place. On Monday, collaborating with the police, Cecil had security cameras installed, remotely monitored twenty-four-seven. They also put in a panic button. She and Will travelled to and from work together, and the security guards in the Rose building were alerted to the death threat.

Ace won his fourth game, and on Wednesday would be playing in the quarter final. He was three matches away from achieving the Golden Slam.

On Tuesday night, Eliza opened her laptop, ready to call him. Will was giving her space, making them hot chocolates in the kitchen. It had become a routine. 'We're like an old married couple,' he'd said.

'Will,' she'd replied, 'I've often said I'll never get married. But honestly, if I did, you'd be the one.'

When Ace's face popped up, Eliza congratulated him – again. 'This is beginning to feel like *Groundhog Day*.'

'It is. And much as I love seeing you on my screen, I'm now desperate for the real thing.'

'Me too.'

'We could do something about that. Eliza … how would you fancy a trip to the Big Apple? If I make it through to the final?'

She pictured it. The idea of getting on a plane by herself was both seductive and terrifying. But surely it would be easy to organise without her stalker discovering she was attempting to flee the country.

'Are you sure I wouldn't put you off your game?' she asked, hesitantly. 'And if you lost, everyone would probably blame me. Including you, maybe.'

'I already have Merle's eyes boring into me. Yours would encourage me; they'd buoy me up.' He opened his own blue eyes wide. 'Please?' He rounded it all off with a cute smile.

She laughed. 'That's not fair.'

'All the other wives and girlfriends are here.'

'Oh, a WAG! I'd have to practise my Victoria Beckham pout.'

'Your lips are prettier.'

'And I'd need overlarge sunglasses. Is that the look? Hey …' She had an idea. 'Could Will come too?'

'What? Why? Can't you go *anywhere* without him?'

'At the moment, no.'

'Oh, I see. Well … I guess so. There's space in the box.'

'Excellent.'

And so it was decided. If he made it through, they'd fly out on Saturday, the day before the final.

Chapter 24

Ace sailed through the quarter final. The semi was much tougher, stretching out to five sets, but he held his nerve, and after sending Britain's collective blood pressure through the roof, was finally victorious.

On Saturday morning, as Will and Eliza stocked up on reading material in a Heathrow bookshop, Ace was again front page news:

ONE MATCH AWAY FROM SPORTING HISTORY said the *Telegraph*.

ACE COMES UP TRUMPS AGAIN! said the *Mirror*.

They flew first class on Rose Air, and that afternoon checked in at the Plaza. Their penthouse suite, its two floors connected by an elegant staircase, had sweeping views over Central Park, and Eliza watched Will with a fond smile as he explored, exclaiming over the gilded grandness of it all. Eliza and Harry always stayed here when they visited on business.

'Seriously?' he mouthed, as the white-gloved butler opened tall glass doors leading onto an enormous private terrace overlooking the New York skyline.

The hotel was a short car ride from Flushing Meadows. Ace was staying in one of the official tournament hotels, a few blocks over.

That evening, as Eliza and Will sipped Manhattans beneath the blazing chandeliers of the Champagne Bar, she said, 'Clare told me I needed a break – she was so right. I already feel more like my old self.' She gazed around her, sighed with pleasure, and raised her glass in Will's direction. 'Here's to Ace's win, and to escaping London and its sickos.'

Will clinked his glass to hers. 'And to Romeo. May he rest in peace in pussycat heaven. And you look gorgeous, by the way.'

She was wearing a red silk sleeveless dress, and her hair, tamed with her magic wand, rippled pleasingly and co-operatively all the way down her back.

'Look at your eyes, outsparkling these crazy chandeliers in anticipation,' he said. They were expecting Ace any minute. As it was the final tomorrow, he'd told them he could only stay for an hour or so.

This being the Plaza, and New York, fellow guests either didn't recognise Eliza or pretended not to. The same couldn't be said when Ace entered the lofty bar. Heads whipped round, necks were craned, and mouths dropped open as he walked across the room, dressed in a crisp white shirt and chinos, a wide but embarrassed smile on his face.

A rush of emotion hit; Eliza squealed and leapt up. He held out his arms and she flung herself into them. He squeezed her tight, lifting her off the floor.

Someone started to clap. A few more joined in, and then the room was filled with applause and whistles and hoots.

'Oh, how bloody gorgeous,' said Will. 'God bless darling America.'

'I can't believe you're here.' Ace's voice was muffled against her ear. 'I've missed you so much.'

'I'm so, so happy to be here.'

'Will!' he said, one arm still around Eliza, holding out his other hand.

'Just manning the drawbridge,' Will said, shaking it.

Ace eyed Eliza's drink. 'Sup up, princess, I've only got an hour.'

As they left the room, holding hands, there was another round of applause, and good luck wishes, Ace acknowledging them with warm smiles.

'I'll text you,' Eliza mouthed to Will, and was delighted to see a cute guy from the next table asking if he could join him.

Ace idly stroked Eliza's shoulder and kissed her hair. Over the past hour, her sleek waves had been whipped into an anarchy of riotous curls, which now spilled across Ace, and the pillows. 'I've missed you so much,' he said.

She'd been drifting off – it was past midnight back home. 'Me too.' She opened her eyes and met the little dragon's stare. 'Sorry, dragon, if you were shocked at that display of unbridled passion.'

'I suppose I should go,' Ace said, playing with her hair in the way she remembered. It seemed like forever since that last time, at her flat. 'Merle will have a stopwatch on. I'm glad Will's here. It's nicer for you to hang with him than Merle. She's not a lot of fun, right now.'

'His cat died,' blurted Eliza. 'In an accident.'

'What? Oh, I'm sorry. He was really fond of it, wasn't he?'

'Yes. I'm so glad Will could come with me. To be honest, we've both had a time of it. This is exactly what we needed.'

Ace looked around him at the palatial bedroom. 'Hm. How many families could you feed for a month for the price of one night here, Eliza? Or perhaps you should let them eat cake?'

She snorted. 'Just doing my bit for New York's Covid recovery.'

He shook his head. 'Sheesh. If the paps snap me here I'll be outed as the last word in hypocrisy.'

'Ace, seriously. Once Excalibur's set up, I'll be donating. A lot.'

Their time was all too soon up, and as they kissed goodbye, Ace said, 'My phone will be switched off tomorrow. Don't contact me until after–'

'… you've won,' said Eliza, touching his dragon.

Ace

There was a tap on his hotel room door. He let Merle in. He'd returned from the Plaza seconds ago, and here she was, already back on his case.

She sat down in an armchair, pulling her plait forward. Her dark eyes fixed him with their gaze.

Ace perched on the bed and resumed wrapping overgrip round the handle of a racket. It was a ritual. It calmed his nerves, and only he knew exactly how he wanted the grip to feel. He had four left to do, of the nine newly strung rackets he'd take with him tomorrow.

'Nice evening?' Merle asked, finally.

'Fantastic,' he said, not pausing in his task. 'They're in the penthouse at the Plaza, would you believe? You weren't wrong when you said she's from another world.'

'They?'

'Will's here too, remember?'

'Hm. He's not writing about you again, is he? You want to watch what you say around him.' Ace paused in his wrapping. She raised her eyebrows. 'Be careful who you trust.'

'No, he's not writing about me. He's just company for Eliza. She's … well. She doesn't enjoy being alone, right now. As you know, there's a lot of hate out there.' He resumed his task. 'Will called you "magnificent", by the way.'

'Did he now?'

He glanced up – there was a small smile on her face.

'I suppose he's all right. But Arthur … don't get too carried away with all your new rich and famous friends. Remember who you are, where you come from.'

'Two new friends. Two.'

She nodded at his racket. 'Stop that for a minute.'

Ace braced himself as she came to sit beside him on the bed. 'Pep talk time?'

She took his hand and held it in her lap. 'Arthur. Whatever the outcome tomorrow, I want you to know, I'm so proud of you. I know it hasn't been easy. Your determination, your drive; the way you've learned to focus your mind … after everything that happened, what you've overcome.' She swallowed.

This was most unusual. And slightly unnerving.

'Merle …' he said, as a lump formed in his throat. 'Mum–'

'Let me finish. You'll win tomorrow, I know it.' She paused, and looked into the distance. 'But … it won't be an easy win. There will be something … unusually challenging about it. Some … threat.' She closed her eyes, as if trying to dismiss an image.

He laughed. 'Well of *course* it won't be easy – it's Nokovic!' He deliberately ignored her prophetic undertone. It didn't do to encourage her when she was like this.

'You've beaten him before, and you can do it again.' The formidable Serb was the number two seed. Her eyes locked on his. 'If for whatever reason you falter, look at me–'

'And Eliza.'

She frowned. 'If that helps.' She sat up straighter, released his hand. 'We've had lots of good luck messages.' Her tone was lighter, and her troubled expression brightened into a smile. She moved back to the armchair. 'They're mostly from sponsors and such. Did Hector text you?'

He nodded, and picked up his phone. 'Yes …' He reread his foster father's message: *All the very best for tomorrow! Sorry I can't be there, but I'll be at home cheering you on and I know you can do it!! With love from Hector (Dad).*

The lump in his throat swelled again as he read the apologetic 'Dad', enclosed in brackets as if to say, *Is it okay if I call myself Dad? Sorry I wasn't a better one.*

Ace returned a simple thumbs up.

There were more good luck messages; he scrolled through, not bothering to open them, only reading the first words:

Good luck! You can do …

Best of luck for tomorrow …

Smash it, Ace! We're all …

He opened one from Eliza, received ten minutes ago:

Before you switch off your phone, lovely Ace, thanks so much for tonight, it was very special and YOU are so very special to me. I'm sending you all my love and all the luck in the world and I'm SO excited to be there for you tomorrow, my eyes won't leave you for one second! I KNOW you'll do it. Hugs, kisses, all the things and more, E XXX

He smiled. *But still*, said that insidious little voice, *sending you all my love* isn't *I love you*.

He shushed the voice. And then sucked in a breath as he read the next message:

Good luk bro I'll be waching
Lockie

'My god.' He looked up at Merle, his eyes wide. 'Lockie!' He was overwhelmed with relief. His foster brother was alive and well, and communicating with him again after a year and a half of silence.

'*What?* Let me see.' Merle beckoned quickly with a hand.

He passed her the phone.

'*Lockie* …' She closed her eyes and blew out a breath that would have stripped a dandelion clock.

Joy was blossoming deep inside Ace, filling a space that had been empty for so long. Lockie was thinking of him. He'd been keeping up with events. Ace hadn't been consigned to his past, after all.

'He'll be watching.' His smile grew wider. 'Lockie and Eliza will both be watching. And you, and Tristan, all rooting for me. How could I possibly lose?' Then the smile faded. 'Don't answer that. Forget I even said it.'

The cloud that had drifted over Merle's face lifted, and she laughed. 'You and your superstitions. Remember, you control the magic, not the other way round.'

'If only. Still, I do have this little guy.' He touched his dragon.

'Well,' she said, standing up, waggling a finger at him, 'it's bedtime for you, young man. Don't forget to set your alarm. Sweet dreams, and do the calming exercises.'

Ace was soon in bed. His kit was ready, his alarm was set. He was as fit as he'd ever been, mentally prepared, and he had the good wishes of all those people he cared about, plus many anonymous millions more (America seemed to like him too).

He spread out his arms and legs, still appreciative of a king-sized bed with crisp, smooth hotel sheets, after years of sharing a rickety old bunk bed with Lockie. At one time they'd had a room each, but after Lockie's suicide attempt his foster brother hadn't wanted to be alone in the dark.

Ace beckoned sleep, nudging away thoughts of tomorrow's match by thinking instead of Lockie. *He'll be watching!* What time would the match start in New Zealand? About breakfast time. He was always subconsciously aware of the time in that country at the bottom of the world.

He wondered, was Lockie in a hostel, a house? In a city, on a beach? Was he still surfing? Did he have a job? Friends?

Lockie had saved up to travel by winning surfing competitions, and, much to their mutual amusement, being scouted as a model for surfing and beach gear. With his tousled, sun-bleached locks, sky blue eyes and a shy half-smile the camera interpreted as somewhere between aloof and cool, he certainly looked the part. As one lusty photographer had said, he was probably the only boy in Cornwall who looked drop-dead gorgeous in a wetsuit, even before he rolled it down to his waist. She'd labelled her folder of Lockie photos, *Sex on a surfboard.*

Ace smiled in the dark as he remembered Lockie telling him the photographer had said it was an invitation, as well as a label.

'And what did you say?' Ace had replied, chuckling in anticipation of Lockie's answer.

'I said it was sweet of her to offer, but no thank you. Then I ran away.'

When Lockie had first taken himself off to New Zealand, Ace had tried to contact him day after day. But all his emails, texts and messages had gone unanswered. Lockie had cut himself off completely.

Ace understood his need to get away, but at the same time couldn't comprehend why he'd ghost the person he'd been closest to, who knew the truth of what he'd been through. Lockie had no one else. Merle and Hector had let him down, his mother didn't care, he had no idea who his father was, no brothers or sisters … his only friends had been in the surfing community. Ace had attempted to find out if any of them had heard from him, but they hadn't.

He picked up his phone from the bedside table and typed in a reply:

Lockie, your message means more than all the others put together. Thanks bro ☺☺

Chapter 25

Ace

Left sock on first; right sock on second. Left shoe on, right shoe on. Tie the right shoe, tie the left. It had to be done this way.

Across the locker room sat his Serbian opponent, Dejan Nokovic. Normally good friends, the rivals now avoided each other's eye.

Ace's knee was jiggling up and down. He frowned at it. *Stop.*

He touched his dragon, shut his eyes, breathed deeply. *In … out. In … out.* He had to trust that these crushing nerves, more ferocious than ever before, would disappear once he was on court.

An hour and half ago he'd forced down his perfectly balanced meal, his stomach shrinking away from the food as Merle commanded, 'Eat, Arthur. Eat.' Now, he took a sip of his water, and had trouble swallowing that down too, along with the nausea. But he had to stay hydrated.

Thank god – the officials had arrived, the wait was over. Ace glanced across at Nokovic. The Serb met his eye, and nodded.

It was time.

Eliza

The air in the Arthur Ashe stadium crackled with anticipation. The world's largest tennis venue was filled to capacity – it held almost double the numbers of Wimbledon's centre court.

Eliza and Will were sitting in the players' box, behind Tristan and Merle. Representatives from Ace's sponsors were also in attendance.

Tristan kept turning round to chat, but Eliza was too nervous to concentrate on the conversation. She felt sick. How must Ace be feeling, facing this? She remembered the Euro football final, the three England players who'd missed their penalties. The pressure – the weight of England's hopes on their shoulders; the Wembley crowd, all those people watching in pubs, special outdoor venues, at home. But those players had been part of a team. Ace was all alone. There was only him. She couldn't begin to comprehend what that must be like.

Merle was in a world of her own, sitting still as stone, focusing her energy on the empty blue space of the court below.

A voice rang out over the loudspeaker: '*Ladies and gentlemen. Welcome to the men's singles final of the US Open, 2021. Please welcome, from Serbia … Dejan Nokovic!*'

There were loud cheers, and cameras flashed as the smiling Serb appeared out of the tunnel, waving to the crowd.

'*And from Great Britain … Arthur Penhalagon!*'

The volume of cheering increased markedly as Ace followed the Serb into the arena. He waved in response to the cheers, then looked up to the players' box. He gave Eliza a smile; she went to blow him a kiss, but halfway to her mouth her hand stopped and she waved. Blowing a kiss felt inappropriate for such a momentous occasion.

He nodded to Tristan and Merle. He looked composed; together. Ready.

The two players unzipped their bags, fiddled with their rackets, sipped their water, arranged their gear … Ace organised his just so. He carefully positioned two water bottles beneath his seat so they pointed towards one end of the court. Why? He was so cute, with his superstitions.

Ace won the coin toss. He touched his dragon, made his way to the base line, and signalled to the ball girl.

After the warm-up, the noise in the stadium gave way to a highly charged silence. Ace bounced the ball five times (another superstition – *always five for the first serve, four for the second*), fixed

Nokovic with a stare, and launched the first ball of the US Open final high in the air.

❀

Only when Ace won the first set 6–2 did Eliza's nerves begin to ease. As the players took a break, Ace reorganising the bottles beneath his chair, she finally let go of Will's hand, which she'd gripped tightly all through the first set.

'Eliza,' he'd said. 'For goodness sake, there isn't a camera lens in this stadium that isn't zooming in on you every time Ace wins a game. And you're holding hands with me.'

Neither player had so far lost many points through unforced errors. The Serb's serves were as powerful as Ace's, and there were long, nail-biting rallies as they both held their nerve.

Ace had smiled just once, briefly, in response to the crowd's squeals of delight when he'd played a winning shot backwards through his legs. Between points, he often glanced at Merle, whose stillness was uncanny. And between games, he'd look up at Eliza. She'd removed her oversized sunglasses, the better to let him see her eyes. His own face remained expressionless.

The hush descended again as the second set began. Before long, Ace was two games up. He began to dominate; his confidence was clear to see. He won the set 6–3. If he bagged one more set, Ace would make sporting history.

Forty minutes later, Ace was 4–3 up in the third set, and the crowd was sensing victory – though Eliza didn't want to jinx things by entertaining that thought; not yet.

As Ace made his way to the base line after the end swap, the crowd went silent, and Will told the overexcited sponsors to shush. Ace took up position, bounced the ball five times, stared at his opponent, threw up the ball … and served it into the net. With a small frown, he examined his racket, testing its strings.

He bounced the second ball four times, looked up, launched it, swept his racket down … the ball went into the net.

The crowd groaned. No one enjoyed a double fault.

Ace moved across and prepared to serve again. The delivery was solid; the Serb returned it to Ace's backhand and he played a deep shot, attempting to pass his opponent, but Nokovic reached it and dropped the ball just over the net. Ace launched himself towards it, connected with it, but mis-hit the ball which flew out, narrowly missing the umpire.

'*Love thirty*', she called, smiling at Ace.

As he returned to the baseline, Ace again examined his strings.

Eliza's angst had returned with a vengeance. Something didn't feel right. She got the strongest impression that Ace had, very suddenly, started to lose his nerve.

She fixed her eyes on him and focused her mind, aware that her lips were moving: *Stay strong, Ace. You're SO close to doing this!*

He lost the next point through an unforced error. A shot that should have been an easy winner instead landed in the tramlines.

Ace's expression had changed. Normally inscrutable, there was now a hint of fear. She saw him quickly scan the crowd as he returned again to the baseline.

Love forty.

He served, and the Serb, perhaps knocked off kilter by Ace's sudden lapse in form, hit the return into the net.

Momentary relief.

The next point progressed into a rally, and as Eliza watched Ace lurch around the court, she was reminded of a scene in a movie … what was it? She racked her brains.

Of course. That first Harry Potter film – the Quidditch match, when Professor Quirrell sat in the stands murmuring a curse, attempting to knock Harry off his broom. That was how this felt. As if Ace had suddenly lost control of his racket. And from the way he kept glancing into the crowd, she guessed that something, or someone, had put him off his game.

Eliza scanned the spectators in the direction he'd been looking, but they were too far away for her to make out any faces.

Ace lost the rally, and the game. It was four games all, and Nokovic was serving.

Ace's first return went into the net. He hit the second out by a long way.

The crowd had gone quiet. The atmosphere was awful; Ace's consternation – his sudden loss of focus – was obvious to all. Eliza felt sick.

She leaned forward and tapped Merle on the shoulder.

'What?' Merle snapped, not moving.

'Something's upset him. What do you think's happened?'

Merle didn't reply, but Tristan turned round. 'Yes, something's not right. Something's afoot.'

'Afoot, yes,' growled Merle. Still she hadn't moved.

'What the feck's going on?' said Tristan.

Ace lost the game, and the players went to change ends.

'Will, my man,' said Tristan. 'Would you mind swapping seats? I'd like a little conflab with Eliza.'

'Sure.' Will hopped over, sat down next to Merle and smiled at her. 'How are you doing?' She ignored him, staring resolutely ahead, muttering under her breath.

'What's bothering him?' Eliza said to Tristan. 'Something's knocked his concentration for six.'

'I don't know. But look, I think you might be able to help nudge him back on track.'

'How?'

Tristan shared his plan. It was a very simple one. He thought it might work.

It was worth a try.

As Ace and Dejan made their way to their baselines, the crowd erupted. Eliza felt their positive energy as they attempted to infuse Ace with strength and nerve and resolve.

Ace touched his dragon and glanced up to the players' box. Eliza saw his disquiet. His panic. His eyes went first to Merle, then moved to Eliza.

She held his gaze, made a heart with her two hands, and mouthed slowly and deliberately: *I LOVE YOU*. And then she did it again, with a wide smile. *I LOVE YOU, ACE.*

He blinked, and there was a tiny smile.

The game went to deuce … then Ace served two ferocious aces. He was back. Five all.

Next game, Ace won every point, breaking Dejan's serve.

It was 6–5. Ace was serving for the match. The championship. The Golden Slam.

They swapped ends again, Ace doing the things with his bottles, his towels, changing his racket … back in his normal routine. The fear she'd seen, that strange loss of control, had vanished.

'The power of love,' said Tristan into her ear. 'Never doubt it.'

Eliza didn't think too hard about whether she'd meant those words. She surely did. Ace was everything she could ever want in a man. She was the luckiest girl on the planet. Her family loved him; her best friend loved him. Heck, *everyone* loved him.

'You really think me saying *I love you* fixed whatever it was?'

'Well of course it did,' said Tristan. 'Whatever evil just tried to undo him, you stopped it in its tracks. Love always wins out.'

'What do you think it was? Did he see something?'

'Some*one*,' said Merle, turning round at last. 'Who may or may not have been here in person.'

Tristan and Eliza looked at her in confusion.

'The mind plays tricks in these high-pressure situations,' she said. 'A face in the crowd may deceive. Thank you, Eliza, for grounding him. I appreciate it.' She turned to face the court again.

Tristan pulled a face at the back of her head. '*Maith thú.*'

'Sorry?'

'Gaelic. For well done. A tick from Merle is a hard-won thing.'

The two players walked out, and Ace looked up to the box again. Eliza put both hands over her heart, and Ace returned a small smile.

The applause was deafening, and the umpire had to ask for quiet – twice.

Eliza gripped Tristan's hand, and saw Will grasp Merle's. She didn't respond, but Eliza could sense her energy, her willpower, slicing through the air, flowing into Ace.

All hint of Ace's nerves, confusion – that heart-stopping wobble – had fled.

He served an ace, and then another.

Thirty love.

Dejan won the third point, and then, after a nifty lob from Ace that saw his opponent hurtle into the boundary, it was forty fifteen.

Two match points. Two championship points. Two Golden Slam points.

The tension was unbearable – a thick, palpable thing, like a giant supernatural beast hovering over the silent stadium. Eliza couldn't bear to watch; she wanted to close her eyes, or cover them with her hands. Maybe if she wished too hard, pictured him winning, it would in fact make him lose?

And now you're making no sense at all.

Ace served; Nokovic played a fierce return and ran into the net. Ace flipped up a lob, and Nokovic ran backwards, racket held high, ready. He brought it down, smashing the ball … it clipped the net and paused, while the gods decided what to do with it.

Then it dropped – onto Nokovic's side.

He's done it! Oh my god – he's done it!

Tristan, Will and Eliza leapt out of their seats like a trio of jack-in-the-boxes, screaming, while Merle dropped her head into her hands and remained unmoving. The crowd went berserk.

Ace fell to his knees, a stunned look on his face. Eliza thought he was about to cry again – tears were running down her own face, and Will's, and Tristan's, and probably Merle's, although hers was still hidden – but he got back onto his feet and raised his hands above his head. He lifted his face to the sky, and on it was a smile that dissolved Eliza's insides. She could see the pressure evaporating, like a mist lifting, and the sunshine streaming in.

He ran in to the net and the two players hugged, then Dejan took Ace's face in his hands and kissed him on both cheeks, before raising his hands above his head and clapping, encouraging the crowd to roar louder.

Ace went over to the front row of spectators below the players' box. He handed his racket to a young boy, pausing to shake his hand. Eliza knew she would never forget the look on that little boy's face. As the ear-splitting cheers continued, people reached out to touch Ace, and he held out a palm, swiping hands as he quickly climbed up through the rows towards them.

He met Eliza's eye; she was cheering, clapping, crying; the emotions were overwhelming. He was nearly level, but she pointed to Merle and he diverted, enveloping his foster mother in a hug. Merle seemed to be in shock … stunned, unable to grasp what Ace had just achieved. She stared at his face and shook her head, blinking.

'We did it, Mum,' he shouted above the cheering.

Merle nodded, still incapable of speech.

Then, as Will clapped him on the back, he jumped onto Merle's seat and up to Eliza's level. He laughed at her tears, then gently wiped her cheeks before wrapping her in his arms and lifting her off her feet. She took his gorgeous face in her hands and kissed him, and the crowd went even wilder.

'I love you too,' he said against her lips. 'Thank you.'

He put her down, and then said, 'Again,' so she kissed him some more.

'I'm not normally one for PDAs,' she heard Will say to Tristan, 'but this, I don't mind at all.' Then she spluttered with laughter as Will added, 'You do know it was me who got them together?'

Merle's voice, evidently functioning again, cut in sharply. 'Get back down there, Arthur. *Now.*'

'On my way,' he said, after hugging Tristan. Then he kissed Eliza one more time, squeezed Merle's shoulder, and ran back down the steps to the court.

A podium had been speedily erected, and an interviewer and uniformed officials stood waiting, along with Dejan. On the other side of the net, ball girls and boys were lining up, one waving the Stars and Stripes. On a pedestal sat the gleaming silver cup and the runner up's trophy.

As Ace came onto the court, the cheers grew louder again and music blared from speakers. The interviewer waved him to her side. Ace was presented with an envelope containing $2.5 million. Or paperwork to that effect. Did they even still do cheques?

'Don't you love America?' said Will, back by Eliza's side. 'Money first, silverware later.'

At last, Ace was presented with the trophy, by tennis great Stan Smith, and he held it high as the cameras flashed. There was an on-court interview, the players praising each other and thanking their teams and all the fans who'd supported them. In the ranks of spectators, Serbian flags and Union Jacks waved in response.

Ace teared up as he thanked 'my incredible mum, Merle Innes, for taking in an unwanted little boy and dedicating herself to turning him into a champion.' Then he thanked Tristan, 'my coach, dear friend and quite often my agony aunt.' He turned towards Eliza. 'And my beautiful, incredible girlfriend, Eliza. You've changed my life. You're amazing. I love you.'

With tears in her eyes, she blew him a kiss.

'And finally,' he said, looking into the camera, 'my brother, Lockie. I miss you, bro. Please – come home.'

Chapter 26

Ace, Merle and Tristan stayed behind for a press conference, while Eliza and Will returned to the Plaza. Eliza had invited Merle to bring everyone back to their suite for an impromptu celebration on the roof terrace.

She discussed arrangements with the butler.

'May I enquire as to your budget, Ms Rose,' he asked discreetly.

'There isn't one. Just make everything extra special.'

Before they changed for the party, Eliza and Will opened a bottle of champagne from the bar fridge and took it out onto the terrace.

'*What* a day,' he said, flopping onto a sofa and tossing back his curls. He gazed out at the view. 'Would you look at this place. So familiar from the movies, yet it's even better in real life. Can you second me to New York, please?'

'Yes, it is even better. But no.'

As dusk thickened the air, a thousand windows in the skyscrapers dwarfing the Plaza glowed yellow. The traffic noise on Fifth Avenue far below dissipated as it floated upwards, reaching them as a quiet hum. Beyond, the trees in the darkening hollow of Central Park were already turning gold as autumn gathered momentum.

'Wasn't Ace amazing?' she said (again).

He put an arm along the back of the sofa. 'It's official, then? He loves you, and you love him.'

She met his eye. 'Tristan asked me to say it. But I think I do.'

'You *think*? Don't you know?'

'Will,' she said, smiling. 'Now is not the time for a deep delve into the meaning of love and the various iterations thereof. He's absolutely gorgeous, and probably the nicest, most genuine, inspiring human being I've ever met. I'm beyond happy to be his girlfriend.' She nudged him. 'And he *really* knows how to kiss.'

'I see. Well, aren't you the lucky one.' He raised his eyebrows. 'Best ever? Truth only, please.'

She blinked. 'That's unfair. I don't have to answer.'

His brown eyes returned to the view, but she saw his mind drifting off ... drifting back. He sighed, and said:

> '*A man had given all other bliss,*
> *And all his worldly worth for this,*
> *To waste his whole heart in one kiss,*
> *Upon those perfect lips.*'

Eliza shivered. 'Ooh, is that Tennyson? Arthur and Guinevere?'

'Yes, Tennyson. But no – the wasted heart belonged to your other boy. Lancelot.' He met her eye again. 'Is it okay if I bring a friend tonight too?'

'Friend? What friend?'

'A guy I met in the Champagne Bar. He's a journalist, writes for *Time* magazine. To be honest, I don't think our meeting was a happy coincidence; I reckon he's after a scoop. But he's cute.'

'Cute, huh?'

'I'm trying to move on. If mostly failing.'

Poor Will. She squeezed his knee. 'Of course you can. I'm in the mood to grant you anything. Apart from a job in New York. Invite whoever you like.'

◈

It was a magical evening, one Eliza knew she'd remember every detail of, for the rest of her life. Ace hardly left her side as they celebrated his Golden Slam against the breathtaking backdrop of Manhattan by night.

Tristan and Ace brought a few tennis player pals; the sponsors came along with their partners. Ace invited his technician and his lovely wife, plus a locker room attendant who'd taken good care of him. There was Merle, Will, and Will's new journalist friend, Jonas. He had little round spectacles, wiry brown hair and a beard, and began the evening speaking in an intense manner about politics to anyone who'd listen, and finished by dancing on a table, lip synching to Taylor Swift's 'Welcome to New York'.

Fairy lights twinkled in the trees sitting in tubs around the terrace. The butler had organised the sound system, and Eliza chose a party playlist. Waiters laid out platters of lobster, smoked salmon blinis and dishes of caviar. Also mini hot dogs, burgers, and slices of pizza. This was New York, after all.

Bottles of champagne sat in gleaming buckets of ice. Ace had been presented with a replica trophy, and this sat in pride of place in the middle of the food table.

'What am I supposed to do with this?' he asked Eliza, eyeing a dish of caviar with its tiny scoop.

Pleasantly tipsy, she dipped the little implement into the fish eggs and spread them on the back of her hand. 'You can eat it off my hand, and if there's any left at the end, we'll find somewhere else for you to lick it off.'

Ace looked a little shocked. 'Honestly? I'm not sure I'm ready for all this.'

'Too late,' she said, running her fingers through his hair. 'You're a multi-millionaire now. Welcome to the world of decadence.' She kissed him on the mouth.

'I meant to tell you,' he said, when she let him go, 'I had a good-luck message from Lockie. First time I've heard from him since he ran away to the Antipodes.'

'Oh! Hence the plea to come home?'

'Yes. I've been checking my phone, no congrats as yet. Oh my god,' he said, distracted, as Abba's 'Gimme Gimme Gimme' came on and Merle hauled Will into a space big enough for dancing. Since the match, she'd unwound like a ball of wool hurtling down a hillside. Her hair had been liberated from its plait, and it frothed round her shoulders like a silver cloud. She was wearing a purple sequined dress, and was taller than Will in her high heels.

Ace shook his head as he watched Merle tossing her hair, gyrating her hips, Will enthusiastically mirroring her moves. She waved Ace over, but he declined. 'I'm done with exercise for today,' he said to Eliza. 'I've earned a rest.'

'Oh really? That's disappointing.'

'Ah. Apart from the type where I'm allowed to lie down,' he said, squeezing her waist.

As the song finished, Merle joined them. 'Eliza, can I have a private word?' It was like being summoned to the headmistress's office.

'Of course.' Eliza widened her eyes at Ace, who gave a small *search me* shake of his head.

They moved away from the others. Merle smiled. 'Thank you for your support today, Eliza.'

A burst of relief. 'Oh, I wouldn't have missed it for the world! What an amazing experience. You deserve many congratulations too.'

Merle put a hand on her arm. 'My life has been all about Ace, these past years. I know I'm overprotective–'

'I understand.'

'No, I don't think you do.' Her expression turned serious; her aura darkened. 'The death of someone so deeply connected can unhinge us, Eliza.'

Death? What?

'But it puts us in touch with the universe for a while. Opens us up. We see things, hear things – notice things that otherwise would go unremarked.' Those dark eyes locked on Eliza's. 'You'd give anything to have him back.'

Eliza's heart stopped. Everyone else faded into the background, and there was only this all-seeing, all-knowing woman, filling this rooftop with her crushing presence.

'You made a deal,' said Merle. 'It's beyond me now. But maybe it's not beyond you. You can still stop it.'

Ace appeared at Eliza's side. 'Chrissakes, Merle,' he said in a low voice. 'You're weirding Eliza out. Leave her alone. She's been brilliant, and nothing like this night will ever happen again.'

'No, it won't,' said Merle. 'Not if *she* doesn't–'

She stopped, and gave Eliza another intense stare, before making a beeline for Will, as Beyoncé's 'Single Ladies' blasted out.

Ace put an arm round Eliza. 'I'm so sorry about her. What could she *possibly* have against you now?'

All Eliza could do was shake her head.

'So – am I staying the night?' he said, nuzzling her hair.

Eliza was still attempting to slough off Merle's words, her miasma. How could she possibly know about Eliza's wish? About her relationship with Kit? Unless … was she messing with her mind, wanting to scare off her rival for power and influence? Ace was her meal ticket, after all.

Barbie nudged her.

Could Merle have sent her? *Surely not.*

'Well?' prompted Ace.

'Of course you're staying,' she replied, firmly shutting that door in her mind. She wouldn't let anything spoil this perfect day. 'And wonderful as all this is, I'd quite like everyone else to go away now.'

'Me too. What are your plans for tomorrow?'

'Oh, I think we're on the red-eye home. How about you?' She hadn't thought that far ahead.

'Can you postpone?'

She laughed. 'Well, it's my own airline, troubled though it is, so that might be possible. Why?'

'Well, Cinderella – how would you like to go to a ball?'

'Ball? What ball?'

'The Met Gala, of course. We're in New York, it's tomorrow, and my biggest sponsor bought a table. Now I'm US champ, I apparently earn an invitation.' He grinned. 'See? I can do glamorous too.'

Excitement fought panic. 'But … it takes *months* to get a look for the Met. I have no gown, what about my hair? What about–'

'Calm down. My people spoke to your people.' He chuckled

at his own words. 'Your Rose colleagues have organised for some fashion magazine person to bring dresses for you to choose from, first thing. Hair and make-up are being sorted. It's all in hand, anyway, and you've got this suite for another night. So … are we going?'

'Well, this is quite a surprise.' The Met Gala. It sunk in. 'My god, Ace. You've just out-celebbed me.'

'I'm a proper king now.'

'Ace, and King,' she said, hugging him.

'And I'm promoting you, from Princess to Queen.'

❀

Eliza had drunk deep of joy and champagne. But she wasn't *drunk* drunk. Just on a high, ecstatic for Ace.

She smiled at her reflection in the gilt-framed bathroom mirror, which, she thought, remembering Ace's Marie Antoinette quip, wouldn't have looked out of place at Versailles. She was glowing, a result of champagne, happiness and … expectation. Her body was sizzling with it.

She'd changed into a lace cami. Technically 'sleepwear', but … well. Sleep was the last thing on her mind. She quickly rubbed in a few blobs of moisturiser, fanned her hair over her shoulders and headed for the bedroom, where her champion, her king of the world, was waiting.

She stopped in the doorway and gazed at him, his golden hair on the pillow, his broad shoulders, a muscled arm slung across the empty space next to him. His eyes were closed, his lips curved in a contented smile.

Eliza slipped into bed, lifting his arm and laying it across her. 'Finally,' she said quietly. She tilted her face up to his, brushed his lips with hers.

He gave a sigh, then a small, adorable snuffle.

He was fast asleep. Exhausted. Wiped out.

Eliza ran a finger down his cheek. Ace didn't stir. It was hardly surprising. Her spirits sank, but she didn't have the heart to wake him, in spite of her …

What am I supposed to do with this?

She rolled onto her back and stared at the high, moulded ceiling, then through the sheer curtains at the diffused lights of Manhattan. Her eyelids grew heavy …

Don't go, she whispered. *No … stay, don't leave, not yet …*

'Eliza,' came his voice. 'Eliza,' louder.

A hand on her shoulder, shaking her gently. A voice, breaking through. 'Eliza, you're dreaming …'

No. It isn't a dream.

She moaned softly. 'Please, don't stop …'

'Eliza.'

She turned towards him, not opening her eyes. 'Touch me,' she said, reaching for him, guiding his hand. '*Here.*'

Afterwards, Ace remained quiet. He hadn't uttered a sound during those brief, intense minutes. He'd tried to slow her down, but she'd been on fire.

'Good morning, King of the World,' she said, stretching, properly awake now. 'Shall I order us up some coffee?'

'There's a machine.'

'There's a butler.' When he didn't laugh, she added, 'Joking. Shall I make it?'

'Good idea.'

'What's the time?' she said, and checked her phone. 'Not yet seven. Early! Maybe we don't need to get up just yet.' She trailed her fingernails lightly down his chest. 'When are my fairy godmothers due?'

'You need to speak to your people.' His tone was distracted.

'Oh, never mind. People can wait.'

She looked up at him. He was staring out of the window.

'Is everything okay? I suppose you were on such a high yesterday … bit of an anti-climax?'

He turned to her, a slight frown on his face. 'I don't know. I guess it's still sinking in.'

'Let me say it, yet again.' She gave him a squeeze. 'You did it. You're the best tennis player the world has ever seen. You achieved something no man has ever done before. It was an incredible performance …'

She thought back, and the question left her lips before she could stop it. 'Ace, when you lost those two games in the final set …' He tensed, but she'd started now. 'You seemed to lose focus for a while. I just wondered … you don't have to tell me …'

'It happens,' he said, after a pause. 'I served a double fault; it knocked me off balance. Sudden attack of self-doubt. I was thinking, you'll never do this. These players have been at it for years; you're just the fluky new boy, an imposter. Or my success had all been down to Merle's force of will. Or something, but not my talent. I guess I lost my sense of self for a moment there.' He smiled at her. 'Until I looked at you.'

Eliza melted. She laced her fingers with his and kissed his hand. 'The power of love, Tristan said.'

But she sensed – there was something he wasn't telling her. There had been more going on than a dip in confidence. That loss of control, the way he kept looking into the crowd, as if he could sense its malevolent source.

What, or who, had he seen?

Chapter 27

Eliza

The dress she chose was simple, compared to the elaborate ensembles she knew would be on show. The theme was 'In America', which was wide enough that her beautiful gown, close-fitting and made of golden silk, could be described as reminiscent of old Hollywood. Maybe. If anyone asked.

It was off the shoulder and tapered to a short train. She was supplied with a rib-crushing undergarment to give her the requisite waistline. An elaborate necklace on loan from Tiffany offset the simplicity of the dress, and the hairstylist pulled her curls up into an artfully constructed high ponytail that swung down her back. Her eye make-up was gold, and her cheekbones were highlighted with fine glitter.

While Eliza was attended to by a steady procession of ladies in waiting – stylists, hair and make-up people, nail people, jewellery people – Ace was being interviewed by Will's *Time* journalist pal Jonas, who'd taken advantage of Merle's loosening up to bag himself an hour of the new super-champ's time. Then the photographer posed Ace on the rooftop, for what would no doubt be a stunning portfolio of shots of the tennis king against the New York skyline.

For the gala, Ace refused to entertain the idea of anything other than a standard, if exquisitely tailored, tuxedo, declaring the men's fashion ridiculous.

'People might think you've got no imagination,' said Eliza, as their limo took them to the Metropolitan Museum of Art that evening. 'But they're wrong. I know what's under that shirt.'

They joined the queue to ascend the famous staircase, as crowds jostled to glimpse the rich and famous. While always a focus of attention in London, here, as neither an actress, a singer, a New York Name or a sportsperson, Eliza felt like a nonentity. Comfortably un-famous. It was nice.

The same couldn't be said for Ace, who was creating a sensation as he was efficiently ushered from one glamorous TV presenter to the next. The Americans loved his bashful acceptance of their congratulations, his quaint hint of a Cornish accent, his confusion when asked about his fashion choices, and the way he was telling everyone how beautiful his girlfriend looked tonight.

Finally, they were inside. It was cocktail hour, and the boss of Ace's major sponsor introduced them to a group of US sporting superstars. Having spent the past half hour reverting to something approaching his former fish-out-of-water self, Ace now joined in the conversation with enthusiasm.

Eliza had no clue about US sport, and was happy to take a back seat. She looked around her, celebrity spotting. In spite of her regular attendance at awards events and suchlike, she'd never seen this many spectacularly beautiful women in one place. Their skin glowed, their smiles, with their perfect teeth, were dazzling; their limbs were sleek, glistening, toned. What did you have to eat, drink, do … *spend* to look like that?

Freaks of nature, really. The thought made Eliza feel slightly better about herself. She felt like a moth, albeit a pretty one, compared to these iridescent butterflies.

But the men? Meh. Few compared to Ace, and as a result he was attracting a great deal of female attention. She realised, this was the first time she'd been on a proper date with him, in public. She really had been turning into a recluse. Her mood dipped as she remembered why.

Her mouth suddenly dry, Eliza put down her champagne and

went in search of a glass of water. As she headed for the bar there was a tap on her shoulder, and a voice spoke in her ear. 'Honestly, the riff raff they let in here these days. Did you bribe your way in, Lizzie?'

She whirled round, her mouth dropping open. 'Oh my *god*!'

'Hello, Snow White,' said Rob, his brown eyes twinkling. 'Nice dress – you look like an Oscar.'

'Rob! What on *earth* are you doing here?' Her face broke into a huge smile. 'But how brilliant that you are!'

They hugged, and it went on for a while. She dropped her head onto his shoulder. Oh … the warm familiarity of him.

'Hey, watch it with your lipstick,' he said, pulling away.

He was wearing a white suit, the jacket lapels cut on an unusual bias, with a black shirt and no tie. His shiny dark curls, longer than they used to be, were slicked back, a few left free to flop appealingly over his forehead.

'You look *insanely* cool,' she said, giving him the once over. 'Very NYC. How come you're here? RoseGold's entertainment budget surely doesn't stretch to this?'

'God, no. I'm just a plus one. But I was already in New York, for the tennis. The TV chaps got me tickets.' Rob had always been a tennis fan, like Harry. 'I spotted you in the crowd yesterday. I nearly texted you … thought about it, but …' his smile dimmed, 'it didn't feel right. You were so intent on your new man.' He looked over at Ace, who had his back to them.

'Oh gosh, yes. It was probably the most nerve-wracking afternoon of my life.'

'So, Lizzie …' He searched her eyes. 'You've gone from *probably a non-starter* to fully loved up in the space of two months?'

Had she said that? Yes, she had.

He waited for her response.

'He's really something. You *have* to come and meet him.'

'Do I?'

'Absolutely. I've told him all about you.'

'Really? *All*?'

'Just … you know. How we were. How you've been my pal forever.' She bit her lip. 'Will's here too, back at the hotel.'

'Yes, I spotted him. How come?'

'Just for company, really. And …' The need to confide was overwhelming. Rob always lifted her spirits. 'I'm afraid I've been the target of abuse. Mostly online, but some pretty scary stalker-y stuff too.'

'Stalkery?' Rob's brow creased in concern.

'Someone sending things – really horrible things – with threatening messages.' She swallowed. 'Well, death threats, actually.'

'What the fuck, Lizzie?' He took hold of her hand.

'Back home, I feel like I'm constantly being watched. So I don't much enjoy being alone right now. Will's been a great help, so I guess … this trip is his reward.'

'I saw the trolling, and all that bollocks Ace's ex said about you.' He looked over at Ace again, and released her hand. 'When I saw her in the crowd yesterday, I wanted to stuff a bunch of sour grapes down her nasty little throat. Why is she flogging her dead horse of a career, anyway? She didn't even make it through the qualifiers.'

'What?' Eliza looked at him in surprise. 'She was watching?'

'Yes, in the players' area, just in front of our box.' He gave her a wry smile. 'What really hurt was that she didn't mention me in your history of sexual predation.'

Eliza snorted, then frowned. Was it Catriona who'd put Ace off his game?

She glanced over, and saw Ace watching them. 'Come and meet him.'

'Okay.' His eyes went over to the bar entrance. 'But before you introduce me to yours, I'd better introduce you to mine.'

Yet another stunning woman was crossing the room. Eliza recognised Letitia from the photos. Like the ones she'd obsessed over when Rob had cast her in *My Dark Soul*. It was a face to stop traffic, to hush conversation. In Greek times, it would have launched a thousand ships.

And Letitia's body … my god. So Barbie wasn't a physical

impossibility, after all. Her dress was gauzy, bordering on invisible, demonstrating the fact that she could achieve that shape without the help of miracle-working underwear. Nothing was left to the imagination, apart from what lay beneath two tiny heart-shaped diamanté clusters on her chest, and another on the sheer fabric between her thighs.

As she made her way over, eyes were popping like champagne corks. If Eliza had considered herself a pretty moth before, now she felt like one of those little brown ones that fly out of your wardrobe.

'Eliza – we meet at last!'

There was nothing guarded about Letitia's megawatt smile. Which was quite surprising. Not only had Eliza been Rob's long-term partner, she'd also engineered a significant setback in Letitia's acting career, when she'd overruled Rob's decision to cast her in *My Dark Soul*. An entirely professional decision, based on the fact that she, Will and Kit felt her luminous blondeness was all wrong for the role.

Maybe Letitia's lack of wariness was to do with the fact that she'd been the 'other woman', and Eliza the cheated-on partner sitting alone and sad in her flat across the ocean. But revenge had been sweet – wielding her power to banish Letitia had been deeply satisfying.

She remembered Kit's words: 'Neatly done, Eliza.'

Kit! Oh my god. Her dream had flashed into her consciousness.

Letitia was waiting for a response.

'Good to meet you, Letitia. You look spectacular. I feel *ridiculously* overdressed!' *Oops.*

'And I just feel ridiculous. My studio wanted me to wear this.'

Rob placed his hand in the small of Letitia's back. 'Small' also applied to the waist that went with it. Eliza tried not to look at his hand but failed, and her heart died a little as his fingers tightened.

'Imagination's overrated,' he said, giving Letitia a wink.

What had Chess said? *We should hate her, but she's actually nice.*

Well of course she was nice. Rob would never be serious about someone who was just a beautiful face. But that thought only made her feel worse.

'Come and meet Ace.'

'Oh my gosh, yes!' said Letitia. 'I was so excited to watch the final. Great that it coincided with the Met Gala so I could do both.'

'Letitia's filming in the UK; she's just popped back here for a few days,' said Rob. 'She's doing a Marvel – female lead, a real bad-ass bitch.' His pride as he looked at her was clear to see. 'Letitia's a brilliant actress.' His eyes met Eliza's. 'She can make you believe she's anyone.'

'I *love* England,' Letitia said. 'It's just *darling*.'

'Bless our quaint little hearts,' said Rob. 'Let's go meet your man, then, Lizzie.'

Chapter 28

Ace

Ace tried to speak usefully about basketball – he enjoyed the game, and it was an honour to meet the top NBA players – but his eyes kept drifting over to where Eliza stood talking with Rob. He recognised her ex, even though this was a far smoother version than the one in that photo on her kitchen wall.

Rob's suit was … imaginative. Unlike Ace's. His shiny hair was slicked back, his smile engaging, his eyes twinkly, and his date was the most spectacular woman in the room. Possibly in America.

Rob's hand moved to the blonde's waist. What there was of it. Ace couldn't help staring. He wondered how much of her was real; unsculpted. Perhaps all of her, but then he'd thought that about one of the Kardashians they'd seen earlier, until Eliza had explained.

Eliza smiled at Ace, and everyone else in the room faded away. Not one of these women came close. They were so overdone. Fake. All the make up, the eyelashes, the injected (apparently) lips, the hair, the nails. He got that they needed to look this way for the cameras, but it was difficult to spot what lay beneath, what they were like. And he discovered he didn't really care about finding out.

Eliza's personality shone through, lit her up, whether a vision in gold or the frizzy haired, hungover version of this morning.

She was coming towards him, followed by the blonde, and then Rob. The blonde's gaze settled on the back of Eliza's head, and Ace spotted a fleeting malevolence – a narrowing of her feline eyes, a barely imperceptible crease in that buffed forehead. He experienced a moment of empathy as his eyes moved to Rob's bright, self-confident grin.

'Ace!' said Eliza, hooking her arm through his. 'I'm so excited for you to meet Rob.' She brought him forward. 'My partner in crime since I was very tiny years old, my best pal forever. And this is Letitia. Letitia is an actress.' From her tone of voice, she might as well have said 'peasant'.

'Rob, Letitia, meet Ace. The new King of the W–'

'Stop, Eliza.' Ace put an arm round her waist and smiled down at her. 'Just "Ace", or I'll get embarrassed.'

'Embarrassed?' said Rob. 'Fuck – why would you be? I'd be milking it!'

Ace flinched at his accent. Public school, all the way.

'Hearty congratulations.' Rob held out his hand, and Ace shook it. 'That was the most incredible performance. And that atmosphere – never known anything like it, and I'm a Wimbledon regular.' His eyes flicked over to Eliza, and they exchanged a brief smile. 'Missed it this year, but yesterday more than made up for it.'

Ace was picking up strong Harry Rose vibes. He wondered if Harry had been disappointed when Rob and Eliza split.

'You were there?' he said.

'Absolutely. Cheering you on to victory.'

'You were *amazing*!' said Letitia. Her beautiful eyes held his.

Ace blinked. 'Thanks.'

'Nice that you two are official, now,' said Rob. 'Eliza and I had to creep around for a while too.' He gave both women the benefit of a cheeky grin. 'Bloody pain, going out with celebs, isn't it? All the media attention.'

'Too right,' said Eliza. 'From gossip mag darling to slut shamed in the blink of an eye. Again. But hey – I have my very own special hashtag now: ditch the rich bitch.'

Letitia laughed. A little too heartily.

Ace shook his head. 'It's not funny. We need to push back against

254 ● Olivia Hayfield

this stuff; the hate. Eliza's more or less moved in with her friend because she's scared to be on her own.'

'With Will?' said Rob. 'Because of your stalker?'

Eliza went still.

'*Stalker?*' Ace repeated. 'What?'

Eliza didn't meet his eye. 'That mugger, remember?' She looked up at him, and he read the expression in her eyes: *Not now.*

Eliza had a stalker. And he hadn't known (but she'd told Rob?), because she hadn't wanted to worry him, to put him off his game. Thanks to his new-found fame, thanks to *him*, her life had been turned upside down. She was the victim of cyberbullying, the target of hate, ripped apart in the gossip magazines.

Attempting to keep the dismay off his face, he said, 'Ah yes, I remember. Shall we talk about something more worthy of our time? Letitia, what sort of things do you act in?'

But there was no time for further chat, as an announcer asked guests to please take their seats for the performances and dinner, and everyone began to move towards the doors.

'Do you know who you're sitting with?' Letitia asked Eliza.

'Nobody spectacular. Looks like I'm with the money, rather than the fame.'

'I should do a speedy place-name swap,' said Rob. 'Remember Gil's wedding, Lizzie?'

Lizzie?

Eliza's eyes flicked to Ace's, before she said, 'I remember.'

Poor Rob. It was clear to Ace that, whether he'd bagged the most beautiful woman in Hollywood or not, he was still in love with Eliza. He imagined how that would feel, to lose her, but still see her, all the time. And now, with someone else.

But as they made their way to their tables, Ace remembered the name she'd breathed in her half-sleep this morning. *No ... stay, don't leave ...* as she'd reached for him ... *Please, don't stop ...* before he'd woken her from a dream.

Not his name. Not Rob's.

Kit.

Eliza chatted all the way back to the hotel, about the people she'd been sitting with, the outfits she'd seen. 'Cara Delevinge – wow, that was brave. Did you see Rihanna and her boyfriend?'

He had. 'Some way to go before I understand fashion.'

Back in her suite, he poured them a nightcap. Will had gone to bed.

Eliza was still buzzing with it all. As she related a story someone had told her about Harry and Meghan, he found it difficult to concentrate. He wanted to ask about her stalker – he needed to know more about what had happened. But bringing up the subject would spoil the mood. Eliza was on such a high. He gazed at her, his eyes travelling down from her high ponytail, which swung as she talked animatedly, to her porcelain shoulders above the gold of the dress; the swell of her breasts, the seductive curve of her waist …

He went over to where she stood looking out at the view of Manhattan. 'You might need help with this,' he said, lowering the zip on her dress, kissing the back of her neck. She leaned back into him, sighing.

He slid the dress down over her hips, then turned her round.

She stepped out of it. '*Not* the sexiest of undergarments,' she said, looking down at the flesh-toned stretchy whatever-it-was, reaching from her chest to halfway down her thighs. 'Give me five minutes.'

Ace smiled as she headed upstairs. He'd won the Golden Slam, he'd taken Eliza on a memorable date – their first proper one – and now they had the whole night ahead of them. No pressure, no training or work tomorrow, and Ace was wide awake. Tonight there would be no speedy descent into oblivion.

Quite some time later, she was practically purring as she snuggled into his chest.

'I love you so much,' he said softly.

She tried to mumble something, but failed as she fell fast asleep.

❀

They woke early, the rising sun winking at them from between the skyscrapers. The traffic was already humming down below, the intermittent sound of horns drifting upwards in the morning air.

Eliza smiled at him sleepily. Ace pulled her closer, and she moved her limbs until she was in a position where they could pick up where they'd left off the night before – a slow, dreamy version.

Later, Ace made them mugs of coffee and brought them back to bed. He sipped his espresso, appreciating the flavour. Everything in life tasted so good right now.

'Eliza,' he said, as she sat up, stretching her arms over her head. 'I'm sorry to bring it up, but it's playing on my mind.'

'Oh? What is?'

'Your … stalker.' She tensed. 'Is it online?' he asked.

She gripped her mug tightly with both hands. 'No. Deliveries in the mail; flowers to the office. I thought they were from you, but no. Instead of a romantic message there was a note asking why I was still alive.'

'Shit.' The coffee suddenly tasted bitter. 'That's sick.'

'Not as sick as stabbing Will's cat.' Her bottom lip began to wobble, and she turned her head away.

A sense of dread struck him dumb.

'Romeo's death wasn't an accident.' She turned to face him again. 'Also an email with a doctored photo of Rob's late wife, implying I was to blame for her death, and that there would be retribution – like, from beyond the grave. The message was, *The Dead are Not Dumb*.'

He repeated the words. 'What does that even mean?'

'And two dolls, in my mailbox at the flat, with fake blood on them, both dressed in mini versions of my clothes. With notes. One said the same, *The Dead are Not Dumb*. The other said, *He broke my heart … I will break you*.'

Ace's blood was running cold. He knew Merle protected him from all the crazy stuff, from fans' attempts to reach him, but he'd never experienced a death threat. The thought of anyone harming Eliza …

'No one's going to hurt you,' he said fiercely. '*No one*. Fuck – I can't believe this, and all because of me.'

She stared down at the sheets. 'There's a chance it may *not* be because of you. We've been assuming it is …'

'We?'

'Will's been with me all the way. And Rowan helped. He got me to think about whether it could be someone with a grudge, out for revenge.' She gave a humourless laugh. 'I've collected a few enemies along the way. We passed the list of names on to the private investigator–'

'There's a detective?'

'Organised by Cecil – Rose's COO. She's found out pretty much nothing.'

All this had been going on without him knowing. Ace's stomach was churning with a mixture of rage and fear. Dark thoughts were gathering, clamouring for attention.

'But, that first doll,' Eliza continued. 'It was a reference to Kit …'

Kit.

'… to how he died. The doll had a knife in its neck. Like … like Kit did.' She swallowed. 'And Amy – some people think she killed herself, because of Rob and me. Neither of those are anything to do with you. It's someone who knows how to mess with my head. Dad said maybe it's someone who's still obsessed with Kit, who blames me for his death.'

'Harry knows too?'

'I freaked when I found the first doll. He talked me down, got me all that security the next day. That day I saw you, when I'd just been mugged. Which may or may not be connected. Who knows?'

'What did the mugger look like?' Ace held his breath.

'Impossible to tell. They were wearing a mask and hoodie. But there's a CCTV image – they were small. A young teenager, or maybe a tall child, the PI said.'

He released the breath.

'You know what's just as awful as the death threats?' she said quietly. 'The feeling that I deserve this. Like, it's karma.'

'What?' He pulled himself up sharply. 'Come on, this isn't like you. You're a rational person.'

She continued as if he hadn't spoken. 'My half-brother, Stu, once said I leave a trail of dead bodies and broken hearts. I've never forgotten that.'

He stared at her. He still had so much to learn about this woman. 'Half brother? Who's that?'

'One of Dad's little surprises. He's dead. He was an alcoholic, got violent when he was drunk. Thumped Kit, once. He did try to sort himself out, but he failed. Our family basically washed our hands of him. So maybe I played a part in his death too.'

Ace took the mug from her hand, put it down and pulled her into his arms. 'Hey, you need to stop this. Like you said, someone's messing with your mind, giving you dark thoughts. Don't let them.' He stroked her hair, kissed her head. 'And I won't let anybody hurt you.'

Eliza pressed her fingers to her eyes, but tears leaked out. 'Kit *did* die because of me. I can't stop thinking about it.'

Ace couldn't help it. He'd been unable to stop thinking about that man, too. The words just tumbled on out again. 'You said his name in your sleep yesterday. Right before you asked me to touch you.'

She was wiping her eyes with the sheet. 'God, I'm losing it.'

'Eliza – did you love him?'

She carried on dabbing at her face, avoiding his eye.

'Please tell me, I'm trying to understand. Were you in love with Kit?'

She sniffed, and finally lowered the sheet. 'Yes.' She stared at her hands. 'I did love him. But I don't think I was *in* love with him. What we had didn't fit into any boxes. Not romantic love; not love for a friend. Not physical love. It was … a deep connection. I felt lost when he wasn't around; I still feel lost. We were soul mates.' She sighed, briefly closing her eyes, calmer now.

But he just couldn't let it rest. 'Not physical? So why were you moaning and saying his name? You were so turned on. And why did Will tell me it would be hard, competing with a dead guy?'

Her eyes flew to his. 'He said *what*?' She huffed a breath. 'Look, Will's being weird about it, I don't understand why. He wasn't like this when Kit was alive.' Her words held a mix of exasperation and hurt. 'Perhaps it's grief, I don't know. He needs to stop.'

When Ace didn't reply, she carried on. 'I think … maybe talking to you about Kit might help sort things out in my own mind. Would you be okay with that?'

He wasn't sure he was ready for this but … the guy was dead. 'Sure. Go ahead.'

'Turned on?' She gave him a watery smile. 'That's pretty embarrassing. I'll be honest, because you deserve that. Kit was … very seductive. *Everyone* fancied him. And yes, I was strongly attracted. And we almost hooked up, at uni, but … that was when I discovered I had an issue with intimacy. So it went nowhere.'

'And after – when you'd overcome your problem?'

'I was with Rob by then. And honestly? It was just as well. Kit was completely without boundaries–'

'What does that actually mean?'

She gave a low laugh. '*Mad, bad, and dangerous to know.* He did it all, with everyone.'

'Jesus.'

'I guess he was a free spirit–' She stopped, then said, as if to herself, 'But no, he wasn't. Because Fate wouldn't set him free.'

Ace frowned. 'How did Will cope?'

'He learned to live with it. Just before Kit was murdered, I came to understand why he behaved like that. Maybe he'd have changed his ways if he hadn't died, but he did. So …'

'And what did you find out, that helped you understand him?'

'Childhood trauma. His father was a violent man – he killed Kit's mum, when Kit was a boy. He only told me that the day before he died. And my …' She closed her eyes for a moment.

'And your mum too,' he said quietly, caressing her shoulder. 'I read Terri's article.'

She nodded. 'Yes. Kit's childhood messed him up; he was incapable of forming loving relationships, never let his … lovers close. He refused to even believe love was a thing.' She sighed. 'He said it was just a fancy word for desire, or the need to control. For him, sex was nothing to do with love.'

'I see.' Ace paused. 'And … what did you mean by Fate not setting him free?'

'Cruel cruel Fate.' Her eyes moved to the view out of the window. 'Remember what I told you about our last night at Oxford? Kit seemed to understand how time works – in a different way to how you and I perceive it. He got how time and Fate are connected, and he had this uncanny ability to sense the future. He somehow knew he was destined to die young. I was the only person he told.'

'Not Will?'

'No. I told Will, after. So there he was, living that wild life, taking things to the limit, believing – *knowing* – it would be over soon, all the while trying to make sense of existence, of death. And it all went into his brilliant writing …' She squeezed her eyes shut. 'He seemed so self-assured, so cocky.' When she opened them, the tears were back. 'But underneath he was confused … scared.' She lifted the sheet to her eyes again.

Ace had a strong sense of things unfinished, unresolved. 'So – what I'm getting is, he was the right guy, at the wrong time.'

'Oh.' She lowered the sheet, staring at him. 'I never thought of it like that.'

'Makes sense to me.'

She leaned her head on his shoulder and was quiet for a while. 'Thanks for listening. It's best we share these things, right? Get them out in the open.'

'Sorry I pushed you; it was just … that dream of yours–'

'But dreams are nonsense,' she said. 'People get mixed up in them, the brain's wires get crossed. It might have been an Ace-Kit mash-up, perhaps.' She managed a cheeky smile. 'Wow.'

Her expression turned serious again. 'Ace – look. Will was so wrong. You're not competing with a dead guy. You two are very different. Kit didn't give a toss about people; he was quite self-obsessed. He only cared about his work. And me, and Will. That was it. You care about everyone, you have one of the best hearts I've ever known. You're a bright light. Kit was mostly in a dark place.'

Ace thought about Rob, wondering how he'd coped with Eliza's relationship with Kit. The 'soul mate' who wasn't Rob.

'I liked Rob.'

'Oh, yes. Rob. I knew you would.'

'How did he get on with Kit?'

Eliza exhaled. 'Big problem. But then … Rob's very competitive. Kit used to laugh about it. But the only time things got seriously nasty was when Rob tried to tone down Kit's writing, to make it more commercial, less … inflammatory. I told Rob to back off, to leave Kit's words alone. He hated that; how I prioritised staying true to Kit's work over Rob's ratings-and-money targets. I think that, and Letitia, were what did for me and Rob.'

She looked at him, raising her eyebrows. 'How did you like Letitia?'

'All right.' He grinned. 'Not too hard on the eye.'

'Pft.'

'I'd say a blonde bombshell actress is very Rob. But he's still crazy about you, poor bloke. I guess she'll ease the pain.'

'He's not–'

'Yes, he is. Anyway,' he said, finally feeling himself return to an even keel, 'sorry for going on about Kit. Blame it on my enduring insecurity. No writerly genius here – all I can do is smack a ball.'

'Silly.' She gave him a little punch on the arm. 'You could have anyone you wanted, now. *Anyone*.'

'Only you. And as far as this stalker goes – sorry to mention that again, but I have a plan. Soon as we're back, I'll take you to the beach cottage. We'll only let the necessary people know we're there. You can work remotely, if you have to; I'll just chill, do the odd bit of training, move the foundation forward. And I can start my search for a place near London. How does that sound?'

'Like heaven. And I can help with Excalibur.'

'Great. I'll text Merle, make sure the cottage is empty. Sometimes she lends it to friends.' He picked up his phone, and his eyebrows shot up. 'Hey – a message from Lockie.'

Eliza leaned over, peering at the screen.

You did grate Art Im so proud. congrads bro

He smiled in delight. 'He was watching!'

She gave a small laugh. 'Spelling's not his forte, then.'

Ace's smile vanished and his expression darkened. 'And you'd be borderline illiterate if you'd been fucked over like he was. You really have no idea at all what goes on in the real world – do you?'

Her mouth dropped open as he threw back the covers, left the bed and headed for the bathroom without a backward glance.

Chapter 29

Eliza

Eliza stared at his back as he strode across the room, his striking tattoo sending a timely reminder to tread more carefully with this man. A man who was fiercely protective of those he cared for, and angered by society's neglect of the disadvantaged, the ignored, the unwanted. Who intended to do something about that, perhaps for more personal reasons than she'd realised.

Welcome to the world of decadence. Here she was, entrapping him in her penthouse-tower, like some wicked enchantress diverting him from his noble quest. Which included holding the rich and powerful to account. Like Harry. Like her.

Before his incarnation as Ace, he'd been Arthur, about whom she knew little. While Ace could now tick the main Eliza boxes – career goals, family, best friend, ex-boyfriend, soul mate – she could tick only two or three of his. His tennis goal (achieved), his strange, antagonistic foster mother, and his tennis pro. In his cobbled-together foster family, he'd made mention of a 'useless' father, an off-the-rails sister, and that brother who inspired such loyalty, even though he'd run off to the ends of the earth more than a year ago and had ignored Ace ever since.

She knew nothing of Ace's roots (and neither, it seemed, did he). He was still mostly a mystery to her.

As the hiss of the shower reached her from beyond the bathroom door, she mulled over that burst of anger. She sensed it wasn't only a reaction to her flippant comment about Lockie's typos, or even about Ace's resentment of her privileged upbringing. Maybe she shouldn't have been so honest about Kit. She'd thought it would clear the air after the awkward dream moment, but he still seemed to be brooding about it. Why?

She wondered whether to join him in the shower, then decided against it. Maybe he needed space, to think on the things they'd talked about. The stalker, the death threats. Kit.

She twisted the ring on her finger and smiled sadly. 'You're still causing trouble,' she whispered.

She put on her robe and went downstairs. Will was sitting on the sofa reading the *New York Times*. He closed it and patted the seat beside him. 'Sit. Tell me *everything*.'

She gave him the Met Gala goss – who was there, what they wore, who was even more beautiful in real life, and who was in fact a bit of a minger.

'I put Elon right on his space colonization plans.'

'You *didn't*.'

'Rob was there. And Letitia. They were at the tennis too. And … oh yes. So was Catriona. Rob saw her.'

'Really? Yikes.' He counted on his fingers: 'Two, three – possibly *four* from our list of suspects, within assassination distance! Sorry,' he said, as she frowned at him. 'So, how did the Rob-Ace meet-up pan out?'

She smiled. 'I think they liked each other. I knew they would. Ace's eyes nearly popped out when Letitia came over. God, she's sex on legs, isn't she? And she's starring in the new Marvel.' She paused. 'Will – I just remembered. She's been in London.'

'Really? That's … interesting.'

They stared at each other.

'You know who she reminds me of?' said Will.

'Barbie? Marilyn Munroe?'

'The woman who shot your dear papa. Your aunt Merry.'

Eliza's mother's sister, Meredith McCarey, had been Harry's

mistress for a while, way before Eliza was born. Many years later she'd been all over the media following her arrest for attempted murder. Eliza and Will had been at Oxford at the time.

'She *does* look like her!' Eliza said in surprise. 'Perhaps she is in fact another unexpected cousin.' As Will's eyes widened, she added, 'No – I'm joking. Aunt Merry never had children. I think. I guess it's a look. The blonde hair, the hourglass figure, the sa … *shay.*' She wiggled her hips. 'Anyway, how was your evening with Jonas, hm?' She flicked her eyebrows up and down at him.

'Oh he's *so* intense. I'll be glad to shake him off, to be honest.' Then he dialled down the drama. 'I should probably warn you, the *Time* piece is out on Friday, and obviously I won't be able to get at it, or even see it. Neither will Merle, which is only right and proper. But Jonas is a far-left Democrat and not a fan of our government. I'm going to take a guess Ace was encouraged to let rip at BoJo and Co, and that Jonas will focus on that part of the interview, rather than Ace's thoughts on racism and inequality and what have you.'

'Heck.'

'Oh!' He sat up straighter. 'And I Zoomed with Terri. *Amazing* response to Ace's column. They've been inundated with enquiries – some of them Names with a capital N. Even a royal – but she wouldn't tell me which one,' he said, as Eliza opened her mouth to ask. 'Companies wanting to get their logos on it, chuck money at it, have a seat at the table. *The Rack*'s set up a web page with a contact form. They're logging it all, ready for when Ace is back.'

Eliza sighed. 'Damn. No, I mean … it's good. It's just that he's taking me to Cornwall, and he really deserves some time off.'

'Cornwall? For how long?'

'A week.' She smiled. 'And then Ace is going to look for a place to buy near London.'

'Yep,' said Ace, appearing on the stairs. 'Going to find me my very own castle, Will.' He grinned. 'Fit for a king.'

Eliza was glad to see he'd loosened up again.

Will struck a hunched-over peasant pose. '*Well, I didn't vote for you.*'

Ace laughed. '*You don't vote for kings.*' He proceeded down the rest of the stairs and across the room, then kissed Eliza's hand with a flourish.

'*Well*,' said Will. '*How do you become king then?*'

'I can't remember the next bit. Something about the Lady of the Lake and Excalibur – *farcical aquatic ceremony*?'

'Oh, I get it, we're doing Monty Python again,' said Eliza. 'What a couple of dweebs you are.'

Will stood up. 'Shall we hit the breakfast buffet?'

'I thought we might take a walk in the park,' said Ace to Eliza. 'If we do the hats and sunglasses, we might not be recognised.'

'I'll leave you to it, then,' said Will. 'Insert appropriate don't-want-to-be-a-gooseberry quote here, because I'm all out of them.'

'Order something up,' said Eliza. 'Whatever you want.' She looked at Ace. 'Hot dogs for breakfast?'

'Why the fuck not?'

⚜

'Hey, sorry about earlier,' he said, as they entered the green space of Central Park. 'I over-reacted. Guess you touched a nerve.'

'No, it's fine. And I've probably been over-princessing; letting off steam, I suppose.' She slipped her hand into his. 'It's been so special, being here with you. I'll never forget a minute of it. I wish we didn't have to leave, but I'm really looking forward to Cornwall.'

'Merle says the cottage is empty. But …' he grimaced.

'But what?'

'She's acting weird again. Asked me not to go, practically *begged* me, but wouldn't say why. It drives me nuts when she's like this. She was muttering about fate again.' He put on a Merle voice. '*Can't fight it. Have to let things play out.*'

A sense of dread Eliza had been barely aware of suddenly tightened its grip.

'I think she's still worried you're not serious about me,' he went on. 'And maybe she thinks you'll scoff at our little shack, when you're used to super-yachts and mansions.' He tutted. 'I'm twenty-six, at the top of my game, about to launch my foundation, soon to be a home-owner, and *still* she treats me like I'm twelve.'

'Ace, were those her actual words? The part about letting things play out?'

He looked at her. 'Pretty much.'

Sometimes you have to go with the flow. Let things play out … It's down to fate.

'What's wrong?' he said. 'You look like you've seen a ghost.'

'Not seen – heard. In here.' She tapped her temple.

Kit's name hung in the air.

'We just need to get ourselves down there,' he said, after a pause. 'It's going to be magic.'

'I can't wait.' She tried to shake off the unease. 'You can show me your old haunts – where you grew up, went to school. I have so much to learn about you. Not in a nosey way, in a getting-to-know-you-better way.'

He put an arm round her. 'Unrelentingly boring, I'm afraid. Crappy education, good at hitting a ball. That's about it.'

'No, silly, you're so much more.' She turned to look at him. 'You know … I opened up to you, about Kit. It was hard, but I think it helped. If there's anything you want to share with me …'

He didn't respond. His eyes were hidden behind his wrap-around sunglasses.

'Because I was thinking, after you huffed at me – I don't know much about the other you, the one before you starting winning absolutely everything.'

Still he didn't respond.

'You said before, about things that happened in your family … bad things?'

'This way?' he said, looking at a sign.

'Sure.' They took the path towards the lake. 'Lockie, for example. He's obviously special to you. You said you nearly lost him. Is it okay if I ask what happened there?'

Ace glanced at her, then ahead again. 'It's not my story to share. I'd rather not.'

'But he's thousands of miles away. And I won't repeat it, obviously.'

'Maybe he'll come home. Though …' He sighed. 'Perhaps he's better off where he is, if he's made a fresh start.'

'He was … abused?'

Ace was silent.

'Okay. Look, I do have some understanding of abuse. An uncle sexually harassed me as a teen, and my father treated women so badly it put me off marriage for life. I wouldn't let men physically close for a long time. I had panic attacks when Rob … well. You get the picture.'

He was staring at her in surprise.

'So there we go,' she said. 'I don't think we should keep quiet about these things, cover them up. We shouldn't be ashamed – it's not *our* fault. If we say nothing, the perpetrators get away with it, right? If we get it out in the open, it's healthier.'

'So that's what was behind your … intimacy issues?'

'Let's not mince words. I was afraid of sex because I'd been assaulted, and because my dad used women badly.'

'I see. I'm so sorry. Thanks for telling me.' He gave her a squeeze. 'It's something I want Excalibur to get involved with. Talking about abuse, and mental health. Especially for young people – because of Lockie. I like what you just said, about not being ashamed. Will you be part of it? Excalibur?'

She smiled. 'Of course. I was hoping you'd find me a place at your table.'

'I'm surprised, though, about you and Harry. You seem pretty close.'

'Oh, we are. Because I had it out with him, told him what his behaviour had done to me. So, rather than snapping at me when I remark on your brother's crappy spelling, why don't you tell me what happened, so I can understand you better?'

'Stop,' he said, halting. He looked around him. 'We need a hot dog.'

Her mouth dropped open. 'Well – that wasn't the answer I was expecting!'

'I want to answer properly, but I need a hot dog.'

'Right there.' Eliza pointed to a cart with a green-and-white-striped awning, visible through the trees. They bought one each, Ace making Eliza swear not to tell Merle, even though he was on a break.

Eliza eyed the pink sausage topped with swirls of mustard and dollops of onion relish, wrapped in a white roll, all sitting in a stripy serviette. 'Jesus, it looks absolutely disgusting.' She bit into it. 'Holy mother of god! That's divine.'

They found a secluded bench. Ace was still wary of being recognised, but the people passing them – joggers, skaters; mums, dads and nannies pushing buggies while speaking on their phones – didn't give them a second glance.

'Can you take these off?' Without waiting for a reply, Eliza reached up and removed his sunglasses. 'I want to see your eyes.'

'Okay. Look,' he said. 'I get what you're saying, but I find it really hard to talk about. Because … I feel guilty. So does Merle. It's like we dropped the ball, with Lockie. We didn't spot how hard things had got for him. The fencing – I was starting to do well, we were travelling a lot. And all the while, he was really vulnerable. Unprotected.'

He rested his hot dog in his lap and stared at it.

She waited.

'He slit his wrists. I found him in the bath.'

Eliza gasped. 'Oh no … Oh god, Ace, I'm so sorry.' She couldn't stop the unbearable memory his words unleashed. The blood; his dying eyes.

'It wasn't a cry for help,' he said, 'it was a full-on suicide attempt. He was in a terrible place. Felt he couldn't talk to anyone, that no one would understand. He was full of shame–'

With an effort, she pushed the image of Kit aside. 'He was abused?'

Ace nodded. 'I found out later, when he could finally bring himself to talk about it. Social Services got involved; Merle and Hector were hauled over the coals.'

'You mean, this was *after* he came to Merle for fostering?'

'Yes. They suggested moving him to a different family, but he wanted to stay, because of me.' He closed his eyes, blew out a long breath, opened them again. They were glassy with tears. 'I swore, Eliza, when I found him in the bath, I'd never let him down again …' He swallowed.

She put an arm round him. 'It's okay, only carry on if you want to.'

His gaze fixed on a young dad with a little boy on his shoulders. He said nothing for a while. Eliza was quiet.

'It was round about then he discovered surfing,' he said, as the father and son disappeared around a corner. 'Merle bought him a board when he came out of hospital, and he was brilliant at it. Started to win all the competitions; it really boosted his self-confidence. He seemed pretty much okay, then, except he constantly wagged school to go to the beach. Hence the terrible spelling.' He gave her a small smile. 'But you should see him ride a big wave. It's poetry in motion.'

'How long ago was all this?'

'Which part?'

'The abuse, the suicide attempt?'

'If you include neglect, it'd been going on forever. His crazy, drug-addicted mum, then in and out of care. He was fourteen when he slit his wrists. After that … a few episodes, but I helped him through them, and Merle was on the lookout too. By the time we left school he was mostly okay, hanging out with his surfing mates, taking part in competitions. And …' He paused and shook his head, fighting a smile. 'He was a lifesaver at the local surf beach, but he had to stop that. My god.'

'Okay – why?'

'All the girls. They kept pretending they were drowning so he'd save them. He spent a whole summer rescuing girls who swam too far out on purpose.'

'That's hilarious.'

'Then later he just upped and left.'

'And you lost touch – why?'

'I think he just wanted to disappear, which is why I've been so worried. He's never bothered much with phones – texting, social media … he can't write properly, which doesn't help. I nagged him for years to at least get his reading and writing sorted, but he didn't give a toss. I guess you don't need it so much for the stuff he's into.'

He smiled, relaxing at last, and picked up his hot dog. 'Maybe he'll come home and you'll meet him. He's not as flaky as I made him sound. He's a beautiful, sensitive soul; extremely shy, but he can be so funny. And he's got this great affinity with nature. Loves the ocean; out in it in all weathers. Lockie's just … different, on another planet half the time.'

He opened his mouth wide and sunk his teeth into his sausage. 'Shit. It's gone cold. I'm going to get another one.' He stood up.

'And your foster sister?' said Eliza, as they set off again. 'Is she important in your life?'

'Nope,' he said, speeding up a little, putting his sunglasses back on. 'If Lockie was Merle's failure, Faye was her full-on catastrophe. Absolute nightmare. The day she fucked off from our house with her weirdo friends was the day we all cheered.'

'Yikes.'

'Okay, are we done with our *My Private Hell* stories? Can we just enjoy our last morning in New York now?'

'That sounds like a good plan,' she said. 'And thanks, I know that was hard, and I'm so sorry about your brother. Must've been really traumatic, finding him. I guess … it's a bit like me finding Kit, except … I wasn't in time to save him.'

'It's odd,' said Ace, 'but I feel like the two are connected. Why would I feel that?'

'Because neither of us can forget? Because we feel guilty?'

Chapter 30

Eliza

Eliza cast a final glance behind her as she and Will waited for the private elevator.

If I could save time in a bottle.

Ace walking towards her in the Champagne Bar, that gorgeous smile on his face; their stolen hour the night before the final. The match – on the edge of her seat, watching her golden boy smash his way into sporting history. Ace waving at her from the podium as tears streamed down her face.

Partying on the rooftop against the backdrop of Manhattan by night; on Ace's arm at the Met Gala. Eating hot dogs in Central Park, Ace finally opening up about his beloved foster brother.

It had been a magical time, but now they were heading home. Merle was insisting Ace should spend a week in London to keep the media (and all those sponsors) happy after his historic win. Interviews, chat shows, photoshoots … Ace was the man of the moment. He'd even been offered pole position on Graham Norton's red couch.

Eliza was still nervous about going back to her flat, so instead would stay at Richmond.

The days passed quietly, and Eliza spent the week working out a plan for Excalibur. Pippa had confirmed availability of an office suite with desk space for six staff, plus a meeting room. (The table was rectangular, so Eliza asked her to order a round one, which felt more appropriate.)

She'd worked through the list of interested parties, and categories were becoming clear. There were companies and charities wanting to be associated with Excalibur because they shared similar goals. Eliza had made a spread sheet and highlighted them in green. Then she'd emailed Cecil about how they might do an audit on those companies, to make sure they cleared Excalibur's high fences. If they did, perhaps they could get the Excalibur tick as an endorsement on their products or services. And the charities could apply to Excalibur for funding.

Then there were those Names who wanted a seat at the table. Sportsmen and women, celebrities, that Royal – exciting! She'd tasked Pippa with background research, to make sure they were genuine in their interest.

Many were clearly bandwagoning. '*Really?*' Eliza said out loud, reading the empty corporate nonsense from a company known for its pathetic wages and terrible work practices. 'I think not.'

There was a rap on her study door, and Harry appeared. 'Got a minute?' In his hand were several sheets of printed paper.

As he sat down on the sofa, his eyes went to her computer screen. 'So you're working for Ace, now?' His tone was irritated.

She gave a nervous laugh. 'Oh, come on, Dad. I'm actually meant to be on holiday, remember? And don't tell me I haven't earned a couple of weeks off.'

'Hm. Fair enough. Be on holiday, then. Do shopping and a show with Clare, or something.'

Eliza's eyes moved to her screen. 'I'm fascinated with how shopping is changing. I honestly think consumerism might be on the wane.'

Harry rolled his eyes a little.

'How's things with Rose Air?' she asked, because she thought she ought to.

'Touch and go.' He crossed one leg over the other and rested his arms along the back of the sofa. Harry really knew how to own a space. 'I think we'll make it through – travel to the US is picking up again. And more to the point, the government was open to a tad more tapping.'

He looked her in the eye. 'Speaking of our friends across the pond …' He passed over the sheets of paper, giving them a displeased flap. 'Friday's *Time* magazine.'

Eliza's heart jumped into her mouth. 'But it's Thursday! *And* they're half a day behind! How …?' But of *course* Harry would know about it. And would somehow be able to access the article which she, Ace, Merle and Will hadn't been allowed to see.

'It's an unfettered attack on the British government. Chrissake, Eliza. What's Ace doing?'

Eliza's heart was thumping. Bracing herself, she began to read.

BRIT KING WINS PLACE IN TENNIS HISTORY – AND AMERICA'S HEART

So far, so good.

The first paragraphs were all about Ace's amazing Golden Slam achievement. A bit about his background … it looked like Jonas had cribbed from Will's *Rack* interview. Photos of Ace on the court, and with Eliza. Arm in arm on the rooftop terrace, arriving at the Met Gala; kissing after his win at the Open. Eliza, 'CEO of media conglomerate Rose Corp, and daughter of its billionaire chairman, Harry Rose', was very much a part of this story.

She skim-read until she reached the part that had obviously riled Harry. *Oh god.* It was only what others had been saying for quite some time, but … She glanced up at Harry, who raised his eyebrows, waiting.

It was littered with damning words – *shambolic*; *incompetent*; *corrupt; cronyism; elitism* … Eliza winced at the references to 'wealthy Tory backers' and 'old-boy networks'. And especially at the 'time for a change' conclusion.

She put the article down. 'Will said Ace was pretty much coerced into saying those things. I'm afraid he's not very media savvy.' The words sounded lame, and implied Eliza had known what to expect in the piece. 'The journalist was a far-left Democrat who wheedled his way in – chatted up Will in the Plaza bar and then got himself invited to our after-match party. He probably threw all those statements at Ace and waited for a nod.'

Harry said nothing.

'I know. Not an excuse. We should've known better.'

'I hear you're planning on Ace's organisation parking itself in the Rose building?'

Eliza swallowed. 'Yes, that's the plan.'

Harry shook his head. 'No. You and Ace? I'm fine with that. But Rose and Excalibur – I can't take the risk. And any assistance you give him–' his eyes returned to her computer, '– not in company time, not using Rose resources or staff, *particularly* not Cecil. Not as a Rose employee yourself. Only as Ace's interested girlfriend, and preferably, not even that.'

'But–'

Harry stood up. 'I've said my piece. I'm sorry, Lizzie. I was fine when it was all about racism and being green and what have you. I'm absolutely *not* fine with it being all about politics. I know it's hard to do one without the other but ...' He sighed. 'It's basic stuff. Charities can lobby, of course, but they need to work *with* the government, not against it.'

He skewered her with his blue-eyed gaze. 'Sort him out.'

Eliza's temper finally found its voice. 'Dad – for heaven's sake!' she said to his departing back. 'What does it matter? Ace is only echoing what so many others are saying?'

Harry stopped. 'Well, let's see, shall we?' He turned to face her. 'Rose Air. Had it been *you* talking one-on-one to the government minister about a bail-out, I'm guessing the outcome might have been different.'

'But ... it was all about keeping jobs, the economic recovery–'

'Just park your bleeding heart and engage your brain instead,' he snapped.

Eliza's jaw dropped open.

'It was all about money. It always is. That, and power – which we, as a media corporation, help endow and maintain. You should know that by now. I'll see you at lunch.'

❀

That evening, Will invited Eliza round before she disappeared off to Cornwall. The setting sun was stretching shadows across the garden as he showed her Romeo's freshly dug grave, on which sat a pot of catnip and a fluffy mouse. There was a wonky cross made from two lashed-together pieces of wood, with Romeo's name messily scratched into it.

Will's pitiful DIY skills made Eliza tear up. She hugged him tight. 'It's lovely. Epitaph?'

'I thought: *Here lies Romeo – a harmless, necessary cat.*'

'Aw, that's perfect. Shakespeare?'

'Mostly.'

Later, as they sat in the kitchen eating ordered-in sushi, Eliza showed Will the *Time* piece.

'Ugh, Jonas,' he said, tucking his hair behind his ears and peering at the reworded version of his own interview. He winced as his eyes scanned the article. 'Sneaky little bastard. The only new stuff here is the politicking. He's spun Ace's words into a web of anti-government rhetoric.'

'I know. Dad isn't best pleased. Says Excalibur can't use Rose staff or facilities. Political conflict of interest. What do you think?'

Will sat back as he considered his answer. 'Hm. I think you should take a stand. Your father isn't used to being challenged. Dear Harry has two business modus operandi: charm, and terror. Normally the charm does the job; it's only afterwards people realise they've been played. He's a clever bloke. The only person I've seen triumph over the tyrant version is Terri – she dares take him on because she knows he respects her.'

'True,' said Eliza. 'She's so principled.' *Usually.*

'Well, he respects you too. You don't want to have to choose between Ace and your father, so tell him, you want Rose to embrace social responsibility. It's a core value for you, and you'll be supporting Ace in his venture. Just reassure Harry that Ace'll dial down the political stuff. Those were mostly Jonas's words, not Ace's. And then keep Ace in line.'

'I can try.'

'He's putty in your fair hands. Now, there's something I want to show you, before you disappear off to the land of tin mines and clotted cream.'

'Oh?'

Will cleared away their plates, then brought over a leather-bound notebook that had been sitting on the worktop. 'I found this in Kit's desk. It's full of ideas for his writing; observations. Not really a journal, more a collection of thoughts. The usual Marley mash-up of genius and nonsensical rambling.'

He passed it over, and Eliza swallowed as she opened it and saw his familiar handwriting – overlarge lettering sprawled across the pages, ignoring the ruled lines. Almost indecipherable, as if his writing couldn't keep up with his thoughts.

'Look – first notes for *Dark Soul.*' Will took the notebook and flicked forward. 'Stream-of-consciousness stuff in his appalling hand, but I've managed to translate from Kit to English.'

He read out: '*Love and Fate battle for a soul. Can love triumph over predestination? Change destiny's course?*'

'Good premise.'

Will pulled a face. 'Predestination – it's a bit biblical, considering he was an atheist.'

'And that he didn't believe in love,' said Eliza.

'He was thinking deep on it all. See here; this is interesting. *If nature abhors a vacuum, Fate loathes a loose end. Soul's ultimate fate pre-determined but returns again and again in "time" (time loops). Universe seeks order from chaos; attempts equilibrium. Soul is influenced by others encountered in that loop. By love? So each loop = different outcome. An end point? Or infinite number of loops?*'

Eliza closed her eyes as she attempted to follow.

'*Which more powerful, Fate or Love? What if soul strong/resilient enough (because person truly loves/is loved) to defy Fate and Death and return to complete its destiny? Each loop in time discrete i.e. don't*'

278 ⁕ Olivia Hayfield

overlap – Soul not aware of past/future loops. Yet – some cognisance – ?? Sense of knowing/recognition.'

Eliza opened her eyes. 'Holy shit.'

'Okay, it's getting away from me now. It's classic opaque Marley.'

'No, it's not. Carry on.' Eliza held her breath, aware of some profound truth hovering just beyond her grasp.

'*What if cataclysmic personal event e.g. untimely death could shatter a soul?*' He glanced up, and she knew he was picturing Kit, the knife in his neck. '*Could a shard lodge in another who was connected (either now or in past) so both could continue to exist in same time loop? While being unaware of fact?*'

Eliza released the breath. This was some out-there thinking.

'I need another beer,' said Will, 'we're veering towards possession. Want one?'

Eliza shook her head and beckoned for Will to pass her the diary. As he went over to the fridge, she reread those words, frowning in concentration.

'It's not *Dark Soul*,' she said, biting her lip. 'This is beyond what he explored in that. It's him; it's Kit. He somehow knows he's meant to die soon. Fate has decreed it; it's predestined. But he's not ready to. It'll be *untimely*, because he's only just accepted love is real, that it exists …'

Will sat down again, took a swig of his beer. '*This*,' he said, taking the journal and flipping to the next page. '*Love arrives in its own time, on its own terms. It will do to us whatever it wants, and there's nothing we can do to stop it.*'

He met her eye, and they were silent for a moment.

'Oh Will. Oh no.' She squeezed her eyes shut against a sudden rush of tears. Kit had finally opened his mind, his heart, his soul to love, only for Fate to immediately snuff him out.

Will sighed. 'Time, eh? Like he always said.'

Eliza nodded, pressing the palms of her hands to her eyes. 'He was wondering … wondering if –' Her voice failed her; she cleared her throat, '– if, in accepting love's power, he might triumph over Fate and live on. Or if Fate won and his soul was taken, if a piece of it could somehow remain here until … I guess until something was resolved?' She lowered her hands. 'And maybe … maybe he was right.'

'And you think this because?' Will said quietly.

'Because I keep sensing his presence.'

And because I wished it.

'Somehow, he's not gone,' she said. 'Something of him's still here.'

Will blew out a breath, then smiled. 'Well, let's face it, Kit was never going to go quietly, or disappear completely.' His expression grew serious. 'But just for a little while, maybe. I hope he can move on. We want him to be at peace – don't we?' He slid the journal across the table. 'Here, you keep it.'

She went to say no, he should have it, but he carried on. 'I think, if he'd known how to love, if he'd *let* himself love …' He met her eye. 'He'd have given it to you.'

'And to you. Love isn't exclusive.' She went to close the journal, then stopped. 'Will – the date.' She pointed to the top of the page. 'He wrote that the night before he died.'

Now she understood those words Will had said to Ace.

Chapter 31

Eliza arranged to meet Ace at her apartment so she could pack what she needed to take to Cornwall. As she walked through the marina, the earthy scent of autumn blew in on the breeze, bringing with it the melancholy Eliza always felt at the close of summer.

She thought back to July, to the Wimbledon final. To when everyone had fallen in love with Ace; the lift he'd given Britain after their hellish winter and spring. Who'd have thought, as she watched that winsome stranger lift the silver trophy high, that two months later (*only two months?*) she'd be heading off on holiday with him, to a hidden cottage on a beach. A burst of anticipation shooed away the melancholy.

At first glance there was nothing sinister in her letterbox. But as she leafed through the mail, she recognized the writing on a plain white envelope. 'Nope,' she said, ripping it into pieces without reading.

The PI had found out nothing useful from the others; one single sheet of paper was unlikely to add to the non-existent clues. And she wasn't going to sacrifice her good mood for another death threat.

Her phone beeped: Ace.

Just parked, 1hr so hope you're good to go XX

'Yep,' she said out loud, picturing the wide blue ocean, golden beaches, a pretty cottage – and Ace's arms. 'I most certainly am.'

After yesterday's lecture from Harry, that upsetting either-or ultimatum, her father had carried on as if he hadn't just blown apart her vision of helping to improve people's lives, as well as producing great things for them to read and watch. Harry assumed she'd do as he asked and put Rose first, as she'd always done. That she'd bring Ace to heel, tell him to find somewhere else for his offices, someone else to help him set things up.

But Will was right – she should push back. And she had everything she needed on her laptop, so they could plan while they were away.

Okay, it may have been cheeky asking Cecil for help. She should have made it a casual verbal request for advice, rather than a work email. Clearly Cecil had grassed her up to Harry immediately. *Traitor.* But he was only doing his job, what he thought best for Rose, as was to be expected. And that was what Harry expected of her, too.

She was going to have to sort out her balancing act.

Ace arrived and swept her up in a fierce hug. 'Nearly three whole days without you. I didn't like that.'

'Me neither.'

He kissed her, and when it seemed he wouldn't be stopping any time soon, she pulled away.

His eyes flicked towards the bedroom, then met hers again.

'Can we go?' she said. 'I honestly don't want to stay in London a minute longer.'

He gently touched her cheek. 'Are you okay? No more …'

'A note. I ripped it up; didn't read it.'

'Shit. Okay, fetch your stuff. And much respect for not letting that get to you.'

'I wouldn't say that.' She smiled. 'But you're here now.'

❀

Eliza felt herself unwind as London's concrete and clamour gave way to the leafy green spaces of Surrey, then Hampshire, then Wiltshire. Ace had rented a Range Rover, considering the Lotus too conspicuous, and as they made their way west Eliza dozed, waking up as they crossed the flat expanse of Salisbury Plain.

'Oh – look!' She sat up properly. 'Stonehenge! I've never seen that before.'

'Seriously?' Ace glanced over at her. 'We could stop? But … damn. I still forget.'

'Shame.' Eliza gazed out at the ancient stones silhouetted on the horizon. 'The only times I've been properly west were when I went to Wales, to stay with Dad's first wife, Katie. I've never been to Devon or Cornwall.'

'That's disgraceful.'

'That's Dad. Prefers the Med and his yacht and his Caribbean mansion.'

Ace smiled. 'You're going to love Cornwall. It's like another country; you'll get that straight away. It just feels different – the light, the ocean, the moors, the folklore. It has its very own fairies and dragons, and will o' the wisps and giants and–'

'King Arthur.'

'Of course. The cottage isn't far from Tintagel.'

'But Arthur never actually lived at Tintagel?' said Eliza. 'I saw a documentary about it.'

Ace tutted. 'Just because some London archaeology professor hasn't found a goblet with *Arthur Rex Lived Here* inscribed on it, doesn't mean he didn't.'

Eliza snorted. '*Rex Arthur vixit hic.*'

'No need to show off.'

'Arthur was conceived at Tintagel though, right?' she said.

'According to the legend, yes. There's evidence of a castle dating from at least the fifth century, maybe belonging to a leader who fought the Anglo-Saxons.'

'Ace – you *do* know your history!'

'I'm not a total ignoramus. And I know my Cornwall.'

'Wasn't his mum duped into sleeping with Arthur's father at Tintagel? We studied *Le Morte d'Arthur* at Oxford.'

'Uther Pendragon. He was lusting after Igraine – *desperate* for her. Merlin cast a spell that made Uther look like her husband, the Duke of Cornwall–'

'I remember. Igraine thought the Duke had returned for a night of passion before resuming some tribal spat. The deal was, if there was a child, Merlin would take it and raise it.' Eliza paused. 'You'd think she'd have known he wasn't her husband, even if he had a lookalike body. I mean, I'm pretty sure I'd know if it was some other guy having his way.'

'Early date rape drugs, maybe. But she went on to marry Uther, so it can't have been too awful.'

Eliza sighed. 'Don't you just *love* the Arthurian myth? The Lady of the Lake, Excalibur, the cool knights; Lancelot rescuing damsels in distress, all swooning in his arms as he snatched them from the jaws of death … '

'It's sad,' he said, 'the way it all vanished after Arthur's death … all the chivalry, the magic …'

'Why did it?'

'Britain was properly getting into Christianity. The old ways were disappearing, the ancient gods and goddesses, slipping between this world and the other one – the magical one …'

'Avalon. Where the Lady of the Lake took Arthur when he died. Where he rests until Britain needs him again.' Eliza looked over at Ace and smiled. 'Now would be good.'

'True. And women were powerful, before the Church put the boot in. You'd have fitted right in. Enchantresses on misty lakes … Okay, I'm in danger of slipping into Monty Python again.'

'Please don't.'

'Afterwards, it was all a bit solemn and worthy. The knights became obsessed with grails and all the other holy things. Merlin, those enchantresses – they were fading away, slipping back to their world. Their time was done.'

Eliza stretched in her passenger seat. They passed a sign, *Welcome to Somerset.*

'There's a pub near here where Merle and me usually stop for food. Should we give it a try, just hope people will give us space?'

'I can't take that risk.'

Ace's face fell. 'Shall I just say it? *Fuck phones.*'

'Too right. What are we doing about food, if we can't eat out?'

'Merle's on it. She's stocked us up with enough to last the week. Nobody needs to find out we're there.'

'But … we'll be walking on the beach?' said Eliza.

'It's not actually on the beach, but it's not far – a ten-minute walk down the cliffs.'

'Cliffs? So it's not actually a beach shack?'

He smiled mysteriously. 'Wait and see.'

A little further on, he pointed out the distant, shadowy form of Glastonbury Tor. 'Welcome to the West,' he said. 'King Arthur Country.'

Chapter 32

Two hours later they were still on this interminable A-road, passing through flat countryside with not a glimpse of the much-hyped ocean to be seen.

Eliza fidgeted in her seat. 'Who knew West was so distant? New York was quicker.'

'Not quite – but not too far now.'

She smiled over at him. 'Sorry. I sounded like Dad there. Stop me if that ever happens again.' They passed a road sign. '*St Columb. St Dennis*. Why so many saints?'

'Many saintly Cornish people. Many magical places they left behind. Our local beach is named after St Constantine. There's a holy well – if you drink the water from it during a drought, it brings rain. So it hasn't had a lot of use, but it could be handy in times to come.'

'Cornwall needs a Saint Ace. You deserve that.' She peered upwards, out of the window. 'The sky does seem bigger here.'

'And the sea's bluer, the horizon's wider.' He took a deep, contented breath. 'Home. Not always a happy place, but me and Lockie had this to escape to ... *Newquay*,' he read out as they circled a roundabout. 'Lockie's stomping ground. It's where they hold the major surfing championships.'

At last they reached the turn-off to the coast.

She read out, '*St Eval. St Ervan. St Merryn*. Oh, what? *Lancelot's Mini-golf*?' Excitement was mounting. This really did feel like entering a land of saints, knights, and wizards.

'See how the sky's changed again?' said Ace. 'Even bigger and bluer? That's how you know you're near the coast. The sky tells you.'

The winding road was now hemmed in by tall hedgerows, beyond which were pretty woodland copses.

'Are there fairies in there?'

'Of course.'

The road narrowed still further, until there was room for only one car. They pulled over to let a van pass. *Galahad Electrical*, it said on the side.

'Um – Ace? Where on earth are we? Where's the sea?'

'A little patience, please, Princess.'

'Queen, you said. Oooh!'

They had crested a hill, and there it was, the glittering, wide expanse of the Atlantic Ocean, stretching away to the hazy horizon. Over to their left was a bay edged with a broad crescent of golden sand.

'That's Constantine Bay,' said Ace. 'It's where we learned to surf.'

Out to sea, breakers were lining up in rows.

'It's beautiful!'

'And this is Trevose Head.'

They were driving out to a promontory. Down below, the deep-blue water was patched with pools of turquoise, and white surf foamed around jagged rocks.

'And now we leave the world behind,' he said, halting at a gate across the road. He leapt out to open it.

'You know, I *can* open gates,' she said, as he got back into the car.

'Sure about that?' He drove through. 'Okay, you can shut it.'

Eliza climbed out, stretched, and was hit by a burst of … she breathed in deeply. Pure, blessed, glorious freedom. The quiet, the solitude, the cool, fresh sea air with its whiff of salt, blowing her hair across her face. She stood by the gate, letting it all wash over her, feeling it sweep away her worries, the last vestiges of city noise and bustle; thoughts of stalkers and haters, pandemics and failing airlines.

'Hey,' called Ace. 'You have to lift the–'

'I know! Just let me have this moment!'

Thankfully, the gate wasn't complicated. A sign attached to it read *Private Property: No Access.*

A short while later they were pulling up outside a whitewashed stone cottage with a slate roof, its front door and window frames painted periwinkle blue. Ace's grin, which had spread across his face as he watched her shut the gate, only got wider.

Eliza's mouth had dropped open. 'You are *kidding* me.'

Just beyond the cottage was a lighthouse, glowing a soft, peachy white in the evening sun.

'Welcome to the lighthouse keeper's cottage.'

Eliza stared, shaking her head. 'It's *gorgeous*! And that is not a shack.'

'It used to be – it was practically derelict when Hector and Merle bought it. This was Hector's other escape from the madness of our family – he'd come up here at weekends, doing it up. He's a carpenter – pretty handy.'

Ace drove around the side of the cottage. 'The coastal footpath skirts us, but the gate puts most people off coming down here to nosey at the lighthouse. I'll park out of sight.'

Ace let them in the front door, which led into a living room lit by that bright, heavenly light that filled the sky here. It was simple, painted white; there was a sea-blue velvety sofa and matching armchair, a wood-burning stove with a pile of logs next to it. A small bookcase with board games stacked on top; lighthouse ornaments, pretty watercolour seascapes on the walls.

They went through to the first bedroom. 'This is our room – mine and Lockie's. Last time I was here it was a lot messier than this.'

On one wall was a poster advertising a local surfing competition. A surfer was barrelling through an enormous turquoise wave.

'Wow. The waves get that big here?'

'That's Lockie, riding the wave that won him the competition the year before,' said Ace, sticking up a corner that had come loose.

She peered closer at the figure slicing across the wall of water, his arms outstretched, long hair flying. His face and body, dwarfed by the wave, were in silhouette.

Ace opened the wardrobe; it was full of junk. He picked up something off the floor – a silver trophy with a figure of a surfer on it.

'Merle's just chucked all our stuff in here. That's sad. She could've put these on display.' He rubbed it carefully with his sleeve and sat it on the windowsill.

'You really miss him, don't you?' said Eliza, touching his arm.

'Until I met you, he was the only person I'd ever properly loved.'

Last on the tour was the neat, bright kitchen. On the table was a vase of sunflowers, a bottle of champagne, and a box of chocolates. A folded note with Ace's name on it was propped up against the champagne.

He picked it up and smiled as he read the words. Then the smile faded to a frown, and finally a head shake.

'Merle?'

'About the food, mainly'

'Can I see?'

He hesitated, then handed it to her.

> *There should be enough food & drink. Enjoy, and try not to lapse too far from your regime! Relax, be happy, let Cornwall work its magic.*
> *Make the best of this precious time. If you need me (you probably will) I can be there in a flash.*
> *Love and light, M x*
> *PS First aid kit in bathroom cupboard*

'Nice, but slightly odd,' said Eliza.

'In a nutshell,' replied Ace. 'Especially the nut part.'

❀

'I'll cook,' said Ace, later, as they sat on a wooden bench in the lee of the cottage, sipping the champagne. The setting sun washed the lighthouse with soft pink.

'Sounds good. What are we having? Pasties?'

Ace rolled his eyes. 'Pasties are for lunch, not dinner. Fish and salad?'

'Lovely. How old is the lighthouse?'

'Eighteen forty-something. It's been unmanned for a long time. Everything's automated. Would you believe, it's actually controlled from a place in Essex?'

'That's kind of sad.' She smiled. 'Hey, imagine being a lighthouse keeper. What a cool job. You could write books and paint and have a cat.' She pictured it, and it seemed like heaven.

'This is still an important lighthouse. There are lots of sea mists in these parts.'

'Of course there are. What's in there?' She pointed to a squat, square building between the cottage and the lighthouse.

'It's an old storeroom. It was a sleepout for a while – Hector put bunk beds in there for us while the renovations were going on. Now it's full of outdoor furniture and surfboards.'

✦

That night, as they lay in bed, beams from the tower swept across the sky above the cottage, lighting up the bedroom every seven seconds (Eliza counted).

'I always liked watching the light,' said Ace. 'But I'll shut the curtains in a minute. They're blackout ones.'

Eliza looked up at his face, lit by a flash. 'Thank you for bringing me here. It's absolutely perfect. What shall we do tomorrow?'

'How about nothing?' said Ace, before pulling her close.

Chapter 33

Eliza woke as the sun was rising, filling the little bedroom with pale dawn light. They hadn't got round to drawing the curtains. Silence embraced the cottage, pierced only by a seagull's mournful cry.

Ace was still deep in the land of sleep. He deserved to stay there a while longer.

As she slid out of bed, she remembered … no ensuite! When was the last time she'd had to traverse another room to reach a bathroom? She laughed to herself. She was Marie Antoinette in her shepherdess phase. The simple life was certainly appealing, when there was a view like that. And she didn't only mean the one out of the window. She gazed at Ace, smiling with affection, then set off on her journey to the loo.

After washing her hands, Eliza opened the bathroom window to freshen up the room. As she latched it, she looked through the gap at the lighthouse, growing brighter as the sun rose higher. It was going to be a beautiful day.

Cool morning air trickled in, bringing with it a distinctive smell.

She froze. Cigarette smoke. *French* cigarette smoke.

The back of her neck prickled.

No. She shook her head at her reflection in the mirror, picking up her hairbrush. It was just her mind, up to its old tricks.

She smelt it again, and unlatched the window, poking her head outside. For a fleeting moment she thought she glimpsed a figure reflected in the storeroom window. The reflection of someone with long, messy blond hair.

No. She'd imagined it. *Surely* she'd imagined it.

As quietly as she could, her heart thumping, Eliza made her way to the kitchen. She slipped the back door key into the lock and turned it, then stepped outside and crept along the side of the house, peering round the corner towards the storeroom.

There was no one around; the crisp sea air carried no smoky smell. Everywhere was very much deserted.

Returning to the kitchen, she brooded as she filled the kettle. 'You can't be here, Kit,' she muttered. 'Not this week.'

She made two mugs of coffee and took them through to the bedroom – Ace was still dead to the world. Too restless to get back into bed, Eliza slipped on jeans and a sweatshirt, and on a whim grabbed her bikini and a towel. *I've never even been in the English sea!* Then, just in case, she added a baseball cap, pulling it down hard over her curls.

Ace stirred as she did up her trainers.

'Sorry – didn't mean to wake you,' she whispered. 'Go back to sleep.' His eyes remained closed.

She went through to the living room, where she hunted for a pen and paper. The sensible, logical part of her brain was telling her to take a nice, pre-breakfast cliff walk; to explore a little, maybe have a swim. The part that made no sense was telling her to make sure Kit wasn't in fact sitting on a rock somewhere below, smoking a cigarette, waiting for her.

Didn't want to wake you! she wrote. *You looked so peaceful. Gone for walk along the cliffs, back for breakfast! XXX*

She downed her coffee, let herself out and walked up the grassy slope to the gate. There was only one person out and about, a woman with a Labrador, heading away from her.

A wooden sign pointed to the coastal footpath, and she set off, striding out along the clifftop, the golden sands of Constantine Bay misty in the distance. She swung her arms, aware of the smile on her face, drinking in the fresh morning air. Life was great. Stalkers and spooks notwithstanding.

Before long Eliza spotted a deep, blue-green rock pool in a small cove below. *It's Cornwall – there has to be a mermaid in there.* She left the main track and scrambled down the rocky path.

The pool was nestled in a promontory beyond a narrow stretch of sand. As she reached it, seaweed in shades of green and purple waved a gentle welcome from beneath the rippling surface. She changed into her bikini, contorting beneath her towel, shivering in the cool air. Then she picked her way carefully down to the crystal-clear water, and dipped in her toes.

Freezing! Cornwall holidaymakers must be a hardy bunch.

She lowered herself in, inch by bracing inch, the seaweed playfully tickling her legs. As she grew accustomed to the temperature, she let out a sigh of pleasure and tilted her face up to the sky, swishing her hands in the pool.

She slipped in further, until the water took her weight, then flipped onto her back, spreading her arms and legs wide, closing her eyes against the sun's dazzle. Her hair floated and swirled around her, mirroring the seaweed.

The mermaid is me.

It was sublime; the cool water caressed her skin, the sun stroked her face. She was at one with nature … until her moment of connection was rudely interrupted by a wave breaking on the rocks in front of her, showering her in icy spray.

She gasped, opening her eyes, then kicked her feet, gliding back to the rocks where she perched, her lower half submerged in the water, her wet hair draped over one shoulder. As she wrung the sea out of her curls, she looked out towards the ocean, and realised the tide was coming in. She should probably head back.

Then she smelt it again. Cigarette smoke. Her heart stopped as a shadow fell across her, cooling the air.

Eliza whirled round. He was silhouetted by the sun, and for a moment she couldn't make out his features. Just the corona of shoulder-length blond hair, his tall, lean outline, one hand on his hip, the other holding a cigarette in long fingers.

'Hey, sorry to disturb you.' He raised his voice against the crashing surf. 'But you should move. Tide's coming in. Go over to the beach, swim between the flags.' He waved his cigarette in the direction of Constantine Bay.

As Eliza's eyes adjusted, his face came into focus. He pushed back his hair, took a drag of his cigarette, then let it dangle between his lips.

Eliza couldn't move, couldn't speak. Her breath, her words – all gone. She opened and shut her mouth like a fish, staring up at him from where she sat, perched in the pool.

'Oh, sorry,' he said, registering her shock. He stepped back and took out the cigarette. 'Didn't mean to scare you, I was just worried you …' His words trailed off as his expression changed. His eyes widened in surprise.

Still Eliza couldn't speak. But she noticed, as her focus sharpened further, those eyes were blue – the colour of the Cornish sky – and turned down at the corners. Not hazel; not round. Her gaze swept over his sweatshirt … jeans … bare feet. He was taller, not as skinny; his chest was broader. His skin was golden, not pale.

Her eyes moved back to his. And they clicked, like magnets.

He blinked. 'You're Eliza. Art's girlfriend. I saw you on TV. At the tennis.'

'And you're …' Finally, she found her voice. 'I'm guessing you're Lockie.'

He nodded.

They stared some more, and Eliza was aware of time stopping, like it had before.

Then his face broke into a smile. 'Well, Eliza, it's great to meet you.' He crouched down on his haunches, holding out his hand.

She reached up and shook it, and his touch – his energy – flowed through her, warming her core, bringing that flame back to life.

'Where's Art?' he said, dropping her hand.

'Art? Oh, Ace. Still in bed.' Her voice sounded surprisingly normal.

Could he sense it? What she was feeling? Deep inside her – beyond words, beyond thought. She already knew him.

'It's our first morning here; I couldn't wait to explore. Ace was tired – we had a long drive yesterday, after all the madness … the tournament, the media stuff …'

She shook her head slightly, trying to get a grip. 'Hey, I'm sorry.' She gave him a weak smile. 'I probably seemed a bit strange, just then. You … took me by surprise.'

'No – my bad.' He smiled back, and his eyes went to her rock-pool perch, her wet hair. 'I don't normally creep up on mermaids.' She laughed. 'But seeing you floating, I was worried you didn't know about the tide. In fact, we need to leave. Right now.'

'Oh – okay.'

Waves were spraying them as the sea crept closer.

He held out a hand as she began to climb out. She took it and he hauled her up, then she stood dripping in front of him, close, and their eyes snapped together again. Neither seemed able to look away.

This was beyond her control. Her past had crashed into her present, in this timeless place with its magic and its mists. She couldn't hope to understand what was happening, she could only let it carry her along.

'Hey – you're shivering.' He picked up her towel, holding it out by the corners. She moved closer and turned away from him, and he wrapped it round her shoulders.

'Thank you,' she said, facing him again.

He frowned slightly as he looked down at her, and the flame burned higher, brighter, filling her with warmth, defrosting her heart.

'Let's go,' he said, scooping up her jeans, T-shirt and hat, balling them up under his arm. Her panties were caught up in the jeans; he pulled them free and tossed them to her with a cheeky grin.

Kit's cheeky grin.

She giggled as she caught them. A little flirtation she could handle; the chaos in her heart and mind would be more complicated to sort out.

'Wait till we get to the path to put your trainers on,' he said, eyeing the waves.

'Where are *your* shoes?' she asked.

'I prefer bare feet. Um, if you're okay with it, can we go find Art … Ace? Soon as?'

'Of course!' She smiled. 'He's going to be beside himself when he sees you. He's missed you so much.'

They set off back to the beach. 'Me too,' he said, hopping from rock to rock, sure-footed as a goat. 'He's the reason I've come back. The *only* reason.'

'When did you arrive?'

'Yesterday,' he said over his shoulder. 'Then I caught the overnight bus to Newquay and hitched a ride up here. I thought the cottage would be empty – Merle told me it was.'

'Did she?' said Eliza, picking her way across, trying to keep up with him. *Strange.*

'When I saw the car I realised it wasn't. Thought I shouldn't knock, so early in the morning. Decided to take a walk, come back later.'

'Ah. So it was you I saw creeping around that storeroom.'

They crossed the slither of beach, the water swirling round their ankles – now she understood his urgency – then stopped for her to put on her trainers.

'Hope I didn't scare you?' he said, watching her.

'No. But I thought, just for a moment …' She paused in tying her lace, looking up at him. 'That's mostly why I freaked, back there, when you appeared behind me. Lockie …' She swallowed. 'You're the spitting image of someone I used to know. A close friend. His name was Kit. He was … like, my soul mate. He died last year. And he smoked French cigarettes.'

'Oh. Right.' He frowned. 'I'm sorry – that's sad. So … what? You thought I was his ghost?'

She nodded. 'I know it sounds crazy, but in a way he's been haunting me. So yes, I did.'

'Bloody hell.'

She laughed. 'No, it's fine. It was just …' She shook her head. 'You're very like him. And yet you're not.'

His gaze was so direct. Ace had called him shy. But there was no awkwardness here.

'Like him how?' he asked, looking at her sideways. *Oh* – a little shyness there, after all. 'And how not?'

'In looks and … your mannerisms. But I guess, quite different people. He was a writer–'

Lockie snorted, ruffling his hair with a hand. 'I can't even fucking spell.'

She chuckled, and bit her lip. Heavens. All crazy-existential stuff aside, Lockie was outrageously cute.

She stared hard at her shoes as she finished tying them, then stood up. 'Please, don't say anything to Ace about that. Let's just say you took me by surprise.'

'For sure.' His face broke into a grin, and then he laughed again.

'What's so funny? Being mistaken for a ghost?'

'No. It's just … your voice.'

'My voice?'

'You're so posh–' He pressed his lips together. 'Sorry – nicely spoken. Can't believe Art's hooked up with a rich girl. He's always been so anti all that. You know, white privilege …'

'Ah, yes,' she said, as they set off. 'I'm known to Ace's fan base as the Rich Bitch.'

'What?'

'But I think Ace has accepted none of us can help the circumstances of our birth.' She raised her eyebrows.

'I suppose not. If you even know what those are.' He shrugged. 'Me an' Art have no clue. Sorry I laughed at you, though. That's horrible, what they call you. And your voice is actually –' he glanced over, 'very pretty.'

She smiled. 'Why thank you.'

Lockie pulled ahead on the steep slope. Eliza's heart was thumping, and it had nothing to do with the exertion. To deflect her confusion, she pictured Ace's expression when he found out what the wind had blown in. She couldn't wait to see it. But she wondered – why hadn't he mentioned the obvious resemblance? He'd seen the photo of Kit.

Back on the coastal footpath, Lockie pulled his cigarettes from his jeans pocket. She recognised the blue box with the curly wisps of smoke.

'Does Ace know you smoke?' she asked, catching him up. 'You'll be aware his body is his temple?'

'No, I only started a year ago.' He looked at the packet in his hand, then stuffed it back in his pocket. 'My girlfriend in New Zealand smoked; I just took it up to keep her company. These were the only ones I liked.'

A girlfriend. So he could presumably bear to be touched, now.

The path had widened, and she fell into step beside him.

'Shall I give up?' he said.

'Yes, you should.'

'Okay. Next rubbish bin, in they go.'

'As simple as that?'

'I'm not addicted,' he said. 'My mum's an addict; I'll never be addicted to anything. Except surfing.'

Would he guess Ace had told her about Lockie's difficult background? About the abuse and the suicide attempt?

'You're giving up because I told you to?'

'Why not? Should never have started. And it's expensive. Especially seeing as I have no job.'

'Will your girlfriend be coming to England?' asked Eliza, nonchalantly.

He shot her a look. 'Ex-girlfriend. So no.'

'Oh, right.'

'She's awesome, though,' he said. 'I was pretty messed up when I left here; she helped fix me.'

'That's great. I hope you haven't broken her heart, leaving New Zealand?'

He smiled. 'Nah. It was only for a while. She knew that.'

'Why did you leave England?'

The smile vanished. 'I was escaping a … a situation.'

'Wait …' said Eliza. The cottage had just come into view. 'I don't want Ace to see us out of the window. We should surprise him.'

Chapter 34

Ace

The mug of coffee on his bedside table was stone cold. Out of the window, the lighthouse was dazzling white, daytime bright. He looked at his phone: 8.47a.m.

When was the last time he'd slept past eight?

He listened carefully, but all was quiet. Eliza had probably gone for a walk. She liked her morning walks.

With London left behind, Eliza was already different. He'd loved watching her unwind yesterday, away from the pressures of her job, the media attention, the insidious online attacks. The stalker. He'd seen the stress floating up, up and away.

And he'd noticed a subtle change in their relationship. Over dinner they'd discussed plans for Excalibur, then had sat in the living room, Eliza already in her pink pyjamas, reading her book. Her usual lively chat had given way to stretches of companiable silence. She was easy with him; happy to sit quietly.

Later, bedtime had been as much about the pre-lights-out cuddle and gentle conversation as it was about making love in the dark, those sweeping beams of light playing across Eliza's pale skin. The all-consuming passion of their first weeks had morphed into something slower, more controlled. A week alone together felt like all the time in the world.

He let out a contented sigh as he stretched. This amazing woman had filled the Eliza-shaped space inside him that had been waiting. Already, he couldn't imagine life without her.

His eyes settled on a watercolour on the wall, of Constantine Bay. It was beautiful – the way Lockie had caught the light, the motion of the waves. He'd been only thirteen when he painted it.

Ace tried to block it, but the darkness crashed in. Here, back in this place … the image slithered into his mind's eye. Hector, in this bedroom, when Ace and Merle were away at some competition. Faye down the hall. Lockie, alone outside in the sleepout. Unprotected. Vulnerable.

No. Ace shook it off. Having Eliza here, filling the cottage with light, with love – he hoped this would exorcise the demons.

He swung his legs out of bed and put on his robe, running his fingers through his hair as he went through to the kitchen. He read the note on the table, which told him, in exuberant Eliza-speak, that she had indeed gone for a walk.

He glanced out of the window, but from here could only see the seaward view. Might as well make a start on breakfast.

He was slicing bread for toast when the back door flew open and she breezed in. 'Good morning!' She shut the door behind her and stood on the mat, her chest, clad only in a blue bikini top, quickly rising and falling.

'Well hello,' he said. 'The sea air obviously agrees with you.'

Her normally pale cheeks were flushed pink; her eyes were sparkling.

'You've been for a swim?' His gaze swept over the damp, salty ringlets spiralling down her back. A blue towel was wrapped around her lower half, secured at the waist. 'You look like a mermaid. Apart from the trainers.'

'Ha! Funny you should–' She smacked her lips together. 'Yes, I did have a swim. Actually, a float. It was *freezing*! But divine.'

'Well, it hasn't done you any harm. Look at you, you're glowing. Whatever's in that water, I want some of it.'

Her smile faltered. 'Yes …' She stepped further into the room, and glanced behind her at the back door. 'That's your Cornwall, working its magic.'

He encircled her with his arms, dropping a kiss on her shoulder. Her skin was warm and salty, and as he traced the curve of her waist above the towel he felt himself respond.

'It's so good to see you looking relaxed,' he said, and bent his head again to kiss her.

She kissed him back, but quickly stopped. 'I'm starving! What's for breakfast?'

'How about me.' He pulled her close again.

'Yum. But can I have some carbs first? Piece of toast? Muesli?'

Ace frowned a little. Normally lively, Eliza was now verging on hyper. Maybe this was the post-lockdown holiday vibe. There were probably people all over Britain behaving as if they'd got a new lease of life.

'Eggs on toast? Bacon?' he said.

Now she stood, listening … watchful. And then there was a soft tap on the door. She went still in his arms.

'Who on earth …?' he said. Surely the press hadn't discovered their hideaway already.

'I'll get it,' she said.

What? How come she was okay with answering a mysterious knock, when the front door to her own apartment was secured like Fort Knox?

'Oh, and Ace?' She smiled, and the pink in those cheeks intensified. 'I found something interesting at the beach. I think the tide brought it in. Probably because you wished it.'

He could only stare at her, nonplussed, as she unlatched the door and opened it, standing aside.

Ace experienced a moment of disconnect, as if time had twisted. Lockie was on the doorstep. He looked the same – tall, blond, barefoot – but somehow different.

Then Ace's brain accepted what his eyes were telling him, and he was walloped by a wave of joy as powerful as the breakers his beloved foster brother loved to ride.

'Hello Art,' said Lockie, and then his wide smile faltered as Ace's eyes filled with tears.

'Oh … hey, bro …' Lockie teared up too. 'Art … mate … it's been too fucking long. I missed you so much.'

Ace finally found his voice. 'I missed you more … *mate*.' He gave a shaky laugh. 'You've obviously been in the Antipodes too long.' He held out his arms. 'You're home. Thank god.'

Lockie stepped inside and they hugged each other tight, slapping each other's backs.

'You found him on the beach?' Ace said, blinking away his tears. Eliza nodded. She looked as if she might cry too.

They pulled apart, and Lockie shut the door behind him. 'First things first,' he said, punching Ace on the arm. 'Congrats – king of the fucking world. Knew you'd do it.'

'Thanks. It still hasn't sunk in. Life was *almost* perfect –' He looked over at Eliza, then back at Lockie, and smiled. 'And now you're back, it is.' He pulled Lockie in for another hug.

'It's good to be back. And hey – don't worry,' said Lockie, also glancing at Eliza. 'I won't intrude. Bloody Merle told me the cottage was empty. I can just head up to Mum's later.' He paused. 'She's still alive, against all the odds.'

'Surprising,' said Ace, his expression darkening. 'But you're not going anywhere. There's two bedrooms here, and I'm not so up myself I need both.'

Lockie looked at Eliza again.

'Yep,' she said. 'Ace can drive you to see your mum, but you must stay here. It'll be fun!' But there was something in her eyes, as if she wasn't quite sure.

'So – you've been in touch with Merle?' Ace said.

'Texted her just before I left, to ask if I could use the cottage. She said fine. Said she'd leave me food.'

Ace and Eliza looked at each other, confused.

Merle knew Lockie was coming?

'You know what?' said Ace. 'I reckon our beloved foster mum's losing it. I guess she's been under pressure, getting me through this year. Anyway, children …' He smiled at the pair of them. 'I was going to make bacon and eggs. Want some?'

'Awesome,' said Lockie. 'Haven't eaten since the plane.'

'Sounds perfect,' said Eliza, hopping up onto a kitchen stool.

Ace watched Lockie as he wiped his bare feet on the mat, then sat down on the stool next to Eliza. Again, he noticed the change. There was the obvious difference – the deeper tan, the sun-bleached hair. He'd filled out; his chest was broader, his arm muscles more defined.

But his manner – his demeanour – was different too. As Eliza and Lockie exchanged another look, Ace registered he didn't seem at all shy of her. Normally, someone as … up front as Eliza would have Lockie retreating into his shell, if not running for the hills.

He watched them some more as he cracked eggs into a bowl. It was as if they were old friends, had known each other forever.

And then he clocked Eliza's expression as she looked at Lockie. Like she was mesmerised, hypnotised.

It was like a punch in the guts.

Fuck.

But then – *of course.* He breathed out in relief. Lockie's resemblance to Kit – *that* must be why she kept staring at him. Ace knew he should have mentioned it, but he hadn't expected Lockie to turn up on his doorstep without warning.

'Where's your stuff?' he said, needing to move things on from this three-way staring game.

'In the front porch. Just a backpack.'

'So,' said Ace, beating the eggs. 'How come Eliza found you on the beach?'

'No, I found *her*.' Lockie smiled at Eliza. 'She was in the rock pool floating on her back, hair streaming out, eyes shut, like fuckin' Ophelia. Another ten minutes and she'd have been cut off by the tide.'

'God,' said Ace. 'Your first day back and already you're doing your girl-rescues.'

'I spoiled her moment.'

'You did!' said Eliza. 'One minute I was enjoying an existential connection with nature, the next you were blocking my sun and poisoning my air with cigarette smoke.' She wrinkled her nose.

'What?' said Ace. 'Since when did you smoke?'

'Since not anymore. Your girl told me to stop.'

Ace looked at Eliza, who gave him a smug smile.

'Wait,' Ace said. '*Ophelia*? Since when have you been into Shakespeare? You hated Shakespeare!'

'Don't judge me,' said Lockie. 'I watched that Netflix Shakespeare thing while we were in lockdown. It was brilliant. I spent a lot of lockdown sitting about watching TV, with Lena. My girlfriend.' He winked at Ace. 'I guess that was something new too.'

'*Girlfriend?* Since when have you–'

'About a year ago.'

'Well, I'll be …' Ace shook his head. 'Smoking, girls, Shakespeare?'

'Travel broadens the mind,' said Lockie. 'You better believe it.'

❋

They chatted more over Ace's eggs and bacon. Lockie described his past year and a half, relating how he'd arrived in New Zealand a few months before the borders had slammed shut. He'd backpacked around the country doing casual jobs like fruit picking, then had parked himself in a west coast surfing paradise. There he'd worked as an instructor, and had met Lena, a local surfing champ. Normally she'd have been travelling the world entering competitions, but of course, everything had ground to a halt.

'How come you didn't run away this time?' asked Ace.

'Man, she was persistent. And there was nowhere to run to.' He gave a small laugh. 'She just wouldn't take no for an answer. But …' he paused, 'in a good way.'

Ace met his eye.

'She …' Lockie's eyes flicked to Eliza.

'Only if you're comfortable,' she said. 'Ace did tell me something of your difficult childhood.' She smiled gently. 'Not much, though.'

Ace noticed it again. The way their eyes locked. His heart missed a beat. But no; the idea was ridiculous. Eliza would never be interested in his semi-literate, jobless, beach bum of a brother. Even if he was the spitting image of Kit.

'Lena and me surfed together,' said Lockie, 'and things just kind of progressed from there. Sounds a bit flaky, but we bonded over the sea. She's Maori. Their relationship to the land and the ocean is so different to ours. She taught me to respect the waves, to listen to them; told me not to challenge them.'

His gaze moved out of the window to the ocean. 'Lena and me getting together, it felt … natural.' He looked at Ace, who nodded. 'And when I said I was leaving, she was okay with that. She got my reasons. Their borders will open next year, she'll be off travelling again. It was a special time, but now it's done.'

He put his knife and fork down on his plate, breakfast finished. 'I'll go fetch my stuff,' he said, standing up. 'If you're really okay with me crashing here for a bit?'

'Not my house,' said Ace. 'But seriously, we're good. Right, Eliza?'

Of course, she was far too polite to refuse. Ace acknowledged that, deep down, he wanted her to mind that their romantic week away had been ambushed by his brother. But as her eyes met Lockie's again, he saw that she didn't mind at all.

'There might be compulsory board games,' she said.

'No worries. Scrabble?'

Eliza burst out laughing.

Ace looked at the pair of them in confusion.

'I might have mentioned my struggle with spelling,' said Lockie. Then he left the room.

Ace looked at Eliza. 'You discussed his spelling?'

'Oh,' she said, flustered. 'Only because …' She frowned at the table in front of her. 'While we were walking back, it came up – writing – because of his resemblance to … ' She got herself together, looked him in the eye. 'Chrissakes, Ace.' Her voice was low, edgy. 'Why didn't you *tell* me?' She looked towards the hallway, but Lockie had taken his backpack into the spare bedroom and all had gone quiet.

How to explain? 'Sorry. I know I should have. I just didn't expect Lockie to show up without warning. But don't …' He held her gaze. 'Lots of people look alike. It's only superficial – he's nothing like Kit. Obviously.'

'That's how the spelling came up. He appeared behind me; he was smoking Kit's favourite cigarette brand.' She paused, emotion playing across her face. 'My god, Ace. I couldn't think straight. I honestly thought it was Kit. Or his ghost. It completely floored me. Then I had to explain to your foster brother why I reacted like that. So he didn't think I was some madwoman.'

'How *did* you react?'

'Just … shocked; speechless. I thought, for the briefest moment, Kit had come back. Because–' Her voice caught. 'Because I wished it, so hard.'

There was a jolt of disquiet as Ace remembered her fingers tracing a path down his tattoo, the intensity on her face, her eyes squeezed shut.

He reached across and took her hand. 'I'm truly sorry. I should have told you. But look. Don't say anything more about it to him. He's fragile. Suggestible. Be careful. Don't …' He wasn't quite sure how to finish. Who was he trying to protect?

'You're overthinking it. He can stay a couple of days, you two can hang out, and then he can be on his way.'

'To where, though?' he said. 'He's homeless. And he hates being at his mum's; it's bad for his mental health.'

'He can stay at Merle's?' said Eliza. 'In fact, why didn't he just go there in the first place?'

'Well … Hector's there too, and things were tricky between the three of them when he left. But Merle wants to make it up to him.'

'Make what up to him?'

'This probably isn't the time to explain,' said Ace, not meeting her eye. 'Let's just take it easy for a couple of days.' Then he smiled and looked down the hallway. 'It's just so bloody fantastic to have him home.'

Chapter 35

Ace

After washing up, Ace poked his head round the bedroom door to see Lockie fast asleep, still fully clothed, his backpack untouched on the floor. He smiled at his foster brother's angelic face, the long blond hair falling across it. The sight took him straight back.

Eliza joined him. 'Aw,' she whispered. 'Look at him.'

Ace ushered her away and pulled the door quietly closed. 'We'll leave him to his jetlag – let's go to the beach. It's pretty big, we can find a spot away from everyone.'

They walked along the cliffs to Constantine Bay, and spent the morning sitting in the lee of a sand dune, reading, talking, swimming … the summer holidays were over now, so the beach wasn't busy; it was mostly locals enjoying their Saturday. Surfers bobbed in the sea, and people walked their dogs.

By lunchtime the clouds had moved in and the wind was picking up, whistling through the marram grass, flicking sand in Eliza's face. The annoying whine of a drone kept distracting her from her book. She sat up and slipped on her jumper. 'It's gone cold,' she said, rubbing her arms.

'It's September. And it's not Bermuda.'

Eliza chuckled. 'True. Shall we go for a walk?'

They headed inland from the beach, cutting across the golf course to the remains of the ancient chapel and its holy well.

'I'm wondering what Lockie will do, now he's home,' said Ace. 'Maybe I could involve him in Excalibur. We need staff, right?'

Eliza gave a small laugh. 'I can't see Lockie behind a desk.'

'Hm. I don't know … I'd love him to join me, and it really is time he learned how to function in the real world. Maybe he should do a year at college, take some sort of course to upskill.'

'You sound like his dad. The poor boy just got off the plane.'

'Sometimes I *feel* like his dad.' He smiled. 'But it's amazing, he seems so much more self-confident. And I mean – Shakespeare? He's changed.'

Eliza glanced over at him. 'How?'

'A lot less nervous around … strangers.'

'Was he really so shy?'

'Painfully. It was mostly about not trusting people. But I guess travelling by yourself, surviving in an unfamiliar country – he probably *had* to overcome his anxiety.'

◈

Back at the cottage, Ace assumed Lockie was up and about when he saw washing hanging on the rotary clothesline. They found him in the living room window seat, peering at the pages of a novel.

Ace let out a mock gasp of astonishment. 'You're *reading?*'

Lockie looked up, and his eyes flicked from Ace to Eliza, then back to Ace. 'Found this on the shelf. I remember, it was Merle's favourite.' He flashed the cover at them.

'Bro, what have you done with the real Lockie?'

'Oh!' said Eliza, '*The Once and Future King* – I *love* that book.' She sat down beside him. 'How far have you got?'

'Not far.' He smiled at her. 'Struggling with the longer words.'

Ace opened his mouth, but Lockie pre-empted him. 'Something else I did in lockdown – learned to read properly. Well, better. What's this word, Eliza?' He pointed to the page, and Ace watched their heads bend together.

'Tiercel. It means–'

'– a male hawk?'

'Yes.' Eliza looked from Lockie to Ace.

'What? How do you know that?' said Ace.

Lockie shrugged. 'No idea.'

Ace blew out a breath. 'So – you can read. Do you need a job?'

'Too right I do.'

Eliza went off to shower, and Ace sat down next to Lockie, mussing his hair. 'Still can't believe you're here. How's the jet lag?'

'Getting there.' He met Ace's eye. 'It's weird, though, being back in this place. The ... ghosts.'

'Yep. Still haven't quite fucked off.'

They went quiet.

'How is Hector?'

Ace shook his head. 'Nothing changes. Although he's been rising up the ranks of the Camelford Fishing Club. Things between him and Merle are still tense.'

He changed the subject. 'Lockie, the reason Eliza and me are here – we're kind of in hiding. She's got a stalker, identity unknown, and she's had death threats. She's been pretty shaken up by it all. We think it's an obsessive fan.'

'Shit, really?' Lockie frowned. 'No wonder she nearly lost it when I appeared behind her.'

'Yes, pretty jittery.' Ace looked sideways at him. 'How do you like her? First impression.'

Lockie grinned. 'Man – she's a fuckin' goddess.'

Ace let out a bark of laughter. 'She really is.'

'So posh, though.' His gaze moved out of the window. 'It's strange, but I feel like I know her from somewhere.' He closed his eyes, concentrating. 'Felt it real strong when I saw her on the beach.' He opened them again and shrugged. 'Probably 'cause I've seen her on TV.'

Ace nodded, but the niggle of worry nudged him again.

'Art – if she's in any danger, like, that death threat ... I'm here. Got no job. Happy to babysit, be a bodyguard, if you need to go off and train or whatever.'

Lockie wasn't only a seasoned surf life-saver, he also excelled at martial arts – something else Merle encouraged him to take up after his suicide attempt.

'Hardly anyone knows we're here,' said Ace, 'and I'll be sticking to her like a leech. But thanks.'

❀

Later, as the sun kissed the horizon goodnight, and beams from the lighthouse began sweeping overhead, they caught up properly on each other's lives, Eliza listening quietly from the window seat. The cottage grew chilly and Ace lit the stove, its flames illuminating the room with their soft glow. They didn't bother putting on the lights.

Ace described his incredible year of tennis, and Lockie, lying on his stomach in front of the fire, told them about Aotearoa, '… its Maori name. Means the Land of the Long White Cloud. I learned a few words from Lena.'

'Can you tell us some?' said Eliza.

Firelight flickered across his face. He smiled at her. 'Kia ora – hello.'

He looked over at Ace. 'Whanau – family. Aroha – love.'

'A-ro-ha,' Eliza repeated slowly, her eyes meeting Lockie's, which glowed amber, reflecting the flames. 'What a beautiful word.'

There was a moment's silence, then Eliza suggested putting on music.

Ace switched on a speaker. 'You choose,' he said to Lockie, who fiddled with the settings on his phone.

Radiohead's 'Street Spirit' began to play, and Ace saw Eliza's intake of breath.

'I remember,' she said. 'Ace told me you were a fan.'

'You too?'

She gave a small nod.

'How about something that isn't a dirge?' Ace said, with a smile he didn't feel.

Eliza left them to talk some more while she cooked a meal; Ace and Lockie washed up, and afterwards, as beams from the lighthouse measured out time in seven-second bursts, the three of them played cards.

Lockie's head started to nod. 'Sorry, can't keep awake.' He stood up and stretched; his T-shirt rode up, and Eliza's eyes briefly settled on the exposed, tanned skin above his low-slung jeans.

Lockie grinned at Ace. 'I'm for Bedfordshire.' It had been Hector's lame little parting shot when they were kids. As he passed the sofa, he dropped a hand onto Ace's shoulder. 'No words for how good this feels. Thanks for letting me stay.'

'Best day,' said Ace.

Lockie's eyes moved to Eliza. 'Goodnight, Ace's missus,' he said, with that remembered shy half-smile.

'Goodnight, Lockie,' she said softly.

Chapter 36

Eliza

A lazy Cornwall Sunday with Ace and Lockie. What could be lovelier?

The only cloud on the horizon – *ha* – was that the weather was changing. The wind that had gently teased them on the beach yesterday had gained in strength, and was now blustering around the cottage. Beyond the lighthouse, banks of grey cloud were building out to sea, and white horses – or were they unicorns here? – were partying on the waves.

The sound of Ace singing Ed Sheeran's 'Castle on the Hill' floated down the hallway from the kitchen. He was making breakfast again. This time he'd promised the full English. Unfettered by Merle, he was letting rip with his food fantasies. 'Sausages!' he'd said, spotting them in the fridge. 'Prepare yourselves for the king of all breakfasts.' He was full of beans – the pressure was off; his brother was home.

Out of the bedroom window, the rotary clothesline, with Lockie's washing still pegged on it, was spinning like a whirling dervish, and a pair of undies flew off and bowled across the grass. Eliza would do him a favour and rescue them, then take in the rest.

She let herself out the front door, retrieved the boxers, and headed for the clothesline.

From the house, Lockie had been hidden. He was sitting on the wall between the lighthouse and the cottage, a cigarette dangling from his mouth.

Eliza halted, staring. Kit, in LA, smoking on the harbour wall just along from where *Janette* was moored.

No. He's not Kit. He's-not-he's-not-he's-not.

She went over. 'So much for giving up, then.'

And in the exact same way she'd known he would, he gave her a look, then hopped down, took out the cigarette, flicked it onto the ground and stomped it out.

'You should pick that up,' she said, as the déjà vu intensified.

You're such a control freak.

Past and present were colliding before her eyes.

He did as she asked. 'Busted,' he said, straightening. 'I was just finishing the pack. I thought you wouldn't see me behind the washing.' His eyes went to her hand, holding his boxers. 'Thanks for rescuing my undies.'

That smile.

Eliza tossed them to him with a grin, and their eyes snapped together again.

It was if she'd entered a parallel universe. Time had gone haywire. Released from its constraints, it was flip-flopping, switching back … looping. Her head was spinning. She could almost hear the echo of Fate's laughter. It was demonic.

Eliza tried to tear her eyes from his; she was spiralling into their blue depths. She forced herself to blink, keeping them closed for a moment, and time recalibrated; the laughter faded away.

Wanting to keep her grasp on reality – or at least, the version she understood – she asked, 'Can I take a pic? Of you in front of the lighthouse?'

He frowned. 'I hate having my photo taken.'

Of course you do.

'Why do you want to?' He scrunched up the boxers and stuffed them in his shorts pocket.

'It's just … I want to show my friend Will. Kit – the guy who looked like you – was his partner.'

'Kit the writer dude?'

'Yes. Will's a writer too; they wrote together. You've probably seen their dramas on TV. Absolutely brilliant, the pair of them.'

He grinned. 'But can they surf?'

Eliza snorted, even as her heart flipped.

Every mannerism; every expression. It was like watching the flickering, grainy images of an old home movie.

A gust of wind blew her hair across her face, and she pushed it back. The wind blew it across again. The universe was full of mischief today.

'I thought Kit was *your* partner,' said Lockie.

'Oh god no – Will's.'

'But you called him your soul mate.'

'He was.' She sighed. 'It's hard to describe. It was a … connection. We just got each other on some deep level. I'm not even sure there's a word for it.'

As she spoke, a few strands of hair blew into in her mouth, and she puffed out a burst of air, trying to dislodge them.

He raised a hand and gently pulled them free, his fingers brushing her lips, her cheek. His touch robbed her of breath, and yet it seemed the most natural thing in the world.

'Guess you really miss him.'

'I do. So much.'

Again, she couldn't look away; she was trapped in his gaze, and the flame burned higher, licking at her walls. 'I'll … just go fetch my phone.'

'We can use mine,' he said, taking it out of his pocket. 'And you should be in it too, if you want to spook your mate properly.'

He came to stand beside her, and she leaned in close as he held up the phone. Her head touched his shoulder and he flinched, moving away.

Puzzled, she looked up at him, and registered the abrupt change.

'Never mind, forget the photo,' she said. 'I know I can be a bit much. Sorry.'

He wouldn't look at her; his eyes were fixed on the ground. 'Eliza –' With an effort, he dragged them up to meet hers. 'He saved my life. When I … when–'

'I know.'

She wanted to touch him, to hold him tight, but she couldn't. Her eyes went to his wrists; he followed her gaze, then twisted his lower arms to face her, and she saw the faint, silvery scars.

'He got me through the darkest times.' His eyes flicked over to the storeroom. 'I owe him my life. I owe him everything.'

'I know you do. I understand.'

'I'm glad you know about … that.' And then at last, he smiled – a beautiful, warm smile. It was like the sun coming out. 'Long long time ago. C'mon, let's do your damn photo.' He raised the phone and, all trace of shyness gone, put his other arm around her shoulder. His warmth flowed through her, pushing open doors that had remained shut, like fire doors, this past year. She closed her eyes, just as he snapped the photo.

Letting go of her, he peered at his phone. 'You blinked. We'll just have to do that again.'

His arm went back round her, gently pulling her close, and this time she put hers around his waist. He took the photo. 'Better,' he said, releasing her and shielding the screen with his hand. 'I'll send it to you when we're inside.'

'Your washing,' she said. The two words seemed so prosaic, after that moment of connection. 'Shall we get it in before any more undies make a bid for freedom?'

As they reached the clothesline he pulled out the boxers, then patted his other pockets saying, 'Where'd I put it?' He took a folded piece of paper from his back pocket. 'Here you go – a memento.' He passed it over, as if it were a shopping list.

She unfolded it to see a pencil sketch of Eliza the mermaid, on her back in the rock pool, arms spread wide, her hair floating around her body.

'I woke up early, stupid jet lag. Drew it to pass the time.'

It was composed of abstract swirls – of water, hair, seaweed; a curved tail – the faintest hint of facial features, and yet he'd perfectly captured her serenity. In spite of the movement in those swirls, the impression was one of stillness, of calm.

It took her breath away. 'This is—'

'Just a little sketch.' He smiled. 'I spoiled your moment, so I thought I'd try and give a bit of it back to you.'

'It's so beautiful, Lockie.'

'How many times in your life do you get to feel like that?'

'You mean at one with nature?'

'No – free.'

'Free?' She laughed. 'Almost never.' She paused. 'In fact, just – never.'

⊛

As Ace proudly served up his king of breakfasts, Lockie dropped the photo to Eliza's phone. She was staring out of the window, watching the ocean's ongoing shift from calm to agitated. She felt the change in her bones.

She messaged Will the photo: *Tell me what you make of this.*

'What shall we do today?' asked Ace, tucking into his food.

'Surf's up,' said Lockie. A gust of wind buffeted the cottage in approval.

'What?' said Eliza. 'Surely you shouldn't go in the sea when it's like this?'

Ace laughed. 'That's kind of the point, city girl. Big waves?'

Eliza bristled a little.

'Not for beginners,' said Lockie. 'I'll head down to the bay after breakfast, give you two some space.'

'Sounds good,' said Ace. He slipped a hand under the table and squeezed Eliza's knee.

To her disquiet, her body didn't respond.

Her phone rang. 'Will!' she said, sending the call to voicemail. 'I'll ring back later.'

Then she listened as the boys discussed past surfing glories. 'Actually, can I come watch? I'd love to see you both do your surfing thing.'

Ace's face briefly fell, then he said. 'Sure. Logistical challenge – three people, two surfboards, no roof rack, but Ace's taxi service is here for your surfing needs.'

'I'll be back in ten minutes,' Ace said out of the car window, as she held the gate open. Lockie was in the front, the surfboards angled across the back.

Returning to the cottage, she called Will. 'Hi! I miss you! How are you?'

'Just fine,' he said. 'How's the Land of Merlin?'

'Oh, it's brilliant. Very magical.'

'And our lovely Ace?'

'All good, thanks.'

He paused. 'So, what is this mind-fuckery you sent? Did you meet some Cornish shape-shifting bogeyman?' His tone was flippant, but she picked up his note of unease.

'It's Lockie. Ace's foster brother, back from New Zealand.' She kept her voice level, matter of fact. 'Bit spooky, the resemblance, don't you think?' She wasn't going to mention the recognition that went way beyond superficial. Not yet; not on the phone. What she wanted was for Will to tell her it was all in her mind. That he didn't detect any true essence of Kit in that photo.

Any trace of his soul.

'His *foster brother*? Shit.' His voice had lost its drama. 'That's quite disturbing. If it wasn't for his eyes–'

'Yes,' she interrupted. 'But the eyes are the most important part, right?' Her voice was less steady now. 'The windows to the soul? And Lockie's are completely different. Plus, he's …' She stopped.

'He's what?'

She'd been about to parrot Ace: *He's nothing like Kit.* But she couldn't, because those words weren't true.

'He's a surfer dude,' she said, instead. 'Can't hardly read or write, thinks I'm far too posh for his brother. He's homeless, he has no family, no job …'

Stop. She couldn't carry on like this. It was *Will* she was talking to. And she needed his help. To stop herself betraying the most wonderful man she'd ever met.

'He's …' She swallowed. 'Will – I'm worried,' she said in a small voice. 'He's–'

'He's a Kit lookalike.' His voice was calming; he'd picked up on her panic. 'Why's he even there? I thought you were having a romantic holiday *a deux*?'

'He just showed up; he had nowhere else to go. Ace is so thrilled he's come home.'

There was a toot from outside.

'I have to go. We're off to the beach.'

'Call me again,' he said. 'And ... don't overthink it. It's just a face, right?'

'Yes, mostly. It's just a face.'

✦

Eliza stood at the edge of the waves, hunched into her waterproof jacket, her hair scraped into a tight ponytail against the wild wind. Ace, his board under his arm, pointed out to sea. There were a few surfers out there, but Lockie, with his long, sun-bleached hair, was easy to spot.

Battalions of grey breakers bore down on the land, releasing plumes of spray as they crested, their booms resounding like thunder round the bay as they toppled and crashed, then rushed up the beach with a hiss.

Salty spray was misting the cool air, coating their hair, and Ace took a deep, appreciative breath. 'Fan-bloody-tastic,' he shouted above the surf. 'Okay if I head in? Stay right here, no one's going to recognize you all wrapped up.' He tucked her ponytail into her jacket, then kissed her quickly on the lips.

'I'm fine. Off you go.'

'Ah, wait,' he said, looking out to sea.

Lockie had picked up a breaker and was tearing across its face. The wave turned green as it rose higher and light shone through it, and Lockie left a streak of white foam, keeping just ahead of the crest.

'He's on a shortboard,' said Ace, 'and he's seen us.' He grinned. 'Wait for it.'

She focused on Lockie's tall form, his arms held wide, his hair streaming out behind him. He was channelling the wave's energy, in his element; she could feel his rush, his sense of freedom.

Then, as they watched, Lockie turned into the wall of water and raced up its face; he was horizontal, his face to the sky, and his board's momentum shot him clear of the wave, high into the air. Then he flipped, turning an exuberant somersault before dropping back and landing perfectly on the face of the wave, which he rode in to the beach, hopping off his surfboard as he reached the sand.

Eliza whooped as he picked up the board and jogged over to them. She was suddenly reminded of Ace, racing up the tiers of seats in the Arthur Ashe Stadium on his way to claim his victory kiss.

'Lockie! That was amazing!'

He flicked his wet hair out of his eyes. 'Can't beat the Cornish sea. Forgotten how fuckin' cold it is, though. Your turn, bro,' he said, clapping Ace on the arm.

'On it.' Ace was passing his gear to Eliza to hold, when his phone rang. He pulled a face at it. 'Merle. Accept or reject?'

'Reject,' said Eliza, as Lockie said, 'Accept. I can ask about staying with her.'

Ace answered, then was quiet.

Lockie looked at Eliza and shrugged, as Ace moved away from them, his face creasing into a frown.

She and Lockie stood side by side, watching the waves. 'I understand why you love it,' she said. 'I get why it helped you.'

'It clears your mind of all the crap. Just me and the sea.' He turned to her. 'Eliza, when we get back there's something I'd like to show you. Cos … I think you'll understand.'

'Sure.'

Ace returned, looking displeased. 'I have to go see Merle and Hector. Now, apparently. By myself,' he added, as Eliza and Lockie went to respond. 'I'll run you back and change, then get it over and done with.'

Eliza asked the obvious question. 'Why does she want to see you? For god's sake, she knows you're on holiday!'

Ace glanced at Lockie, who tactfully headed off towards the car.

'She knows Lockie's here,' he said, watching his back. 'She was doing her mysterious thing again. She's got something to tell me; it can't wait, and it's got to be in person. Just me. Chrissake.'

Eliza nodded, feeling uneasy. What was on Merle's mind? 'You'd best go, then. How far away is it?'

'Camelford? About half an hour. So if I move things along, I should be back in an hour and a half, two max.'

Chapter 37

Ace

Ace turned into in the driveway of Merle and Hector's semi, which sat harmlessly at the end of a quiet cul-de-sac. It looked so ordinary, so *typical*. It was difficult to imagine the scenes that had unfolded behind those PVC windows.

As he turned off the engine, the front door opened and Merle appeared. 'Come in, come in,' she said, looking over his shoulder to where faces had appeared in the windows opposite. He waved hello to the neighbours – and goodbye to any hope of staying below the radar. The residents of Avalon Leys were so proud of Merle's famous foster son; word that he was home would spread like wildfire.

Merle raised her chin at them, and they disappeared. Hector materialised in the hallway, wearing his old brown, droopy cardigan. 'Hello, son … Ace,' he said. 'It's marvellous to see you. Thanks for coming over – I know you're very busy these days.'

Ace looked at his foster father, and the familiar frustration took hold. 'This is still my home.'

'We're so proud.' There was an awkward hug, and a pat on the back. 'I'll put the kettle on.' Hector scuttled away.

Ace went through to the tidy living room. Its bay window was crammed with sports trophies, and over in the corner was the cabinet containing the Celtic sword. Excalibur. Only six months had passed since Ace had last been here, but for some reason he was surprised to find everything the same. Although smaller, somehow.

'I can't stay long,' he said, sitting down on the chintz sofa. 'I don't like leaving Eliza by herself at the moment.' He paused. 'Well, Lockie's there, but ...' he met Merle's eye. 'Why did you tell him the cottage was empty?' He assumed his foster brother's return was why Merle had asked to see him.

She ignored his question. 'Can't stay long? I'd best get straight to the point, then.' She sat down beside him. That was unusual. She had her preferred seat, a wing chair, upholstered in purple velvet.

Merle frowned at her legs, brushing something invisible from her track pants. 'Arthur. I asked you here because it's time I talked to you about your mother. And your father.'

Ace's heart gave an enormous lurch. She'd blindsided him. This was the last thing he'd expected. And he didn't want it – not now, when life was going so well. Maybe not ever. He just didn't want, or need, to know why he'd been abandoned.

He stood up. 'No.' He kept his voice steady. 'Let me have this week. Just me and Eliza, no pressures, no worries. No ... past stuff. Please – just leave us alone.'

'You and Eliza and *Lockie*,' she corrected. 'So no, I can't leave you alone. I have to tell you, and it has to be now. Sit down.'

He stayed standing. 'Why? Why can't you leave me be?'

'*Sit down.*'

He did as she asked. His heart was in his mouth. He didn't want any of this, but past experience had shown, Merle must be obeyed.

'Your mum,' she began. 'She was a friend of mine.'

He said nothing.

'Isla. She was lovely. Talented, pretty, kind. Unfortunately, her talent attracted attention from some people – one in particular – who wanted to exploit that.'

Ace didn't want this conversation, but felt himself being drawn in. 'Talent? What sort – sporting?'

'No. Singing. Songwriting.' Merle looked him in the eye. 'You like her music. Isla. *The* Isla. Her full name, which she didn't use professionally, was Isla Penhalagon.'

He was silent as her words sunk in. 'No. Surely, that can't be …' He stared at her in confusion.

'Before she was famous, she hooked up with a dreadful man; she didn't realise what he was really like, at first. He was a charmer, and rich, and he opened doors for her. But he was a crook. The local drug lord, in fact. Went by the nickname Duke. I'm afraid he got her into drugs. It was how he controlled her.'

Isla? Ace still couldn't take it in.

'Duke had contacts in the music business, because of his despicable trade. He got her noticed, and …' Merle paused. 'Sorry, this is hard. When she became successful, she tried to break free of him. And she begged me to help, knowing if she just left he'd hunt her down, would have no compunction about harming her.'

'My god.' *Was Duke my father?*

'He was evil. *Evil.*' She stopped. 'And no, he wasn't your father.'

Ace let out a breath. 'So what did you do?'

'We waited until Duke was away – he disappeared overseas regularly, sorting his drug deals – and we went to the police. Of course, they were already onto him, but he was far too clever and well connected to get caught. One of the drugs team, an undercover detective – Gryff, I never knew his surname – then worked with us to set a trap. Duke was sorting the big deals at the Glastonbury Festival, would have been 1995. The police planned a sting.'

Merle's gaze drifted out of the window as she thought back. 'Isla was performing, and for her own safety she wasn't told the details. I asked her to get me a VIP pass to the after party, and I gave it to Gryff, and helped disguise him as a band member.' She smiled. 'Short brown Plod hair just wouldn't cut it; I gave him black extensions.' She touched Ace's face. 'Gryff had lovely eyes – your eyes.'

Gryff. My father?

'Anyway, it worked. Gryff got the evidence he needed, all recorded on tape, and Duke was arrested.' Merle took his hand, held it in her lap. 'Thing was …' she smiled sadly, 'Gryff had fallen for your mum. And she was drawn to him too. They left the party together, but Isla … well, she was high. So her memory of the night you were conceived was hazy.'

Merle exhaled, and Ace braced himself for what was coming next. Clearly there had been no happy ending.

'Duke was behind bars, and Isla was finally free. Or so we thought. And Ace–' she pre-empted his question '– you were definitely Gryff's, not Duke's. A fact that later only added to his rage and his need for revenge.'

'What happened?' asked Ace.

'Duke's tentacles stretched far beyond the prison walls. Isla, and her parents, who'd also become involved, were in enormous danger. The police hid them in a safe house. And Isla was amazing – she went cold turkey, kicked the drugs. After the trial, they were all set for a fresh start, thought they'd be able to pick up their lives again.'

Merle was still holding his hand, and she squeezed it. 'But I'm afraid they were wrong. Isla was murdered after Duke was sent down, just a few months after you were born.'

A wave of grief hit him, for the kind, talented mum he'd never known, had rarely wondered about. He acknowledged – that wasn't because he hadn't cared, it was because he'd been frightened of discovering she just hadn't wanted him. Couldn't be bothered. That she'd been like Lockie's mum.

'Your grandparents went into witness protection. It's why you've never met them. For their own safety – and mine – I was never told where they'd gone. They left you with me, as you know, with instructions to only reveal the truth if, and when, I felt the time was right.'

'And that's now? Why?'

'When you became famous, I knew this couldn't come out. It just couldn't. It was all far too sensational. But Duke died, a year or so ago. There's no danger now. As for Gryff–'

Gryff. My father. A police detective.

'– he disappeared; got a new identity, perhaps. He didn't know about you; maybe that's for the best. And as you may know, it was put out that Isla was taking a break for health reasons, then that she'd died of cancer, and nobody questioned that.'

Hector appeared, bearing mugs of tea. He put Ace's down on the table in front of him. 'I thought I should wait. So you know now, son?'

Ace nodded. 'Isla.' He breathed her name. 'I love her songs, always have.' He teared up as the emotion properly hit. 'I can't believe it. Isla was my mum.'

'She loved you with all her heart,' said Merle, tears in her own eyes. 'Everyone advised her to terminate the pregnancy, but she was determined to keep you. And all thanks to the gods she did. Look what you've become.'

'Thanks to *you* …' His voice caught.

'She'd have been so proud, Arthur. I knew you could do all this.' She swept a hand in the direction of the trophies, then batted away a tear. 'I coached you for her sake, as much as for yours.'

'I guess I *am* glad you told me.' A weight he hadn't been aware of was lifting, and in spite of the heart-wrenching story Merle had told, a lightness was filling its space. *She loved you with all her heart.*

'Why now, though? Why not before? If Duke's been dead for more than a year.'

'Time. It was never the right moment. But it is now. It had to be now.' She patted his hand. 'You should be getting back.'

'What?' He was only just absorbing this news. He had so many questions.

'You need to get back,' she said. 'Now.' And then her face crumpled, and she dropped her head into her hands. 'Go, Arthur,' she croaked, and he saw her tears. 'I'm too upset after that. And Eliza and Lockie need you. *GO.*'

Eliza

Lockie came into the living room, where Eliza was curled up in the window seat, watching the ocean again. He was towelling his hair, dressed only in faded jeans and a collection of necklaces.

Her eyes went to the objects nestled in the fine blond hairs on his chest – a shark's tooth, a jade pendant, something carved from wood … and her stomach clenched.

Oh no. Oh *shit.*

He caught her staring. 'They're keepsakes from my travels. See this one?' He came to stand beside her, and held up the jade ornament by its black lace. 'It's pounamu – Maori greenstone. It's a fish hook. Lena gave it to me. Brings good luck and safe travels.'

Her nose was level with his taut stomach. He smelled fresh from his shower.

'It's beautiful.' *You're beautiful.* She reached up and traced the swirl of translucent stone. 'It reminds me of the mermaid's tail you gave me in my drawing.'

She looked up at him; his eyes went to her lips.

'What do you think Merle wanted?' she asked, groping for words, wishing he'd get dressed.

'Fuck knows,' he said, moving away. He picked up his sweatshirt from the back of a chair. 'Fuckin' crazywoman.'

Eliza laughed and shook her head. 'You do swear a lot.'

'Sorry. Should I stop that too?'

'Maybe. What was it you wanted to show me?'

He hesitated. 'I guess … because of Ace, I want you to know me. Properly.'

'Oh, I think I already do,' she said quietly.

He gave her a shy smile. 'Already feels like a long time, right?'

Again, she cast around for words. 'You know what? Ace was talking about getting you involved in Excalibur. As a member of staff.'

'What? You mean, like, in an *office?*'

She giggled at his horrified expression. 'Yep. But now I've seen you ride a wave, that does seem a bit ridiculous.'

He looked out of the window. 'No, it's not ridiculous. Art's ideas are cool, and I always felt like he was gonna be something more than a tennis player. He really cares about people – about everything. Maybe I could get involved, but … zero office skills. I just can't be fucked – sorry – with computers.' He met her eye. 'But he gave me a second chance at life, and I need to give that some respect. If you get me.'

'I understand.'

A lump formed in her throat as she thought about the bond between these two. Their love for each other.

Since meeting Ace, Eliza had been aware of a growing conviction she was destined to be part of his journey, to play a role in something significant, life-changing. But now, she sensed Fate grabbing the reins, wrenching her off course.

Merle's words on the rooftop: *You made a deal … You can still stop it.*

That unease she'd felt in New York tightened its grip some more.

Lockie frowned. 'You okay?'

She attempted to shake off the foreboding. 'Yes, fine. Carry on.'

He sat down on the window seat, facing her, his feet flat on the cushion between them. 'Thing is, I know what I want to do, I just don't know how to make it work.' He hugged his knees and rested his chin on them, looking glum. 'I'd need money to get started, but I'm skint, and I really don't want to do any more modelling.' He looked her in the eye and smiled. 'I *hate* having my photo taken.'

Eliza laughed softly. His smile was so … enchanting.

But it vanished as he said, 'Oh, fuck. That wasn't a hint. No way. Cos I hear you're a bit rich.'

'Yep – rich bitch, that's me!' Her jolly tone implied she wasn't at all distracted by his closeness; by the smell of him, his eyes, his smile, his hair falling around his face in damp waves; his tanned feet, millimetres away from her. 'But Ace isn't exactly poor, now. You're not going to be homeless and starving, Lockie.'

'No–' He pushed his hair back with an impatient gesture. 'I'm not a victim anymore. I'm so done with being *cared for*. It's one reason I left. To learn to take care of myself.'

'I'm sure Ace understands that.'

He stared at her; she stared back.

'What I wanted to show you … come with me.' He hopped off

the window seat and she followed him to the back door, then across the grass to the storeroom. The grey clouds and sea had collided; the air had darkened. The wind was whipping around the lighthouse, hurling cold, heavy raindrops in their faces.

Lockie pulled open the old, warped door. 'After you.' He slammed it shut behind them, and immediately there was silence; the wind, the rain – the world – locked out.

There was one small window, choked with cobwebs and opaque with the residue of salty raindrops. In the dim light she saw surfboards stacked against one wall; there were folded garden chairs and a rusty barbecue. Along another wall was a bunk bed with worn mattresses.

Lockie flicked a switch and a bare lightbulb came on.

'Here,' he said, going over to the bunk bed. There was something leaning against it, draped in a sheet. 'These are what I wanted to show you.' He carefully pulled off the sheet and looked at her, nervous, waiting for a response.

Eliza's breath caught. He'd uncovered a stack of canvases, the one in front depicting an enormous wave breaking on a stormy ocean. Like his little sketch, the seascape was composed of abstract swirls, this time painted in thickly layered oils. She could hear the boom of that wave, feel the rushing of the wind; smell the salt, sense the immense power in that breaker. The colours ... wild greens, blues, turquoises; the spray flying off the wave's crest contrasting with indigo clouds slashed by streaks of gold where the sun was breaking through. The energy of it, the exuberance; the magic of its light.

Eliza was spellbound.

The paintings stacked behind were similar – impressionistic seascapes, depicting the ocean's different moods.

He came to stand beside her. 'What do you think? Are they any good?'

The uncertainty in his voice, the complete absence of self-belief, finally unleashed feelings she'd been attempting to suppress since she'd first locked eyes with this man.

'They're *incredible*.' Her voice was quiet, almost a whisper, as if anything louder might break the paintings' spell. 'Oh Lockie, who needs words when you can paint like this? I feel them *here*.' She put a hand on her heart.

His face broke into a smile that melted her.

She looked into his eyes. 'They show me your soul.'

Eliza was lost, defeated. *Fate loathes a loose end.* There was no fighting it.

'And ...' She took a breath, and the words tumbled out. 'I want to kiss you so bad that it hurts.'

His blue eyes widened.

'I needed to tell you that. I just ... I can't help it, I can't stop it.'

Love arrives in its own time, on its own terms ... and there's nothing we can do to stop it.

She touched his hand, and after a few seconds his fingers wrapped around hers.

He stared at the floor. 'Because I remind you of him. Of Kit.'

'No ... no. It's ... I can't explain. Who *can* explain it? Why we fall for someone.'

'But why would you? When you have Ace.'

'Fate, maybe.'

He lifted her hand, twisting the silver ring on her finger, frowning at it.

'I feel like you're my missing piece,' she said.

His arm came round her, pulling her close; he tilted her face up to his and kissed her, and she gave in to it, letting it all overwhelm her – the truth – that she was meant to be with this man. This beautiful soul. With, maybe, a shard of another beautiful soul somewhere deep inside him.

Chapter 38

'Wait, Eliza – stop. I can't …'

'I know,' she whispered, against his lips. 'We don't want to hurt him–'

'Not here. Not in here.' His eyes went to the bunk bed. 'I want to kiss you, but not in here.'

She registered the look on his face. 'Oh god. Is this where …?'

He moved away from her and pulled the sheet back over the paintings. 'Yep,' he said, tucking it in around them. 'Fucked over good and proper. Many times.' He tried to keep his tone flippant, but his voice cracked on those last two words.

He met her eye, his expression dark. 'I stored my paintings right here, against this bed, as a *Fuck you*.' Then he took a deep, calming breath. 'Sorry, swearing again.'

'That's okay. Swear all you like.' If ever she'd felt at a loss for words, now was that moment. She wondered whether to ask what had happened, but he was moving towards the door.

'Let's go. How about I show you where I used to paint.'

'Whatever you want, yes.'

He let them out, back into the weather, which had deteriorated still further. She went to sprint through the rain to the cottage, but he grabbed her wrist. 'No – this way.' He looked towards the lighthouse.

'What? You paint in there?' she said, her voice raised against the clattering of the rain on the storeroom roof.

'Well of course I do. Where else am I going to get natural light like that?'

Eliza was profoundly relieved to see the smile back on his face. She looped her arms round his neck, burying her face in his shoulder, breathing him in. 'Thank you for showing me your paintings. You're so talented.'

It felt as if she'd been trying on all those other men for size, and none had been quite right. But this one … here he was. Her perfect fit.

'Lockie, I–'

'We should talk,' he interrupted, his expression troubled. Raindrops clung to his long eyelashes like tiny diamonds.

'I know. But we should also …' She gently pressed her lips to his. For a moment he resisted, then his arms came round her and the kiss went on, and on, and the wind howled and the rain grew heavier, soaking them, and she was oblivious to all of it.

He stopped. 'Lighthouse.'

They raced hand in hand through the deluge, up the hill to the tall, white tower. At the entrance, Lockie jingled the set of keys in his hands, selected one and let them in. 'Up for a climb?'

She craned her neck, pushing back her wet hair, following the dizzying spiral of the staircase which led up and up, like a stairway to heaven, its destination invisible from the ground.

They started to climb, their footsteps echoing off the old stone walls. Small windows at intervals cast dim light onto the worn steps and metal handrail.

'Stop!' she said halfway up, her chest heaving. 'I need a rest.'

He came back down, pausing on the step above hers. His eyes went to her lips, and he smiled. 'I'm good at resuscitation.'

'So I hear.' She met his gaze, and suddenly felt a little faint. 'I understand you were every girl's favourite life-saver.' She stepped up, and he kissed her.

But then he stopped, and the doubt was back. 'Eliza – please – tell me what's going on in your head.' The jokey tone was gone. 'Don't you love Ace? You said it, at the tennis match. In front of the world.'

Her heart dropped, and she closed her eyes for a moment as reality barged in. 'I know this sounds awful, but … no, I don't.' Tears threatened as she pictured Ace's face, his warm smile. 'I thought I was falling for him, he's so … well, he's perfect. But now I realise, I was swept up in it all, being the girlfriend of such a wonderful man. Britain's hero. He's perhaps the best person I've ever met.'

So how can we possibly do this to him?

'Tristan, his coach, asked me to say those words – something had put Ace off his game. He thought it'd help, and it worked. But honestly, that's the only time I've ever said it. And we've only been together two months.'

Lockie nodded, frowning. 'I remember that wobble he had.' He looked as if he might cry too. He blinked, and then blinked again. 'He's the best person you've ever met. He's everything I'm not. He works so hard; knows what he wants, what he believes in. He's a champion of the world, of the people. Why the fuck would you want me … as well? Instead?'

She looked at him, trying to find the words. 'Shall we carry on?' Peering upwards, she could see the brighter light coming through the lantern room windows.

'My head told me to love Ace,' she continued as they climbed, 'but my heart wouldn't listen. I don't feel that connection … in my soul.' She sighed. 'I know it's a cliché; I do love him in a way – I'm so fond of him – but I'm not *in* love with him. I didn't realise then, but I do now, because … I've never felt like this before.'

It was true. With Rob, love had sparked, grown, ebbed and flowed, over time. Lockie had bowled her over; claimed her heart and soul within one short day.

'Not even with Kit?' Lockie said over his shoulder.

She hesitated. 'Oh. Maybe, in a way, but our time together was all out of whack. We both had so much baggage to deal with, and just when we got there, he was taken.'

'What happened? What did he die of?'

'He was murdered.'

Lockie stopped, turned, and stared. '*Murdered?*'

'I'll tell you about it, but not now.'

He held her gaze. 'Shit.'

They emerged into the lantern room. Enormous panes of glass framed by a square latticework were being lashed by the wind and rain; they could barely see out.

'I love it up here,' he said. 'Even when – maybe especially when – the weather's like this.'

'How come you're allowed?' Eliza asked, circling the enormous lamp on its pedestal.

'I badgered the hell out of Ross, the maintenance guy. He traded me a key for a painting.'

Eliza completed her circuit and stopped in front of him. 'Lockie, I know this is wrong, but it feels so right.' She swallowed. 'Be honest. How do you feel about me?'

He smiled. 'Wipeout.'

'Wipeout?'

'It's when a wave destroys you. Knocks you off your board. That's how I feel.'

'Oh.' She smiled back. 'That doesn't sound so good.'

'Well, it's a problem, obviously.' He dropped a kiss on her head. 'And you … you're from another planet. I think, who the fuck *is* this girl? How can I possibly know her? It's been two days.' He gently pushed back her wet curls. 'But somehow I do. When I saw you in the rock pool … it was like I'd been waiting for you.'

'Maybe you were.'

He traced her lips with a finger; his pupils dilated and his expression changed. 'Man, I can't wait to paint these lips,' he said, his voice low. 'You, in oils, in the rock pool. All this crazy hair floating about.' He lifted a long, wet curl to his lips, then drew it slowly across his mouth, sucking the rainwater from it. 'You know – I thought it was Ace calling me home. But maybe it was you, a siren, luring me onto her rock.'

A shiver ran through her and she swallowed again, unable to tear her eyes from his. 'No,' she said, with what little breath remained. 'I was in my tall London tower, waiting to be rescued.'

'By who, though?' He raised his eyebrows. 'You know – maybe you don't have to choose between us. Why should you have to?'

He bent his head and kissed her, and … there was something different about it.

Holy fuck. She *remembered* that kiss.

She pulled away, her mind and senses reeling. 'Lockie! What are you saying?'

'Sorry.' He shook his head, as if coming out of a trance. The seductive tone was gone. 'Don't know where that thought came from.'

Oh, I think I do.

'I'm not a princess, or a siren. I'm just a girl. And no. Much as I adore your brother, I would not enjoy a *ménage à trois*.'

'Neither would I. That's not what I meant.' He rubbed the back of his neck, looking confused. 'I don't actually know what I meant.'

She searched his eyes, and now saw only Lockie. 'Forget you said it. I have.' She needed to slow this down, to take a minute. 'So – where's your painting stuff?'

'Oh, right. In here,' he said, still looking disorientated. He went over to a large cupboard on the back wall and pulled open the doors. 'It was quite a mission, carting all the gear up the steps.' Inside were neatly stacked boxes, an easel and blank canvases. He peered inside a box. 'This'll all be way out of date,' he said, holding up a Kit Kat. 'I used to nick stuff from Merle and hoard it up here. I never got over the need to grab food when I could.'

He took out some flat, square cushions.

'Do you paint sitting on the floor?' There was no furniture in here.

'No, I sit out on the walkway. I do the preliminary sketches out there to get the sea's mood – the sounds, the smell, the sky. Then I come inside and try and put it all on canvas.'

He carried the cushions over to the foot of the huge windows, dropped them and sat cross-legged on one, gazing through the rain-spattered glass to the churning ocean beyond. She sat down beside him and drew her knees up to her chest, hugging them, rubbing her arms.

He ran an eye over her damp jumper and jeans. 'You're cold.' He smiled, and after a moment said, 'Maybe … should we get you out of these wet clothes?'

She smiled back. 'We should.' She took off her jumper then lay back on the cushions. He undid her jeans and carefully pulled them off.

'Your skin's so pale,' he said, trailing cool fingers across her stomach. 'And your hair's so …'

'Red?'

'Like fire.' He arranged it around her shoulders, pulling curls forward, draping them across her body, his fingers brushing her skin, leaving heat in their wake. 'Fire and snow.'

Her pulse was racing. 'Are you painting me, or …'

'I think I'm worshipping you.'

She laughed quietly. 'You're a bit wet too. Better take those off.'

He stripped down to his boxers, then lay down next to her and swept her wild tangle of wet hair aside. He met her gaze, and she nodded.

The rain battered the windows and the wild wind buffeted the tower as he kissed her lips, her neck; moved on down her body, gently setting light to it, and she lost herself in his touch, which flowed beyond her skin and her senses to her heart and her soul. He moved on top of her and she wrapped her arms and legs around him, no longer aware of what was her, what was him.

And then everything clicked into place; time was stilled. She dimly recognised … *that dream*. And then she slid, helpless, into ecstasy.

'Open your eyes,' he said, and his own burned gold as they fixed on hers, before closing as he held himself deep inside her, and she gripped him tight, as if she'd never let him go. When he opened them again, they were the calmest blue.

❀

'When should we tell him?' Eliza said a while later, shattering the magic. 'And how?'

'We tell him together,' said Lockie, stroking her hair. 'Tonight. We have to – there's no way he won't notice. And I don't want to be ...' He trailed off, and shook his head. 'Man, this is fuckin' ...'

'*Take me up, Cast me away,*' whispered Eliza, tears filling her eyes. 'How about ... we wait until tomorrow? We have one last night, the three of us. Cook a nice dinner, sit by the fire. You two can share memories, whatever, I'll just listen. Let's give him that?'

Lockie considered it. 'Okay. But can you not ...'

'I won't. I'll find a reason to say no.'

'We should go, he'll be back soon. Look – it's stopped raining. I'll take you out on the gallery before we go down.'

When they were dressed he led her outside, and they stood gazing out over the grey-green ocean. She shivered, chilled by her wet clothes, and Lockie cuddled her from behind, his chin resting on her shoulder, rubbing her arms as she gripped the rail. The wind had dropped and the sky had calmed, and over to the west, a rainbow arced across the sky, one end in the ocean, the other on the land.

'See?' said Eliza. 'The old Cornish gods understand.'

Lockie pointed, and she saw the Range Rover heading towards them in the distance.

Chapter 39

Ace

Ace told his phone to stop. He'd been listening to Isla on the drive back, and his heart was in pieces. On her final album she'd sung a cover version of John Lennon's 'Beautiful boy', with the word 'Daddy' changed to 'Mummy', and tears brimmed as he pictured his 'talented, pretty, kind' mother rocking him, singing to him.

He would tell Lockie and Eliza when he got back. If he couldn't cry on their shoulders, then whose?

The rain and wind had moved on, and in their wake had left a glorious rainbow. Perhaps it was a sign – from Isla? He hadn't been unwanted. And his father had loved his mother, put his life on the line to save her. He'd given up his identity for her sake. Perhaps, if Isla had lived, Gryff might have come back for her when it had been safe to do so. And then he'd have found out about their child. Him.

Ace looked towards the lighthouse, and noticed two tiny figures on the walkway outside the lantern room. It must be Lockie and Eliza. He remembered, Lockie had scored a key off the maintenance guy, Ross. For all his shyness, his brother could charm the seagulls from the sky when he put his mind to it.

Lockie had used to paint up there, and Ace wondered if he'd shown Eliza any of his work. Probably. He frowned as the figures disappeared inside. He suspected she'd connect with those strange seascapes, would immediately get what Lockie was expressing, the same way she got books, and poetry. And Radiohead.

As he pulled up outside the cottage, the pair of them appeared out of the lighthouse entrance. Eliza hurried across the grass, waving. He exited the car and held out his arms; what he needed right now was an enormous hug.

'Hi!' she said, putting her arms round him. 'I hope everything's okay? What did Merle want?'

He pulled her closer, saying nothing, inhaling the salty smell of her wild hair.

But she resisted a little. 'Sorry, I'm wet. We got caught in the rain.'

'How come? Did you go for a walk?'

Lockie joined them; his hair hung round his face in damp, blond waves. He saw Ace looking at it and gave it an awkward ruffle. 'I gave Eliza the tour – it pissed down between the storeroom and the lighthouse.'

'Storeroom?' said Ace, as they headed for the cottage. 'What were you doing in there? Explaining the technicalities of the short and long board?' But he knew the answer.

'Showed her my paintings.'

Ace looked at Eliza.

'Your brother's so talented,' she said, not meeting his eye. 'He needs an exhibition. And I know the perfect spot.'

'What?' said Lockie. 'Where?'

'The Rose Building, in London. We have an art gallery. I'm thinking – the launch of Excalibur. We hold it there. Invite *all* the money, all the A-listers.' Her mind was taking off, as it did when she was inspired like this.

She looked at Lockie. 'A proportion of your sales go into our charitable funds. See? Then you can be part of Excalibur, but you won't have to sit at a desk. And your career will be launched, directly into the stratosphere, because collectors and rich-listers will be demanding more. You *can* be an artist, Lockie.'

Lockie was looking at Eliza like she'd saved his life. Ace's heart died a little as he watched her struggle to tear her eyes away.

'What do you think, Ace?' She hooked her arm through his as the slope dipped towards the front door.

I think I know why Merle told me to get back here pronto.

Fuck.

'I think I need a beer,' he replied. 'And I'd like to explain why Merle wanted to see me. I'd also like to put Excalibur on hold for now. We're on holiday.' He glanced at Lockie. 'Remember?'

'True!' said Eliza, heartily. 'Beer it is. I'll just get out of these wet things.'

Eliza and Lockie went off to change, and Ace uncapped two beers, poured Eliza a wine and lit the fire. He sat down beside it, thinking. His head told him, Lockie was a beautiful man, endearingly shy. It was a killer combo women always found irresistible. Why should Eliza be immune? Plus, he was the image of the dead boy she couldn't let go of. Her soul mate. Little wonder she was … intrigued.

But this was Eliza, who, according to her closest friend, never let her heart rule her head. Never acted on impulse.

He was grateful to his own head for also reminding him of Eliza's status as CEO of a media giant. A powerful, driven woman, who carefully considered the repercussions of every decision she made. Ace had had major doubts about his own worthiness but, well – Lockie! A broke, uneducated drifter. The idea that she'd risk her public image, already shaky thanks to Catriona, for a fling with Lockie? It was unthinkable. And – his eyes narrowed as he drank deep of his beer – he'd warned her not to mess with Lockie's fragile mind.

And Lockie? Would he really betray Ace? Of course he wouldn't. Ace was all he had in the world. The only person who properly loved him.

So what, exactly, was going on here?

Eliza

Eliza sat on the edge of the bed – this queen bed she was sharing with Ace – her face in her hands. Ace knew. Somehow, he knew. He'd guessed there was something … he wouldn't know what, just that there was something. The air between the three of them had changed. She could almost see the swirls of tension and emotion eddying about in it, like the shapes and colours in one of Lockie's paintings.

She went over to the wardrobe and stared at her clothes. What should she wear for one last, quiet evening before all hell broke loose? Before she told Ace she was finishing with him because she'd fallen in love with his brother, the person who meant everything in the world to him? Before that world found out, in due course, that she'd dumped Britain's beloved hero for a penniless, unknown artist whose only claim to fame was being able to turn somersaults on a surfboard?

Viewed like that, from an outside perspective, it was madness.

What would the British press say? She'd be toast. Literally. They'd burn her at the stake.

She thought about Harry, about Rose. She couldn't do it. There was too much at stake. She let out a tiny, hysterical laugh. *Stop it.* She was losing her mind.

What if …

Kit's voice in her head: *Why would you mind if the person you loved most, loved the other person you loved most … Depends if you think fidelity's important. Maybe it isn't.*

But it was to her. She'd grown up with a two-timing father, she'd seen the harm that could cause.

And anyway, she wasn't in love with Ace, she knew that now. It would be unfair to string him along. She'd been in love with the *idea* of him, she liked him so much, found him physically attractive. Very. Plus, he was a 'top chap' in her father's eyes – at least, until he started politicking. Her father's hearty approval most certainly hadn't helped her objectivity.

But Ace hadn't touched her soul.

Her phone, displaying Will's smiling face, brought her out of her trance. Did she want to talk to Will right now? No. She needed to suspend time, just for this evening. To do what she'd agreed, let the three of them enjoy this night together, tucked away from the world.

She rejected the call.

It rang again immediately, and a message flashed up: *ANSWER – EMERGENCY.*

She told herself to relax. Will turned everything into drama.

She texted back: *Real emergency or Will emergency? Not the best timing.*

The phone rang again. Okay, presumably a real emergency.

'Will, what's up?'

'Are you all right?' came his voice, sounding breathless.

'Everything's fine, if getting somewhat complicated. You?'

'Your stalker,' he said, his voice serious. 'He … she, they, whatever. They're in Cornwall. You *must* tell Ace. We should let Harry know too. We need to make sure you're safe.'

A chill ran through her. Instinctively she looked towards the window. It was still open. She went over and shut it.

'What makes you think the stalker's here?' she asked nervously.

'After our call, this morning …'

Was it only this morning?

'… I couldn't stop looking at that photo you sent. It was weirding me out. I know we said about the eyes being different, but–'

'You saw Kit in it.'

He was quiet for a moment. 'I came over to your place. I wanted to get the journal back. Shit, Eliza, you could've warned me about the new alarm. Put the fear of god into me when it started beeping.'

'How did you … the code?'

'Well clearly it was going to be Kit's birthday or the day he died. I got it on the second go.'

She laughed. 'Am I that obvious?'

'Yes. So I found the journal, settled down to read the pertinent parts – the parts that have been doing my head in since I saw that photo – and a bit later went to make myself a coffee. Then I noticed the ripped-up note.'

'Oh.' *Oh shit.*

'You didn't read it, I'm guessing.'

'No. I took the decision not to, for the sake of my mental health. What did it say?' She braced herself.

'Sorry I read it, but I worry about you.'

'What did it *say*?'

'It said, *See you in Cornwall.*'

There was silence as the words slithered in.

'You've seen no one suspicious?'

'No.' She felt sick.

'Who, exactly, knows you're there?'

'Dad and Clare, you, Pippa, Merle … Hector, I guess.'

'Merle,' repeated Will. 'But she has no reason to hate you now. Ace won all the things.'

'But perhaps she does,' said Eliza, thinking out loud.

You will break his heart. I will break you. Eliza and Lockie were about to break Ace's heart.

'Warn Ace,' said Will. 'And lock everything up.'

'I will. I'm with two strong lads; I'm feeling pretty safe. But thanks for the warning.'

'One last thing.'

'Yes?'

'The journal. I've read it again.' She heard him swallow. 'I have a sense of things unresolved. I think he's restless. I can't hope to understand, or explain. But whatever you decide, wherever this strange path through time leads you, I'll be there for you. Always. For Kit's sake too.'

Tears sprung into her eyes. 'Oh Will, that means so much. Thank you.' She paused. 'Okay, you've been honest, so I owe you the same.'

He sighed dramatically. 'You've fallen for him?'

'I have. There's no fighting it. I can't explain; it makes no sense, unless you go all esoteric and that is *not* me; at least, it never used to be. But recently …' She thought of Harry and his near-death experiences; of Kit's words on time, the soul, Fate; on love. 'I guess I've become more open to it all. Will, something deep inside is telling me I'm meant to be with Lockie–'

'Lockie?' he interrupted. 'What sort of a name is that?'

'It's Cornish, short for Locryn.'

'Better.'

'And I discovered today, he's not just a surfing dude. Though … oh Will, you should see what he can do on a surfboard.'

'Bloody love to. Continue.'

'He's an artist, a brilliant one. He showed me his paintings, and they told me more about him than any of the conversations we've had.'

'A painter? How divine. And have you kissed him?'

'Will! Am I allowed no secrets from you *at all*?'

'Correct, you're not.'

She huffed. 'Yes. We have kissed. And yes, at one point the kiss was very familiar. But then it wasn't. If you get me.'

'Right. I think I'm getting the picture.' He sighed, this time without the drama. 'Poor Ace. When will you tell him?'

'Tomorrow. And then I guess we let the dust settle before we let anyone – anyone at all – know that Lockie and me are together.'

Explaining it to Will brought her back to an even keel. Suddenly it didn't feel so impossible, so colossal. She was finishing with someone she'd been dating for a mere two months, and then, whenever it felt appropriate to do so, would start to date his foster brother. Ace was a decent, rational human being who cared deeply for them both. He wasn't the sort to harbour revenge, to be bitter. He'd come round; he'd understand. They'd all be best friends for life.

The smile back on her face, she thanked Will for warning her about the note, and ended the call.

When she returned to the living room, the sun was setting, streaking the Cornish sky with shades of red. She remembered the stalker, and at once those colours took on a sinister hue, and the long shadow of the lighthouse falling across the cottage rekindled her unease.

Lockie was in the window seat drinking beer, watching the sunset, and Ace was on the sofa. He patted the space beside him. 'I poured you a wine.'

She sat down. The room looked so cosy, the flames from the fire casting flickering shadows onto the whitewashed walls. She looked at the two men, and her throat constricted.

'I want to share with you both what I learned today,' Ace began.

Right. She'd put off the stalker news for now. Nothing should spoil this evening.

Lockie was still looking out of the window.

'I learned who my parents were; Merle told me everything.'

Eliza let out a gasp.

'Quite a surprise,' he said. 'You remember Isla, the singer from these parts? Turns out she was my mum.'

Neither Eliza nor Lockie said a word. Eliza stared at Ace in astonishment.

'Unbelievable, I know,' he said.

'*Isla?*' said Eliza. 'That's … incredible.' Her heart sank as she anticipated the media frenzy, should this get out.

Ace explained about Isla's drug lord partner, the sting at Glastonbury, the detective who'd fallen in love with her, Ace's birth, the sad ending.

Still, Lockie hadn't said a word; his eyes remained fixed on the horizon.

'What a heart-breaking story,' Eliza said as he finished. 'I can hardly believe it. And you love her music.'

'Always have.' And then she saw the tears in his eyes. 'Merle said …' he choked out, 'Isla wouldn't terminate, wouldn't give me up. She wanted me. She loved me.'

'She did,' said Lockie, quietly. 'She did love you.'

There was silence; Ace lifted his head. 'What?'

'Mum told me. Duke – he was Mum's supplier. He was an evil piece of shit. Mum knew Isla 'cos they were both addicts, both Duke's women. Mum used to brag about it, with Isla being so famous. But she was properly pissed off when Merle and Isla got Duke sent down. I remember her ranting about it, in one of her rare lucid moments.'

'Wait,' said Eliza, attempting to make sense of what he was saying. 'Lockie – you *knew*? You knew Isla was Ace's mum?'

Her head was spinning. How could these two have been so close, and yet Lockie hadn't told Ace about his mother?

344   ❀   Olivia Hayfield

'Lockie?' Ace stared at his foster brother, his face pale.

'She made me swear not to. Said she'd tell you the truth about … if I ever did.'

'"She" being your mum?' said Ace, looking bewildered. 'Or Merle?'

Lockie shook his head. 'I can't–'

Abruptly he stood up and left the room, without looking at either of them.

Ace went to follow, but Eliza put a hand on his arm. 'Leave him, he's pretty upset too.'

He sat down again. 'He knew. I can't believe it. He *knew*.'

She thought hard. 'He must have had good reason not to tell you. Maybe it was too dangerous, if Duke's gang was still active? Perhaps it would have put Merle and Hector in danger – and you? I don't know. But obviously he has a reason.'

Eliza was desperate to follow Lockie, to find out what was going on in his head. But she couldn't. Ace was feeling betrayed – Lockie had kept this from him. And the betrayal was only going to get worse.

Eliza leaned her head on his shoulder and hugged him tight. 'Whatever happens, whatever you find out, Lockie loves you so, so much. I learned that from him today.'

'And you?' he said, tears still in his eyes. 'Do *you* love me?'

She couldn't add to his hurt. But she couldn't lie, either. 'You know how deeply I care for you.'

He didn't respond.

She saw a way out. 'Will rang. Sorry, I know it's the last thing you want to hear, but it's important. The stalker – he or she knows I'm here, in Cornwall. Remember that note I ripped up at the flat? Will pieced it together.'

Ace frowned, then shrugged. 'You've got a fencer and a martial arts expert here with you. No deranged fan's going to hurt you.' He turned to face her, looked her in the eye. 'But I think tomorrow, Lockie should leave. I need to be alone with you, to work things out. We need to talk … don't we?'

Eliza nodded. *He knows.*

Chapter 40

As the sun rose over the lighthouse keeper's cottage, Eliza was already wide awake, waves of anxiety washing over her as she contemplated the day ahead. Ace had fallen asleep in her arms last night, and it had torn at her heart as he'd held her tight, making no move to kiss her.

Her phone on the bedside table, still on silent, was displaying all manner of notifications, but she ignored it. *I'm on fucking holiday!* The burst of anger let her know how tense she was.

Then she noticed her father's piercing blue eyes staring out of her phone. *DAD* said the white lettering.

Dad?

She took the phone into the living room. 'Dad? Bit early – I'm on holiday, remember?'

There was a short silence, then he said, 'Right. Early enough that you haven't seen this morning's news?'

'What?'

'Two takes on this media bomb, before you have a look. Firstly, someone's out to bring you down. Your stalker, I'd surmise. A stalker with a drone and a powerful telescopic lens. The second … well, Lizzie.'

'What?' she managed to croak out, as Harry's displeasure made itself known via the tone of those last two words.

'It may be a tad hypocritical for yours truly to be berating you for cheating on such a wonderful partner, but still. Words fail me, I'm afraid.'

Eliza felt faint. She sat down on the window seat with a bump. 'What's come out?'

'Photos. Of you and someone who looks disturbingly like your Kit, who they're saying is Ace's foster brother.'

'Oh no. *No.*' She put a hand to her throat.

'Much talk of Britain's beloved hero being used and abused by everyone's favourite bad girl. With his own brother. A male model, apparently. A surfer?' He paused. 'That was where I started to think they'd made it up. But I *would* like to hear your side.'

It felt as if her airways were closing up. 'They'll roast me, Dad. What am I going to do?'

'The truth please, Lizzie.'

'That *is* the truth. What you said.' She took some breaths, tried to swallow down the panic. 'I came down here with Ace, and I met his foster brother, who looks like Kit, yes. But it's not just …' Should she try to explain? Would he understand?

'Dad – it's fate. Remember those conversations we had about fate?'

He made a small *tsh*. 'Explain.'

'When I met Lockie, it was like I knew him, and not just because he looks like Kit. It's so much more than that. We just … recognised each other.'

'You fancied each other.'

'No!' The word exploded out of her. 'Come on, you know me better than that.'

'You met a good-looking guy who reminded you of Kit. Clare told me how he's always on your mind; how you can't let him go. You've clearly got in a muddle and–'

'Stop! No. You're so wrong. You know I've never, ever, given my heart easily. But Lockie – I knew the moment I set eyes on him. Nothing like this has ever happened to me before.' She willed him to understand.

He didn't respond.

'Didn't it happen to you? With any of those women? All those wives?'

'Your mother,' he said, after a pause. 'Yes. I suppose that was how I felt when I met Ana. Like I knew her already.'

'Then you know –'

'But Lizzie, it didn't last. We had a few good years and then it turned bad. You have to think with your head. Someone in your position. *Think*, Lizzie. A pro *surfer*? A working-class boy from Cornwall? No, not even that – a boy in and out of care homes, foster homes; not one GCSE to his name–'

'What? How–'

'Cecil. Look. This stops *now*.'

'Eliza?'

Her heart jumped into her mouth. Lockie had appeared in the doorway, still in a rumpled white T-shirt and boxers, rubbing the sleep from his eyes. There were shadows, like bruises, beneath them. He pushed back his tangle of hair. 'You okay?'

'Dad, I have to go. I'll take a look at the media; we'll have to decide what to do.'

'You'll need to step down for a while.' Harry's voice was grim. 'Your reputation's in shreds. Shreds of shreds.' He gave a small laugh. 'Like father, like daughter. I'll make Cecil acting CEO. I'll be in touch.'

My father just fired me.

Harry ended the call, and it felt as if she'd been cut off – severed – from her family, from her work, from Ace. Tears began streaming down her face.

'What's happened?' said Lockie, coming over. 'Hey, please don't cry.' He sat down and put an arm round her. He was still warm from his bed, and she curled into his chest, closing her eyes. The panic began to recede. Things were turning to shit, but this was meant to be. This was what mattered.

'We'll get through this,' he said, stroking her arm, kissing her head. Then his hand stilled. 'Art.'

Eliza opened her eyes and saw him standing in the doorway, dressed only in his jeans, his phone in his hand. 'Merle's sent her daily media round-up.' His voice was flat.

She tried to read Ace's expression. There was hurt, and anger. But most of all, that familiar bewilderment.

'She also said –' he looked at the phone, '*Don't hate them. There was nothing anyone could have done.*' His eyes narrowed. 'I'd beg to differ on that last point. Eliza – obviously I don't know you at all. Too soon, I guess.' His gaze moved to Lockie, and his expression changed again. 'But you? You'd do this to me?'

Eliza flinched at the hurt in his voice.

The most important thing was to save his relationship with Lockie. 'It's all my fault,' she said. 'I … I led him on–'

'Stop,' said Lockie. 'Don't.' He looked at Ace. 'I was lost the moment I set eyes on her. Can't explain.'

Eliza began to cry again. This thing that had happened between them, it was so beautiful. But yet again, time and fate were playing their twisted games.

'We wanted the three of us to have one last evening together before we told you,' Lockie went on, 'but Merle's news about your parents scuppered that.'

Ace just shook his head, his eyes moving between Eliza and Lockie.

'Mum told me Isla was your mother,' said Lockie. 'I didn't tell you because … I couldn't. Because she told me something else, too. Only two other people know. We couldn't let you find out. We just couldn't. *She* held it over me. Said if I didn't do as she wanted, she'd tell you.' His breathing had become shallow, and there was a note of panic in his voice. Abruptly, he stood up.

Ace shook his head again. 'No idea what the *fuck* you're talking about. And I doubt I want to. I think you should leave. But first, maybe you'd be interested to see these?' He moved closer and thrust his phone in Lockie's face. 'Look at them. *Look at them*. You too, Eliza. Read the words.'

The Sun's website's read: *OH BROTHER – ELIZA'S AT IT AGAIN!* The opening sentences drew parallels between Eliza's relationship with Will and Kit, and her new 'hot threesome' with Ace and Lockie.

The *Daily Mail* spun it as a betrayal: *ELIZA'S LOVE TRYST WITH ACE'S BROTHER.*

Both websites had identical photos, and when he showed them another page it became clear the same three photos had been sent to all news media.

Eliza and Ace lying in the dunes of Constantine Bay, kissing.

Eliza and Lockie kissing passionately in the rain outside the storeroom.

Eliza and Lockie on the lighthouse walkway, his arms around her waist.

The copy swam before Eliza's eyes; she couldn't take it in. Just the odd word: *unfaithful, betrayal, cheat, romantic hideaway* … and something in the *Mail* about Ace no doubt regretting his impassioned appeal to his long-lost brother to come home.

The colour drained from Lockie's face, and he sank back onto the window seat.

'Please, Ace,' said Eliza. How would she ever find her way back from this? 'Don't blame him. *Please–*'

There was a noise from the kitchen. She froze.

'Ace?' whispered Eliza.

A figure appeared in the doorway. A woman with spiky blue hair and glittering dark eyes, dressed in a black vest, long skirt and Doc Martens. She bristled with piercings – a chaotic mismatch of rings and studs ran up each ear; another hoop encircled her lower lip. There were studs in her nose and more crawling up her temples, mirroring the line of her sharp cheekbones.

The shocking impact of all that metal was softened by her huge, liquid eyes. As they swept over Ace and Lockie, Eliza saw the emotion swirling in them, flitting between dark and light, like sun and shade on a windy day.

'Hello, boys.' Her low, velvety voice drew out the words. 'It's been far, far too long.' Her lips curved into a smile.

Eliza was breaking out in goose bumps. That was not the smile of a sane woman.

So, here you are. My stalker. She frowned. *Where do I know you from?*

'Faye,' said Ace, his voice calm. 'Showing up like the spectre at the feast. Again. And there was me thinking you'd finally done us all a favour and fucked off for good.'

Faye pouted. 'That's not very nice. Especially in such *refined* company.' She smirked at Eliza. 'Greetings, rich bitch.'

Her gaze moved to Lockie, and her expression changed. 'Hello, my beautiful angel,' she said softly. 'Why did you run away? I've missed you so much.'

Lockie was silent. All remaining colour had drained from his face.

She turned back to Eliza. 'I thought our Lockie here was the illiterate one, but it seems you can't read either. Shame. If you'd read my note, you might have escaped your sad fate here today.'

'What do you want, Faye?' said Ace. He was attempting to sound bored, but Eliza could sense his fear. There was fear in Lockie's eyes too. Why? What did this woman have over these two strong men that they were looking at her like this? Like a pair of rabbits caught in her headlight eyes.

'What do I want?' She cocked her head and put a finger to her chin, relishing the attention. 'Hmm. Well, Art. For one, I thought it was time you met your son.' She threw her voice over her shoulder. 'Come on in, Dread.' She lowered her voice. 'His nickname. Suits him.'

A boy of ten or eleven entered the room. He had dark-brown dreadlocks and wore a black hoodie and jeans. His face was arresting – blue eyes, olive skin, full lips. And in his hand was a metal contraption, like a gun. Eliza looked properly. It was a crossbow, and it was primed, and loaded with a lethal-looking arrow.

And he was pointing it at her.

'No,' said Lockie. 'Faye … no.'

'Son? What are you talking about?' said Ace, his eyes fixed on the crossbow.

'They were good times, eh, boys?' said Faye. 'Such a shame Merle put a stop to our fun.' She turned her gaze on Lockie, and ran her tongue over her lips. 'Wasn't it, my angel? But you're back!

How wonderful. And now Art is so, so famous, neither of you will be wanting your dirty little secrets shared with the world, will you?'

She raised a finger. 'Oh! Apart from the one we shared this morning. Dread, here, is quite the expert with his drone and his laptop. Also an absolute genius when it comes to trolling. Very useful. He can spread hate and secrets at the click of a mouse, right, son?'

She fixed her gaze on Eliza again, and her eyes narrowed with spite. 'He put the wind up you good and proper, didn't he? Shame you didn't heed the warnings to fuck right off from Art. And then fucking Lockie too! What an absolute slag. But there you go; in the end that was your biggest mistake, darling. You cheated on Art, and that's what's going to bring it all crashing down. His career, your career, your stupid Excalibur thing.'

The boy nodded. His eyes flicked between Faye and Eliza.

How long did it take to destroy a child's sense of right and wrong, to turn him bad, Eliza wondered, then clocked herself asking philosophical questions with a crossbow aimed at her heart.

'Where do I know you from?' she said, her palms sweating.

'Tesco's. But at least I got you another wine. And this here is your mugger who forgot to grab your purse.' She slapped the boy hard on the arm. 'That was stupid.'

Eliza flinched, squeezing her eyes shut, but the boy managed to steady himself and the crossbow.

'Fuckin' hell, Mum,' he muttered.

Faye went over to Lockie, bent down and took his face between her hands. 'My beautiful, beautiful Lockie.' She sighed, then kissed him on the lips, lingering. It was as if Lockie had turned to stone.

At last, Ace unfroze, but Faye was up in a flash.

'Nope. I learned how to kiss Lockie and stay alert, remember? Oh boy, did we have some lovely times,' she said, stroking his hair. 'I taught you well, and you were goood. So, so good.'

'Faye,' Lockie said, finding his voice, and his resolve. He smacked her hand away. 'Just stop. Go back to whatever group of weirdos you live with now. We'll pretend we never saw you. That you haven't stalked Eliza, made death threats. Leave. Just fuck off.'

'No,' she snapped. 'You'll *never* be free of me.' Her tone changed again, and she blinked doe eyes at him. 'No one will ever love you like I do. Think of those nights together, remember how we loved each other.'

'You *abused* him!' shot Ace. 'He was *thirteen*, Faye. A *child*. He was completely vulnerable, and you seduced him, you *raped* him, again and again, until he tried to kill himself.'

Eliza sucked in a breath. *Faye was Lockie's abuser.*

'He was full of self-loathing,' Ace went on, his voice charged with suppressed rage, 'so ashamed he couldn't bring himself to tell anyone. He *hated* you. He hated himself. What you did to him was sick, unforgivable.'

'Well,' Faye said, unperturbed, 'after *you* dumped me, what was a girl to do?'

'But you're his *sister*!' blurted out Lockie.

Ace went pale. 'What?'

Faye paused, smirking as Lockie's words sunk in. 'Half sister,' she corrected. 'And how was I supposed to know? Nobody bloody told me Art and me had the same mum, until the Flake by the Lake – your excuse for a mum – told *you*, Lockie. And then we kept it as our little secret, didn't we?'

Faye was Isla's daughter?

She ranted on. 'But to be honest, I mightn't have cared, if I'd known. Art was only a *half* brother, and we'd never met until Merle's. We had fun, right, Art?'

Ace was staring at her in disgust. 'You're insane.' His eyes moved to Dread. 'And he is not my son. He could be anyone's – you had every guy within a ten-mile radius.'

'That was after. A girl's gotta save her pride *somehow*. But no. He's yours. Merle sent me away to have him, swore me to secrecy. Never a good idea to cross Merle. When I came back to Camelford I left him with this bloke I'd hooked up with – a traveller. He fucked off, but the community looked after him when I wasn't there.'

She turned back to Lockie. 'And then, when I came back, I fell in love, didn't I, Lockie? You were so beautiful, and shy and sweet. My angel.'

He flinched, and edged towards the window as she held out a slender white hand.

Lockie looked at Ace. 'She said, if I didn't let her into my bed, if I didn't … if I didn't *touch* her –' His breathing was shallow; he was hyperventilating, '– she'd tell everyone you'd raped your own sister. But then, after … after I–'

'It's okay, Lockie,' said Ace gently. 'Deep breaths.'

Eliza's eyes were travelling between Faye (manic), Lockie (petrified) and Ace (quietly furious). She wondered if she'd entered yet another parallel universe. Surely this wasn't happening. It was as if she were seeing it all play out from the sidelines, as if she'd left her body.

Faye stroked Lockie's hair again. 'I love you so much, Lockie. You came back. You have nowhere to go. We can find somewhere. Be together. Just like old times.'

She turned to Eliza. 'Once *she's* out of the way. Are you going quietly, or do I have to see you off properly?' Her eyes settled on the crossbow.

'Faye,' said Ace, his voice controlled, calm. 'Tell … Dread to put the weapon down. Why did you even bring it?'

'A girl needs protection, right, Eliza? Guess you thought these two would do it for you?' Her voice turned vicious, and her face contorted as she hissed, 'How *dare* you. How dare you seduce not one, but both my boys. *My* boys. I couldn't have Art, once Lockie told me about the sister thing. Fair enough. Bit gross. But Lockie?'

Again, her expression was flitting between over-bright and dark. Now, it snapped to light, tender. 'I love Lockie like you will never love him. I would *die* without him.' She gazed at him. 'The last two years have been *hell*.'

Her eyes turned dark. 'I saw you, yesterday. I *saw* you. Like I say –' she flicked a hand in the boy's direction, 'Dread here is a demon with the drone. In spite of the rain. Although I decided a photo of you two shagging in the lighthouse would be a bit much, even for *Sun* readers.'

Eliza gasped, and glanced at Ace.

His face contorted with anger, and he made a move towards Faye, then stopped as Dread raised the crossbow.

'Don't shoot the messenger,' Faye said, holding up her hands. 'Shoot the rich bitch.' She looked at Dread. '*Do it*. Shoot the rich bitch.'

The boy suddenly looked terrified. 'No, Mum.'

'Remember, Dread,' she said, as if explaining to a four-year-old, 'how we've talked about this. Planned it. How they *both* need to pay. Art took from me what I loved most in the world.' She glared at Ace, her eyes brimful of pure, unfiltered hate. 'Now *he's* going to learn how that feels. And remember why he even exists. Because my stupid mum betrayed my darling father. With a *cop*. Got him sent down.'

'You knew?' said Ace.

'Of *course* I knew. Your arrival changed *everything*. It's one reason I set out to break you. But that was mostly because …' Her tone changed again. 'You split up me and Lockie.' Her eyes filled with tears as they moved to Lockie.

He shook his head and stared at the floor.

She turned back to Ace, blinking quickly. 'You have no clue about any of it, do you? Well, let me enlighten you, *Brother*. When our idiot mum got herself killed, Merle took you in but I was sent away. You got a loving home, I got years in *care*. If ever there was a word that wasn't. But when I proved too hard to handle, Merle stepped up, for the sake of our mum.'

She squeezed her eyes shut for a moment. 'But she didn't *tell* me, did she? That you were my *actual* brother. I thought …' Her voice wavered, and she swallowed. 'Here's someone who might love me. A foster brother. He's nice. *Really* nice.' She smiled hesitantly. 'We were friends at first, weren't we?'

Ace nodded, and his expression briefly softened.

'When we grew up, I wanted to show you *properly* that I loved you. You weren't so keen – hurtful, that was. Shame it only happened once. But then Lockie arrived and told me who your mum was. Though, to be honest, I preferred him anyway. Just like Eliza here does.'

Ace winced.

A fierce anger had now ignited in Eliza. This woman was like a terrible virus, infecting everyone she came into contact with.

'And when you found out about me and Lockie,' Faye went on, 'you made Merle send me away again. Now that was very, very mean of you.'

'But you came back,' said Lockie.

'She gave me yet another chance, for my mother's sake. She kept on trying, on and on.' She laughed. 'Silly woman.'

Her expression changed again. 'I did try, at first. To be normal, to fit in. To be good. But ... my feelings were so *strong*, I couldn't help it.' She took a shaky breath. 'I just wanted someone to love me. I wanted *you two* to love me. I wanted that so bad. And I wanted to show you both how much I loved you.'

Ace gave her a long look, then shook his head and turned to Lockie. 'I'm so sorry, for leaving you alone with her and Hector all those times.'

Faye let out a shrill laugh. 'Hector! What a clueless loser.'

'I should have tried harder to make Merle see sense.'

'Oh, Art. So many reasons to destroy you.' Her vulnerability had vanished. 'And I nearly did it, in New York. I wanted to trash your dream, and I wanted the *world* to see you fail. But *she* stopped me ...' She pointed a finger. 'Because, you – you stupid, stupid, man – believed her *lie*.'

'No!' said Eliza. 'It wasn't a l–'

Faye cut her off. 'But this time, me 'n' your son have humiliated you good and proper. Ace Penhalagon. Snapped up like a trophy by the rich bitch, only to be dumped for his even cuter brother. Shame.'

Faye was psyching herself up, embracing her hate, funnelling it towards Eliza, who grew numb with fear.

'You see, Dread? Isn't Eliza Rose just the *worst* kind of privileged, entitled princess? And so very slutty with it. She totally deserves to die.' She waved her hand at her son. '*Do it.*'

'No, Mum. I can't …'

'Oh for chrissake.'

It was so quick, Eliza didn't realise what was happening. Faye whipped out a knife from her deep pockets, flicked it open and hurled herself at Eliza. Time slowed down as she was caught in the malevolent, deadly glare of those dark eyes.

Ace launched himself at Eliza, pushing her out of the way, and she staggered backwards, knocking into Lockie, who grabbed her round the waist and spun her away from Faye.

'Oh, fuck,' said Faye. 'That wasn't meant to happen.'

Ace lurched forward, then slumped across the window seat. The knife was embedded in his back. In the blade of his sword tattoo.

Faye put her head on one side, looking at the knife. 'Or maybe it was.'

Chapter 41

Time stood still, and Eliza was aware of the four of them, like a tableau, staring at the slumped form of Ace, the knife in his back, his arms splayed across the window seat.

Lockie released Eliza and shot towards the boy, but he'd already thrown the crossbow to the floor. Dodging Lockie, Dread pushed Faye in the direction of the door. 'Go, Mum. Run!'

Faye turned her glittering eyes back to Ace, tutting, as if he'd inconvenienced her. Then she gazed at Lockie before, with a swirl of her black skirt, she fled the room.

Ace's face had turned grey; sweat was breaking out on his forehead. He was watching Eliza, his eyes panicked.

'I can't move,' he said, and then he groaned, his face contorting with pain. He ground out the words: 'Is it in the sword?'

Blood was oozing from the wound. Eliza's eyes met Lockie's. *Don't tell him.*

'It's still in your back,' Lockie said. He crouched down beside Ace. 'We mustn't touch it.'

Eliza dialled 999 with shaking hands. She looked at the boy; he was standing still, indecisive, his frightened eyes moving between Ace and the doorway.

'Stay where you are,' growled Lockie. 'And disarm that thing.' He waved an arm at the crossbow.

The boy nodded.

'Ambulance … and police,' Eliza said into the phone. 'Trevose Head lighthouse, the keeper's cottage … a stabbing …'

Lockie put his face close to Ace's. 'Help's on the way, Art. You're gonna be okay.' His voice was calm, reassuring.

'The knife's still in the wound,' said Eliza down the phone. She went quiet, answered a few questions from the dispatcher, then repeated their instructions to Lockie.

She wondered whether to say who the stabbing victim was – would it hurry things up? But no. She couldn't trust anyone, anymore. She gave a false name.

Lockie took Ace beneath his arms, supporting his weight, talking softly to him. He lowered him carefully to the floor and rested him on his side, gently bending his top leg, positioning his arms.

The boy grabbed a cushion from the sofa, darted forward and lay it beneath Ace's head.

Eliza watched in disbelief. This couldn't be happening. Not again. That sense of déjà vu. Kit's life ebbing away as she and Will begged him not to leave.

No. She wouldn't let it happen again.

But she shivered as she remembered Merle's words: *You made a deal.*

'Please tell them to hurry,' she pleaded down the phone, then ended the call.

'I'll be right back,' Lockie said. 'You –' he nodded at the boy, 'stay there.'

The boy shook his head. 'I don't *want* to go with her. I want to stay with Ace … with my *dad.*'

Lockie sprinted out of the room. Eliza watched him leave in confusion, then turned her attention to Ace. His eyes had lost focus, and her heart missed a beat as she noticed a dribble of blood at the corner of his mouth. The knife must have punctured something inside.

She knelt down and pulled the arm of her pyjama top over her hand, dabbing at the blood, wiping it away. The little crown motif on her sleeve was stained red. Then she gently kissed his forehead.

With an effort, he fixed his eyes on hers.

'I'm so, so sorry,' she whispered, as her tears spilled over.

He tried to move his head, but she put her palm against his cheek to stop him. 'Hold on, Ace. Hold on.'

How long would it take the ambulance to get here? Panic was rising in her gut.

No. Be strong for him. Keep him with you.

She took his hand, holding it tight; with her other she brushed his hair back from his clammy forehead. 'You *must* hold on. The paramedics are on their way. Please, please, stay awake – stay with us.'

What could she say, to make him stay?

'Ace – I love you, I do.' It *wasn't* a lie; she had so much love for him. 'What I feel for Lockie will never change that. And you're *everything* to him; we both need you. The three of us – we love each other, we have a future together. You have so much to give the world. We're not going to let you go. You have to stay.'

Lockie was back, and Eliza's eyes widened in fear as she saw Faye in his grip. She glanced over at the crossbow – the boy had taken out the arrow.

Lockie shoved Faye in front of him, towards Ace. 'Save him,' he said. 'I'll do whatever you want. Be with you. Me for him.'

Faye turned her gaze on him, and the hope in her eyes was pitiful. 'You mean it?'

'Lockie,' said Eliza. 'She can't do anything. We can't touch the knife.'

'Shut up, bitch,' snapped Faye, turning her attention to Ace's wound.

She closed her eyes and touched the inked skin on one side of the knife blade, whispering beneath her breath. A few seconds later her eyes flew open. 'No, it's too strong. It's stopping me …'

'What is?' Lockie was almost beside himself.

'It's too powerful. Art – stop your stupid protection thing, I'm trying to help!'

Ace spoke, his voice barely above a whisper. 'No. Don't touch me. Lockie, Eliza …'

Lockie motioned to Faye. 'Move!'

She stood up and backed away. Lockie knelt down in her place.

'Give me … your hands.' Ace's breathing was shallow, laboured.

Tears streamed down Eliza's cheeks; she sensed he was leaving them, she'd been here before. 'Don't go, Ace, please don't go,' she sobbed.

Lockie grasped Ace's hand, held it tight.

'Eliza …' Ace whispered.

She grasped his other hand, raised it to her mouth and kissed it. Her hot tears ran over his ice-cold skin.

Mustering what little strength he had left, Ace brought their hands together, pulling them into his chest, channelling all his remaining energy into his words. 'If … if I don't …' His face twisted with pain.

'Stop, no,' said Lockie, his voice hoarse. 'You're going to make it. Remember when you found me, and you kept me awake all that time, until help arrived? You talked to me; you told me I was loved, that I deserved to live. Now *you* need to stay awake, stay alive.' He began to cry as Ace's eyes rolled into the back of his head. 'Your life's worth so much more than mine, no fuckin' way are we gonna let you go …'

Ace was trying to speak. 'Be … be together.' There was a barely perceptible squeeze of their hands. He could no longer focus his beautiful eyes on them. Their light was fading, dying …

A stillness settled over the room. No one breathed, as they sensed the change in the air.

'No …' said the boy.

Lockie loosened his hand and felt for Ace's pulse, then put his fingers to his neck. 'No. *No*. It's not possible, it can't be …'

'Sorry,' said Faye. 'I tried.' She gazed at Ace, emotions flitting across her face again. 'Unfortunate. But you called the police, right? So I'd best be going.'

In a flash, Lockie flew at her, knocking her to the floor. He flipped her onto her stomach, twisting her arms behind her, one hand on her neck, rage pouring out of him. 'You *bitch*; I'm gonna fuckin' *kill* you …'

'Lockie!' said Eliza. 'Stop ...' She shook her head, willing him to be calm.

He stared at Faye's head, breathing quickly, then said to the boy, 'Get something to tie her up with.'

Dread disappeared into the kitchen.

Eliza was still holding Ace's hand, which had gone limp. She stared at his face in disbelief, at his lifeless eyes, and gently closed them. Apart from the pallor and another dark-red trickle at the corner of his mouth, he could have been asleep.

But he was dead. And he'd died because of her. Faye had killed him, but he'd died saving Eliza.

This remarkable man died because of me.

The boy returned with a length of string, and Lockie bound Faye's wrists, yanking the twine tight as she writhed beneath him, moaning Lockie's name. He ordered her to stand up. Meekly, she did as he asked.

He pushed her roughly ahead of him towards the hallway.

'Lockie, I didn't mean to,' she whined, as he shoved her again. 'You saw what happened, I didn't mean to ...'

They disappeared, and Eliza heard a door slam. Moments later Lockie returned. He lay down next to Ace and wrapped himself around him, burying his face in his brother's neck, crying inconsolably.

Eliza reached out to comfort him, then stopped. *This is all my fault.*

The boy stood awkwardly in the corner. 'I'm sorry,' he said in a small voice. 'I'm really really sorry, for all those things I did. She made me, she–'

'Not now,' said Eliza. 'Please ... not now. Don't worry, we'll take care of you.'

She heard a vehicle drawing up outside. *You're too late.*

But it wasn't the ambulance. Merle appeared in the doorway, filling the space. She stopped dead, taking in the scene in front of her. Lockie cradling Ace's lifeless body, his face buried in his shoulder; the knife embedded in the tattoo. Eliza sitting beside them, numb with shock. The white-faced boy in the corner.

'Where's Faye?' she barked.

Lockie didn't respond, didn't even acknowledge her arrival.

'Tied up in the bedroom,' said Eliza.

How did she know Faye was here?

Merle came over and stood looking down at Ace. She sighed as her eyes filled with tears. 'Our wonderful Arthur. Britain will never see the like of him again. Fate's a cruel mistress, is she not, Eliza?'

She could only nod.

'It's not your fault,' said Merle, dropping a hand onto her shoulder. She turned those dark eyes on Lockie, his face still hidden. 'Or yours.' Still he didn't respond. He'd retreated to a place where only he and Ace existed.

'Is it mine?' asked the boy.

'No, Dread, it's not. 'This was all …' she paused, '… inevitable. I just didn't expect it to happen so quickly.'

Merle knows the boy.

Chapter 42

Harry and Clare organised a house rental for Eliza, off the beaten track, where the press couldn't find them. They helicoptered down and stayed for a few days. Clare's gentle, wise words were a great help, while Harry seemed mired in disbelief. 'These things that happen to you and me, Lizzie,' he said.

The police interviewed Eliza; Faye was being held on remand. There was speculation she'd be mentally unfit to stand trial.

Harry attempted to assert some control over the story being told. The Rose media release gave the bare bones: twenty-nine-year-old Faye Morgan who, as a teen, had spent time in the same foster family as Ace, had attacked Eliza with a knife. Ace had been stabbed trying to save her and, tragically, had died at the scene. Faye, who had a history of mental illness, had been arrested for murder.

That much was official. The rest varied from newspaper to TV channel to website, but all speculated that the drama at Trevose Head Lighthouse had been sparked by Eliza's 'romantic involvement' with Ace's foster brother, Locryn du Lac, with whom, according to an ex-boyfriend, Faye was infatuated.

Lockie was staying with Merle. He answered none of Eliza's calls. She texted him – text after text – telling him none of this was his fault, and that she loved him.

He replied only to the first one: *I betrayd him. Please leav me alone.*

Four days after Ace's death, Will drove down, and Harry and Clare left.

The funeral was for 'family' and close friends only, at St Pedroc's chapel up on Bodmin Moor. Merle kept the venue and date secret from the media; there would be a memorial service for the tennis world in London in a fortnight's time.

Eliza and Will arrived a little late. She was constantly aware of how she was being talked about, if not as the villain of the piece, then at least as the spark that ignited the bonfire.

Low clouds trailed fingers of mist across the moor, blurring the outline of the old stone chapel.

'Suitably atmospheric,' said Will, attempting to ease Eliza's nerves as they exited the car.

They sat in a pew at the back. Eliza spotted Merle, Hector, Lockie, Tristan, and … Dread. Sitting next to Lockie. But the dreadlocks were gone, and in their place were dark brown curls.

She fixed her eyes on Lockie, ignoring the stares as word of her arrival spread, like a whispered Mexican wave. His hair was tidy; he wore a smart jacket. His neatness made her heart ache.

Merle met her eye and smiled. She leaned in to Lockie and whispered something; Lockie turned round.

Eliza heard Will's intake of breath.

Their eyes met, and Eliza's tears broke through. Lockie gave her a sad, shy, ghost of a smile, then turned back to face the front.

The coffin was already in position. Beside it was a photo of Ace – that warm smile, those gorgeous blue eyes. She stared at her handbag in her lap, blinded by her tears, groping for a tissue. *He died because of me.*

The vicar's opening words washed over her; all she was aware of was Ace's coffin, Lockie's back, and Will's hand gripping hers.

After a hymn, Merle gave a moving eulogy, speaking of Ace's extraordinary career, his achievements, his dreams of using his fame to help others.

Then Lockie made his way to the pulpit. He spoke quietly, not looking up from the piece of paper he unfolded. His hands were shaking.

'… first person to care about me … saw me through the most difficult times … saved my life. Was an inspiration to me, to everyone who ever knew him … had so much to give, so many ideas, was committed to improving the lives of those less fortunate …'

He ended with a plea, that Ace's good heart would live on, that his dedication to helping others would never be forgotten, would be his legacy.

He met Eliza's eye. She smiled through her tears and nodded, and there was a tiny smile in return, before he returned to his seat beside Merle.

She sought him out afterwards, outside the chapel, ignoring the disapproving stares. Droplets of mist were swirling in the air, clinging to their hair.

Will stood tactfully aside.

'Lockie?'

His eyes met hers, and she saw the despair in their depths.

'How're you doing?' he finally said.

Terrible. All I want is to be with you.

'Getting through, somehow. But you – are you managing?'

He shook his head. 'No. Can't sleep. Been surfing a lot.'

'I hope it helps?'

'A bit.' He stared at his feet. 'When are you going back to London?'

Please ask me to stay. I can stay a while longer.

'I don't know. I guess … soon? What will you do?'

He met her eye for a second, then his gaze went over her shoulder to the misty moor beyond the chapel. 'Might take off again.'

No! Please … please don't leave.

'But you'll come back?'

The silence stretched out.

To stop herself begging him to stay, to stop the tears, she waved Will over. 'This is my friend Will. He's been looking after me.'

Will's disquiet was clear as he approached. 'Lovely to meet you,' he said hesitantly, holding out a hand, 'if under such sad circumstances.'

'It's okay, Will knows it all,' said Eliza.

Lockie shook Will's hand.

'I'm so very sorry about Ace,' said Will. 'I didn't know him long, but I loved him to bits. He was an exceptional person.'

'You're Kit's … friend,' Lockie said, staring at Will, still holding his hand. Then he smiled, and there was no trace of shyness – none at all. 'Hello, writer boy.'

The autumn light touched his eyes, turning them gold.

Will went still, and after a moment said, 'Hello, painter boy.'

Eliza watched their eyes lock.

Then Lockie blinked, dropped Will's hand and turned to her. 'Shall I call you?' The hesitancy was back. Lockie was back.

Eliza breathed out. 'Of course. You must. Whenever you want.'

'I can't … see you. You understand? It wouldn't be right.'

Her own despair threatened to swamp her. It was rising, swelling, like a tsunami. 'He wanted us to be together, Lockie,' she said quietly. 'You heard him.'

He shook his head, his eyes on the ground again. 'He died because of us. Because of what we did.'

'*No*,' shot Will. Lockie looked at him in surprise. 'I won't let Eliza follow this self-flagellating path to loneliness again. She's had a horrendous time, and she deserves some love and light in her life. And if that means you casting aside your misplaced guilt, then that is what you must do. Think on that, Lockie.'

Lockie looked at Eliza.

She nodded. 'Yes, please do think on that.'

Merle was making her way over, with Tristan and Dread.

Eliza met her eye. 'Those were beautiful words, Merle. Thank you for saying what we're all feeling.'

Merle nodded.

'Hello, Eliza, Will,' said Tristan. He shook his head slowly. 'I can't believe it. Still hasn't sunk in.' There was no accusation in his words.

'I'm so sorry …' said Eliza, swallowing down more tears.

Lockie was shuffling his feet; his eyes were darting about. He looked desperate to escape.

Tristan gave a sigh as dramatic as one of Will's. 'You two.' He looked between Eliza and Lockie. 'I have some inkling of what happened, so I do.'

Eliza went to speak, to block this conversation, but Tristan carried on.

'You lost the power of rational thought.' He fixed his green eyes on Lockie. 'You couldn't fight it.'

Lockie glanced at Eliza, then nodded.

'Don't be beating yourselves up, now. Our lovely man Ace wouldn't want his two favourite humans to be unhappy for too long on his account.'

'He's right,' said Merle. 'And now we're off to the pub. Probably best if you continue to lie low, Eliza.'

'I'll take her home,' said Will. He looked at Lockie. 'And I'll be seeing you.'

◈

'What can I do?' said Eliza, as they sat in the kitchen lunching on cheese sandwiches and a pot of tea. She had no appetite for hers. She wished they could have gone to the pub for a pasty with Merle and Tristan and all the others. Washed it down with a few scrumpies, or whatever strong alcoholic drink assisted the drowning of sorrows at Cornish wakes.

She felt as if she'd never be able to go out in public again. Never be one of the crowd in a pub. And if she did venture out, she might just be stoned as an adulteress.

'I'm so worried about Lockie's mental state,' she said. 'He's suffered from depression in the past.'

'Merle will keep a close eye, I'm sure.'

'I keep replaying it all. Everything that happened. Wondering at what point I could have stopped it. Tripped up Fate. Is that even possible?'

Will shook his head. 'I don't know. The decisions we make. Those little moments that can change the course of our lives.' He smiled, trying to cheer her up. 'Like, what if I'd asked you out, that first year at Oxford.'

368 ⊛ Olivia Hayfield

Her eyebrows shot up in surprise. 'What? You only *pretended* you fancied me. It was a big act. All that *Shall I compare thee to a summer's day* stuff.' She chuckled at the memory. 'It was Leigh you liked.' Leigh Walters was Eliza's old economist uni friend, now working for Rose in the US.

'Yes, I did like Leigh too, but no, it wasn't an act.'

Her smiled faded. 'Then why …'

'Because I knew you liked Kit. Also, once I'd got over the initial crush, I decided you were far too princessey. *Extremely* high maintenance. Not for me.'

Eliza let out a belly laugh, and was aware of how good that felt.

'And by the third year, it would've felt like shagging my sister.' He grimaced. 'Oops. Sorry.'

Eliza had filled him in on Faye's relationship to Ace, swearing him to secrecy.

Will hurried on. 'And then, when I finally embraced my gay side, I went and fell for bloody Kit. Seriously – what kind of tragicomedy was I?'

'Did you like Lockie?' she said, nervously.

He gave her a long look. 'Which version?'

'You saw it?'

'And felt it.' He shook his head. '*There are more things in heaven and earth …*' Then his expression changed, and his eyes slid away from hers. 'Eliza, there's something …'

She frowned. 'What?'

'Kit's journal. I wasn't quite honest with you. In fact,' he took a breath, 'I did something unforgivable. All I can say in my sorry defence is that I've been an emotional mess since he died. I wasn't thinking rationally.'

'I understand.'

'Thing is, the journal–'

'I haven't read it all,' she interrupted. She wondered what else Will had discovered in Kit's words.

'No, it's not what's inside.' He gave her a sad smile. 'I didn't find it in his desk. The police took it, during the murder enquiry. They told me it was sitting in the middle of his bed. With a note. They returned both to me soon after.'

His words sunk in. 'You'd already read it? Before we cleared out his things?'

'Yes. Some time ago.'

She sat back in her chair and blew out a breath. 'Well. That explains a *lot*.'

'I haven't finished,' said Will.

'Oh?'

'The note.' He reached into the pocket of his jacket, hung over the back of his chair. Eliza's stomach twisted as she took the yellow post-it note from his hand, saw Kit's familiar scrawl.

For Eliza, if I don't make it
With all the love in the world
Yours literally forever
Kit

The writing blurred as her tears came back. *With all the love in the world.* In the end, he'd believed.

'I've known you were right all along,' said Will. 'He foresaw his own death.'

When she didn't reply he said, 'I thought you'd be angry with me.'

She shrugged. 'You kept it because you wanted to understand him.'

He studied her, his head on one side. 'You've changed. I've seen it.'

She sniffed and wiped her eyes. 'Changed? How?'

'Softer.'

She pulled a face. 'You mean I've been crying a lot.'

'No. It's more than that. A lot more. Since you met Ace.'

Eliza went quiet, twirling Kit's ring on her finger. 'I do feel different. My priorities have changed.' She looked up. 'But after this past year, losing Kit, and now Ace, how could we *not* have changed? '

Chapter 43

Merle phoned to ask Eliza if she'd like to help scatter Ace's ashes before returning to London. After talking with Lockie, she said, they'd decided to do this up at Dozmary Pool, the lake on Bodmin Moor where the two boys had loved to play together. Where Lockie had lived, on and off, with his mum.

She told Eliza how Ace had taken Lockie under his wing, way back, years before Merle had fostered him. They'd met during one of Hector's fishing trips, when he'd taken Ace along. The two boys had become friends, spending time together when Lockie was home from his periods in care. Ace would cycle up to the lake with a backpack full of food for Lockie.

It had been Ace who'd persuaded Merle to take Lockie in, when she already had Ace and Faye to look after.

Eliza realized – Lockie had been taken away from his mother, only to end up in a foster home where he was abused by a mentally unstable sexual predator. No wonder Ace had felt such a burden of responsibility, after the suicide attempt.

'It's the lake or Wimbledon,' Merle said. 'And honestly, I can't face the paperwork. Not comfortable with white-man tennis club committees.'

'I think Ace would like to stay in Cornwall,' said Eliza. 'And yes please, if you're happy to have me there, I'd love to come.'

'More Cornish mist – excellent,' said Will three days later, as they parked in the fishermen's car park. It was a grey autumn day, cold and still, low cloud drifting across the water. 'I'll take a stroll. Who knows what manner of mythical maiden I might encounter in the mist. Does this lake have a lady?'

'Apparently it does. Lockie's mum.'

Eliza had chosen the floaty, leaf-green dress she'd worn for that Sunday lunch at Richmond, on a sunny summer's day that felt like the distant past. Ace had said she looked like a Celtic princess. She arranged her cashmere pashmina around her shoulders and flipped out her hair, which hung loose.

Making her way to the lakeside, she spotted Merle, Hector, Lockie and Dread, on a jetty where rowing boats were moored.

Lockie, in jeans and a black jumper, came to meet her. 'Hello.' He smiled a shy smile. 'You look beautiful.'

'He loved this dress.' Her bottom lip trembled.

Lockie opened his arms and she sank into them, closing her eyes. They held each other close. 'I hate being without you,' she said into his chest, overcome with emotion. 'It really hurts – I'm missing you so much.'

Hector coughed awkwardly. 'Shall we go?'

Lockie helped Eliza into the boat, and she sat in the stern with Merle, who was wrapped up warm in a silver puffer jacket. Hector was up front with Dread, and Lockie was rowing. In Merle's lap was a purple velvet drawstring bag.

Eliza averted her eyes. It was impossible to accept that Ace's warmth, his vitality, had been reduced to ashes.

They were quiet, alone with their thoughts. Only the light splash of the oars and the occasional cry of a water bird broke the muffled silence. The shore was soon obscured by low cloud.

'Will you be able to find your way back?' asked Eliza, who'd lost her bearings.

'I grew up here.' Lockie indicated with his head. 'Over there.'

Eliza peered through the mist, but couldn't make out the lake edge.

'Here?' said Lockie to Merle.

She nodded, and Lockie rested the oars. The boat bobbed gently, drifting.

Merle opened the bag and took out a beautiful white urn. 'Lockie, love,' she said, unscrewing the lid, 'you meant so much to him. You go first.'

He leaned over the side, gently tipped the urn and shook it, and a stream of ashes flowed out onto the water. He passed it back to Merle then took off his fishhook pendant, held it over the water and let it fall. He bowed his head. 'Go safely, Art,' he said, his voice soft. 'I'll always love you. My brother forever.' His shoulders were shaking; he was crying. A knife was twisting in Eliza's heart.

Merle tipped in more ashes, speaking quietly under her breath. Then she passed the urn to Eliza, who stared at it, remembering how they'd scattered Kit's ashes in the Thames on a moonlit night not so long ago. *Why are the most beautiful souls taken before their time?*

'Wait, Eliza,' said Merle. She fished in her pocket. 'Here.' She dropped the dragon necklace into Eliza's hand, then beckoned to Lockie. 'Swap places with me.'

He swiped at his cheeks and sat down beside Eliza. 'Go ahead,' he said, resting a hand on her shoulder.

She tipped the urn, and more ashes spilled out onto the water. Then she let the gold necklace trickle through her fingers. The little dragon fell into the lake with a quiet plop, glinting as it sank beneath the waves, a final farewell.

'Goodbye, lovely Ace,' she whispered. 'I was so lucky to–' She choked on the rest, overwhelmed by tears.

Hector and Dread took their turns, then Merle put the urn back in its bag.

But it seemed they hadn't finished. Hector picked up something wrapped in sacking from the floor of the boat, and opened it to reveal an ancient-looking sword. The sword tattooed on Ace's back. Excalibur.

Eliza gasped as the mist around them was shot through with magic.

'It meant so much to him, when he was a boy,' said Hector.

'You do it, Lockie,' said Merle. 'Throw it high and far.'

Take me up. Cast me away.

Time seemed to stop again, as they floated in a solitary wooden boat on this dark lake, Lockie holding the bronze sword. What was its story? Its magic percolated through Eliza's skin, coursed along her veins and seeped into her bones.

Lockie stood up, one foot on the seat and the other on the floor of the boat, gripping the sword in his right hand, his left held out in front of him. He leaned back, then quickly raised his arm, flinging the sword high into the air where it spun slowly, once, twice, tracing an arc before hitting the water and disappearing beneath the waves, which stilled as the lake was suddenly becalmed.

There was a strange, otherworldly silence. No one moved, until a puff of wind skittered across the water, and time was unpaused.

Lockie sat down, and Eliza rested her head on his shoulder. Ace's face swam in front of her.

'I'll row us back,' said Hector.

'One oar each,' said Merle, moving beside him, patting his knee. 'Thank you for giving up the sword.'

The mist was lifting, and the air brightened and warmed as Hector and Merle rowed. Eliza looked at Dread, who was facing the shore. He was an odd, quiet boy, but that was hardly surprising. Eliza sensed a bond had already formed between him and Lockie.

'Have you visited your mum?' she asked Lockie.

His eyes went to a far point across the lake. 'Yes. She's happy in her own little world. Not necessarily this one. I'll go see her now.'

Merle nodded. 'Take as long as you need.'

'Shall I come?' Eliza asked.

'No,' said Lockie. 'It's too sad.'

Will was waiting for them.

'It was so beautiful,' she said, as he helped her onto the jetty.

Lockie followed her out and took her hand. 'Come with me. Ten minutes, okay Will?'

He nodded.

Lockie led her away from the lake into a small woodland. It was damp and mossy, and smelled of wet earth. The cool air was still, silent; not a single bird was singing.

Without a word he kissed her, tenderly at first, then it became passionate … desperate. She sensed his goodbye.

Eliza's walls were gone. Burned down; obliterated. This man held her heart, her future, in his hands.

'Please don't leave,' she whispered.

'I can't be with you.' He leaned his forehead against hers. 'Everything hurts too much. I've fucked it all up so bad.'

'You haven't. It's not your fault. You heard what Merle said.'

He didn't reply.

'Lockie – you have to make peace with yourself.'

'I need to show him I'm sorry. To make amends.'

She reached behind her waist, to where his hands rested, and brought them forward. She turned his palms face up, pushed back his sleeves.

They looked at the silvery scars.

'I know it hurts,' she said. 'It's unbearable. But remember what you said before. He gave you a second chance at life, and now he's saved mine too. We need to respect our second chances. We mustn't waste them. And what were his last words?' She fought back the tears. She needed to stay strong. 'Say them.'

He was quiet.

'*Say* them!'

'Be together.'

'Be together. We need to hold on to those words. His last wish, Lockie.'

He said nothing.

There was no point in pushing him. 'Do what you need to do. I have to think about my future too.' She smiled sadly. 'My father sacked me. Britain hates me.'

He frowned. 'Jesus.'

'Shall we run away?'

He gave a small laugh. *At last.* 'Tempting.'

She sighed. 'I'd love to be that spontaneous person, but I'm not. Lockie …' She stroked his hair back from his face. 'Time will make things right. Have faith.'

Chapter 44

Eliza spent a quiet, reflective week at Richmond before returning to St Katharine Docks. Rose Corp staff were informed she was on 'garden leave' while they waited for the media frenzy to die down. Although she was no longer CEO, she'd continue working on RoseGold projects. Harry was reinstalled at The Rose, in the top-floor throne room.

Eliza worked from home. Her only visitors were Will, Chess (who by her third visit had stopped pursing her lips), and her cleaner.

'I have little appetite for any of it,' she said to Will, as they looked through scripts Rob thought might have potential. 'Honestly, if this were medieval times I'd just go live in a pretty little abbey in the countryside.'

'Get thee to a nunnery,' said Will. 'Don't worry – a couple more months' penance and we'll relaunch you.'

A week later she ventured into the office, where she received big hugs from Pippa and Terri, and furtive glances from almost everyone else. She read their minds: *Our beloved Ace died because of you.*

It was too hard. Everything was too hard.

Passing Kit's photo that night she said, 'What have we done?' There was no answering voice in her head.

She wanted to talk to Terri properly. It was important her mother's closest friend knew the truth. Over lunch she explained what had happened, as best she could, without including her theory as to why she'd immediately fallen for Lockie. She didn't want down-to-earth Terri thinking she was a flake.

'Fuck,' said Terri, when Eliza described Faye's attack. 'I was about to make some sarcy comment about your love affair with drama, but … no. I'm so sorry, love.'

Eliza swallowed. 'Everyone thinks I'm a terrible person. Is there anything we can do? Something in *The Rack*?'

Terri shook her head. 'No. Think about it. The truth isn't going to help this time. Not even Will could spin this pile-on in your favour.' Her face creased into a frown as she toyed with her food. 'Eliza. I don't get it.' She met her eye. 'It's so out of character for you, risking everything for a fling with a pretty surfer boy. Ace's foster brother; his best mate. Behind his back. What the fuck were you thinking?'

Out of character.

Eliza sighed. 'It sounds like I'm avoiding responsibility for my own actions, but it was Fate.'

Terri cocked an eyebrow. 'Fate. Really?'

'And it was *not* a fling. I love him, more than I've ever loved anyone. I always will. He's my …' She stopped. How could she ever explain? How could *anybody* understand?

'I've changed,' she said, 'because of all this.' She waved a hand to convey the chaos of the past year. 'I've stopped caring about Rose Air, about strategic plans and profits and I *hate* spread sheets. The only part I care about is RoseGold. I'm honestly all good with Dad sacking me as CEO.'

Terri was briefly lost for words. Her mouth opened and shut. 'Is this the same Eliza Rose who dumped the love of her life because she was married to her job? Who always puts her career ahead of matters of the heart?'

'No. It's not the same Eliza Rose. That's my point.'

'Right.' Terri sat back in her chair, shaking her head. 'And this lad, Lockie–'

'He's an artist, as well as a surfer. He paints the most breathtaking seascapes.'

'Right,' Terri said again. 'So … what. You're just waiting for him to swoop in on his white charger and carry you off, away from corporate hell?'

Eliza smiled. 'Something like that.'

❀

In late November, Covid decided it wasn't done. It mutated again, into a new, super-efficient variant: Omicron. As Harry quaintly put it, the virus was munching its way through the Greek alphabet like a crazed Pac-Man.

Will caught it, and got off lightly, his symptoms little worse than a nasty cold. He went into isolation, but had already passed it on to Eliza.

Kit, Ace and Faye all had starring roles in her fever dreams. Eliza died several times over.

'That was bloody horrible,' she said on the phone to Will, when she finally tested negative.

'This year really can get in the bin with the last one,' he said. 'Come over, let's wallow together in our post-Covid exhaustion.'

It was a Saturday morning and, having just had one of her where-would-I-be-without-Will moments, Eliza googled Battersea Dogs Home and clicked on 'Meet the Cats'. Two hours later, she took Casper out of his carrier and rang Will's doorbell. It would appeal more to his sense of drama if the cat was in her arms.

The ginger puss nuzzled her neck. He really was the most affectionate little boy, very different to his snooty predecessor. And she was sure Will wouldn't mind that he had only one ear.

'Hi Eli– Ohmygod.'

'Here you go, William. Cat needs home. Boy needs cat.' She passed him over. 'Meet Casper.'

Will wanted to rename him Vincent, in honour of his 'mono-ear and gingerness', but Eliza said he shouldn't be further confused by a new name on top of a new home.

Casper was sitting in an armchair washing himself, and Will and Eliza were drinking tea, when Merle called. Eliza's heart leapt into her mouth. News of Lockie? He'd responded to none of her texts; she had no idea where he was. She'd been terrified he might return to New Zealand, currently known as the Hermit Kingdom – seemed appropriate. But it remained shut, and she wondered if he was staying at the lighthouse cottage. Perhaps Merle would tell her.

'Hi, Merle! How are you?'

'Had bloody Covid, so's Hector, but all better now. You?'

'Same. Have you heard fr–'

'No. I'm not ringing about Lockie. I'm ringing about Ace's will.'

'Will?' Eliza repeated in surprise.

Will raised his eyebrows; Eliza shook her head.

Merle explained that Ace had made a will during initial legal discussions about his foundation. He'd left half his considerable fortune to Lockie, and the other half in trust for Excalibur.

'Eliza – I know you and Ace got some way down the road to setting up Excalibur. How would you feel about carrying on with that? I'm thinking we'll rename it the Ace Penhalagon Memorial Foundation, and we'll focus on helping disadvantaged youth – on providing sports facilities and mental health resources. I think that's what he'd have wanted.'

'Yes.' Eliza forced the word out past the lump in her throat. 'One hundred per cent, yes.'

They arranged a date for a Zoom call with the legal team, then ended the call.

'You've gone pink,' said Will. 'What gives?'

She explained. 'That's it,' she finished. 'That's my future. I'm done with being a corporate queen. From now on it's just RoseGold and Ace's foundation. It feels so, so right.'

'And did Merle give you news on painter boy?' Will asked carefully.

'No. But Will – he can do that now. Paint. Properly. Ace left him half his money.' She smiled. 'Finally, the universe appears to be playing ball.'

❀

Over the Christmas break, Eliza sat Harry down and told him that once her garden leave was finished, she wouldn't be returning to head up Rose Corp. 'You're back in charge.'

While she knew he was entirely satisfied with the resumption of his reign, news of her abdication came as a shock. She explained how recent events had changed her, shifted her priorities. She'd been so young when she'd taken on the CEO role, and unprepared for the level of attention she'd been subjected to. Being constantly in the spotlight, forever judged, had taken its toll.

But, she said, those events had also made it clear what mattered to her – her passion for drama, and her commitment to Ace's legacy. The Ace Penhalagon Foundation for Youth.

Taffy for short.

'*Taffy?*' said Harry.

'Just ignore the P. Taffy's easier for teens to remember, especially the website and helpline. Friendlier.'

'But it's Welsh!'

Eliza rolled her eyes. 'Dread – you remember, Faye's son? He's our junior consultant. Definitely deprived and undoubtedly in need of mental health support. Our perfect sounding board.'

Dread, whose probable relationship to Ace was still a secret, was being fostered by Merle, who reported he was difficult, but bright. She'd also let slip that he was learning to surf.

Eliza wondered who was teaching him.

She showed Harry the mock-up of the Taffy logo – a dragon wrapped around a Celtic sword.

'Also a bit Welsh,' said Harry with a smile. 'But nice. Well done, Lizzie.'

She hugged him. 'Thanks for understanding. And not minding too much?'

'I very much do, but I'm not going to stand in your way.' He sighed. 'I'm hurtling towards my dotage, though. Who's next after me, if not you? Call me old-fashioned, but I want it to be a Rose.'

'Chess?' said Eliza. 'Super-bright, knows the company well.'

'Not strictly a Rose,' said Harry. 'But a reasonable option.'

'Mac? Actually, no.'

'And also not a Rose.'

'Also not a man, you mean?'

'Come on, Lizzie. My unenlightened days are in my distant past. You and Clare have seen to that.'

'True.'

'Mac's pregnant, apparently.'

'What?' said Eliza. 'Who …?'

'Sperm donor. It's a boy. Going to be called James.'

'How do you know all this?'

'Rob told me.'

'Ah.' She paused. 'You know – if you could bear for it to be a non-Rose, Rob would be a fantastic CEO. And he'd love it. Ambition's his middle name.'

'We'll see. Good to have some viable options, but hopefully I'll be occupying the throne for some time yet.'

Chapter 45

Four months later

Eliza's footsteps echoed around The Rose's lofty art gallery as she checked everything was at the required level of perfection, ahead of this evening's launch of Taffy.

All the paintings, including several by Britain's best-known artists, were for sale, with proceeds going to the foundation. Merle had sent up those seascapes from the storeroom, and they hung together, beautifully lit. She wouldn't elaborate on her communications with Lockie, saying only that he was 'still in hermit mode'. 'Time, Eliza,' she'd said. 'I know you understand time.'

Ranks of polished glasses twinkled on a table; name tags were lined up on another. Eliza peered at them – it was a *Who's Who* of British money and celebrity. She smiled as she spotted *HRH* on two labels. *I don't think they'll be needing name tags.*

She saw *EDWARD ROSE* and *MARIA ROSE*. Eliza was thrilled that her half-siblings would be here tonight. Maria had flown home from Cambodia especially.

Her heart skipped a beat as she spotted: *LOCRYN DU LAC – ARTIST*. Merle had assured her Lockie was aware of his invitation, but apparently he'd told her – no. An event like this would probably be his idea of hell, anyway.

Eliza left the gallery. Danny had gone into battle with her hair again, and emerged triumphant. Now she just needed to change and do her make up.

'There was a courier delivery for you,' Pippa said, as Eliza passed her desk. The PA was brimming with excitement at the thought of the evening to come, all those celebs. 'It's in your office. Oh, and it's very big.'

The words *FRAGILE – OPEN WITH EXTREEM CARE* were written in black marker on the well-wrapped package.

Her heart thumping, she found a pair of scissors and carefully cut away the cardboard and layers of paper, then removed several metres of bubble wrap, revealing ….

Her hand went to her mouth and she burst into tears. Eliza as a mermaid, floating on her back in rippling blue-green water, purple seaweed waving below her; her hair drifting, swirling, her arms spread wide, eyes closed; her lips curved in a serene smile.

His voice behind her. 'Does that mean you like it?'

❀

Later, when Lockie had kissed away the last traces of her tears and they remembered where they were, and why, Eliza said she wanted to show him a special part of the exhibition. She swallowed a laugh as she led Lockie through the outer office, where Pippa was pretending to type something important.

Eliza hooked an arm through his. 'Pippa, I guess you've already met Locryn – Lockie. He's Ace's foster brother. And my …' She looked up at him, wondering what to say.

He gave her a sweet, heart-stopping smile, and the words arrived of their own accord. '… my soul mate.' She blinked. 'But don't repeat that.'

'I won't,' said Pippa, beaming, 'but I'm veeerry happy to hear it.' Her Welsh accent was always more pronounced when she was excited. She held out a hand. 'Welcome to Rose, Lockie.'

'Thank you,' he said, shaking it. 'And for letting me hide in Eliza's office.'

Pippa blushed. 'Any time, luvvie.'

The art gallery was only two floors down, so they took the stairs, and as their footsteps echoed in The Rose's cavernous stairwell

Eliza was reminded of the lighthouse steps on that wild, stormy September day.

These past weeks she'd been holding those memories at bay, locking them away for some time in the future when she was stronger. Trying, so very hard, to carry on, one day at a time, as her conviction grew that Lockie was lost to her. Her only way of coping had been to focus on work, to keep busy, as she had after Kit's death. Silence and inactivity were the enemy; at the end of her long days, obsessing over every last little detail of Taffy's launch, exhaustion had been her friend, ushering in sleep's soothing oblivion.

But often she'd wake in the early hours, and in the quiet of the night the tears would make it through, soaking her pillow. Tears for Ace, and for Lockie, in his private hell, overwhelmed by his betrayal of his brother.

And as Ace's ashes drifted, suspended in the waters of that dark lake, some settling, perhaps, on that magical sword, Eliza had wondered if she'd ever know happiness again.

Lockie stopped as they reached a landing. 'It's like …'

'The lighthouse,' she said. 'Is that where you've been?'

'Yes.' He took her hand and pulled her to him. 'When I was in there, painting that picture, I lost all sense of time and … of myself. Like when I surf; there was just the sea and the sky, the colours and the light, and the images in my head, of you. It was like I was … I don't know. Channelling something.'

She nodded. *Like Kit and his writing.*

'And when I finished, I couldn't remember painting it. The picture kind of … created itself. It only became mine when I signed it. And when I did, in that moment, I got a real strong sense of …' He closed his eyes, and when he opened them again, they were full of tears. 'I felt like Art understood. It was like coming out of a tunnel, into the light.'

Eliza was choked; she had no words. One day, she'd explain. Maybe.

❀

As they entered the gallery, Eliza asked the staff to give them ten minutes, then led Lockie over to a display that explained Taffy's mission, and the bringing to life of Ace's vision. There was a series of blown-up photos of Ace: career highlights, and some of him as a boy, with quotes lifted from his interview with Will and from Ace's column for *The Rack*.

'This is wonderful,' said Lockie, as they stood in front of a photo of the two foster brothers arm in arm at Constantine Bay, surfboards vertical beside them. 'You've done him proud.'

'Merle, too,' said Eliza. 'She sorted the pictures.' She slipped her hand into his. 'My life is all about him, now. And you.' She caught sight of Will's signature on the beautiful tribute he'd written to Ace. 'Oh, and not forgetting Will. I'm carrying on with the film and TV, too. You remember Will?'

He smiled. 'Of course I remember Will.'

'And now for the other star of the show,' she said, leading him across the room to where his seascapes hung, their vibrant colours swirling with movement in the spotlights. 'How does that make you feel, Lockie?'

'Honestly?' he said. 'Fucking terrified.'

❀

There was much initial awkwardness when guests read the name tag clipped to Lockie's lapel that evening. And there were an awful lot of double-takes and concerned headshakes among those who'd known Kit. But once the champagne began flowing, along with goodwill for Ace's legacy, things eased.

Lockie had been buttonholed by an art critic, and Eliza smiled as she watched him sweep a hand across the painting they were discussing, only for the art critic to ignore it and gaze at Lockie instead.

It was understandable. 'Christ almighty,' Terri had said earlier, when she'd clapped eyes on him for the first time. 'You lose the devil-boy Marley, only to land the Angel fucking Gabriel.'

An arm slid round Eliza's waist. 'Love me a room full of Brit celebs. It's like the Met Gala but with real people.'

'Hello, my joint-second-favourite boy.' She kissed Rob's cheek, and they hugged.

'Who's first favourite?' he said. 'Let me at him.'

She nodded in Lockie's direction, and Rob's wide smile disappeared in a flash. 'Holy shit,' he said, colour rising in his cheeks. 'You are *kidding* me.'

She sighed, and put a hand on his arm. 'He's nothing like Kit. He's really shy, and right now, so far out of his comfort zone I've no idea how he's holding it all together.'

'That's as maybe, but … fuck.' Rob shook his head. 'That's still pretty unhealthy, Lizzie.'

'It's a long story, and one I'm not quite sure you'll believe. But I look forward to sharing it with you.'

Rob was still staring. 'So – it's all true? I thought maybe it was press bollocks. It makes more sense now, but … seriously, how did you wind up cheating on your perfect Ace with his foster brother?'

'I can't really explain. Not in words that sound like they came out of a sane person's mouth. The universe moves in mysterious ways. I love him. And I want you two to be friends.'

Sensing their gaze, Lockie turned, and his eyes met Rob's before he resumed talking to the critic.

'Blue eyes,' said Rob.

'Yep. Like I said, very different to Kit.' *As far as you're concerned.*

They went quiet. 'How's Letitia?'

'On location. Sends her apologies.'

'She seems very nice. Not entirely good for the self-esteem, but–'

'Lizzie …' Rob looked down at his feet, then at a wall of paintings, then at Eliza. 'She's pregnant. We're engaged.'

For a brief moment it was as if she'd been stabbed in the heart. And then a hot, jealous rage threatened to overwhelm her. But as quickly as they'd arrived, the emotions flew.

'Rob – that's wonderful! You'll be the *best* dad. And your baby's going to be so not-ugly. Congrats!'

Will appeared. 'Greetings, Robert. Why are we congratulating you?'

'I'm going to be a dad.' His eyes moved to Eliza. 'And a husband.'

Will gave him an exuberant hug. 'That's excellent news. At last, a happy ending for a RoseGolder.'

He spotted a new arrival. 'Oof. Look at Yorkshire's favourite son. Why are the best ones always taken?' Eliza assumed the pretty blonde in the spectacular green dress was Rowan's wife.

Harry, Clare, Maria and Eddie had also just entered the room. 'Here's the clan,' she said. 'Dad hasn't met Lockie yet.' She took a steadying breath. 'Wish me luck, boys.'

Eliza made her way over, beckoning to Lockie to join her. She hugged Maria and Eddie, then Clare, looking lovely in a lacy black cocktail dress. Eddie was still pale, she thought. He'd recently recovered from a serious tussle with Covid, including a few days in hospital.

Harry's astonished expression as Lockie joined them made Eliza laugh out loud. 'Dad – he's very different to Kit.'

'I should darned well hope so,' said Harry, shaking Lockie's hand. 'No father would have let Kit near his daughter.'

Lockie smiled. 'Only Eliza for me. No one else.' He put an arm round her waist. 'Ever.'

'Brave words,' said Harry, clapping him on the shoulder.

Eliza rolled her eyes, registering how happy she felt – it had been a long time.

'Lockie,' she said, 'why don't you show Dad and Clare your work?'

Maria and Eddie also went along, and Eliza made her way over to Merle and Terri. Merle was wearing a magnificent full-length purple coat made from something shiny. The two women were talking animatedly, and Eliza attempted a straight face as, behind their backs, Will pointed at them then made a heart with his hands.

'Well, that didn't touch the sides,' said Terri, contemplating her empty champagne glass. She glanced around for a waiter.

'Abracadabra,' said Merle, handing her a full one.

'What the fuck?'

Eliza chuckled.

A little while later, Lockie and the family joined them. Eliza slipped her hand into Lockie's and he squeezed it. Clare caught

Eliza's eye and gave her a smile loaded with approval. *He's lovely!* she mouthed behind his back.

'Have you met Merle?' said Terri to Harry. 'Ace and Lockie's foster mum.'

'An enormous pleasure,' he said. 'I do hope we can entice you to Richmond. I could do with a spot of coaching, and I'd love to share memories of Ace's great tennis moments.' He gave her a sad smile. 'I'm so sorry for your loss. What a remarkable player he was. And ...' he glanced over at Eliza, 'a remarkable person. True to his own spirit.'

Merle swallowed. 'Your daughter's worked magic tonight. You should be proud.'

'I am. Proudest father ever.'

Merle put her head to one side, regarding him. 'I *could* coach you, but my lessons don't come cheap. They have that extra something. I could be persuaded for–'

'A mill?' said Harry. 'Two? For Taffy, of course.' He frowned, and muttered, '*Taffy?*'

'How do you like Lockie's paintings?' asked Eliza.

'Oh – they're amazing!' said Clare. 'What a talent.'

'Thank you,' said Lockie. He gave Clare a shy smile, and Eliza watched her step-mother melt.

'We bought two,' said Harry. 'And Will bought one.'

'That was lovely of you,' said Eliza, looking over at Will.

'No, not *that* Will,' said Harry. 'Lockie, do you think you might paint me?'

Lockie's eyes widened, and Eliza let out a bark of laughter.

'Seriously. I'm quite bored with that exaggerated-shoulders thing in the board room. And it makes me look rather mean. Now I'm back in the driving seat, perhaps it's time for an update. Something more abstract might suit my advancing years.'

Will waved Rowan and Emma over, and introduced them.

'Rowan,' said Harry, as the writer did a double-take at Lockie. 'What an absolute pleasure. Big fan.' He turned to Emma and kissed her cheek. 'Lovely to see you again. You're looking appropriately green tonight.'

'It's a privilege to meet you, Harry,' she said, looking confused, 'but we've never met before. Rowan and I are quite reclusive, up on our farm.'

'Are you sure?' said Harry. 'Well, that's *very* odd. I could have sworn …'

Merle cackled as Emma said, 'Pretty certain I'd have remembered.'

'Congrats on all this,' Rowan said, touching Eliza's arm. 'Yet again you've overcome a huge level of shite to produce something spectacular. I was gutted about Ace. I'm so bloody sorry. The stalker …'

'Wasn't even on our list,' said Eliza. 'Which may surprise you, considering its length.'

Harry put an arm round Eliza's shoulder. 'Yes, you deserve all the congratulations, Lizzie.' His gaze travelled from Eliza to Rowan to Lockie. 'Speaking from experience, I can confirm one should never be constrained by regret. Make peace with your conscience, atone where you can, then move on. There's nothing we can do to change the past.'

Eliza met Lockie's blue eyes.

'You sure about that, Dad?'

Who's Who?

FROM CORNWALL

Arthur 'Ace' Penhalagon: King Arthur (Arthur Pendragon), legendary king of Britain in the late 5th or early 6th century

Isla Penhalagon: Queen Igraine, King Arthur's mother

Gryff: King Uther Pendragon, King Arthur's father

Duke: Gorlois of Tintagel, Duke of Cornwall

Merle Innes: Merlin the magician

Hector Innes: Sir Ector, King Arthur's foster father

Locryn (Lockie) du Lac: Lancelot du Lac, Knight of the Round Table, close companion of King Arthur

Flake by the Lake: The Lady of the Lake; raised Sir Lancelot in the fairy realm

Tristan Knight: Sir Tristan, Knight of the Round Table

Faye Morgan: Morgan le Fey (enchantress)/Morgause. King Arthur's half-sisters

Dread: Mordred, King Arthur's nephew or (illegitimate) son

THE ROSE FAMILY, FRIENDS AND COLLEAGUES
(introduced in *Wife After Wife, Sister to Sister,* and *Notorious*)

Eliza Rose: Queen Guinevere (previously Queen Elizabeth 1st)

Harry Rose: King Henry VIII

Clare Rose: Catherine Parr (sixth wife of Henry VIII)

Maria Rose: Mary Tudor, eldest daughter of Henry VIII

Eddie Rose: King Edward VI

Francesca (Chess) Studley-Lisle: Lady Jane Grey (Queen of England for nine days)

Mackenzie (Mac) James: Mary, Queen of Scots

Will Bardington: William Shakespeare

Kit Marley (deceased): Christopher Marlowe (Elizabethan playwright)

Terri Robbins-More: Sir Thomas More (16th-century lawyer, judge, philosopher)

Cecil Walsham: William Cecil, Lord Burghley; Elizabeth Ist's chief adviser

Rob Studley: Lord Robert Dudley, Earl of Leicester; Elizabeth 1st's favourite

Letitia Knowles: Lettice Knowles; granddaughter of Henry VIII's mistress Mary Boleyn – probably

Rowan Bosworth: King Richard III

Emma Bosworth-Snow: Elizabeth of York; wife of King Henry VII and mother of Henry VIII

A note from the author

When I was eight years old and called Susan (not yet a Sue, and many years before becoming an Olivia), I read an enchanting book called *Green Smoke*, by Rosemary Manning. It was about an eight-year-old girl called Susan, who went on holiday to Constantine Bay in Cornwall. There she met a dragon who had lived at the court of King Arthur (he was a very old dragon), and over the course of Susan's holiday, sometimes in his cave on the beach, sometimes flying her on his back to Tintagel, the dragon told her magical tales of that king, of Merlin the magician, the Knights of the Round Table, and Camelot.

My belief in this book was so absolute that when my family visited Cornwall, I spent an afternoon standing outside a cave at Constantine Bay calling to the dragon. While the underdeveloped logical side of my brain told me there was no dragon, the part that believed in magic knew he was real, and I vividly remember the crushing disappointment when no puff of green smoke appeared out of the mouth of that cave.

Those tales of King Arthur hold a special place in my heart and in the British psyche. They speak to us of something lost – of magic, enchantresses, chivalry, noble deeds and quests. Of dark forests, turreted castles and misty lakes.

Legend says that when Britain needs him again, Arthur, not dead, but asleep on the Isle of Avalon, will awake and reunite the country; that he'll recreate Camelot with its knightly virtues. (As Eliza says, now would be good.)

Since I began writing my historical retellings (this is the fourth) I've wanted to reincarnate King Arthur in the modern day. Post-Brexit, post-Covid Britain felt like it needed an intervention; it was time to wake him up.

Along with *Green Smoke*, my other inspiration for this book was T.H. White's *The Once and Future King*. It's a beautifully written fantasy loosely based on Sir Thomas Malory's 1485 work *Le Morte d'Arthur*. (Malory's version of the tale is the one with which we are probably most familiar, although let's give a nod here to *Monty Python and the Holy Grail*.)

Why did I make Arthur a tennis champ? I think we're all suspicious of politicians, so I decided not to make him an MP. Many of today's heroes are sporting greats, but I know sweet FA (pun!) about football, so that was a non-starter. A day watching Wimbledon, however, with champagne and strawberries, is my idea of heaven, so I thought I'd reincarnate Arthur as a tennis god. Incidentally, to date, nobody has yet achieved the Golden Slam in the men's singles.

If you haven't read my earlier retellings, you may be wondering why the other major characters are based on the Tudors. Ace needed a Queen, and when I was considering how to reincarnate Guinevere, Eliza from *Sister to Sister* whispered, *Choose me!* Again and again. When you create a world and grow to love its characters, it's hard to let them go, so I gave in to her demands. I'd always felt she deserved a Part Two, plus the prospect of pitching her father, my modern-day Henry VIII, against King Arthur was irresistible.

Thank you to everyone who's helped me with this book, especially fellow author and friend Catherine Robertson, who recommended T.H. White and read an early draft of my manuscript. She's been an amazing support ever since *Wife After Wife*, and even appreciates my puns.

Thanks to my agent, Vicki Marsdon of High Spot Literary, who infuses me with positivity and motivation – and those are sometimes more difficult to muster than words. Thanks to designer extraordinaire Cheryl Smith for the fabulous cover, and to Giles Portman for his thoughts on the two-handed backhand.

As ever, thanks to my husband Michael, and my daughter Helena and son James, for all your love and support. I hope one day to book the lighthouse-keeper's cottage at Trevose Head for a family holiday.

And most importantly, heartfelt thanks to you, the readers who spend your precious book-reading time in my world. I'm so grateful for your support, and if you've enjoyed this book, or any of my novels, I would be beyond grateful if you could leave a rating (or even a review) on Amazon, Goodreads, TikTok; a photo on Instagram, whatever – it all really helps.

There's more on my books and me at oliviahayfield.com and suecopsey.com, including a sign-up form for my (rare – I promise) newsletters, and blog posts about the real people behind my reincarnations. All my books are available in paperback and as ebooks, and *Wife After Wife*, *Sister to Sister* and *Notorious* are also available as audiobooks.

Congratulations for making it to the end of this note.
Love, light, and happy reading!
Sue (Olivia) XX

WIFE AFTER WIFE

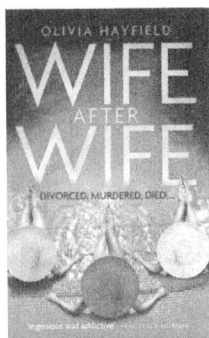

*A wickedly entertaining and utterly absorbing modern take on the life and marriages of **Henry VIII** – if he were a 21st-century womanising media mogul rather than the King of England.*

Master of the universe Harry Rose is head of Rose Corporation, number eighteen on the Forbes Rich List, and recently married to wife number six. But his perfect world is about to come crashing to the ground. His business is in the spotlight, and not in a good way, and his love life is under scrutiny. Because behind a glittering curtain of lavish parties, gorgeous homes, and a media empire is a tale worthy of any tabloid. And Harry has a lot to account for.

Link to Amazon: https://amzn.to/47LI17d
Or scan the QR Code

SISTER TO SISTER

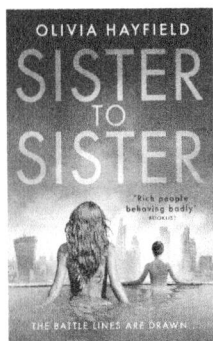

*Based on the turbulent reigns of **Tudor queens Mary and Elizabeth**, this is a compelling tale of love, power and betrayal.*

Following the scandalous revelations about his love life, disgraced media mogul Harry Rose has stepped down from Rose Corporation. His bright, ambitious daughter Eliza must navigate life as its new queen, but Maria, her dark, difficult sister, is standing in her way.

And then there's the distraction of the twinkly-eyed – and married – Rob, and the unresolved death of Eliza's mother,

Ana. After a stellar start, things take a turn for the worse, and ultimately Eliza will have to make a choice: career, or love?

Link to Amazon: https://amzn.to/3TfvODe
Or scan the QR Code

NOTORIOUS

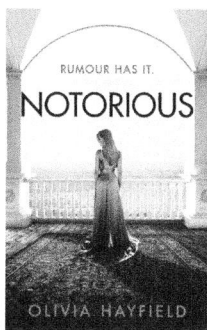

An escapist page-turner based on history's greatest unsolved mystery – the disappearance of the Princes in the Tower – and the royal enigma that was Richard III.

Everyone's heard of the Snows. Rock singer Belle, her husband Teddy – acclaimed actor by day, notorious party animal by night – and their five children.

All Emma Snow wants is to escape her celebrity family and lead a quiet life away from the spotlight. Now she has it all – her dream job as a journalist, the perfect boyfriend in Henry Theodore, and an adorable cat called Perkin.

But Emma can't shake her feelings for her father's protégé, enigmatic playwright Rowan Bosworth. She's never sure whether he likes her, or if she's a pawn in one of the twisted games he likes to play.

When her little brothers vanish and the finger of blame is pointed at Rowan, Emma is determined to uncover the truth. But to do so she must delve into the dark past of her celebrity family – and once and for all decide whether to think with her heart or her head.

When you're surrounded by rumours, it's difficult to see the truth.

Link to Amazon: https://amzn.to/3Tc7tOM
Or scan the QR code

Olivia Hayfield is the pen name of writer, editor and history nerd Sue Copsey. Sue grew up in England and worked in publishing in London before moving to New Zealand. She wanted her children to grow up somewhere with lots of wide open space, and beautiful Aotearoa has plenty of that – but not a lot of history.

So now that her Kiwi kids have flown the nest, Sue and her husband ping pong between hemispheres. Sue loves spending summers in her homeland researching the locations and characters that feature in her novels.

Queen, King, Ace is Sue's fourth historical retelling, following bestsellers *Wife After Wife*, *Sister to Sister*, and *Notorious*. Sue is also an award-winning writer of children's books. She lives in Essex and Auckland.

Printed in Great Britain
by Amazon